Simon stepped nearer. "I haven't forgotten the past either...."

"But apparently the memories that loom largest in my mind differ from the ones looming largest in yours."

The sudden feral hunger in his eyes called to the dark wildness that Louisa had suppressed inside her these many long years. "What do you mean?" she asked, her breath hitching in her throat.

"I remember long waltzes and longer conversations. I remember a time when you did trust me."

"Before I discovered how false your attentions were, you mean."

"They were not all false," he said softly. "And you know it."

As he bent his head, a frisson of anticipation swept her. "What do you think you're doing?" she asked, though she very much feared she knew.

"Finding out if you taste as good as I remember." Then he covered her mouth with his.

TO PLEASURE A PRINCE

"Jeffries's sparkling dialogue takes center stage in an emotional, highly sensual and powerfully romantic story. . . . All the characters have such depth they simply leap from the pages."

—Romantic Times

"[T]he parallel courtships of the Tremaine and North siblings engage throughout. Readers will eagerly await the third brother's story."

—Publishers Weekly

IN THE PRINCE'S BED

"A traditional Regency told with sparkle and energy. . . . The chemistry among all the characters—not just the hero and heroine—ensures that there's never a dull moment in this merry romp. . . . The attraction between the protagonists is electric, and it's consistently entertaining to watch them juggle their various secrets. Fans of historical romances will find the simple pleasures of this novel irresistible."

—Publishers Weekly

"Delightful, sensual, and poignant, Jeffries's latest brings humor and pathos to a richly peopled tale. This is a delightful start to a new series featuring a trio of heroes to die for."

—Romantic Times

Also by Sabrina Jeffries

Never Seduce a Scoundrel

One Night with a Prince

To Pleasure a Prince

In the Prince's Bed

Sabrina Jeffries

Only A Duke Will Do

POCKET BOOKS
New York   London   Toronto   Sydney

An *Original* Publication of POCKET BOOKS

POCKET BOOKS, a division of Simon & Schuster, Inc.
1230 Avenue of the Americas, New York, NY 10020

This book is a work of fiction. Names, characters, places and
incidents are products of the author's imagination or are used
fictitiously. Any resemblance to actual events or locales or persons,
living or dead, is entirely coincidental.

ISBN-13: 978-1-4165-1609-5
ISBN-10:   1-4165-1609-3

This Pocket Books paperback edition September 2006

10 9 8 7 6 5 4 3 2 1

POCKET and colophon are registered trademarks of
Simon & Schuster, Inc.

Cover and stepback illustration by Alan Ayers
Handlettering by David Gatti

Manufactured in the United States of America

For information regarding special discounts for bulk purchases,
please contact Simon & Schuster Special Sales at 1-800-456-6798
or business@simonandschuster.com

To artist Ursula Vernon and doll lover Carlota Sage,
who never cease to make me laugh.

And to all the crew at Mr. Toad's Coffee—
thanks for keeping me supplied with
the best coffee in North Carolina!

Family Tree

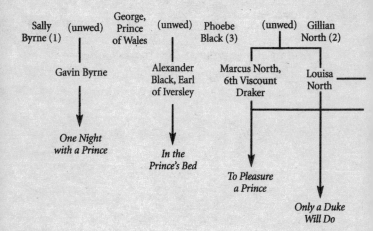

Sally Byrne (1) — (unwed) — George, Prince of Wales — (unwed) — Phoebe Black (3) — (unwed) — Gillian North (2)

Gavin Byrne

Alexander Black, Earl of Iversley

Marcus North, 6th Viscount Draker

Louisa North

One Night with a Prince

In the Prince's Bed

To Pleasure a Prince

Only a Duke Will Do

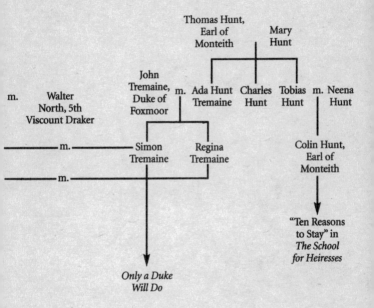

Thomas Hunt, Earl of Monteith — Mary Hunt

John Tremaine, Duke of Foxmoor m. Ada Hunt Tremaine   Charles Hunt   Tobias Hunt m. Neena Hunt

m. Walter North, 5th Viscount Draker

———— m. ———— Simon Tremaine   Regina Tremaine

———— m. ————

Colin Hunt, Earl of Monteith

Only a Duke Will Do

"Ten Reasons to Stay" in *The School for Heiresses*

Chapter One

London
April 1821

Dear Cousin Michael,

Do you know the Duke of Foxmoor who recently returned to England? I've heard such differing accounts of the scandal surrounding his departure that I hardly know what to believe. The two ladies most affected, Lady Draker and Lord Draker's sister Louisa, say nothing of it. Does the duke mention it around other gentlemen?

Yours fondly,
Charlotte

Nothing had changed in seven years.

And everything was different.

Simon Tremaine, the Duke of Foxmoor, stood on the granite gallery above his sister Regina's gardens and warily surveyed her guests. Perhaps *he* was merely different. Before his term as Governor-General of India, he would have known precisely how to handle this assembly of the brightest and best of English society.

Now he felt like a stranger in his own country.

A screeching sounded in his left ear, reminding him he was not the only stranger. He reached up to scratch his pet monkey's belly. "Yes, Raji, parties here are very different from those at Government House in Calcutta, are they not?"

No native orchestras playing with more enthusiasm than skill, no rich curries and peppered soups, no tropical palms dripping with coconuts. Here it was all practiced harpists, French sauces, and yew hedges dotted by beds of primrose.

And a host of new faces to attach to names, a host of new Members of Parliament to assess at this fete celebrating the birthday of the king's bastard son.

"Regina could have warned me she meant to invite every bloody MP in the kingdom to her husband's celebration," he told Raji. "I am surprised that Draker allowed it. There was a time when he would have barred his estate to this lot."

Simon started for the steps leading into the lamplit gardens, then froze as his gaze fell on the dark-haired woman who stood near the bottom.

Draker's sister, Louisa North. Who was also the king's bastard. And the very female who'd had him banished to India.

Regina had made it clear that her sister-in-law would be at the fete, yet expecting Louisa to attend and seeing her in the flesh were two entirely different things.

Especially when she looked like *that*.

Responding to the sudden tension in his master, Raji chattered madly. Simon nodded. "Yes, she was pretty before. But now . . ."

Sometime during his years abroad, the socially awkward innocent who had haunted his dreams had blossomed into a refined beauty.

Simon groaned. Why hadn't her fruitless years on the marriage mart dulled her jeweled eyes or her sparkling laugh? Why hadn't her rich meals at court transformed her lush figure into a stout one?

She wasn't the least bit stout, damn her.

But different, yes. Her appealing country-fresh features were now schooled into reserve. Even her China blue gown was restrained, a quietly elegant bit of female trickery that only hinted teasingly at the full glory of her curves. And gone were her girlish curls, replaced by a sophisticated swirl of black locks that begged to be taken down and kissed—

Bloody hell. How dared she still have this effect on him? His grandfather would turn over in his grave. After Simon's reckless behavior with her, the aging Earl of Monteith had been livid. Simon would never forget what he'd said on Simon's last visit to him before leaving for India.

I knew you would prove as worthless as your father, pursuing pleasure before duty. Did you learn nothing from my training? You're too much a slave to your passions to ever govern a country successfully.

Damn him and damn his "training." Simon had proved his maternal grandfather wrong in India, where, except for his blunder at Poona, he had governed with skill. And now he would prove the man wrong in England, too, Louisa or no Louisa. He only wished Grandfather Monteith had not died before witnessing Simon's triumph.

Raji danced restlessly on his shoulder and Simon rubbed the monkey's shoulder to soothe him. "Yes, scamp. It's best we join the crowd before anyone, especially Miss North, sees me eyeing her like some starving Hindu contemplating a bowl of rice." He strode toward the steps.

"Your Grace!"

Simon turned to see a Castlemaine servant hurrying along the gallery. "My lady told me to watch for you," the man said as he reached Simon. "His Majesty asked that you join him in the rose garden at once."

Deuce take it, someone else he didn't want to see. Simon's correspondence with his ex-friend had been limited to Indian government affairs. "What does His Majesty want?"

The servant blinked. "I-I don't know. I was just sent to fetch you." He eyed Raji warily. "Shall I put your creature in his cage first?"

"Raji attended over thirty balls in India. He will be fine." Simon dismissed the servant with a nod. "Tell His Majesty I will be along presently."

"Very good, sir," the servant said, looking distinctly uneasy as he rushed off.

Simon didn't care. Let the king wait, the way he had made Simon wait all these years to continue his political career.

He started down the steps, only to realize that his way was blocked by Louisa and the elderly lady with whom she conversed. Good God, it was Lady Trusbut. He would know the bird-loving baroness anywhere. No one else would carry a feathered fan *and* a feathered reticule, not to mention the usual feathers in her gown and coiffure that made her look more like a poulterer than the wife of an influential member of the House of Lords.

When the harpists began a new piece and Lady Trusbut turned her head to listen, he noticed that she even wore a brilliantly plumed artificial peacock nestled in—

Damn. Raji!

Even as Simon thought it, he grabbed for his pet, but

Raji was already scampering down the steps after the one thing that could tempt him to misbehave. Fake birds.

With great glee, Raji climbed Lady Trusbut's back and dove into her coiffure after what he saw as a toy.

Simon dashed after him with a curse, wincing when Lady Trusbut screamed . . . and kept screaming as Raji leaped about her head, tugging on the ornament firmly attached to Lady Trusbut's hair.

"Raji, no!" he ordered, but his voice was drowned out by the panicked ones of guests who ran to her aid.

Meanwhile, Louisa was trying to coax the monkey onto her arm as Lady Trusbut lapsed into a sobbing chant, "Get-it-off—get-it-off—get-it-off—"

"Raji, come here!" Simon barked as he neared them.

This time both his pet *and* Louisa heard him.

Although Raji ignored him, Louisa did not. Her head whipped around, her eyes briefly filling with shock. Then her features smoothed into a composed mask. "I take it that this creature is yours."

"Afraid so." He scowled at his pet. "Come down this minute, you scamp!"

Simon reached for him, but Raji shrank back, taking the peacock with him and eliciting another screech from Lady Trusbut. For a monkey, Raji possessed a remarkably well-developed sense of self-preservation.

"You're making it worse, Your Grace," Louisa said. "He's afraid of you."

"The only thing he's afraid of is losing that bloody bird," Simon snapped, irritated that she could call him "Your Grace" as if they were strangers.

"Oh dear, oh dear." Lady Trusbut grabbed at her head, then squealed when Raji dug in harder. "You mustn't let that creature destroy my favorite peacock!"

"It's all right," Louisa said, "I'm sure we can find something else for him to demolish."

She glanced about, then grabbed a cup from a passing footman. After dipping her finger in punch, she held it up to the monkey. "Ooh, smell that, Raji. Doesn't that smell delicious?" She drank from the cup and smiled broadly, easing her finger closer to the monkey. "Yum, very sweet."

Raji leaned near enough to lap her finger, first warily, then eagerly. She held the cup higher, and Raji reached for it with one hand, his other clasping the bird.

Louisa drew the cup back. "Oh no, dear boy, you must come here for it."

As soon as Raji leaned toward the cup, Simon reached up to pry the monkey's fingers from the peacock. Raji looked torn, but in the end the punch won and he leaped onto Louisa's shoulder.

Lady Trusbut gasped, but Louisa didn't so much as flinch. With admirable calm, she coaxed the monkey into her arms and handed Raji the cup.

As Lady Trusbut frantically repaired her hair, Simon told Louisa, "Let me have him." The rascal was sure to head straight for Lady Trusbut's peacock once he had downed the punch.

But when Louisa held Raji out, the monkey grabbed her bodice and wailed.

"Apparently, he doesn't *want* to go to you," she said, arching one raven eyebrow as she cradled Raji against her breasts.

"Of course not," Simon muttered. His lucky devil of a pet drained the cup, then shot Simon a smug look. Little traitor. "Half the men in this garden would give their eyeteeth to be where that imp is right now."

A blush spread from Louisa's cheeks down her neck to

the very breasts that pillowed Raji's head, making Simon's pulse thunder like an elephant run amok. But the calm gaze that met his was as remote as if they'd never met. "If you don't like where your pet is at present, perhaps you shouldn't take him to parties."

"Dear Lord!" Lady Trusbut, who was repairing her coiffure, held up a hand smeared with blood. "That beast has wounded me!" Then she promptly fainted.

As Simon cursed, Louisa ordered, "Get my smelling salts."

"Where are they?" Simon asked.

"In my reticule." Louisa tried to juggle Raji and the empty punch cup. "Oh, never mind. Here, take your monkey." She thrust Raji into Simon's arms.

Raji dropped the cup, but when he eyed the prone Lady Trusbut and her peacock longingly, Simon manacled his wrist. "No, you don't, you rascal."

Louisa was already wafting smelling salts under Lady Trusbut's nose as other females crowded 'round on the graveled path to help. Simon felt like an intruder. Again. "Excuse me, ladies, but I had best remove Raji to his cage."

No one paid him any mind, except Louisa, who glanced up at him. "Yes, Your Grace, you may run along now. We have this under control."

Run along now? A hot retort leapt to his lips, but Raji struggled to get free, and Simon could not stay to argue. "Please make my apologies to Lady Trusbut." He strode off through the crowd.

Ignoring the whispers around him, he hurried up the steps, then back inside, his temper swelling. "You would think the chit and I were complete strangers," he growled as he stalked toward Draker's enormous library, where he had left Raji's cage. *"You may run along now, Your Grace—* how dare she dismiss me as if I were some bloody servant?"

Simon glared at Raji. "And you had to make it worse, didn't you? Had to make me look like a fool in front of her. Countless Indian balls without an incident, and you choose my first English fete to make a spectacle of us both."

With Raji loudly protesting his master's firm hold, Simon entered the library. "Next time I whittle anything for *you,* scamp, it will be a pair of shackles." It was an idle threat; Simon rarely even caged Raji. Which was probably why the rascal shrieked in outrage as Simon carried him toward his prison.

"I had forgotten that you whittled," said a painfully familiar voice behind Simon. "Used to make such a mess in my drawing room."

Simon groaned. Bloody hell. First Louisa, now this.

Slowly he faced the king, who had just entered the library. "Your Majesty." As Simon bowed, Raji in hand, he steeled himself for an awkward confrontation.

"Sprightly chap, isn't he?" The king nodded to where Raji still protested his impending retreat from good society.

"He is generally better behaved." Simon thrust Raji into the cage, but only when he handed his pet the gaily painted bird that was his favorite toy did Raji settle down, stroking the carved creature with paternal affection.

George sidled nearer to peer into the cage. "Did you whittle that toy of his?"

"Whittling helps me think."

"Scheme and plot, you mean."

Simon eyed him warily. "A skill you made good use of, as I recall."

"True enough." The king swept his gaze down Simon. "You look well."

"So do you." Actually, George looked like a bloated whale. A lifetime of debauchery showed in his puffy features and pallid skin.

"You never used to lie to me, you insolent scoundrel, so don't start now."

Simon choked back a laugh. He used to lie to the king with painful regularity—it was how he had advanced his career. But no more. "Fine. You look like hell. Is that what you wanted to hear?"

George winced. "No, but it's the truth, isn't it?"

"Truth depends on your perspective." Simon closed Raji's cage, wondering what the king was up to. "As my aide-de-camp used to say, 'It is better to be blind than to see things from only one point of view.'"

"Don't give me any nonsense you got from that half-caste Indian," George snapped. "You're not a nabob eager to hold lectures about his travels and entertain the frivolous with his pet. You and I both know you have a greater destiny."

As Simon's fingers stilled on the lock of Raji's cage, he kept his tone carefully even. "You sound rather sure of that."

"This is no time for games. I know you went to Parliament yesterday. You're taking stock, aren't you?"

Simon did not deny it. Or reveal that a mere hour with his old cronies had illuminated how much his time in India had altered his ideas about politics. Ruling with paternalistic indulgence had worked fine for men of his grandfather's day, but the French Revolution and American defection had changed people's expectations.

Unfortunately, the old guard had responded by digging

in their heels and instituting draconian policies that only stirred up more trouble. They needed to listen to the discontented voices. And that meant overhauling the House of Commons so that it represented more than just the wealthiest landowners.

Not that Simon intended to let his old allies know of his new ideas. He must tread lightly at first. The old guard did not respond well to suggestions of reform—he would have to reassure them that his measures would not mean an overthrow of the government. Slow, moderate change was the only thing they could embrace.

Simon turned to find the king eyeing him uncertainly. "You do still mean to pursue your lifelong ambition, don't you?" His Majesty searched his face. "Everyone expects you to follow Monteith's fine example."

Then everyone could go to hell. Because although Simon's ambition was as healthy as ever, he did *not* mean to pursue it by following his grandfather's *fine example,* living a life of hypocrisy and secret moral corruption.

Or by falling right back in with the king and his machinations. His Majesty was unpredictable at best and dangerous at worst. "I haven't yet decided—"

"Of course you have." He cast Simon a sly glance. "Or you wouldn't have served your full term as Governor-General. You'd have returned to England once you tired of the heat and snakes and troubles with the natives. But you stuck it out when a lesser man would've said, 'I have wealth and rank. Who needs politics?'"

Simon bristled. "I stuck it out because I pledged to do so."

"And because I said you would have no political future unless you did."

Clearly His Majesty meant to press the issue. "Yes. But

I served my term faithfully, and now you owe me your unqualified support in my bid for prime minister. Just as we agreed."

With a cunning smile, the king circled Simon. "Ah, but that isn't exactly what we agreed to, is it? I said if you went to India, I would not oppose your reentry into politics upon your return. There was no mention of support."

A sharp burst of anger seared Simon's gut. Though he was not surprised that His Bloody Majesty was splitting hairs, it hampered his plans for England. Much as he hated it, permanent change would require the king's complicity.

But he'd be damned before he'd beg. "Then I am on my own. Thank you for clarifying that detail." He turned for the door. "Now if you will excuse me . . ."

"Wait, damn you. I only meant that if you do want my unqualified support—"

"I will have to do as you say." Simon paused as he reached the door. "The last time you dangled your 'unqualified support' in front of me, I ended up banished." Thanks to one reckless kiss and a handful of false promises. "Forgive me if I have lost my taste for currying your favor."

"Don't be impertinent, Foxmoor. You know damned well that what happened with Louisa was your fault. I told you *not* to make her believe you would marry her. Was I supposed to look the other way when you defied me?"

Apparently they were going to have this discussion, regardless of Simon's wishes. Shutting the library door, he faced the king. "You gave me an impossible task. Court her, but not court her. Coax her to go off alone with me so you could meet with her, but not tell her why." He took a steadying breath. "I could not accomplish your aims by remaining aloof."

"I *thought* you would behave like an honorable gentleman."

With Louisa, whose voluptuous mouth had haunted his dreams even then? "Even I have limits."

George eyed Simon assessingly. "She's much altered from the young woman you knew then, don't you think?"

The abrupt change of subject put him further on his guard. This way lay quicksand. "I could not say. We barely had time to speak."

"She's more comfortable in society, more confident." He scowled. "*Too* confident, if you ask me."

"Trouble in paradise, Your Majesty?" Simon said dryly.

George glowered at him. "Your sister has told you about it, I suppose."

"Regina and I do not discuss Louisa."

The king began to pace. "The willful chit is driving me insane. She refuses every suitor, says she's never going to marry. At first I didn't believe her, but she's twenty-six and still hasn't let a man near her."

He shot Simon a dour glance. "Then there's her activities. I didn't squawk when she was over at that blasted Widow Harris's school, giving the girls advice on how to behave at court. I figured it would keep her busy, since Louisa took my daughter Charlotte's death very hard, as did we all. But now she's got herself mixed up with reformers, and she's hieing herself off to Newgate—"

"The prison?" he said, curious in spite of himself.

"Exactly. She and her London Ladies Society go with those Quakers from the Association for the Improvement of Female Prisoners in Newgate to bring aid."

That surprised him. Louisa had never struck him as the sort to pursue reform, much less the unsavory kind of reform. "And her brother allows it?"

"Draker approves, damn him. Even lets Regina go off with her. The fool thinks it's good for them to do something 'useful' and 'worthy' with their time."

Simon shrugged. "Charity work *is* a time-honored pastime for ladies."

"Unmarried ones? Who should not have their tender minds besmirched by the debaucheries they might witness there?"

Remembering his one visit to Newgate years ago, Simon shuddered. The man did have a point. The inmates he had seen had acted little better than animals. And to think of Louisa there . . .

But it was none of his affair.

"And when Louisa isn't trotting off to Newgate, she and her London Ladies Society raise funds for the Association."

"That's why she was speaking to Lady Trusbut."

"Oh, she wants more from Lady Trusbut than money. She wants the silly featherhead to join the London Ladies Society so that—" George stopped abruptly.

Simon's eyes narrowed. "So that what? What is wrong with Lady Trusbut joining Louisa's charitable group?"

The king glanced away. "Nothing. Except that they're trotting about the prisons, of course."

That clearly was not what worried the king. Not that it mattered. "Why would your daughter's new pastime possibly concern me?"

His Majesty's gaze swung back to him. "Do you still fancy Louisa?" When Simon tensed, George added hastily, "What if I were to say you could have her?"

A thrill coursed down Simon's spine that he ruthlessly squelched. This was a trap. "I am sure Louisa would have a strong opinion about that."

"Perhaps if she knew. But I intend this arrangement to stay between us."

Simon dragged in a sharp breath. "If you think I will once more play—"

"I'm not suggesting anything underhanded; this time I mean marriage. She needs a husband to keep her safe. And you're the logical choice."

"Me!" The suggestion staggered Simon. "You cannot possibly be serious. What happened to your assertion years ago that she should marry for love? That I was incapable of it?" Which just happened to be true, unfortunately.

"I thought she'd find someone. But she hasn't, and I fear she never will."

"Unless *I* marry her?"

"Exactly. Wed her and bed her and get her with child. Do whatever's necessary to keep her safely at home."

Simon burst into laughter. This was *not* the conversation he had expected to have with His Majesty. "Surely you see the irony. Me and Louisa . . . married . . ."

"You found her attractive enough once." His face clouded over. "Or did her request that you be sent off turn your tender feelings to hatred?"

His amusement vanished. "I have no feelings for her one way or the other."

Liar. He had tried to hate her. His anger, twisted with a healthy dose of frustrated lust, had consumed him during those early days in Calcutta. He had spent his nights in lurid fantasies, imagining her at his mercy, reduced to begging his forgiveness and offering all manner of erotic favors. But hard work and the challenge of being Governor-General had eventually burned off his anger.

He'd thought he had subdued his lust, as well—until today. Not that it mattered. He would not allow Louisa, with her seductive mouth and refreshing boldness, to distract him from his ambition this time. He had learned his lesson.

Besides, George was clearly hiding his real reasons for wanting Simon to marry her, and that made involvement with her dangerous indeed.

"I do not hate Louisa," Simon said, "but under the circumstances, marrying her would be unwise. Even if I wanted to, she would balk. She has clearly lost any interest she once had in me." Galling but true, judging from her reaction upon first seeing him.

"Yet she's still unmarried. And blushes whenever your name is mentioned."

He ignored the sudden leap in his pulse. "Does she?"

"Why do you think I'm approaching *you* with this proposition? Because I think she secretly still has feelings for you."

"Then they are very secret indeed." The damned female had acted as if he were any bloody gentleman she might meet at a party, instead of the first man to ever kiss her. "I certainly saw no sign of them earlier."

"You will. Put that charm of yours to work. God knows you're more eligible now than ever, after your heroic actions at the Battle of Kirkee."

He sucked in a harsh breath. "Yes, wasn't it heroic of me to close the stable door after the horses had escaped?"

The king eyed him with a curious gaze. "You acted on good intelligence. No one blames you for what happened at Poona."

No one but himself. Because no one but him recognized the enormity of his misjudgment. He might have prevented the razing of Poona if only—

But going over and over it did no good. He had

learned from it, and now he meant to make good use of what he'd learned. And to make amends for his error. That was only right.

"The point is," the king went on, "Louisa still cares for you—I'm sure of it. And if you got her to fall in love with you once, you can do it again."

The tantalizing appeal of that alarmed him. He did not need the likes of Louisa North in his life right now. "Ah, but I don't want to do it again."

"Even if I make sure you're the next prime minister? Liverpool needs to resign after the mess at St. Peter's Field. Even the other ministers acknowledge that it would soothe the populace to see him step down."

And the other ministers were even worse than Liverpool, but they could be dismissed if Liverpool was gone. Judging from the MPs Simon had spoken to, the general feeling was that the entire current government needed dismantling.

Perhaps change was finally in the wind. Perhaps the time had finally come to sever the dead wood before it brought the English oak crashing down.

But that didn't mean Simon could trust George with the axe.

"And what will you do if Louisa refuses to marry me or claims I broke her heart a second time?" Simon asked. "No. I will not risk my career yet again." He stalked toward the door.

"At least take time to think about it," the king said. "If you do this for me, I swear you won't regret it. And if you don't . . ." George trailed off meaningfully.

Bloody hell, the king still had the power to make a great deal of trouble. But why would he resort to threats over Louisa marrying? It made no sense.

Perhaps Simon should learn more about the situation before he burned any bridges. "I will consider it." At least until he learned the king's motives.

Since he clearly would not get the truth from George, that left only one other source—Louisa. Perhaps *she* knew what prompted the king's concern.

Whether she would tell him was another matter. He would have to be careful in his questions, but he *would* get answers. Because he dared not proceed with his own plans until he knew exactly what the king was up to.

And how the tempting and dangerous Louisa North played into the equation.

Chapter Two

Dear Charlotte,
   I have never heard anything but rumor about
what happened between Miss North and Foxmoor.
And what gentleman would dare ask the duke about
it, after the Battle of Kirkee? Any man whose words
can incite a tiny force of sepoys to fight and triumph
over a vast enemy is no one I'd want to tangle with.
                                        Quaking in my boots,
                                        Your Cousin Michael

So the Duke of High-and-Mighty was still causing trouble. That did not surprise Louisa in the least.

The monkey, however, was something of a shock. And who on earth brought a monkey to a social affair? Only someone arrogant and sure of his welcome, someone who liked to pay compliments that would make any woman blush—

"How bad is it?" asked a plaintive voice.

Louisa jerked. She was supposed to be examining Lady Trusbut's head, which presently lay in her lap. "I haven't found it yet."

She and the baroness sat in Castlemaine's drawing

room. Surprisingly, after recovering from her faint, the woman had put herself entirely into Louisa's hands, even lying down on the damask sofa when they'd entered so that Louisa could look at her scalp while a servant fetched Regina. Given this unexpected opportunity to make her case to the woman, Louisa should *not* be woolgathering about Simon.

Good heavens, she mustn't think of him as "Simon" either. He was the Duke of Foxmoor to her now, nothing more. If she'd had any sense seven years ago, she would have realized it then, no matter what dribble he spouted about her eyes and her hair and how he felt—

Felt, hah! The man had no feelings. Those were reserved for lesser mortals than the great duke. She'd been a fool ever to believe otherwise.

But she really ought to thank him. Because of him, she'd taught herself to be wiser, modeling her behavior on that of Regina and the ladies at court. These days the duke wasn't the only one who could hide his true feelings behind an unreadable smile. Though it had taken Louisa years to learn how to restrain her volatile emotions, she'd done it, by heaven. And tonight she'd triumphed, handling the mighty duke himself with ladylike reserve.

Now if only her hands would stop quaking and her insides quivering and her blood raging through her veins.

She scowled. It wasn't fair. How could that manipulative scoundrel still heat her up with just one unsettling glance from those searing blue eyes? She didn't need this. She'd finally gained her chance to speak privately with the skittish baroness, and that lying devil wasn't going to ruin it for her.

"I can't find the wound," Louisa said. "And the monkey seems to have left some odd-looking bits of chaff."

"That's birdseed, dear," the baroness twittered.

"Birdseed?" The woman had birdseed in her hair, for heaven's sake!

"My birds are messy eaters," Lady Trusbut said as if that explained everything. "But at least they don't attack people for no reason."

"Yes, birds make lovely pets." When they weren't depositing their feed in one's hair.

"Do you keep birds?" Lady Trusbut asked, brightening.

She kept cats. They liked to *eat* birds. Probably not the best thing to mention. "My brother keeps swans," she hedged.

"No one 'keeps' swans, my dear," Lady Trusbut said disparagingly. "They're ornamental, and ill-tempered, besides. But a pretty canary will entertain you with song for hours with nary a complaint. Or there's the finch, with its . . ."

As Lady Trusbut waxed poetic about her friendly flock, Louisa picked her way through seed chaff and wondered how to steer the conversation back to the London Ladies Society. She didn't want to frighten the baroness off, after all.

Louisa finally found the source of the blood and dabbed at it with her handkerchief. "Your wound isn't very bad. Just a scratch."

"It hurts like the dickens," Lady Trusbut protested.

"I'm sure it does," Louisa said soothingly. "As soon as Regina comes, she'll put ointment on it. She volunteers at Chelsea Hospital, you know."

"I shall probably catch some vile disease from that odious monkey."

Louisa stifled her impulse to point out that Lady Trusbut could catch something just as easily from her birds.

"You were very brave, my dear. I wouldn't have made it out of the melee otherwise. How clever of you to tempt the creature with punch! I could never have thought of it. I'm not quick on my feet. My canaries always say so."

"Your canaries talk?"

"Don't be silly—they're canaries. But that doesn't mean I can't understand what they think." Louisa was still trying to decipher that, when Lady Trusbut added, "I'm sure they would agree that your capture of that willful beast was magnificent." Lady Trusbut tilted her head to peer up at Louisa. "Did you learn that sort of quick thinking from your little group?"

At last, the chance she'd been waiting for! "I've learned many things from the fine and dedicated women of the London Ladies Society."

"How long have you been a member?"

"Three years. I was the one who established the group."

Lady Trusbut made a tsking sound. "A young lady like you should be thinking about marriage, not reform."

Louisa tensed at the familiar criticism. "I think about both. But since I can only find time to do one, my conscience dictates that I choose the latter."

Her conscience . . . and her raging terror. Although it was true she could do more good as a reforming spinster than as some overbearing lord's wife, it was really the thought of what marriage wrought that kept her from it.

Childbirth. Doctors. Blood and horror.

After what her beloved half sister, Princess Charlotte, had endured . . . she could never live through that. No matter how often she told herself that women bore children safely every day, the bloody birth she'd secretly witnessed preyed on her mind. If even a princess could die in such agony, surrounded by the best doctors, anyone could suffer the same, including her.

A shudder wracked her. No man was worth that, even—

Louisa scowled. *He* was certainly not worth it, the scheming scoundrel.

Fiercely, she renewed her efforts with Lady Trusbut. "If you should hear the call of conscience yourself, the London Ladies would be honored to have you."

"Isn't your group affiliated with that Quaker Association I hear about?"

"Yes, the one run by Mrs. Elizabeth Fry."

Lady Trusbut shook her head. "I don't approve of Quakers. Edward says they despise anything with feathers."

"Edward" was Lord Trusbut, who'd apparently found the perfect way to discourage his eccentric wife's participation. "They merely disapprove of extravagant dress. I doubt they dislike feathers in particular. And the London Ladies Society doesn't just have Quakers. Mrs. Harris is a member, as well as several of her graduates and ladies of rank." She reached into her reticule. "I have here a list of women who—"

"Mrs. Charlotte Harris? Headmistress of the School for Heiresses?"

Louisa bit back a smile to hear the popular nickname for the school where she'd once given aid. "Well, it's actually the School for Young Ladies."

"Mrs. Harris keeps birds, doesn't she?"

Good heavens, the woman had only one note. "She recently acquired a parakeet, I believe."

"Parakeets are delightful, very chatty." Lady Trusbut hesitated, as if thinking, then smiled up at Louisa. "Very well, I shall donate funds to your group. 'Tis the least I can do after you saved me from that imp from hell."

Money. Louisa sighed. "We'll be most grateful for the donation, madam, but we'd be even happier if you'd join us."

"Oh, I don't know. Edward would disapprove."

Before she could answer, a male voice spoke from the doorway. "Nonsense. Surely any gentleman would approve of Miss North's charitable organization."

Startled, Louisa glanced up to find her nemesis watching them. Oh no, why was *he* here? And how long had he been standing there?

As she went to tuck her list into her reticule, her curst hands started shaking and the list floated to the floor.

Simon bent to retrieve it, then scanned it swiftly. "An impressive roster of ladies you have here, Miss North. Members of your group?"

Refusing to answer, Louisa held out her hand. "If you would please—"

"Certainly." A smile touched his lips as he handed her the list.

He was probably laughing at her for her clumsiness. Simon would never be clumsy, oh no. Not the clever duke.

When his gaze fixed on her with the unerring instinct of a tiger scenting prey, she had to struggle not to blush like the girl she'd once been, swept off her feet by a dashing scoundrel. Until she'd discovered there was nothing "dashing" about having the Duke of Foxmoor dash one's heart against the rocks.

"As you can see," Louisa said tartly, "Lady Trusbut is fine now, so we won't keep you from the party."

"I don't mind," he said. "I came to apologize for my pet's behavior."

Lady Trusbut sat up and smoothed her skirts. "Kind of you to think of me, Your Grace."

"It's the least I could do." Taking her hand, he brushed a kiss across the top.

The courtly gesture brought a smile fluttering across the woman's lips.

Louisa stifled a groan. Apparently Simon had this annoying effect on every woman.

How she'd prayed that he would return to England worse for wear—sunken-eyed and gaunt, with skin burnt a leathery brown by the harsh Indian sun. Instead he looked every inch the conqueror arriving home to widespread accolades. His perfectly tailored evening attire accentuated his lean and muscular frame, and his days in the sun had tinted his skin a golden hue perfectly complemented by his sun-streaked blond hair.

"Allow me to explain Raji's actions," Simon went on. "You see, he loves toy birds, so he could not resist the chance to pet yours."

"P-pet it?" Lady Trusbut squeaked. "H-he wasn't trying to mangle it?"

"Absolutely not. He considers birds, real or toy, to be his playmates." Simon arched one eyebrow. "He prefers canaries, though I am not sure why."

Sly devil. He must have heard Lady Trusbut gushing over her birds.

Lady Trusbut cocked her head, pigeon-like. "Canaries are delightful, very amiable and sociable. I happen to own several."

"Do you? Raji would certainly enjoy seeing them."

"Then perhaps you should bring him to call on me sometime. If you're sure he won't hurt them."

Simon bowed. "He will be on his best behavior, I assure you." He shot Louisa a conspiratorial glance. "But I hope you will allow me to bring Miss North, as well. Raji seems to respond better to her commands than mine."

Louisa blinked. What in heaven's name was he up to now?

Before Lady Trusbut could answer, he added, "I forgot, that's probably impossible, since your husband disapproves of Miss North's charitable efforts."

"I-I didn't say that," Lady Trusbut protested, looking confused.

"I assume that if he would disapprove of your joining her group, then he disapproves of their charitable work."

The way he kept pounding the word "charitable" gave Louisa pause.

And flustered Lady Trusbut. "Well, no . . . I mean . . . my husband is a good man. He does believe in Christian charity, but the Association is so very political, you see, and he doesn't think that politics is a woman's purview."

Louisa gaped at her, shocked that she had actually discussed the group with her husband. All this time she'd thought Lady Trusbut was simply ignoring her appeals for support.

Eyes narrowing, Simon glanced to Louisa. "What does she mean by 'political'?"

Louisa stared him down. "We believe Parliament should institute certain reforms in the prisons, sir. And we aren't afraid to tell the MPs our opinions."

His gaze probed hers. "I see."

She squirmed on the sofa. Why did she have the feeling he "saw" more than she'd said? Did he know about their other plans? No, how could he?

Simon smiled at Lady Trusbut. "Then I understand your reluctance, madam. Some men are particular about their politics, so you would not want to risk your husband's wrath by joining such a group. Men of the oppressive sort—"

"My husband isn't oppressive." Lady Trusbut sniffed. "He's a kind, generous man!"

"Yes, of course." He lowered his voice. "Don't worry, we will keep your secret safe. We will not let him know you associate with Miss North and her dangerous companions. We would not want to be the cause of his abusing you—"

"I tell you, sir, you've misunderstood my husband entirely!" Lady Trusbut stood to face the challenger to her husband's honor. "You shall come to call, and you shall bring Miss North. Come Saturday, when Parliament isn't in session, and then you'll see for yourself how accommodating my husband can be."

Simon nodded, eyes gleaming. "Thank you, I will do that." His gaze flicked to Louisa. "Assuming that Miss North will honor me with her company."

Half-dazed, Louisa rose to her feet. Had the duke really just manipulated Lady Trusbut into giving Louisa an audience with her and her husband? But why? What possible purpose could it serve him?

Before Louisa could answer him, Regina swept into the room. "Oh, there you are, Lady Trusbut. You seem to have recovered nicely."

Her pride further soothed by the attention of a duke's very popular sister, the baroness touched a hand to her hair. "Miss North has been quite solicitous of me."

Louisa smiled at her sister-in-law. "I told Lady Trusbut that you probably had some healing ointment for her injury."

"Yes, of course." Regina waved her hand toward the door. "If you'll just come with me to our stillroom . . ."

Lady Trusbut hurried to her side, but when Louisa started to follow, Regina shook her head. "No need for you to stay inside, my dear." She nodded to her brother. "Accompany Louisa back to the party, will you? You might as well make yourself useful now that your pet is under wraps."

"I would be honored." Eyes gleaming, Simon held out his arm to Louisa.

She hesitated, but the last thing she wanted him to know was how much he unsettled her. Besides, she needed to find out what the wily fellow was trying to do. This would be an excellent test of her self-control. If she could stay unruffled with Simon, she would finally be free of him.

Yet the mere act of letting him lead her from the drawing room did fluttery things to her insides. Heavens, but he was finely made—she could feel his muscles bunch beneath his merino coat. He'd always been a virile man, but now . . .

Clearly, he hadn't spent the last few years behind a desk. His shoulders were broader, and his physique more finely developed. Where he'd once been Adonis, he was now Zeus, and as confident of his power as that imperious god.

He stood aside to let her pass through the open door leading to the gallery, then laid his hand briefly in the small of her back as he came up behind her. A shiver of forgotten pleasure skittered down her spine.

Oh dear. When would her body learn the lessons her heart had—that he couldn't be trusted? Would she have to be doddering on the edge of the grave? Because clearly her body was leaping for joy to have him near.

Dratted, witless body. She must teach it to behave.

When he offered her his arm again she barely laid her hand upon it. Surely she could control her thumping pulse if she just didn't touch him.

Unfortunately, he noticed her reaction. Seizing her hand, he pressed it more firmly to his arm. "I promise you, I did not bring any diseases back from India."

"I didn't think you had," she said, hot color flooding her cheeks. It was time to show him she wasn't the naïve girl he'd deceived all those years ago. "But I am wondering what new scheme you're engaged in, Your Grace."

"Scheme?" he echoed as they headed for the steps leading to the gardens.

"That nonsense with Lady Trusbut, coaxing her to welcome me into her home. What are you doing? And why are you doing it?" She shot him a questioning glance, but his eyes remained fixed straight ahead.

"You helped me with Raji, so I decided to help you with the baroness."

"You don't even know what I'm trying to do with her," she said.

"Perhaps you should enlighten me."

That put her instantly on her guard. "Why would I want to do that?"

His gaze swung to hers. "We were friends once."

"We were never friends."

His eyes searched hers, brooding, hot . . . intoxicating. "No, I suppose not." Settling his gaze on her lips, he lowered his voice. "Friends do not kiss, do they?"

Her pulse was positively hammering. "Friends do not lie and betray each other. We were pawns in His Majesty's game. Or I should say, *I* was a pawn. You were as much the chess master as he."

"And you got your just revenge on me for it," he said tightly. "So can't we put the whole incident behind us now?"

Leave it to Simon to regard as a mere "incident" the event that had changed her whole life. "In case you haven't noticed, I *have* put it behind me." She released his arm as they neared the garden steps. "Now if you'll excuse me . . ."

But his attention had shifted to a spot beyond her. "Come," he said abruptly, holding out his arm again. "Let's take a turn about the gardens."

"I can't imagine why I—"

"Look down there," he said under his breath. "Every guest is watching us, waiting to witness the explosion, especially after what happened earlier with Raji."

She followed his gaze, and her heart sank. He was right. The crowd below had grown eerily silent, bent on not missing the "explosion," as he put it.

While no one but their respective families knew the full extent of the antipathy between Miss Louisa North and the Duke of Foxmoor, they did know he'd once seemed on the verge of offering for her before abruptly and mysteriously accepting the post of Governor-General and hieing off to India.

Gossip had run rampant immediately after, snippets of which had drifted back to Louisa. Theories had ranged wildly: she'd jilted him and broken his heart; he'd jilted her and broken her heart; His Highness had inexplicably disapproved of the match and broken both their hearts.

"You have two choices," Simon said with an edge in his voice. "You can take a turn about the gardens with me to show that we are on good terms, which might end the speculation. Or you can give me the cut direct, thus ensuring that we are gossiped about for the next year at least. Which is it to be?"

She hesitated, but she really had no choice. "Why, Your Grace," she said in a syrupy voice as she took his arm, "I'd be honored to walk with you."

A faint smile tugged at his lips. "I rather thought that you might."

As they descended the stairs, people stared and whispered. Drat them all! She'd succeeded with her reform efforts because of her unblemished reputation and her avoidance of scandal. It had taken years at court for her to live down the rumors—not just about her and Simon, but her possible illegitimacy and the scandals her mother and brother had engendered in her youth.

She'd made a useful life for herself, behaved with consummate decorum, and learned to control her worst impulses so no one would compare her to her wanton mother. But it could all unravel with one pull of a loose thread.

How horrible it would be to have the gossip start up again, just as the London Ladies were on the verge of shaking up the stuffy lords and their backward ideas—

"Are you all right?" he asked.

"Fine," she said tersely.

"You look as if you just swallowed a toad."

Her gaze shot to his. "A t-toad?"

"They eat toads in India, you know," he said, his face utterly expressionless.

"You're joking."

The corners of his lips twitched. "Not at all. They eat them with mustard and marmalade. And a drop of Madeira to kill the poison."

"Poison?"

He led her down a path bordered by daffodils and daisies. "Toads are poisonous if you don't add the Madeira. Everyone knows that."

"Now I'm sure you're bamming me," she said with an unsteady laugh.

But his tall tale had relaxed her. People were finally returning to their conversations, deprived of the scandalous spectacle they'd expected.

"That's better," he said in a low voice. "I can't have them think I'm torturing you."

"No, that wouldn't serve your public image, would it?" she said lightly.

"Or yours." When she glanced up at him in surprise, he added, "A reformer must worry about her public image, too, I would imagine."

She sighed. She'd forgotten that he read minds. He'd always had an uncanny ability to know exactly what she was thinking.

No, that was silly. He merely gave that impression—it was his forte. It was how he manipulated people so successfully.

And yet . . . she couldn't shake the sense that they were beginning exactly where they'd left off. He walked beside her as if he'd stepped right out of her memories and into Castlemaine's gardens. Even his scent was the same as back then—an intoxicating blend of brandy, sandalwood, and soap.

And she'd forgotten how charming he could be. If she closed her eyes, would she be whisked back to those heady nights during her come-out when he'd danced with her more often than was proper, teasing her and tempting her?

Of course not. Those nights had been an illusion. And so was this.

Careful, Louisa. Nothing good ever comes of being friendly with the Duke of Foxmoor.

If she didn't take care, she would find herself swept into his latest scheme. Only this time, she had much more to lose than her heart. And she refused to let the duke take something from her ever again.

Chapter Three

∞

Dear Cousin,
  I know perfectly well you would not quake in your boots for anyone. Besides, Foxmoor did not look so fearsome at Lady Draker's fete; he had a monkey who quite got the better of him. Though come to think of it, the monkey did vanish later—perhaps Foxmoor had the last word after all.

  Your gossipy cousin,
  Charlotte

*S*imon knew exactly when Louisa erected her defenses against him again. He'd thought she was softening, but judging from her patently false smile and the way she nodded regally to everyone they passed, the moment was gone.

Bloody hell, she'd turned into quite the prickly female. Because of him?

Or because of her new activities? He couldn't help noticing as they neared two prominent MPs that the men cast dark glances in her direction. Glances that turned wary when they fell on him.

She had said that her organization wasn't afraid to

voice their opinions about prison reform. Just how forcefully did they express them? Surely not strongly enough to annoy the old guard.

Though it might explain the king's inordinate concern for her "safety." Politics was involved. Now all Simon had to do was learn how.

He smiled at her. "I haven't yet thanked you for helping me with Raji."

"Why on earth did you bring him, anyway?"

"It is an outdoor affair, and Raji enjoys the occasional party."

"Ah, but *you* don't usually enjoy the occasional fiasco. The duke I used to know would never have risked annoying potential supporters to please his pet."

"People change," he snapped. *He* was supposed to be running this inquisition, not *her,* for God's sake.

"Do they?" When he bristled, she added, "I confess I was surprised you even own a pet, let alone an exotic one."

"Why?"

"Because pets require care, and a man of your position has little time for such."

"Unfortunately," he said dryly, "no one informed Raji of my busy schedule before he decided to adopt me."

She blinked. "Adopt you?"

"He belonged to my aide-de-camp's Indian wife, who died . . . tragically. Colin was too distraught to care for him, so he brought the little chap to the funeral, meaning to give Raji to her family. But as soon as the rascal saw me, he latched on and would not let go."

And guilt had compelled Simon to keep him. Oddly enough, even though Raji served as a painful reminder of Simon's misjudgment in India, the creature had also been his salvation in that bleak time. "He's been with me ever since."

"That doesn't sound like you, either."

He flashed her a rueful smile. "True. Yet here I am, monkey in tow. What is a man to do?"

Her features softened. Then she jerked her gaze from his and cleared her throat. "So what are your plans?"

He could hardly tell her they rested on what he found out from *her*. "I am not sure. I only arrived in England three days ago. Why do you ask?"

"Have you been to Parliament yet?"

"Yes."

"Then I have my answer."

He didn't pretend to misunderstand. "I do come from a long line of statesmen on my mother's side."

"And on your father's side," she quipped, "a long line of pompous, ne'er-do-well dukes."

He chuckled. "I see you have grown far too friendly with my sister."

"Oh yes, though she talks more about your mother's illustrious relations than your father's. It's a shame that men cannot inherit titles from the mother's side, because you would have been the perfect heir to your grandfather Monteith, the famous prime minister. And apparently, he thought so, too. From what Regina says, the old earl groomed you most carefully to follow in his footsteps."

His amusement vanished. Did his sister have any idea what that "grooming" had entailed? God, he hoped not. He would rather she didn't know about that humiliating time in his life. Fortunately, she'd had far less contact with their autocratic grandfather than Simon had.

"Yes, I suppose you could say that," Simon bit out.

"When I was not at Eton, I spent much of my time with him, preparing for a political career."

"That's why everyone expects you to be prime minister."

He eyed her closely. "And you? What do *you* expect of me?"

He'd meant to turn talk back toward discussion of her group, but her spine went stiff as a palanquin pole. "Nothing. Except that you and I can be civil."

"We're being civil now." He chose his words carefully. "If you want, I could even help you with your charitable group. Since it dabbles in politics—"

"We don't dabble," she said stoutly. "We're serious about our aims. One way or the other, we mean to convince Parliament to reform the prisons."

One way or the other? Just how political *was* her group? "It's a good cause."

"If you only knew the horrors those poor women suffer." Her fingers dug into his arm, and her voice sounded haunted. "It's time something was done about it. And just because a few idiot MPs trot off to the king to complain about me influencing their wives is no reason for us to stop promoting our cause."

Ah, so *that's* what had the king so agitated. Still, trying to marry her off was rather extreme. "Perhaps the gentlemen feel that a young, unmarried woman should not be involved in prison reform."

"Only because my spinsterhood prevents them from vilifying me publicly."

He shot her a surprised glance. "What do you mean?"

"They can't complain that I neglect my husband or children, as they do with Mrs. Fry. My freedom to dedicate myself wholly to my cause makes it hard for them to criticize. Especially since they know in their hearts that my cause is just."

"I see." So the king wanted her married off to destroy her Joan of Arc appeal. Which meant that any man who agreed to His Majesty's bargain would probably gain a significant political advantage.

Good God, what was he thinking? He would be mad to consider marrying Louisa. *Let* her activities make things sticky for the king with Parliament. George deserved it for the havoc he routinely wrought with his private peccadilloes and personal vendettas. As long as the king didn't actively oppose his return to politics, Simon could still achieve his aims. It might take longer, but—

Right. Probably *much* longer. After seven years, half the House of Commons was new, and the other half remembered Simon only as the man who'd taken a lengthy jaunt to India on his way to the top. Without the king's support, he would have an uphill battle to become prime minister, much less institute any changes in policy. So he had to give the king's bargain serious consideration.

He needed a wife anyway, didn't he? He glanced over to where Louisa walked beside him with uncommon poise. Being a lady-in-waiting to the late Princess Charlotte had given her polish, taught her to be less impulsive. She had handled the situation with Raji masterfully. And her interest in reform was admirable, as long she stayed out of politics.

Or allowed her husband to govern her activities. Yes, if Simon married her, he could steer her toward pursuits better suited to a prime minister's wife. He might even tap her unbounded enthusiasm for his own aims.

You just want her in your bed. It was his grandfather's insidious voice, snide with contempt.

He stiffened. All right, so perhaps he did want Louisa in his bed. The hunger to possess her gnawed at his groin and surged through his veins. Who in his right mind would *not* want to possess the sloe-eyed beauty, to kiss that pale, lilac-scented throat and feel the pulse quicken beneath his tongue? That need not change anything. If they were married, he could better control his desires. Keep them from spilling over into his politics as they had last time.

You are too much a slave to your passions. He stifled a curse. Grandfather was wrong; he would prove that.

But before he considered taking up with Louisa again, he had to determine how serious she was about never wanting to marry.

He steered her toward a deserted path while broaching a subject to distract her. "I gather that Lord Trusbut is one of the gentlemen making protests."

"Actually, no. We think he might support our aims. If we could make him see that we're not trying to 'over-throw' the government or any such nonsense—"

"—then he might let his wife join you. And use his in-fluence for your cause."

"That's our hope, yes."

"Understandable," Simon said as he led her farther from the main crowd, praying that she didn't notice.

But Louisa was too busy wondering about the duke's astonishing interest in her group to notice where they wandered. Perhaps people *did* change.

And perhaps she was a fool even to think it. Simon never did anything without a purpose; she just hadn't fig-ured out what it was yet. "Did you mean what you said about taking me to call on her?"

"Of course."

She eyed him closely. "But why? And don't give me that poppycock about repaying me for helping you with Raji."

He shrugged. "Lord Trusbut's support is as important to my aims as it is to yours. I see no reason why we cannot combine forces."

"Except that I don't trust you." The minute the words left her mouth, she cursed her quick tongue. It wasn't a nonchalant, devil-may-care thing to say.

He must have realized it, too, for he halted beneath a wide-stretching oak to search her face. "I thought you said you had put the past behind you."

She fought for calm. "That doesn't mean I forgot the lessons I learned from it."

A Chinese lamp hanging from the oak's low limb sent light dappling his golden hair, glinting in his brilliant eyes. Suddenly she realized that although they could still hear the sounds of the fete, they were essentially alone, cut off from the crowd by a stand of birch trees.

He stepped nearer. "I have not forgotten the past, either. But apparently my memories differ substantially from yours."

The sudden feral hunger in his eyes spoke to the dark wildness that she'd suppressed inside her these many long years. Her breath hitched in her throat. "What do you mean?"

"I remember long waltzes and longer conversations. I remember a time when you *did* trust me."

"Before I discovered how false your attentions were, you mean."

"They were not all false," he said softly. "And you know it." He reached up to seize her chin in a firm grip.

As he bent his head, a frisson of anticipation swept her.

"What do you think you're doing?" she asked, though she very much feared she knew.

"Finding out if you taste as good as I remember." Then he covered her mouth with his.

Heaven help her. He certainly tasted as good as *she* remembered. Memory catapulted her back to the first time he'd kissed her, with a magical tenderness that had captured her heart. But this wasn't then, and this kiss wasn't that one.

Firm, hot, lush . . . it was as exotic and thrilling as the India he'd commanded. The way his mouth commanded hers now, demanding a response.

And like some half-wit schoolgirl, she gave it, letting that secret, feminine part of her thrill to the fact that he could still desire her after what she'd done to him.

To *him!* How about what he'd done to *her?* She wrenched her lips free. "That's enough, Your Grace," she said, struggling to sound cool and unruffled.

"Not enough for me," he murmured as he bent his mouth to hers again.

She wriggled away. "We're done now, sir."

Severely shaken, she turned to hurry down the path, eager to escape before she revealed how much he affected her.

His rumble of a voice came out of the darkness behind her. "Very wise of you, Louisa. You wouldn't want me to find out that you have not put the past behind you after all. I might take advantage."

A pox on him for reading her mind! She should ignore the taunt and walk away, but his arrogance was so annoying—

"You're wrong." She whirled on him. "I assure you I have outgrown you utterly."

With a maddening lift of his eyebrow, he strolled up to her. "Then why are you rushing to get away?"

"I don't want anyone to see us alone together and start up the gossip again."

"No one is here, and no one is coming." He cast her a mocking smile. "Admit it, you are merely afraid to let me kiss you."

"Clearly I am not afraid, for I—"

"—barely gave me time to brush my lips over yours. That was not a real kiss." He shrugged. "But I understand—you dare not give me a real kiss or you might discover you still have feelings for me." His gaze drifted to her mouth. "Unless you simply don't know what a real kiss, an intimate kiss, is like."

An *intimate* kiss?

She'd once foolishly let some naughty fellow at court give her an "intimate kiss." It was disgusting, and she'd hated it.

A slow smile touched her lips. How better to cure herself of any lingering attraction to Simon than to let him give her one of those messy and embarrassing "intimate" kisses?

"Oh, very well." She stepped nearer and lifted her face to his. "I suppose you won't rest until you have your 'real' kiss. So let's get to it, shall we?"

For a second he stared at her, clearly not sure what to make of her sudden capitulation. Then his eyes narrowed and he took her mouth again, this time delving inside it with his bold, searching tongue.

Oh no, she'd made a rather significant miscalculation. Apparently one's enjoyment of an "intimate" kiss depended upon the man's proficiency. And Simon was definitely proficient. Far too proficient.

She moaned. Why hadn't anybody warned her that an intimate kiss meant this series of sleek, silky forays into her mouth that sent her pulse into a gallop? Shouldn't somebody have cautioned her that such a kiss could send her straight for trouble?

He thrust deeply, fiercely, his kiss an irresistible prelude to seduction. Delicious. Swoon-worthy, even though she never swooned.

But apparently he actually expected swooning, for he slid his arm about her waist to steady her. Unless it was just to draw her closer. And she ached to have his hands on her, craved the feel of his embrace.

She spread her hands over his chest, and then, emboldened by the savage pounding of his heart, slipped them up around his neck. How long had it been since a man had made her feel wanted? Desired?

So very long. Too long.

She'd thought she could swear off men, but Simon had made a mockery of that with just one kiss. Just as he'd made a mockery of her silly hopes years ago—

Shaken by how easily she had succumbed, she tore her mouth from his. "Why are you doing this?" she whispered.

"Why are you letting me?" he said in a low rumble.

The soft kisses he brushed along her cheek and jaw and throat made her positively dizzy. "Because . . ."

Because I'm a fool.

Although he'd proved she hadn't put him behind her, she didn't dare let him know it. "Because I figure it's best that we get it over with."

He froze. "Get what over with?" he breathed against her neck.

Struggling to subdue the foolish clamor in her chest,

she drew back. "Your insistence on a real kiss. Now that it's done, *we* are done."

"The devil we are." His breath came quick and hard as his eyes blazed at her. "Don't try to claim you weren't affected."

She pretended to think. "You know," she said slowly, "I really wasn't. It was an interesting experiment, mind you—"

"Experiment!"

"—to determine for myself if I have outgrown you. What a relief to find that I have." Buoyed by her success at hiding her true feelings, she slipped from his arms and added with a smile, "It appears you no longer have any influence on me, Your Grace."

His flinch at her formal address gave her a small measure of satisfaction. Until he dropped his gaze to her burning lips. "You could have fooled me."

Though her smile wobbled, she was determined to have the last word. "Oh, I'm sorry, I didn't mean that how it sounded. You kiss quite as well as any of my previous suitors. But I have aims that don't involve you, no matter how well you kiss." She lifted her chin. "And I still don't trust you."

"You always were eager to think the worst of me," he snapped.

"You're only angry because you've lost the power to twist me about your finger. Well, society may fawn over you, but *I* at least know what you are."

He met her gaze squarely. "You know nothing about me. You never did."

Something in his voice made her want to believe him. But she'd learned only too well that his silver tongue lied with consummate skill. "I know enough."

She pivoted to stalk up the graveled path. From now on, she'd have to be more careful. No private encounters with Simon. No long walks where he could taunt her into things.

And no kisses. Certainly no intimate kisses! He was just too good at them for a woman's peace of mind.

Chapter Four

❦

Dear Charlotte,

If Miss North and Foxmoor are as much at odds as rumor says, then perhaps she stole the duke's monkey to annoy him. Though I cannot imagine what she would want with a monkey. Monkeys make poor reformers, you know.

Your fellow gossip,
Michael

Frustration knotted Simon's insides as Louisa flounced away. The impudent chit had learned to be sophisticated in more ways than one during his absence. Someone had taught her how to kiss. Very well. Too well for his sanity.

And she dared to call that kiss an "experiment"? The devil she would!

He had half a mind to go after her and ravage her mouth until she admitted she hadn't outgrown him. But he had his pride, too. He was not about to let her see how far *he* was from outgrowing *her*. He did not want her to know that he craved another taste of her . . . and another and another—

Deuce take her! Kissing her should have blunted his craving, not sharpened it. And why should he care if Louisa had put him behind her? Or had spent the past years learning seductive tricks designed to inflame a man's desires? Or had let some insolent puppy at court plunder that lush, supple mouth?

He did not care. *Must* not care. In the palace, men occasionally stole kisses from ladies-in-waiting, who occasionally let them. Allowing some foolish jealousy to eat at him would only increase his passion for her, and that was unwise. Especially if he meant to take her in hand. He could not have his wife leading him about by his cock.

Wife?

He curled his hands into fists. Yes, wife. He could no longer deny the advantages to accepting the king's bargain. Aside from what the king could offer him, the MPs would be eager to show their gratitude if Simon tamed Joan of Arc.

Though that could prove no small feat. Her father was right—she was as willful as ever. She had merely learned to hide it behind that princesslike smile.

A groan left his lips. How could he actually consider this mad scheme, after what that bloody female had put him through? If she ever found out about it, she would have *him* burned at the stake.

So he would simply make sure she never found out. After all, he would only be doing what was best for her. From the information he had gleaned, she was headed straight for trouble. If he did not marry her, the king would find some other way to control her, and that could not be good.

Besides, no matter what she claimed, she still desired him. Otherwise she would not have leapt to his kiss with the sweet fervor of a temple dancer, her body arching against his, her lavish breasts pressed—

God help him, he desired her even more than before. He ached to strip away her aloof manner, shake the pins from her sophisticated coiffure, and send that ocean of glossy black waves cascading down to her shoulders and breasts and hips. Then he would plunder that seductive mouth as much as he wanted, whenever he wanted, wherever he wanted. He would have it caress his throat, his belly . . . his aching cock . . .

A vile oath left his lips as molten fire heated his blood. Damn it, after everything he had endured because of his unwanted attraction to her, he deserved to have her. The best way to deal with this foolish obsession was to marry her and slake his thirst. Then his craving would ease.

Fighting it for seven years had not worked, so he must conquer Louisa to conquer his passions. Which would give him everything else he wanted, too.

"You're right—my daughter has indeed lost interest in you," said a voice beside him.

Simon tensed. How long had the king been standing there? "I see you still have your talent for spying. And she has not lost interest in me, I assure you."

"It certainly sounded like she has. Granted, I only heard the end of your argument, but she seemed rather sure—"

"Do you want me to marry her or not?" he snapped, relieved that the king had not witnessed their kiss.

George sucked in a breath. "You said you needed time to think about it."

"I have had all the time I need."

The king paused. "The offer still stands, yes."

Simon faced him. "Then we should discuss my terms."

"Terms?" George glowered at him. "I already told you I'd make you prime minister. What more do you expect?"

"The truth. That your daughter is interfering with your politics." Affecting a casual air, Simon leaned against the oak. "That she is making a nuisance of herself publicly. And that any man who marries her will be taking certain risks in his own political career."

The blood drained from George's face. "I can't imagine where you got such a ridiculous idea."

"From your daughter. Who, unlike you, is eager to expound upon her new interest in political reform." Simon crossed his arms over his chest. "Come now, Your Majesty, surely you did not think you could hide it from *me*. I am the one who first learnt that Canning turned down Liverpool, who predicted long before the Cato Street Conspiracy that the Spenceans would cause trouble. So admit it—the London Ladies are no mere charitable group, are they?"

The king hesitated, then sighed. "No, damn you, they're not."

"They're pressing Parliament to reform the prisons."

His Majesty's voice dropped so low that Simon had to strain to hear it. "First those blasted females started coaxing their husbands to raise the issue of reform in sessions. And if a husband refused, they denied him what a man wants most."

"His wife's bed?"

"What good would that do? Half the men have mistresses, and the rest are too old to get their cocks to a stand. No, their creature comforts. Their wives withheld the niceties that make a man's home his castle, like cigars and brandy and newspapers. Some ladies even commanded their cooks to serve bad meals, or instructed the laundry maids to overstarch their husbands' shirts—"

"You must be joking. England's statesmen are being brought low by too much starch in their shirts, for God's sake?"

"You scoff, but a man can only spend so much time at his club." The king stabbed his stick into the packed earth. "Still, the men didn't let it trouble them until the London Ladies became a cause célèbre. And now Louisa is rumored to have a new approach—"

"Louisa was behind this . . . this 'creature comfort' tactic?"

"I heard that she dreamt it up, yes."

Simon burst into laughter.

"It's not funny, damn you," the king grumbled.

"The devil it isn't. Leave it to Louisa to find a 'domestic' way to influence politics. She's a clever girl, I will give her that." And she would be a clever wife, too. Though he would have to outplot her to win her.

The challenge only made him desire her more.

"That clever girl is headed for a fall if she goes through with her new plan."

"And what is that? Having the ladies put peas in their husbands' drawers? Delaying dinner?"

"Putting up her own candidate for the upcoming by-election."

That certainly got his attention. "You cannot be serious."

"I wish I weren't. Mrs. Fry has already put her brother-in-law in the Commons to support their cause, so it *can* be done. But there's a rumor going 'round that Louisa is considering a radical candidate. And you know damned well if she rallies her ladies behind some hothead, we'll have trouble."

Trouble indeed. No ladies association had the political acumen to manage such a candidate. Louisa would merely succeed in getting the old guard's back up, making it harder for him to achieve change in a reasonable manner. Especially with the balance of power in the Commons so uncertain right now.

"She's a loose cannon," the king went on. "But the public likes her. They see the polished lady-in-waiting to their beloved deceased princess selflessly garnering donations for poor female prisoners. They don't realize that those donations may shortly go to whatever ass she thinks will support her cause."

"And if you expose her—"

"Are you mad? The way things are now, she might rally half the rabble behind her. The last time a radical started making speeches and firing up the common people, eleven people died and hundreds more were wounded."

Simon stiffened. St. Peter's Field had been as much the fault of the government as the radicals, but that hardly mattered to Parliament. After that disaster, it had passed the Six Acts and behaved as the old guard always did—digging in its heels. England wasn't ready for radicals. Couldn't Louisa see that?

Of course not. Like Joan of Arc, she saw only her cause. Prison reform was all well and good, but it did not justify political upheaval.

The king grumbled, "Some in the cabinet are so up in arms about her activities that they're talking about trying to besmirch her reputation. They figure if they destroy her credit it will end this nonsense."

But it would ruin Louisa forever. "Surely you don't condone such idiocy."

"No, but if I don't do something soon, it will be out of

my hands." His voice trembled. "If they hurt Louisa, Draker will never forgive me."

"Never mind Draker, *I* will never forgive you." When the king shot him a questioning glance, he scowled. "The bloody asses ought to reform the prisons."

"They ought to do a lot of things, but they don't want to spend the funds. Besides, the Home Secretary is utterly against it on principle, and there's already enough turmoil in the government." His Majesty sighed. "I told Sidmouth and Castlereagh I'd convince her to resign from her society, but—"

"She refused. So she has become a liability for you."

"Damned right! I can't have them think I support my illegitimate daughter putting up radical candidates. I have enough trouble with Parliament already."

And so would Simon, if he pursued this further. Why should he take on such a political liability?

Because he had no choice. He couldn't achieve his aims if Louisa was stirring up the Commons. Someone had to take her in hand.

Which he could do. *If* he married her. God help him, but the idea of taking Louisa in hand stirred his blood. "So you will give Louisa to any man who will solve your problems with your ministers and with Parliament."

"Not *any* man." George scowled. "But you always did like her—"

"And you figured I'd take the bait."

At his dry tone, the king colored. "See here, I only kept the truth from you at first because I was afraid you wouldn't do it if you knew how bad matters were."

Simon shoved away from the oak and dusted off his gloved hands. "When will you learn that I enjoy a good challenge?" Especially when it involved getting the king's temptress of a daughter into bed. Permanently. "Of course, now that I know everything, I shall expect a greater reward than you originally offered."

The king trundled nearer, moonlight glinting off his silvered hair. "If you think I'll *pay* you to marry my daughter, you greedy devil, think again."

"I do not want money."

That mollified George a bit. "Then what *do* you want?"

"Something more concrete than your vague promise to support me. You will make me prime minister, but you will do it on *my* schedule, under *my* terms."

His Majesty looked wary. "What do you mean?"

"I will not wait on your indulgence ever again. By the time I marry, I expect you to have convinced Liverpool to resign as prime minister. On the day of my wedding, I expect you to hand me his resignation letter."

The king blanched. "What if it ends up being soon? I don't know if I—"

"You'd better, if you want me to keep Louisa from participating in that by-election." When the king still looked uneasy, Simon added, "Don't fret yourself—it will take me a while to win her. She is not an idiot; she knows she is treading dangerous ground. She will suspect any statesman who wants to marry her, especially me."

"True," the king muttered.

"Which is why you must stay away from me until she and I are engaged. I will have an easier time persuading her to marry me if she believes you are against it." His tone sharpened. "You should not have any trouble pretending to disapprove of me—you were ready enough to wash your hands of me seven years ago."

A flush touched George's fat cheeks. "I admit it—I shouldn't have been so hasty to listen to Louisa's suggestion of how to . . . discipline you for your error. But it won't happen again. You'll have me firmly in your camp this time."

"Good. Because the next time you give me the choice between exile or losing my future in politics, I will tell you to go to hell. So if I should happen to fail with Louisa, there will be no repercussions to me or my career, understood?"

"You have my word."

"And no repercussions for her, either. If she won't marry me, then you will not try to bribe any other man to court her."

"If you can't have her, no one else gets her, is that it?"

Anger knotted in Simon's gut. "If I can't have her, then she should be free to choose whomever she wants. Not some ass paid for by her scheming father."

"Watch it, Foxmoor," George snapped, "I am still your king. If you think I shall let you dictate to me—"

"Fine. It appears you don't need me after all." He turned to stride off.

"Wait, damn you, wait," the king cried.

Simon halted.

"All right, if you don't marry her, I won't foist any other man on her."

"And you'll keep your idiot ministers from attempting to ruin her reputation," Simon said as he faced the king.

"I'll do my best." The king paused. "But you won't fail with her, will you?"

"No," Simon said. "And you had better tell them that. I expect them to leave Louisa alone until I can secure her." He scowled. "Because if I hear a single slur against her reputation, I will tear their tongues out by the roots. Understood?"

An odd expression passed over His Majesty's face. "Perfectly."

Simon gritted his teeth. He shouldn't have said that; it revealed that he cared more for Louisa than he let on. And he damned well didn't want the king to know it, or he'd lose his bargaining position. "It will not help my career to have a wife with a tarnished reputation."

"Oh. I didn't think of that." The king broke into a broad smile. "By Jove, it's good to have you back and in fine mettle. You always were my best advisor."

"I'm not done stating my terms," Simon said.

His Majesty sobered at once.

Simon strolled back to the king. "Don't let Draker get wind of this. As it is, he will probably oppose the match. So after she and I become engaged, you should profess yourself resigned to the marriage, and then use your influence over him to make him accept it, as well."

"You have more influence over his wife than I do over him," the king muttered.

"In any matter concerning *me*, he is not going to listen to my sister. But he might listen to you if you assure him I have changed. I will not have Draker for an enemy. In my absence, he has acquired a number of useful connections." The sort who were more open to reforming England's election system than Simon's old cohorts.

"I'll do what I can with Draker." George cast him a sullen glance. "Anything else? My favorite hounds? My collection of Rembrandts?"

"Only one thing." He forced himself to sound casual. "I have a friend whose career I have pledged to advance. I will expect you to support my efforts."

The king leaned heavily on his cane. "Who is this friend?"

After hearing the king's slur against his "half-caste aide-de-camp," Simon wasn't about to tell His Majesty the truth. "I'd rather not say until I have finished looking into his situation."

"You think I'll promise to support some friend of yours without knowing who he is?"

God, he hoped so. It would make fulfilling the vow he'd made to Colin's wife so much easier. "You and I have always been on the same side politically. Surely no friend of mine would pose a problem for you."

"I don't know," the king said warily. "Your years in India might have given you any number of unsuitable friends."

"That's the chance you'll have to take if you want me to marry your daughter." If Simon was going to cast himself headlong into the maelstrom that was Louisa North, then by God he would make the king give him what he wanted.

His Majesty hesitated, then said, "Very well, you scheming scoundrel. I'll support your friend if I must."

"I want this in writing, too," Simon persisted. "Every single term."

The king looked startled. "Why the devil should you want that?"

"Because if you renege on your agreement *this* time, I want something to show the newspapers."

"You wouldn't dare." George snorted. "That would be political suicide."

"For you, too." He fixed the king with a cool stare. "A written contract will bind us both. Because I refuse to suffer punishment on your behalf ever again."

"All right, you devil, all right. I'd hoped that sending you to India might curb that arrogance of yours, but apparently I was wrong."

"If you wanted to curb my arrogance, you shouldn't have made me Governor-General of half a continent," Simon pointed out.

"True. After managing India, I dare say you can manage England with one hand tied behind your back. It's what you were born to, after all." A sudden gleam flashed in the king's eyes. "But it remains to be seen if you can manage my daughter. Until you do, your chance to manage England is far down the road."

"Don't worry. As you said, I made her fall in love with me once; I can damned well do it again. And a woman in love is easy to manage."

"As long as you don't fall in love yourself."

A smile touched Simon's lips at the impossibility of that notion. "Didn't you claim I was incapable of love?"

"Ah, but you're still interested in Louisa after all these years, aren't you?"

If the king could be blunt, so could he. "There's a difference between love and desire. You of all people should know that."

George frowned. "You're talking about my daughter."

"Whom you are willing to sell to save your standing with Parliament," Simon growled. "Your fatherly concern comes a bit late, don't you think?"

George flushed. "We're both scoundrels in our own ways, I suppose. Though I still hope you mean to treat Louisa well."

"Of course. I would not marry her otherwise. But fortunately for your purposes, I *am* incapable of love." Grandfather's "training" and traitorous mistress Betsy had taught Simon only too well to wall up his heart. "Which is probably a good thing, since love is a luxury no statesman can afford." In that, Grandfather Monteith had been right, even if the man's method for teaching it was suspect.

The king sighed. "You do have a point. God knows love has never served *me* well."

And Simon would not allow love to ruin his own life and career. He would keep his obsession in its place. As long as he didn't let Louisa wrap him about her finger, the two of them could have a comfortable, amiable, and *honest* marriage, the sort that would help him achieve his aims without being mired in hypocrisy, as his grandfather's marriage had been.

Because Simon meant to prove he could be a better prime minister—a better man—than his grandfather. Then perhaps he could silence the man's insidious voice in his head once and for all.

Chapter Five

Dear Cousin,

I daresay you are right about monkeys being unsuitable as reformers. But I am no longer sure that Louisa and Foxmoor are at odds, for they were strolling through the gardens at Castlemaine with seeming congeniality. So perhaps they have mended their fences.

Your romantic-minded relation,
Charlotte

ust the girls practice their scales in here?" Louisa rubbed her temples and prayed for patience. "I can hardly hear myself think over that infernal racket."

Mrs. Charlotte Harris's head jerked up, sending her flaming curls aquiver, and Regina burst into laughter. Four days after Regina's fete, they sat at a table in the largest classroom at Mrs. Harris's School. Generally Mrs. Harris used it for the monthly teas where she presented her "Lessons for Heiresses" to her graduates on the marriage mart. Today the widow had generously offered the room to the London Ladies Society for their usual Saturday morning meeting.

Morning had long passed, so most of the other members had left. But Louisa was determined to cross *one* item of business off her list, despite her friend Lady Venetia Campbell's musical prodigies and their racket.

"I can't endure this one more minute." Louisa jumped up, prepared to send the girls packing, then caught the knowing glance Regina shot Mrs. Harris.

"You owe me a shilling," Regina said to her friend. "I told you she wouldn't last until the end."

As Louisa blinked, Mrs. Harris fished a coin from her beaded reticule. "In Louisa's defense, we are all very tired. It's been a long day."

"True." Regina took the shilling. "But neither of us is grousing about the 'infernal racket' of three harpists practicing quietly."

Louisa drew herself up. "I was merely saying—"

"It's all right, dear." Mrs. Harris stood. "They've played long enough. I'm sure they've quite worn out Venetia's tolerance, too." She called over to the girls, "Practice time is over, everyone. You may put your harps away."

When the noise stopped abruptly and Mrs. Harris sat back down, Louisa did the same. "Thank you, that's much better."

Regina rolled her eyes. "Pay Louisa no mind, Charlotte. She has been a regular grumpy goose ever since the fete."

"Oh?" Mrs. Harris said. "And what has provoked this unusual behavior?"

"Judging from her extreme reaction to the elaborate bouquets my brother daily leaves for her at my house," Regina said, smirking, "she seems to have developed an aversion to lilies. Which is odd, since they're her favorite flower."

"Is it a severe aversion?" Mrs. Harris's blue eyes twinkled. "Is she sleeping badly? Sighing into her pillow? Croaking out romantic ballads?"

"Very amusing," Louisa grumbled. "I'm tossing the lilies out as fast as they come in, which is what anyone with an aversion to them does."

Mrs. Harris laughed. "And Foxmoor? Has she tossed *him* out yet?"

"No," Regina said, "but she might as well. She avoids him entirely."

"That is absurd." Louisa scanned the list of names on the table before her. "I'm merely too busy with the London Ladies Society to stay home for callers."

"Busy hiding in your room or sneaking out when he comes by, you mean."

"Who is Miss North hiding from?" asked Miss Eliza Crenshawe, one of the offending harpists who strolled with Venetia toward the table.

"I am *not* hiding. I simply don't have time to entertain Regina's brother."

"You're hiding from the Duke of Foxmoor?" Eliza exclaimed. "Are you mad? I would tremble with excitement if that man came to call on me!"

When all eyes turned to Louisa, most of them reflecting Eliza's sentiments, she stiffened. "I'm not *hiding* from anyone." With a stern glance, she tapped her finger on her list. "I've been utterly consumed with figuring out who to choose as our candidate. Which is why we're here, if you'll recall."

That sobered them. "You're right, of course," Regina said. "We had to table our other items of business until we'd investigated further; we shouldn't end the meeting without resolving this one."

Eliza and Venetia wandered over to stand by the window overlooking the school's front drive while the other girls took their seats in a flurry of white muslin.

Louisa closely surveyed the younger women. "You girls do know that this matter shouldn't be discussed outside this room."

They bobbed their heads in unison, wide-eyed but eager to hear more.

"If you don't think you can curb your tongues, even with your family, leave now," Mrs. Harris warned them. "Is that understood, Miss Crenshawe?"

Color stained Eliza's plump cheeks. "Yes, ma'am."

"Let's go on, then." Louisa stared down at the list. "Of the three men we've narrowed this to, I still think Charles Godwin is our best choice."

Regina frowned. "And I still think he's too dangerous. It's one thing to put Mrs. Fry's brother-in-law into office, but if we start supporting radicals, the MPs will accuse us of fomenting revolution. Especially if Mr. Godwin's speeches are as fiery as his editorials."

"I hope they are. Try as he might, Mrs. Fry's brother-in-law hasn't gained us a thing. It's time to shake up those fussy old MPs."

"But a more moderate candidate—"

"Will just be ignored. As Mrs. Fry's brother-in-law has been. Radicals at least know how to get things done." Louisa turned to Mrs. Harris. "Have you mentioned this to Mr. Godwin yet?"

Mrs. Harris had known the man for years, ever since he'd served in the same regiment with her late bounder of a husband.

"No, I didn't want to speak until we made a decision. But I think he'll be amenable. He's already shown himself to be passionate about other reforms."

"Too passionate, if you ask me," Regina said. When the other two raised their eyebrows, she sighed. "But I suppose if you trust him, Mrs. Harris—"

"I do. He's been a good friend to me since my husband's death."

"As good a friend as Cousin Michael?" Regina teased.

Mrs. Harris snorted. "I can hardly call Cousin Michael a friend when he insists upon keeping his identity secret. Stubborn fool. I'm not entirely sure he's really my late husband's cousin, as he claims to be."

"Blast it all—look at that equipage!" interrupted Eliza from the window.

"Come away from there, Eliza," Mrs. Harris chided. "And a lady does not use words like 'blast.' "

"Hard to resist when a phaeton bearing a nobleman's crest is tearing up the school's drive." Venetia peered through the window. "Is that a ducal crest?"

As every eye turned to Louisa, her heart stumbled into an erratic rhythm.

"It must be Foxmoor himself!" Eliza exclaimed. "How romantic for you, Miss North! He's so smitten he rode all this way from town to find you!"

The younger ladies clapped their hands to their breasts and sighed in a perfect paroxysm of maidenly delight.

"Don't be silly." Louisa's own hands fell into a maddening shake, so she buried them in her skirts of spotted pink muslin. "It's probably one of the parents."

Mrs. Harris lifted one eyebrow. "Aside from the fact that no duke would ever deign to enroll his daughter in a school, I doubt any of our parents would drive a phaeton. Those are for bachelors."

"The duke would never ride anywhere after me." When

the others began to grin, Louisa bristled. "It's someone's cousin or suitor." It couldn't be Simon—she'd made it quite clear that she had no interest in him, not now, not ever.

Yet he kept leaving those gorgeous lilies, and with every bouquet the same line: "Surely we can at least be friends," followed by the words, "Yours, Simon." Not "the duke" or "Foxmoor." Simon. As if he'd never wronged her. As if she'd never had him banished.

As if he weren't probably consorting with her enemies even now.

Was that why he'd started this? Had the MPs asked him to distract her from her activities? She wouldn't put it past them—or him, either. Not for one minute did she think he really wanted to be her "friend."

"The phaeton is stopping!" Eliza leaned forward to see better. "A gentleman is getting out. He's wearing a cobalt blue frock coat, light blue pantaloon trousers, and Hessians. I do so love a man in Hessians." She turned back to smile at them, her hazel eyes sparkling. "Especially a handsome one."

"Young, too," Venetia added. "He couldn't be more than thirty."

"Thirty-three," Louisa breathed. When they laughed, she thrust out her lower lip. "*If* it's Regina's brother. Which it probably isn't."

"Look, he has a monkey!" Eliza exclaimed.

Louisa groaned. Wonderful. The dratted man had run her to ground. Perhaps she could sneak down the back stairs to the stables . . . but no, she couldn't leave without Regina.

She turned to Mrs. Harris. "Where are your copies of

the *London Monitor*?" When the schoolmistress blinked, she added, "The ones with Mr. Godwin's articles. Are they in your office? I shall go see—"

"Hiding in there will do you no good," Regina put in. "I know my brother—he will find you."

"Then it's a good thing this has nothing to do with him." Louisa headed for the door. "I told you, I can't be bothered with his visits when we have work to do."

"Regina is right, dear," Mrs. Harris said. "You can't avoid him forever. Just tell him you're not interested, and put an end to it."

"I already tried that at the fete. I made it quite clear how I felt."

"Yet he keeps pursuing you." Regina arched one blonde eyebrow. "You must have been very convincing."

"I can't believe she's avoiding a duke," exclaimed one of the girls.

"I can't believe she's avoiding the man who once governed India." Eliza pursed her lips. "Who cares if he's a duke? My father's third cousin is a duke, and he's an ass."

"Miss Crenshawe!" Mrs. Harris chided. "We don't use the word 'ass,' ever!"

"Sorry," Eliza mumbled.

Louisa stifled a smile, remembering similar discussions with her governess. Eliza, with her reckless tongue and budding country beauty, reminded her of how *she* had been at seventeen: headstrong but naïve, easy pickings for the scheming Simon.

But she was older and wiser now. Surely she could handle one annoyingly attractive duke. And Mrs. Harris was right—she couldn't avoid him forever, not when she lived with his sister. Better to settle her relationship with him for good. "I shall just have to be firmer in my refusal."

"For some men it takes more than once," Mrs. Harris said.

"Especially when the man knows you're lying," Regina said dryly.

Scowling, Louisa faced her sister-in-law. "I'm not lying."

"No? Then why have you been hiding from him? Because you are afraid that you will succumb to his pursuit." Regina's eyes narrowed. "Or worse yet, that you will discover he has changed. You are afraid to see him for what he is."

Louisa snorted. "His claim to have changed may fool you, but not me."

"Did you know that he and His Majesty have been at odds since his return, reportedly over Simon's renewed interest in you?"

The unbidden thrill searing Louisa's veins vexed her, especially when she saw the young ladies regard her with envy and awe. "I hardly believe that His Majesty would disapprove of his old advisor."

"Last night Simon pointedly left White's as soon as the king arrived," Regina persisted. "Marcus witnessed it himself. Doesn't that prove Simon's sincerity?"

It shook her, to be sure. She'd wondered if the king had coaxed Simon to distract her in exchange for some political advantage. But if they were on bad terms—

"Don't you see?" Regina went on. "You have thought him the villain for so long that you would rather hide from your feelings than accept the changed man."

"You're wrong, I tell you," Louisa said. "And I am not *hiding!*"

"From whom?" asked a deep male voice.

She jumped, then whirled to find Simon in the doorway, eyes gleaming. "From anyone," she said, her heart in her throat. "I'm not hiding from . . . anyone."

As Raji chattered and everyone behind her except Regina dropped into deep curtsies, Simon said, "Glad to hear it. Because only cowards hide. And I never took you for a coward."

Heat filled her cheeks. She deserved that; she *had* been a coward. His bold, consuming kiss in the woods had unsettled her, but avoiding the truth never solved anything.

The butler appeared behind Simon, looking flustered. "Forgive me, ladies. I intended to announce His Grace, but he insisted upon surprising you."

"Of course he did." Louisa managed a remote smile. "The duke is nothing if not insistent." Just like his sister, whom he resembled to an astonishing degree, both of them blond, blue-eyed, and bold. Except that Regina's boldness was invigorating. Simon's was just plain dangerous.

Like now, when he was scouring her with his impudent gaze. "You gave me little choice, Miss North. You seem to have forgotten our appointment."

"What are you talking about?"

"You and I are supposed to pay a visit to Lady Trusbut, remember?" Idly, he scratched his monkey's belly. "Raji was looking forward to it. But when I went to the town house to fetch you, they informed me that you were here."

A hush fell across the room. Even the girls knew that gaining Lady Trusbut's support had been a particular quest of Louisa's.

"I didn't think you meant it." She lifted her chin in

challenge. "After all, Your Grace, you have a bad habit of saying what you don't mean."

Ignoring the gasps from behind her, he shifted Raji to his shoulder. "Then give me a chance to prove I have overcome my bad habits."

As if confirming his master's words, Raji chattered madly, clutching a wooden carving of a bird to his furry chest. Painted bright yellow, the toy was clearly well-worn, well-loved. A canary. So Simon *hadn't* been lying to Lady Trusbut about Raji's preference for canaries.

It was a small thing, yet it gave her pause.

Simon held out his arm. "Shall we go? I have the phaeton waiting."

Though the prospect of spending time alone with Simon in a phaeton unnerved her, she dared not lose the chance to snag Lady Trusbut's support. Besides, he could hardly make advances in broad daylight with a monkey and groom as chaperones.

But first she and her ladies had to choose their candidate. "I tell you what, sir. Let me finish my meeting and then we'll go. You can wait for me downstairs."

He tensed, but before he could protest, Eliza burst out with, "Perhaps His Grace should participate, too. He probably knows all your prospective candi—"

"Hush, Eliza!" Louisa cast the loose-tongued girl a quelling glance. "I told you, that isn't a matter for general discussion."

Eliza's face fell. "Oh, right."

Louisa shifted her gaze to Simon. "Especially when we don't know where the duke stands on our issue."

"Nor can I tell you, when you are not forthright with me," Simon countered.

"What do you mean?" she retorted.

He strode into the room. "You said you press your cause in Parliament, but you neglected to say how. I had to hear elsewhere about your unorthodox tactics."

He'd *heard* about that?

They were still gaping at him when he added, "And you certainly never said you are putting up your own candidate for the Commons."

Chapter Six

Dear Charlotte,
*   It would certainly help Miss North if she mended her fences with Foxmoor. Everyone is sure he will succeed Liverpool as prime minister. But I cannot see Miss North as his duchess. She would lead him a merry dance, and I hear Foxmoor isn't particularly fond of dancing.*

*   Your opinionated cousin,*
*   Michael*

*L*ouisa's heart dropped into her stomach. He wasn't supposed to know about their political aspirations. No one in Parliament was supposed to know until the London Ladies marshaled their support. She could think of only one way he'd found out.

But when she glared at his sister, Regina drew herself up stiffly. "Don't look at me—*I* didn't tell him."

"No, she didn't." Simon smiled. "Not for nothing was I once the king's advisor. I know how to ferret out information, especially when it regards politics."

As he handed his beaver top hat to the butler, Mrs. Harris said, "Then surely you realize how unhappy some of your friends in Parliament would be to hear that you're helping us."

"Helping you?"

"By taking Louisa to meet with Lord Trusbut."

"Ah. I hardly call arranging an appointment with the Trusbuts 'help.' But if you're looking for real help, I might offer it. After you convince me I should."

Convince him? The audacity of the man! "We're not interested in your help," Louisa snapped.

"We're interested in *anyone's* help," Mrs. Harris put in. "Especially coming from a man of such stature." She cast Simon an assessing glance. "The question, Your Grace, isn't whether we want your help, but why you're offering it."

"I'm not. Yet. First, I would have to know more about your cause—your aims, your methods—"

"You wish to spy on us," Louisa said.

He cast her a cool smile. "I acquired my other information about your group with ease. So if I wanted to spy on you, Miss North, I would not waste time talking to you suspicious females. I'd be off befriending a less wary member." He nodded at Regina. "Or bedeviling my sister with questions."

"Which, to be fair," Regina put in, "he has not done."

"I came here to fulfill my promise to you," Simon went on. "You were discussing politics, so I pointed out that I could help." He smiled tightly. "But before I endorse any organization, I expect to know its aims and methods. Surely you understand that." When they remained silently wary, he added with a shrug, "Of course, if you do not *want* my help—"

"What exactly would you wish to know?" Mrs. Harris asked.

"Now see here," Louisa put in, "I'm not telling him anything until I know we can trust him."

"Of course not," Simon surprised her by saying. "But why not let me observe the workings of your group for a few days? How could that be a problem?" He arched one eyebrow. "Unless what I keep hearing is true, and the London Ladies Society really is planning some wild revolution."

The others laughed a bit shakily, but Louisa's stomach knotted up. He certainly knew a great deal after only a week. And if the other statesmen knew what he did, that wasn't good. Refusing to let him observe might rouse further suspicion of her group's political aspirations. That wouldn't be good, either.

But if she *did* let him "observe," she'd have to endure his presence.

Or would she? A sudden idea came to her. "What do you think, Mrs. Harris? Would you like the duke to observe your new committee?"

"I'd be honored." Mrs. Harris smiled. "If he doesn't mind riding out here twice a week for meetings."

"Certainly not," Simon said. "I could accompany my sister and Miss North."

"Oh, but I'm not a member of her committee." Louisa smirked.

His face darkened. "Then let me observe *yours.*"

She smiled sweetly. "Mrs. Harris's committee will give you a better picture of our organization."

How lovely to outwit Simon for a change. If he meant to assess their political aims, this would thwart him. And if he was sincerely interested in her group, Mrs. Harris's current task would give him an excellent idea of their activities.

He was watching her suspiciously. "Exactly what does this committee do?"

Louisa headed back to the table. "If you can spare another few minutes, Your Grace, we'll explain."

"Certainly," he said, following her.

He held her chair out with one of his tigerish smiles and she knew exactly how a gazelle must feel to be cornered. She shook off the feeling. She wasn't cornered. She'd found a way to keep him out of her hair for a while, hadn't she?

And thank heaven for that. Look at the handsome scoundrel—he already had the girls blushing and stammering as Mrs. Harris introduced them. Even Venetia turned a bit pink, and no man ever affected her.

What was it about Simon that turned perfectly reasonable females into blithering idiots? Was it his ability to make a woman feel as if he was listening only to her, paying attention only to her?

Or was it simply his air of command? He pulled back a chair for Mrs. Harris with a male grace that was beautiful to behold, every motion deliberate, nothing wasted. And once they were all seated and he took his own chair opposite Louisa, she couldn't help noticing how well he controlled Raji. He tapped the table and the monkey hopped right onto that spot, clutching his toy canary to his white furry chest.

Eliza, who'd finagled the seat beside Simon, uttered a girlish sigh. "Your monkey is just darling, Your Grace."

"You haven't seen the creature lay waste to a woman's coiffure," Louisa quipped. "That darling draws blood if you're not careful."

"Only when presented with the right temptation,"

Simon said. "He thought Lady Trusbut's peacock was a toy."

"Like his little carving," Eliza said. "Where did you get it?"

"Simon probably carved it himself," Regina put in. "He likes to whittle."

"Really?" Mrs. Harris surveyed Simon with new eyes. "It's very good."

"Whittling keeps my hands busy while my mind works through a problem," he said.

Louisa had forgotten that odd habit of his. He'd once whittled her a perfectly charming miniature lily, merely because she'd said she liked them. It was the one reminder of him that she'd kept.

"Did you learn to whittle in India?" Eliza asked.

"No," Simon said with a chuckle. "My father taught me."

Louisa blinked. She had rarely heard him speak of his parents. She'd learned more about them from Regina than she'd ever learned from him.

"Is it true you were the first duke to serve as Governor-General of India?" Eliza asked with stars in her eyes.

"Miss Crenshawe, stop plaguing the duke," Mrs. Harris broke in.

"It's fine." Simon cast Eliza a kindly glance. "And no, not exactly. Wellington served long before me, though he wasn't a duke at the time."

"Simon wasn't the first of our family to go to India, either," Regina put in. "My mother's younger brother served there, too. Uncle Tobias was there as a lieutenant for . . . what was it, Simon? Two years? Before he died of malaria?"

Simon's expression grew shuttered. "Three years." He sat back. "But enough talk of India—I want to know what Mrs. Harris's committee does."

His strained smile gave Louisa pause. All she'd heard from Regina about their uncle was that the poor man had gone to seek his fortune, and instead had died alone. A very sad tale. Was that why it bothered Simon to think of it?

Oh, why did she care? She forced herself to pay attention to what Mrs. Harris was saying.

"We're presently assessing tasks that would provide sustainable income for our convict women while teaching them usable skills," Mrs. Harris explained. "We need one that requires little training, since we lack sufficient volunteers for that. Yet it must pay well."

"How well?" Simon asked.

"Enough to support our projects—the prison school, supplemental clothing and bedding, and matrons instead of male guards."

"Why would *you* have to pay for matrons—isn't that the prison system's responsibility?" Simon asked as he scratched Raji's back.

"It should be." Anger at such injustice burned in Louisa's chest. "Instead, guards are paid out of fees taken from the poverty-stricken prisoners. So of course they're brutes who use their position to bully the women, subjecting them to—" She broke off, remembering the younger girls. "To . . . er . . . their advances."

"And Parliament does not consider it a problem," Regina said. "Despite committee reports, they refuse to institute the proper reforms."

"The Home Secretary claims that we would 'remove the dread of punishment in the criminal classes.'" Just remembering the speech made Louisa's blood boil.

"That certainly sounds like Sidmouth." Simon's voice held an edge. "He equates reform with revolution and radicals."

"And you don't?" Mrs. Harris prodded.

A veiled look crossed his face. "It depends on the reform. But I see why you want to put up a candidate. And if you'll forgive my saying so, I could be of greater use in advising you—"

"Oh yes," Louisa cut in, "I'm sure your fellow statesmen have told you exactly how to advise us."

His gaze pierced her. "Do you suspect me of being an agent provocateur?"

"I can't imagine why I should." Her voice dripped sarcasm. "What could possibly be suspicious about a duke with political aspirations wanting to spend time with female reformers instead of with his chums at his club?"

With a lazy smile, he trailed his gaze down to her mouth. "Even a duke with political aspirations can have a personal reason for wanting to advise . . . a friend."

When that set the schoolgirls to giggling, she tossed her head. "Fine. As long as you limit your advice to helping us with an income-producing task for the convict women, sir, I am happy to hear it."

Eliza cast him an adoring glance. "Perhaps the duke could tell us how to teach the convict women to whittle. Wouldn't that be an income-producing task?"

"Handing knives to prisoners is not a good idea, Eliza," Louisa snapped, annoyed by the girl's hero-worship.

Simon settled back in his chair. "Whittling might not work, but your women could paint someone else's carvings."

"And who will provide us with those? You?" Louisa taunted.

He lifted one eyebrow. "Of course not. But I could supply the paint."

Regina clapped her hands together. "I quite forgot. One of Grandfather Monteith's investments was a paint factory in Leeds. He left it to Simon."

"Every year London toymakers carve thousands of toy carts, soldiers, even Noah's arks with animals." Simon leaned forward, enthusiasm tinting his tanned cheeks a ruddy hue. "There's still a few months before Christmas. If you were to partner with white-wood carvers—"

"White-wood?" Eliza chirped.

"Pine," Louisa explained, surprised that Simon even knew the term.

"You could have the ladies paint toys," Simon went on. "And if you sell them at Christmas, you will make very good money."

Grudgingly, Louisa conceded that it was a good idea. She began to list strategies for carrying it out. "We'll have to find the carvers and someone to transport the paint and train the women—"

An object thunked on the table in front of her. Startled, she looked up to find that Raji had walked across to set his canary before her. "Sorry, Raji," she said, "but if we take on this project, we'll need new carvings to paint."

When he cocked his head as if listening to her, everyone at the table laughed. Then he leaped into her lap.

"Oh!" she exclaimed as he caught hold of her bodice. When she closed her arms about the dear creature, he curled up with a contented sigh. "For heaven's sake, what's this about?"

"Apparently he likes you," Simon said, his voice a low rumble. "And Raji is very particular. Ever since his previous owner died, he's been wary of women."

"Isn't that adorable?" Eliza breathed. "He thinks you're *her* or something."

A lump filled Louisa's throat as she stroked the monkey's fur. "Don't be silly. He just hopes to coax a cup of punch out of me." But secretly she was touched. She didn't bother to examine why too closely. Nor did she meet Simon's gaze, afraid of what she might see there. "Now where were we?"

"Mrs. Harris's committee will head up a project to have the ladies paint toys." Regina tapped a pencil on the table. "But we'll have to take care around the children, so they don't eat the paint."

"There are children in Newgate?" A frown marred Simon's fine high brow.

"Unfortunately, yes," Mrs. Harris said, her expression grim. "The policy is to imprison the youngest with their mothers. Newgate alone contains two hundred eighty seven women and one hundred thirteen children under six, locked up with murderers and highwaymen."

Louisa well remembered her outrage when she'd first seen the pitifully underfed, naked urchins, forced to witness their mothers selling themselves to gain food and clothes for their poor mites.

Thank heaven the Association and the London Ladies had improved matters. But not enough; not yet. She cradled Raji closer. "They even deliver babies in there. Can you imagine? With only one doctor, we have to fight to keep the women from dying of childbed fever or pouring out their life's blood—"

"Louisa, dear, you've made your point," Mrs. Harris broke in, with a glance 'round at her pupils.

They stared at Louisa wide-eyed, clearly never having thought about the perils of childbirth. Simon was watching her, too, a silent question in his eyes. And the last person to whom she wanted to reveal her darkest fear was *him.*

"That's why we *must* have the funds," she said quickly. "If not for the women, then for our children." A smile touched her lips. "They deserve toys, too." She glanced at Mrs. Harris. "Make sure you include that in the project."

"I hate to interrupt, Miss North, but you and I must still visit the Trusbuts." Simon glanced at his watch. "And it's already three-thirty."

Mrs. Harris made a shooing gesture at Louisa. "Go, go. Lady Trusbut is too important to ignore. We can discuss the candidates further on Tuesday."

Simon had already risen to round the table. "What's happening Tuesday?"

Louisa rose, too. "That's when we—" She halted as a devious idea struck her. "That's when you really ought to come observe us. And if you want to help, you can bring your coach and any other equipage you can spare."

"Now, Louisa," Regina warned, "I doubt that my brother would want—"

"He said he wished to observe, didn't he? And how better to observe than from his own carriage? Besides, we could use the extra rigs."

"We certainly could," Mrs. Harris said with mischief in her voice.

"For what?" Simon looked decidedly wary.

Louisa smiled. "Time to leave, don't you think? Although the Trusbut manor isn't far, the hour is getting late. If we're to return before dark—"

"Fine." Simon scooped up Raji's toy canary from

where it lay on the table. "But I expect you to explain on the way why you want my carriages."

He gestured to the door and she hurried out, her smile broadening with every step. If this didn't discourage him from whatever sly scheme he was engaged in with them, nothing would.

Chapter Seven

Dear Cousin,
Foxmoor's love of dancing must have improved,
for he's shamelessly pursuing Louisa. He even agreed
to help the London Ladies, which worries me. Because
if ever a man could spell danger for our political
aims, it is the duke.

Your concerned friend,
Charlotte

*S*imon seethed as he and Raji waited for Louisa outside Mrs. Harris's office. The damned chit had refused
to see him all week, only to trick him into agreeing to
observe the wrong committee once he'd finally cornered
her.

She thought to make him relinquish his pursuit, did
she? Very well, he would let her have her head, but only
for a while. Because to deal with her political dabbling, he
must know how far it went, which meant getting close to
her. Besides, courting a woman was damned hard when
the woman made herself inaccessible.

At least he had her for this jaunt, and for Tuesday's, as

well. He frowned. No doubt she had invented some new test with this business of needing his carriages.

"Ready?" she asked as she emerged from Mrs. Harris's office, wearing a peculiar sealskin hat and a snug little white spencer.

He sucked in a breath. How did the bloody female manage to look so enticing in such prim attire? During his time in India, he'd seen a hundred *devadasis* in alluring saris, yet none of them had looked as enchanting as Louisa in a buttoned-up spencer. None of them had made his blood run hot with wondering about the silky female curves beneath the satin—

"Simon?" she asked, her cheeks pinkening fetchingly beneath his lustful gaze.

"Yes. Ready. Right." Deuce take his vivid imagination. Pray God she stopped resisting him soon, or she would reduce him to begging.

They headed out to his waiting phaeton. Since he preferred to drive and Raji enjoyed riding on the perch, he handed his pet off to his tiger. Moments later, he had his matched bays comfortably trotting along the road back to London.

Glancing over, he noticed that Louisa sat prim and erect, the very picture of his sister at her loftiest. Except that the smile playing about Louisa's pretty mouth was too mischievous for Regina. And too damned tempting by far.

He jerked his attention back to the road before he indulged his urge to ravage that sumptuous mouth out here in plain view of the world. "Why do you want carriages Tuesday?" he snapped, to take his mind off her lips.

"We need to transport some convict women a short distance, that's all."

Then why was she smiling so smugly? "Isn't transportation the prison's responsibility?"

"Yes, but they usually put them in open carts, and we don't want that because—" Her smile vanished. "Well, it's just not wise."

"Let me guess—shackled prisoners in open carts invite public attention. Which means the women are subjected to taunts and insults."

"And mauled by unfeeling men." Her voice grew impassioned. "And pelted by rotten tomatoes and eggs and—" She stopped short as she realized how much she'd revealed. "Anyway, we figured private carriages would be better than carts."

"I'm sure you did," he said irritably. "Especially *my* private carriages. Why subject your own carriages to the whims of a rowdy mob when it would be more entertaining to subject mine?"

"We're not asking you to do anything we're not doing ourselves." She flashed him a challenging glare. "You did say you wanted to observe."

"Yes, I did." And the minx had leapt at the chance to torment him for it. "But much as I enjoy the occasional run through rotten vegetables, I would rather provide coaches more suitable to your purposes."

She sniffed. "If you're suggesting hackneys, we tried that. They won't rent to us at any price. Not for this."

Yet the troublemaking wench was eager to have him expose his own costly rigs to abuse. "Hackney owners will take a risk if given the proper incentive. Like assurances from a duke that their losses will be covered."

Good thing he had a fortune to spare. Otherwise, convincing his skeptical future wife to trust him would eventually drive him into penury.

When she said nothing, he added, "Will that do the trick? Or are you determined to see my carriages ravaged by the mob?"

"This isn't a joke," she said. "Our group is serious about gaining humane treatment for these women."

"Not serious enough." He still chafed at how she'd manipulated him earlier. "Otherwise you would not refuse to make use of my considerable talents where it would do you the most good."

"Stop trying to provoke me into involving you in our political affairs." She folded her hands in her lap. "I know that observing us isn't really your aim."

"It is certainly not my only aim," he muttered.

"What do you mean?"

He hesitated, but it was best to be honest where he could. Honesty had always carried him further with her than deception.

This entire courtship is a deception, his grandfather's voice sneered. *And you call* me *a hypocrite?*

Simon gritted his teeth. It was not a deception—he fully intended to marry her. He was simply hiding his reasons for it because it was the only way to gain what was best for everyone—her included. "Surely what I want is obvious. I want to be with you, Louisa."

She eyed him askance. "Why? Did the king say something to you? He keeps going on and on about my activities—"

"It has nothing to do with the king," he snapped, then regretted the blatant falsehood. But Christ, she drove him to it sometimes. "You are the most suspicious female I have ever met. God forbid a man should try to court you—"

"*Court* me!" Her musical laughter grated on him. "Court me? Fancy that."

"Not the most flattering response," he grumbled.

"No, no, forgive me, I'm flattered, indeed I am." Her shoulders shook with laughter, and she clasped her gloved hands together tightly.

"I can tell how flattered you are. You're practically swooning."

She shot him a mischievous glance. "Would you like to see me swoon?"

"I would like to see you take me seriously. Because this time I have every intention of winning you."

Her eyes darkened. "You really mean it, don't you?"

"I wouldn't say it if I—" He caught himself too late.

"Didn't mean it?" she finished, an arch smile on her lips. "I seem to recall that you said it without meaning it easily enough the first time."

His temper flared. "Things have changed since then. *I* have changed." More than she realized, even if he still had an ulterior motive for courting her.

"You aren't the only one." She sounded as if she were trying to convince herself as much as him. "That's why there's no point to your courting me. I am no longer the naïve little fool who lapped up your every word."

"You were never a fool." He tensed, but could see no way around having this discussion. They clearly couldn't go further without it.

Between Raji's excited chattering and the raised phaeton hood, Simon's tiger could probably not hear them. But just in case, Simon lowered his voice. "I was the fool, Louisa. I thought I could do what the king asked without hurting anyone." His tone grew acid. "Unfortunately, I have an annoying tendency to press far beyond the point when another man would call a retreat."

"Really?" she said coldly. "Do tell."

"I didn't mean to say what I did, I swear." His hands clenching the reins, he stared at the macadam road. "That night when you told me I mustn't see you again until you came of age, I saw my plans crumbling. The words just came out—"

He halted, realizing how feeble it sounded. Yet it was true. Desperate to keep from losing the king's influence, he had spoken the fateful words that had changed his life forever: *Run away with me. I love you. Marry me.*

A second later, he had regretted them. Even in the throes of his youthful ambition, he'd realized he'd gone too far. But he still had not taken them back.

And when her face had lit up and she had said yes, kissing her had seemed perfectly natural. Especially when he had dreamed of it for weeks, had thought of it in the night, had burned to touch her—

"The point is, sir," Louisa said, "I don't care anymore if you've changed. I don't intend to marry anyone ever. Neither you nor any other man."

He refused to believe her. His sister had professed the same desire until she had succumbed to Draker's advances. So if Louisa meant to drive him off, she would have to do better. "Say what you will, you are not the sort of woman to—"

"Dedicate her life to a cause?"

"Give up men. You are too passionate to endure life as a spinster."

"Just because I melted into a puddle when you kissed me seven years ago—"

"And four nights ago," he growled.

"I told you, that was an experiment. It didn't mean anything."

He eyed her askance. "And that is why you avoid me."

His sarcasm thickened. "That is why today you were headed off to hide—"

"I wasn't!" With a furtive glance behind her, she lowered her voice. "My cause is just more important than you or me or what once happened between us."

But a pretty blush stained her cheeks and her hands trembled, which sent a surge of triumph through him. "Prove it."

"I beg your pardon?"

"Prove that your cause is more bloody important than anything else. Let me advise *your* committee. You know very well I can be invaluable to you. And don't give me that rot about not trusting me. If I wanted to ferret out your secrets, I would. But give me a chance, and I can be very useful in helping you navigate political waters. I *want* to be useful to you."

At least until he married her. He had nothing against her admirable group, but they were headed for trouble if they kept listening to *her.* Reform groups that got on the wrong side of public opinion only succeeded in setting back their cause.

Since she was the one pushing them into politics, they would be better off without her. Then they could return to aiding convict women until their reforms could be legislated at a reasonable pace by reasonable men like himself.

And if taking Louisa out of the group damaged their charitable aims, too?

Newgate alone contains two hundred eighty-seven women and one hundred thirteen children, locked up with murderers and highwaymen. Children, for God's sake, under the age of six.

It didn't matter, he told himself, ignoring the squirming of his conscience. Sometimes even admirable causes must be sacrificed to achieve the greater good. He meant to uphold his devil's bargain with the king no matter what that entailed. The sooner he stopped her political meddling, the better for everyone.

He flicked the reins. "If your cause really is more important than 'you or me,' then why not let me advise you?" Shooting her a covert glance, he added, "Of course, if you cannot bear to be around me because our past is too painful or I tempt you to abandon your high-minded ideas about marriage—"

"Don't flatter yourself," she bit out.

"Then make use of me. Seven years ago, I used you for my own purposes. Now it's your chance to use my reckless attraction to you for your political cause."

He felt her eyes assessing him. "How can I be sure this isn't another of your schemes?"

"You can let me prove my sincerity. If you believe that anyone can reform, can't you give me the same consideration as your convict women? What will it cost you to make use of my political connections and knowledge?"

"It could cost us everything if you use what you learn against us."

"Not knowing what you're doing could cost you everything, anyway." That was exactly why he meant to marry her and coax her out of politics. "Besides, I'll be risking my own career by publicly supporting a group that has MPs grumbling."

"So why do it?" she snapped.

"Because I want you," he said in a low voice. "As my wife. And if advising your group is the only way to win you, then that is what I will do."

That brought her up short. She looked as if she

might give him an answer, then blinked and pointed to a wide, elm-lined avenue cutting off from the main road immediately ahead. "That's the turn to Lady Trusbut's house."

Damn, so it was. He took the turn quickly, throwing her against him. When she clutched at his leg for balance, his very muscles leapt at the touch. She started to draw her hand back, but he caught it and flattened it against his thigh. His gaze met hers, and for the merest second he saw his own arousal mirrored in her eyes.

That glimpse emboldened him. As they approached the house, he entwined his fingers with hers. "Will you let me advise you? Or will you condemn me to worshiping you from afar, pining after you alone in my bed, besotted and—"

"What a lot of poppycock." But a reluctant smile played about her lips, and she did not try to free her hand. "I give you a week at most before you tire of courting me and turn your attention to a more suitable female."

"I didn't tire of courting you last time, did I?" He shot her a mischievous glance. "I only stopped because you demanded that I be packed off to India."

"You didn't have to go." Stiffening, she slid her hand free of his. "You could have defied the king, given up the chance to become prime minister, and married me instead. But you didn't."

Cursing himself for having brought up their unsettling past yet again, he halted the phaeton in front of the Trusbuts' impressive Palladian manor, then angled himself to face her. "You're right. I chose exile over marriage. Because like you, I once believed there were ambitions more important than you or I."

She arched an eyebrow. "Surely you won't claim you no longer believe that."

"I no longer believe that one must always choose," he hedged. "There's no reason we can't have both, our ambitions and—" As his tiger leapt down, taking Raji with him, Simon lowered his voice. "—our passions." In the right place.

"In a perfect world we might have both, but in the real world—"

"We *make* the real world, Louisa." Simon climbed out. "If you did not believe that, you would not be a reformer."

He took Raji from his tiger, allowing the scamp to climb onto his shoulder. "So make the world be what you want. What we both want. Give me a chance." He held out his hand to help her down. "Let me be with you."

She stared at his hand a long moment. The sun hung above the horizon behind her head, haloing her in an amber light that also shielded her expression.

But at last she allowed him to help her down. As she hesitated beside the phaeton, with cheeks pink and eyes lowered, he ruthlessly tamped down the urge to kiss her until she yielded everything. If he shamed her on the Trusbuts' doorstep, she would never forgive him.

"I'll think about your . . . er . . . proposition," she said, "and let you know my answer by the end of the day . . . Your Grace."

Scowling, he settled her hand on his arm, then led her toward the steps. "I'll have you calling me Simon before then, I swear. The way you used to."

"That was when you were someone else." She reverted to her calm, detached air. "The Simon I knew was a figment of my imagination. The real Duke of Foxmoor was . . . *is* a stranger to me. And until I know him better, I will treat him like any other stranger I've just met."

Not for long, my clever beauty, he thought as they mounted the steps. *Not if I have anything to say about it.*

Raji climbed across his back, then leapt off. When he landed on Louisa's shoulder, she laughed.

"He has taken a fancy to you." Simon fixed his gaze on her luscious lips. "Much like his owner."

Though she blushed, her gaze was skeptical. "If I didn't know better, I'd think you put Raji up to it."

"I have trained him to do some things, but leaping into your arms is not one of them. His fancy for you and his fancy for birds are entirely his own idea."

The door opened, and the butler ushered them in, taking their cards off to his mistress while they stood waiting.

"Well," Louisa whispered, "let's pray he doesn't take a fancy to Lady Trusbut's coiffure this time."

"As long as she refrains from wearing toy peacocks, he will be fine. Which reminds me—" He dug Raji's canary out of his coat pocket and handed it to the monkey, who clung to Louisa's neck. "It helps if he has his own toy to pet."

"Good," she said as Raji seized his toy. "We need to impress Lady Trusbut."

We? Simon bit back a smile.

"And his lordship, too, of course," she added.

"Which is why I'm here," Simon said.

This would be tricky. They both needed Lord Trusbut's support, but if Simon remembered correctly, the courtly gentleman thought women should be protected from the cold, cruel world at all costs. Which meant keeping them well away from prisons. Not to mention Parliament.

The butler returned to bid them follow him, then headed off at a clipped pace that gave Simon little time to examine the manor as thoroughly as he preferred when assessing adversaries. After a brisk walk down a carpetless hall devoid of portraits and smelling faintly of linseed oil, they were ushered into a private sitting room filled with bird cages, some of them empty, most of them not.

With a smile, Lady Trusbut curtsied while her hoary-headed husband made a sketchy bow over the stout ivory cane he leaned upon. Judging from the grim expression on the baron's gaunt face, he was not nearly as happy that they'd come as Lady Trusbut seemed to be.

The baroness rushed forward, her hazel eyes alight. "Your Grace, we are so delighted to have you." She inclined her head toward Louisa. "And you, too, Miss North, of course. Did your sister-in-law not come with you?"

"We took my phaeton, so there was no room for her," Simon explained.

Lady Trusbut edged closer to where Raji was perched on Louisa's shoulder and peered cautiously at him. "I say, is he really clutching a toy canary?"

"His favorite," Simon said. "Though as you know, he also bears a certain fondness for miniature peacocks."

Lady Trusbut gave a trilling laugh. "He does, indeed." She gestured to a settee littered with yellow feathers. "Please, do stay a moment."

Once he and Louisa were seated together opposite the Trusbuts, who'd each taken a chair, the baroness called for tea. Raji, scamp that he was, immediately settled himself into the curve of Louisa's arm and buried his face in her bodice.

Louisa laughed. "Don't tell me you're choosing *now* to be shy, you little imp. After all the trouble you caused the other night?"

When Raji gazed up at her adoringly, she fussed over him. A sudden pang struck Simon's chest. It was easy to imagine Louisa fussing over his child instead, cooing to his sloe-eyed, dark-haired son or tenderly stroking his curly-headed minx of a daughter. As Simon's throat constricted, he had to look away.

All in good time. You will have that, too, if you can only be patient. A pity he felt far less than patient right now, with the feel of her hand on his thigh still fresh in his memory.

"See here, little fellow," Lady Trusbut told Raji as her husband looked on sullenly, "do not be frightened of us. You're among friends here." Waving her hand in the air, she uttered a series of clicking noises. "Come, Garnet and Opal, Ruby and Sapphire! We have guests!"

As a flock of canaries alighted on her arms and shoulders, Simon quipped, "What? No Diamond?"

"Diamond is ill." Lady Trusbut gestured to a cage at the far end of the room. "He's resting, poor thing. How did you know?"

"Lucky guess," he said, exchanging a glance with Lord Trusbut, who sat grimly silent with his hands upon his knees.

Lady Trusbut took a bird upon her finger. "Come now, Emerald, say hello to Raji."

Emerald did more than that—she sang. Raji's head jerked up, and before anyone knew it, he'd tossed his toy aside and was scampering over to Lady Trusbut.

"Raji, no!" Louisa cried and lunged forward.

But Simon caught her arm. "It's all right. Just watch."

The monkey scrambled into Lady Trusbut's lap, then sat listening, enraptured.

Lady Trusbut smiled. "Look at that, will you? A perfect gentleman."

"He knows the difference between real birds and toys," Simon explained. "He's very careful with real birds. It's the toy ones he loves to death."

Lady Trusbut brought her bird nearer Raji, who visibly sighed with pleasure. When the canary stopped warbling, Simon gave Raji a command in Hindi.

Raji clapped his hands and everyone laughed, even Lord Trusbut before he caught himself.

"What did you say?" Louisa asked.

"I told him to show his appreciation for the song. Certain commands he will only heed if I give them in Hindi."

"You speak Hindi?" Louisa said, clearly surprised.

"Some." Not knowing the language of the people whom one ruled could lead to disaster, as he had learned only too well from the tragedies at Poona. If he had only been able to listen to the gossip in the markets then, as he had learned to do later, perhaps—

No, thoughts like that led to madness. He was trying to make amends for that mistake. This endless reassessing of where he had gone wrong only kept him from focusing his energies on setting things right.

Louisa gasped, jerking his attention to where Raji now reached for the canary.

"Pet lightly, lad," Simon warned, then repeated the command in Hindi.

But Raji was careful as usual, stroking the bird with awe.

"I don't believe it," Louisa breathed. "Look at the little devil. He's in raptures. And so gentle, too." She slanted a glance at Simon. "Not to mention well-trained. Did *you* train him?"

"No, he belonged to a traveling performer before Colin's wife acquired him. Apparently he used to wear a silly vest and red hat." He smiled over at Raji. "But we don't go for such humiliating rot now, do we, chap?"

Raji chattered in answer.

"What did he say?" Lady Trusbut asked in perfect seriousness.

Simon blinked. "Devil if I know. Probably something like, 'When are you going to feed me again, you big sorry lout?' "

"Oh no, surely nothing so impudent as that." Lady Trusbut turned her head to the three birds jockeying for purchase on her shoulder. "What's that, ladies? Yes, I know. The duke is joking. He would never starve his pet, I'm sure."

"Apparently Lady Trusbut's birds talk to her," Louisa murmured.

"Ah," Simon said. "Don't tell Raji, or he'll expect me to interpret."

Lady Trusbut straightened in her chair. "My canaries are very intelligent, sir. They're the jewels in my crown." She flashed her husband a coy glance. "Edward buys me another every Christmas, don't you, dear?"

The old gent's ears reddened. "Cheaper than real jewels, eh, Foxmoor?"

"I imagine so." Noting the indulgent look the baron shot his wife, Simon added, "Though I hear that any expense is worth it to keep one's spouse content."

Lord Trusbut took his meaning readily, for he reached inside his coat pocket. "My wife seems to think Miss North's cause is a good one." With a frown, he removed a slip of paper. "I told her I'd be willing to offer a small donation."

The baron pointedly offered the bank draft to Simon. Ignoring how Louisa bristled, Simon reached for it, but Lord Trusbut did not let go.

"I assume, Foxmoor, that this amount will suffice to put an end to Miss North's attempts to involve my wife with her Ladies Society."

"Edward, please!" Lady Trusbut exclaimed.

"I mean it." The crusty old baron met Simon's gaze dolefully. "I won't have my wife trotting about a prison. And if you care for Miss North, you'll keep her away from prisons, as well. I'm sure you agree, sir, that ladies don't belong at Newgate."

The conversation had just turned tricky, but fortunately not impossible. Simon flashed Lord Trusbut a broad smile. "I do agree with you, sir. Newgate is no place for ladies."

Chapter Eight

Dear Charlotte,

*You have good reason to be wary. By all accounts,
Foxmoor's ambition to become prime minister has
not changed, so if Miss North does catch him for a
husband, she will take second place to his ambition.*

Yours fondly,
Michael

*L*ouisa nearly had heart failure. How dared Simon agree
with that man? Leaning forward, she prepared to give
Lord Trusbut a piece of her mind, but Simon laid his
hand on her arm and squeezed it in warning.

"Newgate is no place for ladies," he repeated. Lord
Trusbut released the bank draft. Simon glanced at it,
frowned, then folded it and tapped it against his knee.
"Indeed, it's no place for women at all. Yet there *are* hundreds there, being treated little better than animals. And
surely you don't approve of that, do you?"

Louisa let out her breath, then fixed Lord Trusbut with
a questioning glance.

Lord Trusbut scowled at them both. "They're criminals. That's different."

Releasing her arm, Simon sat back and cast her an expectant look.

She took his cue. "They're not *all* criminals. Nearly a third are awaiting trial, which means they haven't been convicted. And there are children, too, subjected to the filth and indignities of a prison merely because their mothers were sent there. Surely you don't think children belong in a prison, sir."

"Certainly not, but—"

"Despite what Lord Sidmouth claims, we're not advocating that the women escape punishment. But we've found that if they are given rules and a suitable occupation in prison, they often become law-abiding citizens once they're released."

She chose her words carefully. "But until Parliament agrees to fund permanent matrons and schoolteachers, we need many charity-minded females to provide those services. We'd hate to see the prisoners return to their old ways because ladies like your wife and I aren't there to help."

"And if it's the ladies' safety you're concerned about," Simon added, "I intend to go with them from now on."

"Really?" Lord Trusbut said. "You will accompany them to Newgate?"

Louisa was as surprised by the statement as the baron.

"As often as I can." He fixed the baron with a steely look. "It is a worthy cause. And women will have their little causes, so why not indulge them?"

She didn't like him speaking of prison reform as some female whim, but she couldn't deny the effect his words were having on Lord Trusbut.

The man sat back, rubbing the ivory knob of his cane as if it were a fortune-teller's crystal ball and he thought to find answers in its creamy surface.

Simon pressed his point. "I have taken a personal interest in Miss North's organization. A very personal interest."

That seemed to push Lord Trusbut over the edge, for he glanced over to his wife. "What do you think, Lillian? Is this something you would like to do?"

Lady Trusbut stared down to where Raji chattered at her canary. "Well . . . you see, Edward, many of my friends are joining. And I can't help thinking how sad it is that those poor children must suffer for their mothers' crimes. If I could make myself useful to *them* . . ."

It suddenly dawned on Louisa that the Trusbuts had no children, despite having been married practically forever. Her heart constricted to see how carefully the baroness handled her birds, how gentle she was with Raji.

"We'd be delighted to have you bring a few canaries to the prison sometime," Louisa said softly. "The children would adore hearing them sing."

Lady Trusbut brightened. "Do you really think so? Opal is the best for singing, though Emerald has a fine voice, too." She held Emerald up to eye level. "What do you think, dear? Should you like to entertain some poor children?"

The bird cocked its head, and Lady Trusbut nodded, then flashed Louisa a blazing smile. "She would be happy to go."

Louisa glanced at Lord Trusbut, who was staring at his wife with a haunting tenderness that made a lump lodge in Louisa's throat. Oh, to be loved like that. It might make even the risk of childbearing worth it.

Simon must have seen it, too, for his voice was thick

when he spoke again. "Then it's settled. Lady Trusbut will join Miss North's little group."

Lord Trusbut's gaze snapped to Simon, suddenly fierce. "But she will only go to Newgate if you are in attendance, too."

"Of course," Simon said. "I will ensure her safety at all times."

The rest of the visit passed in a happy daze for Louisa. As she explained the project they were considering, she marveled at how easily Simon laid it out, how firm he was with Lord Trusbut about his assurance that it would be successful. Could this be? Could Simon really be this enthusiastic about their cause?

And could it really be all for her?

She dared not let herself believe that. Yet he'd defended her to an influential lord. He'd even agreed to accompany them to the prison, and before witnesses, too.

Surely it couldn't last. He had more important things to do than squire ladies back and forth to Newgate. Unless he was sincere about courting her . . .

Warmth pooled in her belly at the thought. The devil certainly knew how to tempt her. She should know better than to trust him. Why, Sidmouth himself might have sent Simon to wreak havoc in their midst.

But if so, Simon was going about it wrong, professing publicly to have taken "a personal interest" in their group. The Home Secretary wouldn't like that at all.

As they rose to leave, Simon stunned her by handing the bank draft back to Lord Trusbut. "Surely now you can find it in your heart to be more generous."

Shocked at his daring, she said, "Your Grace—"

"No, the duke is right," Lord Trusbut answered. "If my wife is to participate, I'm happy to oblige."

He invited Simon to go with him to his study, leaving her and Lady Trusbut alone. Casting a glance toward the open door, Lady Trusbut lowered her voice. "His Grace seems very enamored of you."

There's no reason we can't have both. Our ambitions. And our passions.

Louisa managed a shaky laugh. "He's merely helping me because of our family connection."

"Nonsense, my dear. No man is *that* solicitous of his sister's relation for nothing. I can tell a serious suitor when I see one."

Just what she did not need. Or want.

Except when he looked at her. And entwined her fingers with his. And ravished her mouth in the tempting dark of the night—

"Shh, they return," Lady Trusbut warned. As the two men approached from down the hall, she added, "I shall tell my friends Mrs. Peel and Mrs. Canning about your group as well. They are both quite the philanthropists."

Louisa gaped at the baroness's generosity, as well as her astute choice of friends. Robert Peel and George Canning were both MPs who'd leaned toward supporting Louisa's cause. If their wives were to join . . .

Barely able to contain her excitement, Louisa squeezed the baroness's hand. "That would be wonderful—thank you! The three of you should come to call next week, so I can further explain our group's aims."

Then she and Simon took their leave and headed back for London, with dusk settling soft as silk on the sprouting green fields.

Louisa let out a long breath. "I can't believe how well that went! I've been trying to get Lady Trusbut to join for weeks." She gave Simon's arm a playful punch. "But you merely set Raji to work, and she offers to introduce me to her important friends. Isn't that wonderful?"

When Simon didn't answer, she glanced over to where he tooled the phaeton with expert skill, looking pensive. "What's wrong?" Her cheery mood dimmed. "Are you worried Lord Trusbut will change his mind and try to hurt your career?"

"Hardly." When he caught her questioning gaze on him, he forced a smile. "Trusbut's a man of character. If he says he'll support your group, then he will."

"Then why are you upset?"

"I'm not upset. I . . ." He returned to staring at the road, his hands fisting on the reins. "Did you see how Trusbut looked at her?"

"His wife? Yes. I thought it was very sweet."

For a moment, he said nothing. When he spoke again, his voice held a wistfulness that tugged at her heart. "My father never once looked at my mother like that, not in all the years they were married."

She was surprised he would speak of something so personal. "Regina did say your parents were rather formal together."

"Formal?" He gave a harsh laugh. "Cold is closer to the truth. Father spent his time at his club, and Mother with her friends. Her fondness for faro was a sore subject with Grandfather Monteith. He believed my father corrupted his daughter."

"Is that why your grandfather made you his protégé? Because his son-in-law was a dissipated gambler?"

"You could say that." His voice held an odd edge. "It was probably no coincidence that Grandfather Monteith took me under his wing after the second of his two sons died. With my mother married, he had no one left to bully."

"Bully?" His vitriolic words surprised her. "What did your grandfather—"

"He was merely strong-minded," he said quickly, his expression veiled. He cast her a rueful smile. "Like me."

"But not like your father, I take it."

"No. My father had no ambition for anything but grouse hunting and whist. In the early years of their marriage, that fact annoyed my mother." A weary resignation tinged Simon's voice. "By the time she died, neither of them cared enough about the other for annoyance."

"If it's any consolation, neither did my parents."

"Which ones?"

She sighed. "Good point. But it's true of either of my possible fathers. The king's attention to Mama was limited to the bedchamber. And the man who gave me his name couldn't have cared much for Mama, or he wouldn't have let His Majesty carry on a shamelessly public long-term affair with her."

The pity in Simon's face did nothing to lessen her hurt. "I'm sorry, Louisa."

"For what?" She forced reserve into her voice. "It's not your fault that my mother was a . . ." Whore. But she couldn't bring herself to say the word, although she'd heard her brother call Mama that often enough.

Staring blindly at the road, she struggled to regain her composure. Odd how one's past could jump up to bite a person at the most inopportune moment. "You knew Mama, didn't you? She stayed with your family after Marcus banished her from Castlemaine."

He tensed. "I was at school."

"But surely not the whole time." When he said nothing, she added, "Was she as much a . . . wanton as Marcus says?"

He hesitated just long enough for her to know the answer. "No."

"Liar."

His gaze swung to her. "Does it matter?"

"My family's scandalous reputation was one of the reasons you thought me unsuitable for marriage, as you'll recall."

"What makes you think I considered you unsuitable?"

"It was fairly obvious when you left without marrying me. And then didn't write or in any way show that you missed me."

"I did not believe that you would welcome letters from me after how I behaved to you. Indeed, even after I returned, I did not think you would countenance my courting you again. Not until we kissed."

"When I showed myself to be as wanton as my mother."

"Louisa—"

"No, I want to know. Not about you and me—I suppose I understand why you behaved as you did. I want to know about my mother." She took a deep breath. "I've always wondered what she was really like. When I was a child, she was hardly ever there." Because she was perfectly content to ignore her children and her husband for the privileges of being a royal mistress. "Then after Papa died when I was ten and Marcus banished her, I wasn't allowed to see her again."

She swallowed hard. Marcus had only done what he'd thought was right. But it still hurt that in the four years Mama had lived after leaving Castlemaine, she'd made no attempt to see her daughter. That's why Louisa had clung so tightly to her half sister. Because Charlotte had been abandoned, too, left to the indifferent care of her royal father while her mother, Queen Caroline, took lovers abroad.

It wasn't right. No woman should put passion above her children. Better not to have children at all than to treat them with so little regard.

Or die bearing them, leaving them to the fickle affections of their fathers.

They drove in silence, past oat fields glittering greenly in the waning sun. When they entered a section of road near Richmond Park shrouded by overreaching oaks, even the clopping of the horses began to sound muted.

She sighed. "Anyway, I thought . . . you might tell me—"

"Beyond the physical resemblance you bear to your mother, you are nothing like her, if that is what worries you," Simon said.

Worry her? It plagued her constantly, her suspicion that she'd inherited her mother's lustful nature. Simon had no idea how she burned in the night, the places she touched herself as she yearned for what she knew was bad for her.

Then again, perhaps he *did* know. "Didn't you claim just this afternoon that I am too passionate to be a spinster?" she said tartly.

"A woman can be passionate without being a wanton, just as a man can enjoy a good meal without being a glutton. Wantons—and rakes—are gluttons for fleshly pleasure. They're indiscriminate and unable to heed the call of conscience or reason, which often makes them behave recklessly."

"Like my mother."

His silence was her answer.

Something suddenly occurred to her that sent a chill skating down her spine. "Did she ever . . . that is . . . were you and my mother ever—"

"Certainly not. Your mother liked her men much older. When she stayed with us, I was only eighteen, far too young." He stared blindly at the road. "For *her,* at least."

"What do you mean?" What other woman had been eager for a young lover? And why did the thought of a young Simon in the arms of some experienced older woman make jealousy burn in her belly?

"Nothing." He gazed down the road, his smooth statesman's mask firmly back in place. "So you're happy about the results of our visit, are you?"

She wanted to press him, but was half-afraid to know what he meant. "Deliriously happy. It appears you were right—you *can* be very useful to my group."

He flicked the reins. "Does that mean you will allow me to advise you?"

He was certainly making it hard to dismiss his offer. If Simon were the one pushing their reforms in Parliament, he'd win, assuming he could regain the influence he'd had before he'd left for India, and judging from Lord Trusbut's reactions, it wouldn't be long before he did just that.

But was that what he was offering? Or was he just seeking to ruin their political efforts? "You still haven't said how you stand on prison reform."

"I still haven't seen what it entails."

That was precisely what bothered her—the way he evaded her questions.

And the fact that accepting his help would mean being around him, talking to him . . . stirring up the old feelings for him. Feelings she didn't dare act upon.

Her heart thundered in her ears. Was it worth the risks?

Before she could answer herself or him, something large and furry tumbled over her shoulder and fell into her lap. She laughed, relieved to put off the decision a while longer. "Raji, you little devil. I thought you preferred riding on the perch."

"Apparently not when you're around." Simon cast his pet a stern glance. "You should leave the poor woman be. She is not your keeper."

"I don't mind," she said, cradling the adorable creature in her arms.

Simon said something in Hindi to his pet. They were about to pass under a low-hanging branch, and suddenly Raji scrambled up the hood of the phaeton, then leapt right onto the oak and disappeared.

"Damn." Simon brought the phaeton to a swift halt. "The rascal has a mind of his own. I must retrieve him before he scampers too far." He sprang out, then turned to her. "You should come, too. Since he's fond of you, perhaps you can coax him back."

"Of course." She let Simon help her down, then headed into the woods where Raji had disappeared. Simon gave his tiger some orders before joining her.

She could see no sign of Raji, and began to worry that they would never find him. Even Simon's shouted commands brought no results. After several moments of wandering and calling, they reached the end of the woods. Still no Raji.

Simon turned to her. "We'll have to wait until he tires of exploring. Which he will do eventually."

"But he could hurt himself!"

"He's a monkey. You may not realize it, sweetheart, but they actually spend most of their time in trees."

"Very funny," she said, but the word "sweetheart" reverberated through her chest in a most alarming way.

"We might as well wait for him to find us." Simon gestured to a fallen oak. "Let's sit, shall we?"

She shot him a sharp glance. "Wouldn't he find us more easily at the phaeton?"

"Not necessarily." He strode to the log and swept it clean with his leather driving gloves, which he then peeled off and slapped against his thigh. "Besides, I'd rather sit here than on the side of the dusty road, wouldn't you?"

Removing his frock coat, he laid it over the log, then gestured for her to take a seat. The fact that it left him scandalously clad in his shirtsleeves and striped waistcoat didn't seem to occur to him.

Or did it? Suspicion sputtered to life. "What did you say to Raji in Hindi that sent him leaping from the phaeton?"

"I told him to leave you be." Simon tossed his beaver top hat onto the log. "He must have taken it to mean he should run off."

"Fiddlesticks." She planted her hands on her hips. "I saw how well you managed him today; he obeyed your every command. So admit it—you didn't really tell him to leave me be, did you?"

A reluctant smile touched his lips. "You are too clever for your own good."

"Too clever for the machinations of a scoundrel like you," she scoffed. "Now tell me what you said to Raji."

Mischief glinted in his eyes. "I said, 'Go find the bananas.' "

"You know perfectly well there are no banana trees here!"

"Exactly." He strode toward her with clear intent.

A little thrill coursed down her spine. "But he'll get lost or—"

"Don't fret yourself over it." His dark smile made her toes curl in her half boots. "He's been trained to look for a while and then return to his owner."

Torn between laughter and outrage, she backed away from him. "You mean you sent that poor thing on a wild banana chase? That's awful!"

"Trust me, there's nothing Raji likes better than a good swing through the trees." He stalked her with a tiger's easy grace. "Besides, a man has to find some way to be alone with the woman he's courting, doesn't he?"

The words hung in the air, tantalizing her with the forbidden, alarming her with the reality.

Once again she'd made a huge miscalculation. And judging from the predatory look on Simon's face, she'd best beat a hasty retreat.

Chapter Nine

❦

Dear Cousin,
  Why can't Miss North and the duke both pursue their ambitions? Assumptions like yours are why women like myself refuse to marry—because once we achieve our life's dream, we are loath to toss it aside for the dubious pleasures of matrimony.

  Your irate cousin,
  Charlotte

*S*imon wasn't surprised Louisa had caught on to his ploy so quickly—he could scarcely believe she had let him take it *this* far.

She hurried back down the path toward the road. "It's getting late, sir. We should return to town."

She thought to flee him, did she? The devil she would.

Reaching inside his waistcoat pocket, he called out, "Don't you want to know how much money Lord Trusbut donated to the London Ladies Society?"

That made her halt. She hesitated, probably weighing whether to engage the enemy in this cozy spot, but the reformer in her won out over the cautious spinster.

When she faced him, he was dangling the bank draft from his fingers.

Her face darkened. "That belongs to me, and you know it." She held out her hand. "Now give it here."

"'Give it here'?" He chuckled. "That may work for my sister when she deals with your lummox of a brother, but I'm not so easily led." With a grin, he tucked the draft inside his pocket. "If you want it, you will have to come and get it."

Though color suffused her lovely cheeks, her eyes glittered in the rapidly dimming light. "I am not going to play your games," she told him with typically feminine condescension. "Hand me the draft, Your Grace."

His grin vanished. "Call me Simon, and I will."

"Your Grace, Your Grace, Your Grace—"

"I will make you call me Simon if it's the last thing I do," he growled, then lunged for her.

She whirled and ran from him. "I shall never say it now, sir," she called back as she weaved through birches and elms, her bodice ribbons trailing out behind her like a comet's tail.

Fortunately her skirts hampered her speed, so he caught up to her within moments. Snagging her about the waist, he yanked her back against him so hard that he knocked off her hat. "Call me Simon," he hissed in her ear as her sweet derriere nestled against his groin. "Call me Simon or you will never see that draft."

She stopped wriggling, and for a second he thought he had won. Until she brought the heel of her very sturdy half boot back into his shin. Hard.

"Ow!" He released her at once. The bloody female had kicked him!

She turned and slid her hand inside his pocket, jerking

out the draft with a cry of triumph. When she read it, she froze. "Oh my word."

Simon glared up at her as he rubbed his sore shin. "I hope that warms your mercenary little heart."

"Two hundred pounds! Do you know what we can do with two hundred pounds?"

"Hire hackneys?" he grumbled as he straightened.

"Add nicely to our fund for our candidate."

He went cold. Not if he had anything to say about it.

She stared at the draft, a guilty flush touching her cheeks. "Um . . . what amount had Lord Trusbut offered before you convinced him to change it?"

"Twenty." When her startled gaze shot to him, he added, "I strongly encouraged him to add a zero." After promising privately that he would prevent the group from pursuing their political aspirations. Trusbut might be willing to placate his wife's new interest in reform, but he was as wary as the other lords about letting some charitable group trot a questionable political candidate about the country giving incendiary speeches.

"Thank you. It is much appreciated."

Her unwitting thanks troubled his conscience, but he told himself he would make it up to her once they were married.

Contrition shining in her eyes, Louisa folded the draft, then slipped it inside the pocket of her morning gown. "I'm sorry I kicked you. It was most ungenerous of me. This is far more than I expected, Your Grace."

If she called him "Your Grace" one more time, he would take her over his knee. "Surely I deserve more than a mere thanks," he snapped.

She stiffened. "Now see here, I am not the sort of woman to offer—"

"Call me Simon, damn it."

Her eyes went wide. "Oh."

The color suffusing her cheeks gave him pause. "You thought I was going to ask for something else, didn't you?"

She dropped her gaze. "No, I-I wasn't . . . I just thought—"

"That I was going to ask for a kiss. Or something equally scandalous." He stepped nearer. "Perhaps you were even hoping I would."

"Certainly not!" But she couldn't meet his eyes. "I told you already that I have no desire to—"

Taking her off guard, he tugged her into his arms, then kissed her. Suddenly, firmly . . . briefly. When she lifted her startled gaze to him, he said, "There, you have your kiss. Now call me Simon."

A laugh sputtered out of her that she quickly squelched. Her lips formed a prim line once more, but their twitch betrayed her. "I told you, I shan't be so familiar with you." She pushed against his chest. "And I certainly didn't mean for you to—"

He kissed her again, but before she could shove him away, he drew back. "I am happy to give you as many kisses as you please, as long as you call me Simon."

She looked torn between anger and laughter. "You know perfectly well I wasn't asking you to—"

He leaned forward to kiss her again, but she hastily pressed her hand to his lips. "Stop that, sir!"

"Simon," he prompted against her gloved fingers. "Call me Simon, and I will stop."

Another laugh bubbled out of her. "Are you deaf? I told you, I won't call you Simon until I know the real you better."

Imprisoning her hand against his lips, he began to kiss her gloved fingers one by one. "So you prefer that I keep kissing you—"

"You know that's not what I meant," she said in a throaty whisper.

Yet she did not push him away or try to halt him as he unfastened the tiny buttons of her glove and opened it to feather a kiss over the lilac-scented skin of her wrist. When her pulse stammered into a wild thrumming, his own pulse leapt in response. She was not as immune to him as she pretended, thank God.

"You have such pretty hands." He peeled her glove off, kissing every inch he bared. "Such delicate fingers."

Her breath came in a hot, staccato rhythm against his forehead. "Don't be ridiculous. I have short, stubby fingers. That's why I play the harp so badly. Everyone says so."

"Everyone is wrong." He tucked her glove inside his trouser pocket, then skimmed his lips down her index finger to kiss her bare palm. When her fingers flattened against his cheek in a near caress, he exulted. "I remember your harp playing. It was wonderful."

She laughed shakily. "Then you're either mad or tone-deaf, or remembering another woman's harp playing entirely. Regina's perhaps."

"It wasn't my sister's hands I dreamt of in Calcutta. It wasn't her fingers I dreamt of having stroke my cheek." His voice deepened. "The way you are now."

Stiffening, she tried to pull her hand away, but he wouldn't let her, caressing her palm with his open mouth until she softened.

"I don't believe you thought of my fingers for one minute," she said, but the yearning in her gaze showed that she wanted him to be telling the truth.

Oddly enough, he was. "No?" He paused in the midst of nibbling her sweet pinkie to seize her other hand, then rub her ring finger through the glove. "You have a scar on the second knuckle, right here, which you got when a terrier bit you. You told me about it at that dinner at the Iversleys." When she had let him hold her bare hand briefly beneath the table.

"You . . . you remember that?" Her eyes widened to a sultry black that enticed him to lose himself in them.

He stripped her other glove off and tucked it in his pocket. Placing her hands on his shoulders, he tugged her close, plastering her against him from thigh to breast. "I remember everything," he rasped.

Then he took her lips with his, his blood fired with the need to plunder her honeyed mouth. To hell with biding his time, being careful to keep from frightening her off with too much too fast. The only way to shatter her Joan of Arc shield was to remind her that she was a desirable woman, too passionate to languish as a spinster.

Too passionate and too damned luscious for words. She tasted of tea and lemon cakes—so thoroughly English that it intoxicated him, yet as exotic to him as any concoction of almond milk and coconut. And when she opened those soft-as-silk lips, coaxing him in, meeting his tongue thrust for thrust, it was all he could do not to lay her down beneath the birch and elms and satisfy his aching need.

For a woman who seemed to have led a nun's life of late, she certainly excelled at kissing. Just thinking of the men who might have dared to kiss her while he was in India made him kiss her more roughly, more possessively—

She tore her mouth from his, struggling for breath, her hands now buried in his hair. "What else do you . . . remember about our time together?"

At least she didn't thrust him away. "Obviously more than you." The words came out harsher than he'd meant, and he nuzzled her sleek swan's throat. "I suppose you were too busy with those idiots at court to think of me."

"Idiots at court?" she echoed.

"The ones who taught you to kiss so well."

He wished he'd kept his bloody mouth shut when she drew back to stare at him with a wounded expression. "So you *do* think I'm a wanton like my mother."

Damn, he knew how sensitive she was about that. "If I thought you were a wanton, I wouldn't be courting you." When she tried to leave his embrace, he wouldn't let her. "But clearly you learned to kiss from someone."

She glared at him. "And what if I did? How many dozens of women did *you* kiss while you were away?"

"You wouldn't believe me if I told you."

"I'm sure I would." She tipped up her chin. "You probably had a string of Indian mistresses to rival a rajah."

"No," he said tersely. "No mistresses."

Her eyes shone luminous in the fading light. "Then there were ladybirds."

"No ladybirds, either. I have been as celibate as a monk for seven years."

She looked skeptical. "I'm no longer a naïve girl, so you needn't protect my delicate sensibilities. I've seen and heard enough at Newgate to know that men don't usually deny themselves . . . certain things. You can tell me the truth."

"Why would I lie about it?"

"So that I would think you'd saved yourself for me, or some such nonsense."

He cast her a rueful smile. "My reasons were more practical. I did not want to risk exposing myself to disease—or treachery. I had plenty of opportunity to observe the dangers of taking an Indian mistress, especially for a man in my position." Given the alternatives, pleasuring himself had seemed the most prudent.

Louisa, however, did not look convinced. "Then you should get yourself to a bawdy house straightaway, sir."

"I beg your pardon?" Surely she had not just suggested that he—

"I've seen how cranky Marcus gets when Regina is away more than a few days, so I can only imagine how vexing seven years of celibacy must be. Which explains why you're courting a woman who doesn't wish to marry you. You need a less permanent solution, some ladybird or a mistress—"

"I don't want a ladybird." He'd seen enough ladybirds during Grandfather's "training" to last him a lifetime. That was the most important reason for his restraint in India, though he could hardly tell *her* that. "And I certainly don't want a mistress." Not after his encounter with Grandfather's heartless mistress Betsy. He cupped her cheek. "I want a wife. I want you."

As he ran his thumb over her lavish lower lip, it trembled. "But I don't want *you,*" she protested, a hint of desperation in her voice.

"Then why are you jealous of my supposed companions in India?"

He had her there and she knew it, for she blushed.

"We were meant to be together, Louisa." He backed her against a tree, trapping her. "And we both know it. So there is no point to your fighting it."

And flush with his triumph, he lowered his mouth to hers once more.

Chapter Ten

Dear Charlotte,

You know I admire your accomplishments. But surely you are lonely. Yes, your marriage was disastrous, but if you could live your life over, isn't there some fellow with whom you might have been happier? And wouldn't you have set aside your ambitions for this man?

Many apologies from your cousin,
Michael

Louisa groaned when Simon began kissing her again. This was *not* what she wanted, this sweet . . . heady . . . good heavens, he was doing it to her again, him and his hard, heated body flattening her against the elm. How could he annihilate her resistance so easily?

This never happened to her with any other men, only with Simon. Only he seemed able to tempt her to forget her purpose, her fears . . .

"Simon, please," she whispered as he scattered kisses along her jaw. Perhaps if she begged—

A triumphant laugh escaped his lips. "I told you I would have you calling me Simon before the day was out."

Now she'd never convince him she didn't want him. And he would take full advantage of that knowledge . . . as always. "You know my wanton nature so well," she said bitterly.

"Not wanton—passionate," he breathed. "Nothing wrong with that."

Only as long as she kissed *him,* she thought acidly.

If I thought you were a wanton, Louisa, I wouldn't be courting you.

She froze. Could the way to discourage his suit be that simple?

Any man who'd spent seven years celibate to avoid complications or disease wouldn't want a promiscuous wife. And she must do *something* before she found herself married to a man who might take her from her cause so she could bear his children—

No, that mustn't happen. "'Wanton' is exactly what I mean," she murmured against his whisker-rough cheek. "You were right about the 'idiots at court.' They taught me to kiss. And more."

He paused, his mouth against her throat. "More?"

Heart pounding, she embellished the lie. "Yes. I've tried to fight it, tried to hide it, but you've found me out."

He drew back to stare at her, his eyes the searing heat of blue flames. "What are you talking about?"

She hesitated. She risked much by making this claim. After her hard work to overcome her family's reputation, did she dare ruin her efforts?

Did she dare not? Though he'd helped her with Lord Trusbut, that didn't mean she could trust him. His persistent interest in their candidates was alarming. And if she gave in to his advances, only to find they were part of another scheme—

No, she couldn't bear it. Besides, he was the only man who couldn't or wouldn't hurt her reputation. He wouldn't risk bringing scandal down on his sister's family. If he tried, she'd simply tell people he was lying to wreak revenge on her for having him sent to India.

She cast him a brazen glance of the sort she figured her mother would have worn. "After you went to India and I went to court, I was very angry. So I did some things I later came to regret. I allowed several men to sample my affections."

His eyes narrowed. "Sample how?"

"You know—kiss me and touch me intimately, and . . . well, things a lady shouldn't do."

"Like let a man make love to her?" he said coolly.

She fought down a blush. "I-I am my mother's daughter, you know."

"Apparently you are," he said in a tone as unreadable as his expression in the rapidly dimming light. "Though it's odd that such a thing hasn't been whispered about you. If anything, people say you've been a model of propriety."

"I was careful and discreet."

"I see." But he hadn't released her, and she couldn't tell if he believed her.

"It happened at court, so the king was honor-bound to hide it, you know."

That got a reaction. "The king knew about these . . . dalliances?"

The lie caught on her lips, but if Regina was right, the king and Simon were at odds, so Simon would never try to confirm her claim. "Certainly. He had to be the one to hush it up and force the gentlemen to keep their silence." She thrust out her chin. "If you don't believe me, ask *him* about it."

"I would not want to cause you any more trouble," Simon said, an odd note in his voice. "Though I wonder why you would tell me your little secret."

She managed a shrug. "You want to court me, so I thought it only fair that you know I'm not chaste. Before this goes any further, you understand."

"Ah—I do understand. And I am relieved to hear of your past."

"You . . . you are?" She hadn't expected quite that reaction.

Nor the way he was holding her now, leaning into her, his hand stroking her waist with a gossamer touch that made her blood race. His mouth brushed her ear. "Oh yes," he whispered. "I've always desired you. Surely you know that."

That he could say it despite her claim to be a wanton shot a thrill right through her.

Then he ruined it. "And now I need not marry you to have you. That is why you told me, is it not? To let me know you will allow me certain liberties?"

"Absolutely not!" The scoundrel, the cad—

"Care to be my mistress, Louisa?" With his heated mouth still hovering near her ear, he unbuttoned her spencer, then slid his hand inside to cup her breast through her gown. "It is not as if you have anything to lose. And I can be as discreet as any of your other lovers."

A pox on him, this wasn't going according to plan. She tried futilely to shove his hand down. "I wasn't trying to suggest—"

"Of course, I might be wrong, and you might have invented this Banbury tale about your sordid past merely to put me off."

She froze, then drew back to find amusement shining in his face.

The arrogant scoundrel was laughing at her! Oh, she should have known he wouldn't believe her. He was always so dratted sure of himself, always so sure of *her*. She'd wipe that taunting smile off his lips if it killed her.

She forced her hand to press his more firmly against her breast. "Lie about it? No, indeed. I'm only giving you fair warning." Looping her arms about his neck, she undulated against him as she'd seen some of the lewd females at Newgate do to male prisoners.

To her satisfaction, his smile vanished. Only then did she stretch up to kiss him, putting lips and tongue and teeth into it in a kiss as bold as she could make it.

But her triumph was short-lived. His hand moved against her breast, fondling, kneading, teasing. She felt it even through her muslin gown and linen chemise, even through the thin cotton of her stays. The firm caress sent a jolt of sensation right down to her toes, hardening the nipple into an aching knot, dragging a moan up from deep in her throat.

Then he took command of the kiss, too, and she was lost, drowning in the taste and scent of him. The twin assaults of his tongue and hand made her reel, especially when coupled with the rigid pressure of his thigh pressing into the softness between her legs, making her ache for something unknown. She was falling into that heady heaven where only the two of them dwelt.

Half-dazed, she felt him tug out her fichu, then slide his shameless hand inside her gown and chemise and stays to stroke her bare breast. How outrageous!

How delicious. She tore her lips from his in shock, but he didn't even pause in his caresses. With his gaze settling warm as summer rain on her, he thumbed her nipple, wringing a gasp from her lips, making her yearn for more.

"Don't you understand yet?" The stark hunger in his face was a wild complement to the hunger he roused in her breast. "I don't care if you kissed the whole bloody army, if you took one man or ten into your bed. I want you. I have always wanted you. You've been a fever in my blood for years. So I mean to have you. Lie to yourself and lie to me all you like, but in the end, you *will* be mine."

A thrill shot through her as powerful as it was alarming. "Your mistress, you mean?" she asked, her hands tangling in his hair.

"My wife." He untied her bodice and chemise ribbons. "Although I am not averse to having the wedding night before the wedding, believe me."

As she caught her breath, he trailed kisses down her jaw and throat to the exposed swell of her upper breast, then dragged down her layers of clothing just enough to expose one breast.

Her eyes went wide. "Simon—"

"I just want a taste of you. To hold me until we share a bed."

"We are never going to—"

He closed his mouth hotly over her breast.

Heaven help her. What insanity was this? It was far more exciting than the secret fantasies that regularly troubled her nights, far more tantalizing than even her own furtive caresses at night. His tongue was doing things to her nipple that dragged a strangled cry from her throat.

Then his hand rubbed her lower down through her

walking dress, in a most scandalous fashion. Sometimes she touched herself there, too, but it never felt like this ... like she was tinder to his flame, sparking and burning so fiercely ...

"You taste like nectar," he breathed against her breast. "So damned sweet."

She bent her head to bury a kiss in his golden hair. "You feel like ... oh ... heavens ..." Now his other hand worked her other breast through her layers of clothing, and the flames blazed brighter in her belly, coursing through her like wildfire, consuming her. If he didn't stop— "Simon ... Simon ... don't ..."

"Ache for you?" He scattered rough kisses from her breast to her throat. "Need you? Have you any idea what you do to me?"

He angled his hips against the place he'd just been rubbing, and she felt something unmistakably hard bulging against her. "This, sweetheart, is what you rouse in me every time I see you." His lips brushed her ear. "I want to be inside you. I want to prove that passion between *us* is never a mistake. And I can, if you will just give me the chance."

He bent his mouth to her other breast and laved it so deftly, teased it so expertly with his teeth, that she arched against him, lured by the promise of him driving inside her to satisfy her hot, aching urges—

A furry ball dropped onto Simon's head, chattering and jerking his hair and shocking them both out of their sensual haze.

Simon sprang back, eyes alight with frustration as he grabbed for his pet. "Damn it, Raji, you have the worst bloody timing!"

"Or the best timing, depending on how you look at it,"

she whispered. She'd just ventured close enough to the inferno to feel its flames licking at her. Thank heaven Raji had jerked her back.

While Simon wrestled with his angry monkey, she frantically tried to restore her clothing. How could she have allowed Simon . . . what sort of hussy was she, consumed by desires and fires and sweet, heady—

Raji leapt to her shoulder, then turned to snarl at Simon. Judging from Simon's startled expression, his pet had never done that before. "What the deuce are you—" The monkey chattered at Simon so furiously that Simon scowled. "Oh, for God's sake, you can't possibly think I was hurting her."

When Raji threw his arms about Louisa's neck, Louisa clung to him. "I do believe that Raji is staking his claim on me," she said shakily, afraid she could never be serene again after this.

"The devil he is." Simon reached for Raji, only to have his pet slap his hand. Simon glared at Raji. "Now see here, you little scamp—"

"Don't chastise him!" she said as she soothed the agitated monkey. "At least *he* has sense enough to know that we shouldn't be doing . . . these things."

Simon's gaze shot to her, his blue eyes dark as midnight in the dusk. "You're right, of course." A shuddering breath escaped him. "I'm sorry, I got carried away. But I can control myself, I swear. You have to give me the chance—"

"To seduce me? To ruin me?"

"No!" He thrust one hand through his hair. "Of course not. To court you."

"But I don't want you to court me!"

His conqueror's gaze fell hotly upon her. "Yet you melt

in my arms whenever we kiss. Don't try to deny that you desire me, when I can feel—"

"Yes, I do," she said hastily, before his words further tempted her. She hadn't yet recovered from his startling assertion—*You've been a fever in my blood for years.*

Just because he desired her didn't mean she could trust him . . . with her heart *or* her dreams. He hadn't been on the side of reform before—could his sojourn in India really have changed him that much?

She doubted it. And she dared not risk finding out that it hadn't. Last time he'd betrayed her, it had nearly destroyed her. "I'll admit that you tempt me. And you're right—I still feel . . . a connection to you." She stroked Raji's fur, her voice lowering. "But it changes nothing. I'm still determined not to marry. Which is why I've . . . I've made my decision."

He stiffened. "About what?"

"If you're serious about helping us, then you can observe Mrs. Harris's committee. But that is all. Because you and I are never going to work together."

"Damn it, Louisa—" he began and stepped nearer, but Raji started caterwauling.

Clenching his hands, Simon glowered at her. "Take some time to think about it. You are only alarmed right now because of what we nearly did."

"I don't need time. I know what I want." *I know what I have to do to keep myself safe. To stay the course.*

The fury on his face chilled her to her bones. "For God's sake—"

"That's my final decision, Simon." Scooping up her hat and fichu, she took off at a run through the woods, with Raji clinging to her bodice. She had to get back to the road, where the tiger was, where Simon would be forced to behave like a gentleman and she could retreat into the solace of her ladylike reserve again.

Avoiding the groom's curious glances, she set Raji on the seat, then stuffed in her fichu, buttoned her spencer, and donned her hat. By the time she climbed into the rig, she'd hidden the evidence of her shameless encounter with Simon. She could only pray that his groom would be discreet.

She heard thundering hooves coming from the direction of London and in case it was someone she knew, she bent her head to hide her face.

That proved useless when the carriage halted a scant few feet away. Too late, she recognized the crest and silver livery of her brother's equipage.

Marcus leapt out, followed closely by Regina. "Why are you sitting out here by the side of the road?"

"I'm sorry, Louisa," Regina said hastily, "but you know your brother. When he heard that I let you go alone with Simon to Lady Trusbut's, he was furious."

Thank heaven Louisa had returned to the phaeton before Marcus showed up, or he would be pummeling Simon into a bloody pulp right now.

"Deuce take it!" exclaimed Simon's voice from the woods. "Why didn't you—"

Louisa tensed. Leave it to him to choose the wrong moment to make his appearance. Her heart in her throat, she glanced at him, and let out a sigh of relief to find him fully dressed now.

Her brother whirled on the duke with a vicious scowl. "What the hell is going on here, Foxmoor?"

"His Grace's pet ran off into the woods," Louisa said before Simon could answer, "and the duke went to look for him."

That drew her brother's anger back to her. "Oh? Then why is the monkey sitting in your lap?"

She thrust out her chin, well-accustomed to dealing with her bear of a brother. "Because he found his way back while the duke was out searching." She shot Simon a glance as she took Raji into her arms. "You see, Your Grace? Raji is safe." *Please don't make trouble for me,* she begged him silently.

Simon sucked in a breath, and for an instant she feared he'd pronounce her a liar. She wouldn't put it past him— compromising her would probably seem like a good way to force her to the altar. But he was in for a surprise if he tried it, because she would never let Marcus browbeat her into marrying anyone.

Simon let out a breath, then approached them with an expression as unruffled as she hoped hers was. "Typical Raji behavior, I'm afraid. The scamp took a notion to swing through the trees, and I half feared I wouldn't find him." He smiled coldly at her brother. "But he has a fondness for your sister. I should have known he would circle back to her."

"Yes, and he's fine now," she put in.

Though her brother looked suspicious, his stance softened. "Well, neither of you should be out here after dark. The roads can be dangerous."

"Yes." Simon shifted his gaze to Louisa, a wealth of emotion glittering in the steely depths. "We were talking about the dangers of a lonely road earlier, weren't we, Miss North?"

Impudent scoundrel—him and his "dangers of a lonely road." What did *he* know about it? He'd never had to bear a child in blood and horror, never had to risk trusting someone who could easily turn into a tyrant after marrying her. Men had all the power in England. And if you couldn't be sure you trusted the man—

She smiled sweetly. "Speaking of dangerous roads, I might as well ride back the rest of the way with Marcus. You'll be home quicker if you don't have to take me to the town house, Your Grace."

"I don't mind," Simon bit out, his jaw taut with anger.

"I know." She set Raji on the seat, then leapt down from the phaeton before anyone could stop her. "But this will be easier."

Indeed, now that she no longer feared being caught in a passionate embrace with Simon, she wanted to kiss her overprotective brother for coming after her.

As she walked toward Marcus's carriage, she told Simon, "I do hope you enjoy observing Mrs. Harris's committee, sir. And thank you for helping with the Trusbuts. It was most kind of you."

"We'll see you Tuesday, won't we, Simon?" Regina chirped behind her.

Louisa stifled a groan. She'd forgotten that she'd asked him to join them. She could hardly get out of it now.

The cursed rogue knew it, too, for a sudden smile split his face. "Oh, I'll be there. I'm looking forward to it."

Jerking her gaze from his gloating expression, Louisa stepped up to her brother's carriage, but before Marcus could help her inside, Simon added, "Aren't you forgetting something, Miss North?"

She turned toward him, her heart nearly stopping when she saw what he held out to her. Her gloves. The ones he'd tucked in his pockets.

Ignoring her brother's scowl, she walked over to take them from Simon. How she wished she could use them to slap the mocking smile off his face. "Thank you." Hastily, she slipped them on her hands. "I forgot I'd removed them to feed Raji at Lady Trusbut's. I'm so glad you remembered that I'd given them to you."

It was a creaky tale at best, which was why his low laugh made her want to kick him. But at least he didn't try to sabotage her claim. "You're welcome, Miss North. I am always happy to be of service to you."

His eyes drifted down to her crooked fichu, and she thanked the heavens that she blocked Marcus's view of his knowing gaze.

Simon's voice was a rough rumble that stopped the breath in her throat. "Next time we're alone, I'll be sure to leave my pesky monkey at home."

She couldn't mistake his meaning, or the firmness of purpose that darkened his handsome face.

"There will be no next time," she murmured. "I promise you that."

As she headed for Marcus's carriage, she felt Simon's hot gaze scorching her. If he ever got her alone again, the fever in his blood was liable to ignite the fever in hers, and they'd erupt in flames together, burning everything to ash before them—everything she'd planned, everything she'd worked for.

As she, Marcus, and Regina set off in the carriage, she didn't look out the window to see if Simon stood watching them leave. With Regina and Marcus there, she didn't dare.

When she caught her brother scowling, she met his gaze coolly. "Do you have something to say, Marcus?"

"Take care, angel. Foxmoor is still a dangerous man."

"Marcus!" Regina cried. "My brother is not the ogre you paint him."

"No? Have you forgotten how he manipulated even you—"

"That was years ago," Regina said. "He's not the same man he was then."

"I'm not so sure," Marcus said. "He's still toying with my sister's heart."

"Fiddlesticks." Louisa forced lightness into her tone. "My heart has been boarded up against the duke for years. You needn't worry about me with him."

Marcus lifted an eyebrow. "Then why did he have your gloves? I'm no fool, Louisa. I know how a man like him works."

"Probably much the way *you* worked on the many occasions when you and Regina got into trouble before you married her."

Regina's smothered laugh merely made Marcus's scowl deepen. "That was different. Regina and I were in love."

Louisa sighed. She certainly couldn't claim that for her and Simon. Just because they couldn't seem to keep their hands off each other didn't mean they were in love. Reckless, perhaps. Insane, most definitely. But not in love.

"Simon and I aren't taking up with each other again. He has agreed to help the London Ladies Society, but that's all." She flashed her brother a blithe smile.

Marcus snorted. "I saw how he looked at you, like you were a plump partridge he ached to pluck. Has it occurred to you that his sudden interest might be part of a scheme for enacting his revenge on you for what you did to him?"

The chill that coursed through her banished her smile. That had never occurred to her; she'd been too busy looking for some political reason for his behavior. She'd never once thought his motive might be as simple as revenge.

Because he'd said he'd put the past behind him. Because he'd claimed to have recognized that what he'd done to her was wrong.

Because he'd kissed her like a man who meant it.

But his kisses could lie—they had before. Oh, she was such an idiot, not to consider the most obvious reason for distrusting him.

"Ignore Marcus," Regina said. "Simon would never be so diabolical—"

"That's what you claimed seven years ago," Marcus snapped.

"He was a brash young idiot then. Since that time, he has done much good for his country. He learned from his mistakes. I'm sure of it." She glared at her husband. "Even you once admitted that his tenure as Governor-General was above reproach."

A muscle ticked in Marcus's jaw. "That was before he started pursuing my sister again. And before I got wind of—"

When he broke off, Louisa's stomach knotted. "Of what?"

"It's just a rumor, and I can't even be sure it's true, but . . ." Marcus sighed. "Supposedly Sidmouth and his friends were thinking about trying to ruin your reputation irretrievably—by having some idiot compromise you."

The ache in her belly intensified. "And you think that Simon—"

"I don't know, angel. I'm just saying it's possible."

"He would never do such a horrible thing!" Regina protested.

"He might." Louisa cringed to remember him asking if she wanted to be his mistress. He hadn't been serious. Had he?

"It doesn't matter what his motives are," she said tightly. "I don't intend to be alone with him again, so he couldn't possibly ruin my reputation."

"Now, Louisa—" Regina began.

"I mean it, Regina. I know you hope that Simon and I will marry one day, but it's never going to happen. This is best for everyone, I assure you."

Now if only she could convince her silly heart.

Chapter Eleven

~⊷∞⊶~

Dear Cousin,
No need for apologies. As for Foxmoor and Louisa,
if the duke thinks marrying her will enable him to
keep her under his thumb, he is in for a surprise. I
have never met a woman as determined to go her
own way as Louisa.

Ever your friend,
Charlotte

The Monday evening after Simon had last kissed Louisa, he restlessly prowled one of Travellers' drawing rooms. Of all his clubs, Travellers was the only one with a sufficient diversity of newspapers to suit his purposes. But after poring over back issues of the radical press for two hours, he'd lost patience with the task.

Partly because what he had read upset him more than he had expected. But mostly because the same damned female who had haunted his nights now bedeviled his days, as well. He could still taste her lilac-scented flesh, still hear her delicious moans of pleasure, still feel the soft yielding of her beneath his hand.

Bloody hell. He paced between the fluted columns, grateful that the club's inhabitants were in the card room or dining, leaving the drawing room to him. If they saw him so agitated, they would torment him unmercifully with questions.

He'd suffered enough torment already. And what the devil was he to do about it after he had driven her away?

That's what happens when you let your cock overrule your reason.

"Shut up, old man," he muttered at his grandfather's voice. The memories of his grandfather's cynical remarks had not plagued him so in India. Except for the brief period after his misjudgment at Poona, the voices had died once Simon had received word of Grandfather's death, shortly after arriving in India.

But now that he had returned, and Louisa was tying him into knots . . .

He groaned. Grandfather's criticism was well-deserved this time; he had indeed let his cock rule his reason. He had frightened her off. And he could not for the life of him figure out how to regain lost ground.

After her cold leave-taking, he had expected her to avoid his call this morning. Instead she had accepted it like any society lady—with rigid courtesy and impenetrable self-assurance. Only Regina's presence had kept him from grabbing Louisa by her pretty arms and shaking her senseless.

What would it take to convince her to trust him? Kisses and caresses did not work, and she merely twisted his offer of help into an excuse for avoiding him.

Stubborn wench. Bloody female.

"Foxmoor," said a thready voice behind him, and he

whirled, prepared to snap off the head of whomever had dared bother him.

But he choked down the angry words as soon as he saw who it was—the Home Secretary himself. And the man's good friend Castlereagh, the Foreign Secretary.

"Sidmouth," he said tersely.

Sidmouth approached Simon with the cautious care of a hound sniffing 'round a porcupine. As well he should. At the moment, Simon would enjoy spiking the scrawny fellow's nose with a few choice quills.

Sidmouth's gaze flicked to the newspaper Simon had left open on a table, something called the *London Monitor,* published by a hothead named Godwin. The Home Secretary scowled, then shifted his gaze back to Simon. "I hear you've been spending time with that flock of hens who flutter about Miss North."

"My sister is one of that flock, so be careful what you say."

"The king told me in confidence that you mean to curb their activities. Yet I hear you wangled two hundred pounds out of Trusbut for their cause." Sidmouth's pasty cheeks pinkened. "You know they'll use the money to put forth their candidate."

"If they get the chance, yes. But I don't intend to let them."

Sidmouth's thin lips twisted into a sneer. "How do you mean to stop them? By marrying Miss North? When she turns down every suitor?"

"She will not turn me down," Simon retorted. "In time—"

"Time! We don't have time. Every day her group marshals more women to its cause. Before you know it, they'll be supporting several candidates for election, the Commons will be overrun with radicals, and we'll have another Manchester Patriotic Union Society on our hands—"

"And then you will make sure they are arrested or murdered at St. Peter's Field, the way you did the members of the Manchester Society," Simon bit out.

Sidmouth paled and Castlereagh gasped. But before either could speak, Simon added, "No, you cannot do that, can you? Because it is one thing to arrest farmers demanding representation in the government. It is quite another to arrest society ladies trying to clothe prison children and prevent poor women from being raped by their guards."

Sidmouth drew himself up with the haughty condescension he was known for. "Whose side are you on, Foxmoor?"

Only with an effort did Simon gain control over his temper. What insanity had prompted him to speak so bluntly? Probably all his reading about the "Peterloo Massacre," as the radicals called it. In India he had only read the *Times* version, which, though sympathetic to the crowd, had not been nearly as chilling as that of the radical press.

He steeled himself to speak the lie. "Yours, of course."

"I begin to wonder," Sidmouth snapped. "I had thought you meant to step into your grandfather's shoes. But he would have lauded my response to the St. Peter's Field affair. Monteith knew that the people require a firm hand."

"And I am not Monteith," he said tersely. "Nonetheless, you and I do share some concerns. I agree that Miss North and her friends are in over their pretty heads. And if we want to prevent another St. Peter's Field 'affair,' we'd

best fish them out of the pond before they drown us all."
He fixed Sidmouth with a cool glance. "But you must give
me time to work."

So that when this was over, he could make sure lords of
Sidmouth's ilk no longer ruled England with an iron fist.
Simon was certainly never going to tolerate such a man in
his cabinet.

Sidmouth cast him a grudging nod. "Very well. But
only a little, or we will take matters into our own
hands."

The devil they would. Keeping a tight rein on his temper, he nodded. "Now if you will excuse me, gentlemen, I
am late for an engagement."

If he stayed one more second in Sidmouth's presence,
he would say something he would regret. But damn, the
man infuriated him. Couldn't he see that if they did not
deal with those who wanted representation, they would
continue to find themselves at the mercy of angry mobs?

No, Sidmouth was from a different age, still living in
fear of an English version of the Reign of Terror.

Simon strode out of the club, pausing only to retrieve
his hat and cloak from the porter and call for his phaeton
to be brought 'round. He had done all the reading he
could stomach this evening.

He had discovered more than he had bargained for.
He'd hoped to figure out which friends of the London
Ladies Society were likely candidates for the Commons.
Instead, he had read countless articles praising their
work, lauding the good they had brought about despite
fools like Sidmouth.

But that had been the radical papers. There were
grumblings in the more traditional press. Just the usual
complaints about women dabbling in matters beyond

their purview, but unnerving all the same. It alarmed him to think how close they skated to the edge, especially now that they meant to move into politics.

As he headed for home, he thrust his unease aside. Tomorrow he would get another chance at changing Louisa's resolve regarding marriage. Until then, there was nothing he could do.

Besides, he had something else to work on. With his days spent at Parliament or wooing Louisa, and his nights filled with social affairs that he could not ignore if he meant to reenter politics, he'd had little time for researching Colin's situation. But he could not put it off. He had a promise to keep, after all.

As soon as he reached home, he called his butler into his study. "Fetch me another box of Grandfather Monteith's letters." Simon peeled off his coat. "And have one of the footmen bring me a cold supper. I didn't eat at the club."

"Very good, sir."

As his butler headed off, Simon looked around for Raji, whom he spotted dozing in his favorite spot by the fire. The study was the monkey's temporary cage when he wasn't tramping about with Simon. The servants were careful not to release him if the door was closed.

Simon lit more candles and prepared for a long evening of dusty work sifting through Grandfather Monteith's letters, but he had little hope of finding anything. The man had been too wily to leave incriminating documents behind. He had probably burned the pertinent letters as soon as he received them.

Still, he might have missed one. Or an otherwise innocuous letter might refer to someone who could corroborate Colin's claim. Simon had to try.

After his butler returned with the box, Simon settled down at his desk with it. But after a mere hour, his eyes began to glaze over. Damn his grandfather for keeping every piece of correspondence from every lackey. Though Simon could skip some merely by noting the signature, he had to wade through plenty of others. He never knew when a note from the steward might contain an important reference.

Simon had just sat back to eat his sandwich when his butler entered the room. "Lord Draker is here to see you, sir. Are you at home to him?"

Simon had half expected this visit ever since Saturday night, but he was not in the mood for his brother-in-law's lectures now.

Still, he didn't want Draker for an enemy. "Yes, send him in." He barely had time to check that Raji was still asleep before his mountainous relation entered.

"Evening, Foxmoor," the viscount bit out.

"Evening, Draker." Simon caught his butler's eye and said, "Leave us," then rose and strolled to a side table to pour himself a glass of brandy.

After Draker closed the door behind the butler, Simon held up the decanter to him, one eyebrow raised.

When the viscount nodded, Simon poured him a glass, as well, then walked over to hand it to him. "Isn't it a little late in the evening for paying social calls?"

"You know damned well this isn't a social call."

If his brother-in-law could be blunt, so could he. "You were obviously unhappy to see Louisa with me Saturday night." Simon walked back to sit behind his desk.

"Unhappy isn't the word." Draker dropped into a seat before the desk. "But I promised Regina I'd stay out of it." Scowling, he gulped some brandy. "Of course, that was before I heard that you paid a call on my sister today. Bearing flowers. *After* she'd assured me that you had no romantic interest in her."

"She told you that?" Simon set down his brandy glass so hard that some sloshed over onto the desk. Scowling, he mopped it up with the napkin from his supper tray. "Bloody stubborn female—"

"Watch it, Foxmoor, that's my sister you're talking about."

Simon eyed him coolly. "Don't tell me you've never thought the same."

Draker stared at him, then gave the barest nod. "She can be a little difficult sometimes."

"Difficult? Is that what you call it when a woman pretends not to have an interest in you, when you know she bloody well—" Mindful of who he spoke to, Simon modulated his tone. "I am courting your sister. And whether she will admit it to you, it is a fact I have made quite clear to her."

Eyes narrowing, Draker sat back in his chair. "Perhaps she's having trouble believing you."

"Deuce take it, first I get it from her, and now from you." Simon reached for his knife and the block of wood atop his desk, then began to whittle with sharp, angry strokes. "You two make quite a pair—suspicious as hell, always sure that the world is out to betray you."

"Not the world," Draker said dryly. "Just you."

Simon paused to fix Draker with a baleful stare. "I mean to marry her, and this time I do not need your consent. Louisa is perfectly capable of making her own decisions. So you might as well resign yourself to it."

"I'm not resigning myself to anything until I'm sure of your reasons."

"They are the same as any man's who wants to marry a woman," he hedged. "I think she will make me a good wife, and I enjoy her company—"

"And you're in love with her?"

Avoiding Draker's gaze, Simon returned to his whittling with a vengeance. He ought to lie, but lying to her and her family was what landed him in trouble last time, and he meant to go about things better this time. "The king once claimed I am incapable of love, and I fear he is probably right. But I do feel a great deal of affection for her."

"That doesn't exactly reassure me," Draker growled.

"I know. But I am trying to be truthful." His gaze swung to Draker. "I figure you deserve that."

Draker stared him down, coldly, assessingly.

"Perhaps this will put your mind at ease." Setting aside his whittling, Simon removed something from a drawer and flung it across the desk.

As Draker scanned the thick sheaf of papers, an incredulous expression filled his scarred face. "This is a marriage settlement."

"Yes. I had it drawn up last week. As you can tell, she will have a generous allowance, a jointure for our children, a—"

"I doubt she'll care much about that. Well, except for the children." To Simon's surprise, Draker smiled. "Though the existence of a marriage settlement does set to rest one of my suspicions."

"Oh?"

"Never mind." He read over the settlement, then sat back with a smug look on his face. "Rather cocksure about your chances, aren't you?"

"I was until this morning," he grumbled, feeling companionable now that Draker was being decent about the whole thing. "Your sister can be as cold as an arctic winter when she wants."

"Blame Regina for that. Louisa has adopted your sister's old manner to perfection." Draker stared down into his brandy. "I should warn you, Louisa claims to have no interest in marrying anyone."

"Regina said the same thing up until the night she agreed to marry you."

"After I compromised her." Draker's gaze shot to him. "I hope you're not planning anything like that."

"Planning it? No." Simon brooded a moment, before adding, in the spirit of honesty, "But I cannot promise that it will not happen. When it comes to Louisa, I seem to have trouble—" He broke off as Draker's face started to darken. "All I can promise is that I will do my best to avoid it."

Though Draker's expression was still clouded, he did not say anything. He just sat back against his chair and drank his brandy.

After a moment, Simon ventured a comment. "You do not seem as upset as I expected about the possibility that I might marry Louisa."

Draker swirled his brandy. "I can't be upset about something that might not happen. And the truth is . . ." He sighed. "I worry about her obsession with the London Ladies. Theirs is a good cause, I'll grant you. But I can't help thinking—"

"That she deserves more."

Draker's gaze shot to him. "Exactly. There was a time when *I* thought I had no chance of ever marrying. It was a long and lonely part of my life I would not wish on anyone, especially my sister."

"Nor would I." Simon tapped the block of wood, then sighed. "See here, Draker, I know we have had our differences, and I would not blame you for despising me after what I did to Louisa seven years ago. But I am not the same man I was then." He met his brother-in-law's gaze. "I think I can make her a good husband. And I will treat her with the kindness and respect she deserves."

Rising from his chair, Draker set down his empty glass. "See that you do." He leaned on the desk, his massive shoulders set for battle. "Because if you hurt my sister, I swear I will kill you, brother-in-law or no."

Simon met his gaze without flinching. "I understand." Forcibly, he restrained the urge to point out that Draker would only succeed if he did it with his bare hands, because Simon could beat him in a duel of sword or pistols with one hand tied behind his back.

Draker headed for the door, then paused. "I wanted to ask you about one other matter. Ever since Regina heard that your aide-de-camp's name was Colin Hunt, she's been curious to know if it's mere coincidence that his surname is the same as your late uncle who served in India. Regina said she even asked you about it in a letter, but you didn't answer."

Simon's fingers curled around the block of wood on his desk. "It's a common enough name."

"That's not what I asked." He drew himself up. "And I think Regina has a right to know if she has a cousin somewhere, even an illegitimate one."

"I agree." A sigh escaped Simon's lips. "But I am not sure of the answer."

Draker arched one eyebrow. "Not sure? Or not willing to say?"

"Not sure." He gestured to the letters. "I am looking into it right now, as a matter of fact."

"Does he *claim* to be your uncle's by-blow?" Draker asked.

"No." That was the absolute truth, although what it left out was so enormous as to be staggering.

"Yet you are looking into it."

"Yes. I promise that you and Regina will be the first to know when I get an answer." He wasn't about to drop that surprise into their laps without being absolutely certain that he could prove his assertions.

After Draker left, he returned to his desk and took up another letter. Despite his exhaustion and having to get up early in the morning to be at Newgate to help Louisa, he needed to know the truth. Only then could he make amends for his dreadful misjudgment at Poona.

Chapter Twelve

❧❦❧

Dear Charlotte,

    I recently learned that Foxmoor spoke privately to Lord Sidmouth on Monday. It may mean nothing, but given the Home Secretary's acrimony for the London Ladies, I would caution you and your friends to be on your guard.

                                Your concerned cousin,
                                       Michael

The sun had barely lifted its nose above the horizon Tuesday morning when Louisa faced down Brutus the Bully inside the gates of Newgate Prison.

Louisa had privately dubbed Mr. Treacle that, because the guard had been nothing but trouble ever since the London Ladies had hired a matron to replace him, resulting in his reassignment to the men's wards. Brutus didn't like that, oh no. The male prisoners weren't nearly as useful for his lascivious tastes.

If she'd had her way, he would have been dismissed from the prison long ago, but his cousin was Mr. Brown, governor of the prison, so that was that.

Today he was sorely taxing her patience. "You told me last week that eight hackney coaches would be enough," she said.

"To transport the women, Miss North." Brutus tucked his thumbs in the pockets of his grimy waistcoat. "But the guards has got to ride somewhere."

"The guards always ride on horseback alongside."

"Aye. When the women is in carts. But they ain't gonna be in carts today, is they? And we can't risk them escaping."

"They're shackled! How far could they get before a guard ran them down?"

Brutus crossed his thick arms over his chest. "A carriage might break free and be gone before a guard can catch up to it."

Oh, for heaven's sake— She had half a mind to strike the wicked fellow; it was hard to resist when faced with his oily smirk.

Steady, Louisa, steady. Losing your temper never accomplishes anything. She settled for an icy glare instead. "So how many carriages do we need?"

"Dunno. I'm just sayin' that with two guards to a coach—one on the perch and one inside—you'll never get them and sixty women in eight hackneys."

"I told Simon to hire an extra," Regina put in, "but it still won't suffice."

"Reckon we'll have to put the rest of the prisoners in carts after all." Brutus didn't even bother to mask his glee.

"We are *not* using carts," Louisa bit out.

"What's wrong?" Mrs. Fry asked, drawn by the commotion at the gates.

She and the other Quakers had been passing out packets of needles, thread, and fabric scraps so the convict women could make patchwork quilts to sell in Australia, and Louisa hated taking her from her task. Still, the neatly dressed banker's daughter, a woman of forty whose kindly features belied her iron will, often had good success with shaming Brutus into behaving.

After Louisa explained, Mrs. Fry fixed him with her sternest gaze. "I shall take this up with the governor, sir."

Brutus shrugged. "Ain't no skin off my back if you do. And it don't change nothing—there's still too few coaches."

"We can use my carriage, too," Mrs. Harris put in. "Since only Venetia and I came today, we can fit three women more."

The discussion of who else could volunteer their equipages was still going on when Simon arrived.

"Why are carts lined up in front?" he asked as he joined them.

Louisa cast Brutus a glance of pure disdain. "Because Mr. Treacle here is itching to make a public spectacle of these women."

"Ain't my fault that you didn't take into account the guards," he snapped.

"You didn't say I had to." Louisa arched her chin so far forward that the high lace collar of her pelisse robe scratched her throat. "And so help me, if you—"

Simon stepped between her and the guard. "What seems to be the problem?"

In a frock coat and trousers of dun-colored nankeen, Simon was decidedly underdressed for a lord, so Brutus barely spared him a glance. "Too many women for the hackneys."

"Then we'll hire more," Simon said. "Or take two trips."

"Can't. No time. The *Cormorant* sets sail in two hours with the tide. So you gotta use the carts, guv'nor. You ain't got no choice."

Those were the wrong words to say to Simon. Drawing himself up, he said in a cool, awful voice, "I would like to speak to the governor of the prison."

"The governor don't have time for no Quakers," Brutus said dismissively.

"I am not a Quaker. I am Foxmoor. And I want to speak to the governor. Now," he said, every inch the supercilious aristocrat.

It took a second for the name to register, but when it did, it wiped the smirk right off Brutus's face. "F-Foxmoor? The duke?"

"The very one." Without breaking eye contact, Simon gestured to Regina. "That woman is my sister. Miss North is her sister-in-law and my own very good friend. You might want to mention that when you fetch the governor."

"Aye, Your Grace," the man mumbled, then hurried away.

As soon as he'd gone, Simon faced the ladies. "Tell me how this happened."

By the time Brutus returned, Louisa had thoroughly acquainted Simon with the man's general tactics and his dislike for reformers.

Mr. Brown trotted up beside Brutus out of breath, like a spaniel panting to please his master. "Your Grace, it appears there's a misunderstanding—"

"Yes, it appears there is," Simon said in that imperious manner she could never perfect. He flicked his gaze at Brutus as he would at a lowly beetle. "Your man there told us to bring eight hackneys. Now he says there aren't enough."

Brutus regarded Simon with murder in his eyes, but Mr. Brown bobbed his head furiously. "An honest mistake. I shall get to the bottom of it at once."

"An excellent idea, since these ladies and I will now have to use our own equipages. Unless you have another suggestion?" When Mr. Brown opened his mouth, Simon added, "One that does not involve using open carts?"

Mr. Brown shut his mouth.

"I see. And do you have an equipage of your own, sir?" Simon asked.

"Aye," called out one of the guards before the governor could answer. Louisa recognized him as a man of good character, who'd always been kind to the women. "Keeps his barouche out back, he does."

"Good." Simon smiled thinly at the governor. "I am sure you will be happy to add your barouche to the tally, won't you, sir?"

Only with great difficulty did Louisa stifle her smile.

Mr. Brown paled. "Er . . . yes . . . Your Grace, of course."

"Because otherwise I might have to mention your 'honest mistake' to my good friend, the Lord Mayor, and he would not be pleased."

"I . . . I will be happy to offer my barouche, Your Grace."

With a nod, Simon turned to the women, who'd been hastily amassing a count. "How many more carriages do we need then, ladies?"

"Two," Mrs. Harris said, "if we put the children on laps."

"There's some hackneys at a stand in the next street," said the helpful guard. "If you'll vouch for their pay, Your Grace, I'll see how many I can fetch."

Simon handed him several crowns. "Pay them with that, and keep the rest."

Louisa knew it was more than the guard made in a month. His face alight, he thanked Simon profusely before scurrying off.

With a supercilious stare Simon turned back to Brutus. "It appears, sir, that our problem is solved." His voice dripped sarcasm. "So perhaps we should get this going, since the ships are so impatient for our arrival."

Louisa only had time to flash Simon a grateful smile before the guards began the tedious process of loading the shackled women and their children into the carriages.

Oh, how was she to resist him when he did lovely things like facing down Brutus for her convict women? Or informing Marcus that he truly meant to marry her? She could still scarcely believe what her brother had told her last night—that Simon had even shown Marcus marriage settlement papers.

The man's presumption should have angered her. Instead it sent her heart soaring, and all because his attentions had proved not to be a scheme.

She must be insane. She glanced over just as he finished speaking to a hackney driver. He caught her gaze, and the fleeting glance he shot her sent a lightning stroke of anticipation racing along her spine, especially when he coupled it with a smile so dazzling it practically blinded her.

As her breath stuck in her throat, she jerked her gaze away. That was the trouble with Simon—he blinded everyone, the way Lucifer must have done when he'd descended from heaven as an angel of light.

Even Marcus had turned traitor in the wake of Simon's

brilliance. After his talk with Simon, Marcus hadn't tried to caution her further. He'd even admitted he was probably wrong about Simon pretending to court her so he could ruin her.

Unfortunately, Mrs. Harris had related a disturbing bit of news this morning: Simon had been seen speaking privately to Lord Sidmouth right before Marcus had visited him.

Her stomach knotted every time she thought of it. But it could mean anything. Much as it annoyed her, Simon *was* a member of Sidmouth's party. It didn't necessarily follow that he agreed with the man's ideas; there were plenty of Sidmouth's party members who didn't.

But was Simon one of them? Or was this, even the marriage settlement, merely an elaborate deception he'd concocted to destroy her reputation?

Surely not. Surely he knew that Marcus would never allow it. Of course, Marcus's disapproval hadn't stopped him seven years ago—

A pox on Simon! After all these years, he still wreaked havoc in her life. And apparently she was no better equipped to figure out his motives than before. Some men ought to come with instructions, for heaven's sake.

Yet he'd stood up to Brutus for her.

"Miss North?" a guard said, jerking her from her obsessive thoughts. "We've put you in a carriage with the women you taught, if that's all right."

"That's wonderful, thank you." She followed the guard to a hackney. She cast the prison yard a quick glance. Every equipage was filled except Simon's phaeton. Fortunately only one woman remained, tugging a child no more than three years old.

As Louisa debated whether to give up her own seat in

the carriage to the woman, Simon approached the prisoner with a kind smile. "It appears, madam, that you will be riding with me."

Louisa gaped at Simon. He would put a convict woman in his favorite equipage? Truly?

The woman's eyes widened as she took in the phaeton, with its gilded panels, damask upholstery, and spirited pair of matched bays. Simon's identity hadn't yet filtered down to the women, but she couldn't fail to realize that the rig—and its owner—were of superior quality.

She shook her head. "No, sir, i-it's a good sight too nice for the likes of me."

Simon leaned toward her. "Truth is, it's too nice for *me*, too, but I put up with it because the horses prefer it. Makes them feel important, you see. And I have to keep my horses happy, or they dawdle."

Brutus stepped in. "You can't be puttin' her there, Your Grace. A guard's got to be with her."

Simon's look of contemptuous fury was truly awe-inspiring. But he merely said, in a tone of ice and iron, "The guard can squeeze onto the perch with my tiger. Feel free to do it yourself, if you really are concerned that a shackled woman with a child would attempt an escape."

Brutus turned a mottled red as he realized that the duke had called him a liar.

But before he could retort, the convict woman said, "Please, sir, it's all right. My lad here has been ill, and he's likely to . . . spew his breakfast in your lovely coach. We'll ride in a cart. It ain't so bad." Swallowing, she laid her hand on her boy's head. "Them crowds won't throw nothing at a mother and son, I expect."

"They certainly won't." Simon's eyes glinted a steely blue. "Because they'll have to hit me first." And he lifted her, shackles and all, into the phaeton. Then Simon knelt beside the boy. "If your belly starts to hurt, you let me know, and we will stop so you can ease it, all right?"

The boy stared at him wide-eyed, thumb in mouth, then nodded.

Simon picked up the child with such care that it made a lump lodge painfully in Louisa's throat. And why did the boy have to be an adorable cherub whose blond curls jiggled sweetly as he crawled into his mother's lap? It made it too easy to imagine him as Simon's son, off for a ride with Papa. To imagine herself as the child's mother, tucking his head against her breast, straightening his cap, and murmuring soothing nonsense into his tiny ears.

She couldn't tear her gaze from Simon as he mounted the phaeton, a guard climbing onto the perch behind him. She'd never thought of him in terms of fatherhood. Driven by his ambitions, yes. Masterful in his seductions, most definitely. But capable of nurturing a son or daughter? Never.

Until now.

Oh, what was she thinking? She wanted no part of the pain and wrenching screams of childbirth, the cruel doctors with their leeches and scalpels.

She steadied her resolve. No marriage for her, no matter how much Simon tempted her.

Louisa settled into her seat with a sigh of relief. *This* she could handle—her convict women. She'd taught this group to read during their wait for their trials. Despite the gulf in their stations, she felt comfortable with them because they didn't care what she wore or if she spoke her mind. Indeed, they included her in their gossip as the carriages set off.

Amy, a draper's assistant convicted of stealing, leaned

forward. "Is the man who put Lizbeth and her boy in his fancy carriage really a duke, Miss North?"

Martha, the woman next to her, snorted. "You silly goose, why would a duke be *here?*"

When the others teased Amy, Louisa said quickly, "Yes, he's a duke."

"I told you he was!" Amy cast Martha a gloating glance. "Isn't that something? I'll wager Lizbeth never expected to be sitting next to a duke."

"Don't know why not," Martha said. "She probably sat on a duke's lap often enough at the tavern." She nudged Amy. "On more than just his lap, too, I expect."

The other women sniggered, and Louisa frowned. "Ladies, what did we say about avoiding unsavory discourse?"

They sobered at once. "Yes, miss," they replied in unison.

But she couldn't blame them for lapsing into old habits; they were nervous about their futures. And with the hackney curtains drawn, eerily muting the dawn light, the space became a gloomy harbinger of their coming voyage, where they'd be crowded below decks in tiny cells.

Amy cast her a thoughtful glance. "We mean to be good, really we do. But we hear things about what becomes of women who go out on the ships—"

"I know." Louisa, too, had heard the tales. Three years ago, a convict ship had even been kidnapped by pirates. "But if you take pride in yourself, then decent men will treat you with respect."

"And the others?" Martha snapped. "Them's the ones we worry about."

"You must at least try to hold firm to your principles. Because this is your chance for a new sort of life, if you only have the strength to seize it."

"All the same," Martha said, "I'm glad I got my friend to buy me some sponges."

Louisa stared at her questioningly. "Sponges?"

"Don't be talking about that 'round Miss North, you dolt," Amy chided.

"Why not?" Martha said. "Might prove useful to her. And God knows none of them fine gentlemen or ladies is gonna tell her." Martha gazed at Louisa coolly. "Sponges is what you use to keep from having babies. You soak them in vinegar and shove them up inside your—"

"Martha!" Amy snapped. "Don't be so improper-like."

"It's fine," Louisa breathed, her mind reeling. Why hadn't she learned of this before? She'd certainly heard enough about the act itself from the prisoners. She'd even heard of condoms for men, but what use was that if a woman wanted to keep her purpose secret? She could hardly sneak such a contraption onto her husband's . . . thing. "These sponges. Do they really work?"

"Mostly," Amy said. "Preventing children is never a sure thing. You needn't use them anyway, miss—not with the lovely rich man you're bound to marry. He'll have plenty money to go 'round."

"P'raps Miss North ain't thinking of no husband," Martha said slyly. "P'raps she's bent on taking a lover—"

"Certainly not." A blush heated Louisa's cheeks. "I'm only curious because the young women ask me about such things."

The other ladies seemed to accept the blatant lie, but Martha raised an eyebrow as she sat back and crossed her arms over her chest.

Louisa took a steadying breath. "Can't the man . . . well . . . feel the sponge?"

Amy laughed at her embarrassment. "Oh, miss, you

should leave it to the married ladies to instruct the young women about such matters."

"I don't mind explaining it." Martha shot Louisa a piercing glance. "A man don't notice much of nothing when he's doing his business. Long as the woman lays there and lets him do what he wants, he'll never know the difference."

"It's quicker that way, too," said another woman, and they all laughed.

Louisa blinked. That sounded awfully . . . matter-of-fact, rather like the rutting she'd inadvertently witnessed at prisons before she and her fellow reformers had brought order. It certainly sounded nothing like the wild tempest of feeling that Simon's kisses roused in her.

She met Martha's gaze with one that she hoped appeared perfectly innocent. "And where would a . . . young woman purchase these sponges?"

Martha shrugged. "Mrs. Baker's in Petticoat Lane has 'em."

"She even sells a special preparation to soak 'em in, don't she, Amy?" another woman put in.

But Amy had apparently lost interest, for she'd drawn the curtain aside to stare out at the street. "Look at them, the vultures, just itching to let fly."

Louisa drew her curtain aside also and grimaced to see the streets lined with onlookers, some having brought baskets of rotting refuse.

"Why aren't they throwing anything?" Amy asked. "They've got to know who we are. The ship's departures are always in the papers, and they can guess what's going on from the guards."

"Having you in carriages takes the fun out of it," Louisa speculated. Still, the sight of a murmuring crowd

casting black glances at the procession snaked a shiver
down her back.

"It's that duke in front what's keeping 'em still,"
Martha said. "People don't know what to make of the
fancy carriages."

Louisa nodded. Yet she couldn't shake the sense of
foreboding creeping over her, especially when she realized
how many miles they had left. She could only pray that
Simon's stalwart presence would hold the crowd at bay
long enough for the carriages to reach the docks.

Chapter Thirteen

◦◦◦◦◦

Dear Cousin,
    Thank you for the advice, but I am always on my
guard around bachelors. They have this deplorable
tendency to surprise one, and surprises are so very
hard on an aging woman like myself.

                              Your friend and cousin,
                                          Charlotte

*S*imon stared grimly ahead as he navigated the phaeton
through streets clogged with rubbish-wielding dustmen,
costermongers, baker's assistants . . . anyone with the time
and inclination to take their frustration with the government out on convicts. He had a chilly sense that if he
gazed directly at them, the odd spell keeping them orderly would shatter and mayhem would ensue.

As it was, the murmur of voices had been escalating.
How long could an angry mob stay in check? He didn't
want to find out.

Simon set his jaw. This was no place for Louisa or
Regina or the other ladies. Let the Quakers take on prison

reform—they knew how to handle the common people. But just thinking about Louisa confronting that guard earlier spiked fear through his heart.

She would damned well never do it again. If she wouldn't let Simon guide her, then he would make sure Draker received a full account of today's events so that *he* could guide her. Either way, Simon meant to halt her activities.

"Is that the ship?" the little boy at his side lisped, pointing ahead to where several masts loomed high above the river.

"One of them is," Simon said.

"Will I see Papa there?" he asked with the hopefulness of his tender years.

"Hush now, Jimmy," murmured his mother before Simon could answer. Catching Simon's eye, she said, "I told him his father's a sailor."

Whether that was true was any man's guess, but judging from her haunted expression, the father had probably abandoned them long before Jimmy's birth.

Such a thing was probably common, but the sadness of it infected Simon. All right, perhaps he did understand why Louisa felt she couldn't stand back and let such small tragedies routinely occur.

But must she go so far? Holding classes at a prison was one thing; putting oneself at the mercy of this lot was quite another. Or at the mercy of that villainous guard who rode ahead of the phaeton. Treacle reminded Simon painfully of the Maratha bullies who'd pillaged and burned Poona, until the English had arrived to stop them. Or to pick up the pieces, depending on how one looked at it.

The acrid smell of smoke and blood still haunted Simon's nights.

Now the somber procession approached a busy intersection near the docks, and Treacle signaled a halt until they could cross. As they waited, Simon's disquiet grew, especially when he saw Treacle talking with an onlooker.

The bastard glanced back at Simon, and the chap he spoke to scurried off to spread some news among the crowd. Within seconds, low cries erupted throughout the mob like sparks of heat lightning across the Great Indian Desert.

Simon groaned when he caught snatches: "the duke and his mistress" and "Foxmoor's bastard" and "privileges of nobility." It didn't take long to decipher the rest of the tale spreading through the crowd. That he was personally carrying his mistress—presumably the woman at his side—to the docks. That he'd been allowed to circumvent the usual methods by virtue of his being a duke. That he was going to carry his bastard son away with him after his mistress was sent off.

It was a measure of how tense the people were, that they would embrace Treacle's lie instead of considering its absurdity. If any duke had wanted to prevent his criminal mistress from suffering for her crimes, he would have used his influence long before she made it to trial.

But mobs were rarely logical. Nor did it help that his passenger's son shared Simon's coloring.

The intersection cleared, and Simon started the horses going before Treacle gave the order, but the damage had been done. The crowd's grumbling grew to a rumbling, then an outright uproar. Within moments, missiles began to fly.

He heard the refuse hit the carriages behind them, splatting against the panels, startling the horses. As the mounted guards strove to regain order, Simon spurred his steeds to greater speed and the hackneys followed suit. They raced the last mile to the docks amid rotten vegetables and other slop.

Since few in the crowd dared to toss anything at Simon, his passenger and her son were mostly spared, though he did throw his coat over them. Fortunately, once they reached the docks, more guards awaited. They and the mounted ones managed to hold the crowd back so the passengers could disembark without being struck.

But the women couldn't escape the jeering, and as the first of the carriages emptied, a woman in Louisa's group fought back, snarling curses at the crowd.

Simon had just finished lifting his passenger and her son down when he glanced over to see Louisa admonishing the angry woman. He saw a man in the crowd push through the guards and lift his hand, and before anyone could react, the man let his missile fly.

But this was no putrid tomato; it was a large rock.

Simon lunged for Louisa, but it happened too fast—all he could do was watch in horror as it struck. Louisa reeled, then crumpled to the ground.

"Louisa!" Simon vaulted the remaining distance in a panic.

When the man who'd thrown the rock realized it had struck the wrong woman, he ran off, but Simon was too frantic to care.

As Simon reached Louisa, the woman who'd taunted the man fell into hysterics.

"Quiet!" he ordered, fear slamming his heart in his chest. He knelt beside Louisa to feel for a pulse. At least her blood beat steady and strong, though her eyes remained closed and her arm lay limp in his grasp.

"Oh God, she's dead, ain't she?" The convict woman wrung her hands, refusing to leave Louisa's side. "They killed her, and it's all my fault! She *told* me to ignore them, but I just had to give 'em a piece of my mind—"

"She's not dead," he growled. "Now go on, and let us see to her."

A guard pulled the woman away as Regina pushed through. "How is she?"

"I don't know." Simon could hardly breathe past the pressure in his chest. "She either fainted or she's unconscious. Do you have smelling salts?"

"We don't carry our reticules to the prison."

He could well imagine why. "Then I have to get her out of this madness."

"Take the hackney." Regina gestured to the still-open door of the nearby carriage. "I'll see that the phaeton is returned safely for you."

"You should go with me, you and your friends. This is not safe."

"Nonsense," Regina said, "the guards have already got the mob under control. And we need to pass out packets to women who have come from other prisons. Go on. I will be home as soon as I can."

Louisa's pale face alarmed him more by the moment. After carrying her limp form into the hackney, Simon settled Louisa's head in his lap. Sobered by the sight of a reformer being struck low, the crowd thankfully parted to let the carriage pass, and they raced toward the Draker town house in Mayfair. With fear throbbing in his throat, Simon removed her bonnet. As gently as he could, he threaded his fingers through her hair to assess her injuries. The lump swelling on her scalp increased his panic. It was far too large.

Her breathing was steady and even, but that did not reassure him. How could it when her eyes remained shut and her head lolled with every jolt of the carriage? Swearing, he removed the pins from her tightly wound hair and unfastened the top buttons of her pelisse robe. When she still didn't rouse, he removed her gloves and began to chafe her clammy hands, unsure what else to do.

If she ever came out of this, he would make sure she never took such a chance again. He would marry her and lock her up at one of his estates. He would bribe her London Ladies to keep her out of it. He would resort to any method to ensure her safety.

The ride was the longest of Simon's life.

At Draker's town house, Simon climbed out of the carriage with her and ascended the steps.

As he strode inside, Draker's butler approached. "Your Grace! What has happened?"

"Miss North had an accident," Simon snapped. "Fetch her brother at once."

"H-he's not here, sir," the butler said. "He's at Tattersall's for the day."

"Then send for him, for God's sake. And a doctor." He headed for the wide central staircase. "Which bedchamber is Miss North's?"

"The one at the end of the hall on the right."

"Send a footman up with smelling salts." Simon stalked up the stairs with his precious burden.

Her bedchamber proved simple and spartan, with a plain Brussels carpet and modest furnishings. Perfect for a Joan of Arc. He could only pray she did not end up as that famous saint—dead at the hands of her persecutors.

She did not stir even when he laid her on the bed, increasing the vise of terror around his chest. His aide-de-camp must have felt like this when they'd rushed to Poona and found Colin's wife dying of a sword wound to the belly.

The familiar old guilt knotted in Simon's gut, but he pushed it aside. Louisa wasn't going to die—she was not! He would not allow it.

Hurrying to her writing table to fetch the chair, he froze as he spotted what lay beside her inkwell: the lily he had whittled years ago. She had kept it despite his lies and deceptions.

Grabbing the chair, he dragged it back to her bedside, then sat down and tugged off her half boots. Her feet looked so small and fragile in their white cotton stockings. He skimmed his gaze back to her bloodless face. She had to live. She *must*. Life without her . . .

No, he would not consider it. Grabbing her cold hands in his, he prayed. He had never been religious, but he prayed for all he was worth.

He was still praying when Louisa groaned, and her eyelids fluttered open.

She gazed around her, confused. "Why am I at home? And why are *you* here, Simon?"

The vise around his chest eased. She knew where she was! So she couldn't have been hurt too badly, thank God. Swallowing the thick emotion clogging his throat, he squeezed her hands. "Shh, sweetheart. Don't try to talk now."

"Why not?" She frowned. "The last thing I remember, I was coming out of a carriage—"

"Someone threw a rock that hit you and knocked you out."

Confusion knit her pretty brow. "That explains this throbbing." She rubbed her scalp, then winced. "But why would anybody throw a rock at *me*?"

"It was meant for one of the convict women."

"The convict— Oh no, I have to get back to the docks!" She jerked upright, then released a heartfelt moan.

With a curse, he pressed her back down on the bed. "You must rest. At least until I can be sure you are all right."

"But I have to help pass out the packets," she said plaintively, though she closed her eyes.

"You are not going anywhere right now. Regina and the other ladies have matters under control. Besides, you are in no condition to help them. You have a nasty lump, and we will not know how bad it is until a doctor looks at it."

"A doctor!" Her eyes sprang open, and the abject panic in them chilled him. "Absolutely not. I'm fine, really." She sat up, and before he could stop her, swung her legs over the side of the bed and stood.

Rising himself, he caught her just as she pitched forward.

"Bloody hell." He sat back hard on the chair with her in his arms. "Stop that, damn you, before you keel over and add another lump to the first one."

Thank God she didn't resist him, just settled into his lap. "I . . . I really am fine, you know. I only need a minute to . . . to steady my dizziness."

He cradled her head against his chest with an oath. "You are the most stubborn female in creation, do you know that?"

"Surely not." Opening her eyes, she cast him a weak

smile. "There must be someone more stubborn some-where."

"I shudder to think it," he said hoarsely.

She nestled against him, rubbing her cheek against the rough nankeen of his waistcoat. Suddenly she drew back to stare at his chest. "Where's your coat?"

"God only knows. I threw it over my passengers when the mob started hurling refuse. It is probably lying tram-pled on the docks."

A look of remorse crossed her face. "Did those awful people ruin your lovely phaeton?"

He couldn't believe she was worried about *that.* "I don't give a damn if they did."

The irritation in his voice made her wince. "If you don't care about your phaeton, then why are you so angry?"

"Good God, woman, why do you think? I nearly lost ten years off my life when you fell." He nuzzled her hair, his voice thickening. "I don't care about my phaeton or my coat or even the fact that the masses now think I have a mistress and a bastard headed for Australia. I only care about you."

Her face softened, and she began to smile. Until the rest of his speech registered. "Mistress? What are you talk-ing about?"

He explained what he thought had set the crowd off.

She frowned. "That sounds exactly like something Brutus would do."

"Brutus?"

"Mr. Treacle. I call him Brutus the Bully because of how he treats the women."

He tightened his arms about her fiercely. "And that is the sort of vile person you deal with—"

"Better *I* deal with him than the women. At least he knows he can't bully a woman of my rank."

"Oh?" Simon said hotly. "He can only incite a riot to attack you—"

She pulled back with a scowl. "You said the rock wasn't meant for me."

"That scarcely matters. You are the one it struck."

A knock on the door presaged the entrance of a footman, who halted when he caught sight of Louisa in Simon's arms. "I-I beg your pardon, Your Grace. I brought the smelling salts."

With a blush, Louisa leapt from Simon's lap. This time she stayed on her feet rather well. "Thank you," she told the footman, batting Simon's hand aside when he rose and tried to pull her back toward the bed. "But as you can see, it's not needed. I'm fine now."

The footman glanced from Louisa to Simon. "His lordship's doctor wasn't home, sir, so is there another doctor you wish to call?"

"No," she said at the same time Simon said, "Of course."

"Simon!" she cried. "I told you, I'm not going to see a doctor."

Ignoring her protest, Simon strode to her writing table and jotted down the name and address of his own physician. Then he walked over and handed the footman the paper. "If he's not at this address, then he'll be at St. Bartholomew's."

As the footman nodded and hurried off, Louisa darted toward the door. "Come back here this minute! I didn't say you could—"

Simon caught her about the waist, then shut the door and locked it, pocketing the key. "That's enough from you, Joan of Arc." He tugged her toward the bed. "You are not going anywhere until the doctor says you can."

Wrenching free with surprising strength, she backed away. "No doctors."

"Do not be foolish, for God's sake. You might have a fracture or—"

"I don't have a fracture. I'm sure I would know if I did."

"We will let the doctor determine that."

"I don't like doctors!" Alarm suffused her cheeks. "They bleed women on the smallest pretense. Besides, I feel better by the moment." She turned in a slow circle without stumbling once. "You see? I'll be fine. No need for a doctor."

"Let's see what your brother says."

Anger flared in her face. "You can't tell Marcus about this."

"The devil I can't. He needs to know what dangers you and Regina are getting into when his back is turned."

"He already knows."

"I seriously doubt that, or he would never let his wife participate." Eyes narrowing, he stalked toward her. "And you wouldn't be begging me not to tell him. So get back into that bed. Now."

She dropped her pretense. "Simon, you mustn't say anything to Marcus. I know you—you'll make it sound worse than it is."

"Worse!" he roared. "How can I make it sound worse? You nearly got killed!"

She thrust out her pugnacious chin. "And you nearly got killed at the Battle of Kirkee when you weren't even a soldier. No one thought twice about your risking your life, but I must sit at home and do nothing like a good girl, is that it?"

"Damn it, Louisa—"

"You can't tell him. Please."

Muttering an oath, he raked his fingers through his already badly disheveled hair. "He'll find out anyway from the papers tomorrow."

"They've never put it in the papers before," she said with a shrug. "I don't know why they should put it in now."

"Before!" Simon stepped toward her. "You mean you have been hurt—"

"No!" As she darted out of his reach, she hastened to explain. "We've seen the mob throwing things before, that's all. We were never allowed to accompany the carts, but we did meet the convict women at the docks so we could hand out packets. And when we saw what they endured . . ."

She frowned. "It's unconscionable. And the papers never mention it, I assure you. They condone the behavior. That was when we decided it shouldn't happen again."

Casting him an imploring glance, she added, "And if you tell Marcus, he'll refuse to let me and Regina go, and then other husbands will follow suit, and the London Ladies Society will lose half its support—all over some silly rock."

Good, he thought. "Next time it could be a brick the mob throws at you."

"Next time I'll wear a steel hat."

He scowled. "Even if I don't tell Draker, Regina will."

"Fiddlesticks. She's as passionate about reform as I am, and she knows how he'd react. Once she sees I'm fine, she won't say a word."

She probably wouldn't. Regina was every bit as recalcitrant as Louisa.

"Come now, Simon, you don't really want to be at odds with us both, do you?" Louisa's suddenly coy smile made his breath catch in his throat. "And surely you don't want to be at odds with *me.*"

Now she meant to seduce him into forgetting his concern? The devil she would. "We're already at odds, remember? After today, you mean to banish me from your presence. So no matter how angry it makes you, I will keep you safe."

"Perhaps I was a bit hasty yesterday." She tipped up her chin. "What if I were to say that I'll let you observe my committee after all?"

He stared at her a long moment, then said softly, "Not good enough."

"Then what if I were to say you could court me?" She eyed him from beneath seductively lowered lashes. "That *is* what you want, isn't it?"

Good God, yes. That and more. And if he courted her, he could make sure she never risked her life again.

He snorted. Little chance of that. Louisa could get herself into plenty of trouble while he was dancing attendance on her, especially if she kept him dangling for weeks. At least with Draker, Simon had some chance of seeing an end to her activities—assuming that the man wouldn't let the bloody females talk him 'round to their way of thinking.

"I will not risk seeing you end up dead." He took a step toward her. "Now get back in the bed, sweetheart, so I can go see if your brother has arriv—"

She halted his words with a kiss. A very sweet, very tender kiss that sent his blood racing. When she drew back, her eyes glistened the same sultry black as the Indian nautch dancers who'd tempted the soldiers.

To his chagrin, his body leapt to attention just like one of those reckless soldiers. "What do you think you are doing?" he rasped, curling his fingers into his palms to keep from tossing her over his shoulder and carrying her to the bed.

"I'm showing you how nice it can be between us." She draped her arms about his neck, then stretched up on tiptoe to kiss him again, this time skimming her tongue tentatively along his lips.

So innocent . . . so alluring. And he was only human. He had nearly lost her, and now . . .

With a groan, he tugged her close and kissed her deeply, passionately, driving his tongue between her warm, welcoming lips over and over.

When at last he pulled back, her breath stuttered and her temptress's eyes shone up at him. "You see how it could be?" she whispered. "And if you keep quiet about what happened today, I'll . . . I'll . . ." She forced a smile. "I'll let you have as many kisses as you like."

He started to release her, partly out of shock that she would bargain with him using kisses, and partly out of concern for her injury. But she didn't look injured. If anything, she looked—fine. Very fine.

Fine enough to devour in one gulp, with her night-dark hair in a wild tangle about her shoulders and her lips red from his urgent kiss.

His blood beat a steady tattoo in his ears. "Now? Here?" he said hoarsely.

She played with a lock of his hair. "If it takes that to keep you silent . . ."

"Your brother will arrive any moment, and when he finds us together—"

"He won't be back for hours. He left for Tattersall's early this morning, and he never returns from there until late in the afternoon."

But Draker had been summoned—

Oh, right, she hadn't heard that. Which meant that she didn't know how easily they might be caught.

His mind began to race. This might be exactly the opportunity he needed to secure her. To end his torment. To marry her.

He gripped her waist as a plan fell into place. Though he had promised Draker he would not compromise her, that was before watching her nearly die.

"And Regina will be at the prison for a good hour more," she went on, clearly willing to say anything to bend Simon to her will. "Besides, we'd hear either of them enter downstairs in plenty of time to stop kissing."

He doubted that. Nor was he as certain as she seemed to be that Draker would end her reform activities if Simon tattled. But as long as *Louisa* believed it, Simon could get what he wanted—a chance to compromise her.

He'd have to convince her to go far enough to make Draker demand a marriage, but he could do it. Christ, if it meant winning her, he could even endure the beating that her brutish brother would surely administer.

"So?" she asked blithely. "Are we agreed?"

"Not yet. I want more for my silence than a few kisses." He deliberately swept his gaze to where the unbuttoned collar of her pelisse robe exposed a tempting slice of bare flesh. "Quite a bit more."

A blush stained her cheeks a deep scarlet, but she didn't pull away. "What do you mean?"

Bringing his hand up to cover her breast, he bent his mouth to her ear. "Forbidden caresses. Forbidden, *intimate* caresses. I want to touch you. I want to taste you and fondle your bare flesh—"

"That isn't acceptable." She pushed away from him, though her eyes now held a shimmering heat that matched the fire in his belly.

"Then your brother and I will be having a long and very informative conversation about your activities as soon as he arrives."

He loathed pressing her so wickedly, but he might never get this chance again. How better to make her *want* to marry him than to rouse her desires? If he could show her how sweet marriage could be . . .

"I do not mean to take your virtue," he said to reassure her. "Just to have some mutual enjoyment." Enough to compromise her. "When we are done, you can return to being as prickly as you want."

But he would make sure she did not *want* to. Ever again. And surely he could control himself long enough to pleasure her without taking her. He had waited seven years for this; he could wait a short while more for their wedding night.

She glanced away, anger warring with desire in her face. But she was no fool. She knew he meant what he said. She must really be worried that Draker would curtail her activities—and equally determined not to let him—or she wouldn't even consider this outrageous bargain.

At last her gaze swung to his. "You must swear on your honor that you won't ruin me."

"I swear." He merely had to get her so hot and bothered that she lost track of the time.

"And you have to swear that this will be the only time you make me buy your silence with . . . scandalous caresses. Because if you return tomorrow threatening to tell Marcus—"

"On my honor, it will be just this once." Once was all it would take. Unless—"But *you* must promise to let me do as I please. No balking at caresses you think are too intimate. I have agreed not to ruin you." He skimmed his gaze slowly down her. "And that is the only thing I have agreed to."

Panic crossed her face. "But you can't stay here half the day—"

"I will stop when the doctor arrives, all right?" He only prayed that Draker got here first.

"Fine. As long as you send the doctor away when he arrives." When Simon scowled, she added, "No doctor and no discussion with Marcus. That's the agreement."

She thought she was so clever. "You are in no position to bargain, sweetheart," he reminded her.

"If you don't want the offer—" she said primly and started to turn away.

"I'll take it." Giving her no chance to change her mind, he dragged her into his arms.

Chapter Fourteen

❧

Dear Charlotte,
I would hardly call a woman of thirty-two
"aging." Nor can I imagine that all surprises are un-
welcome to you. You are not as unadventurous as you
pretend.

Your *"aging"* cousin,
Michael

*M*adness, sheer madness. Louisa reeled beneath the on-
slaught of Simon's kisses. What had possessed her to pro-
pose this? Clearly, that rock had knocked the common
sense out of her.

But she couldn't let Simon tell Marcus about today. If
her brother knew she'd been hurt . . . No, she dared not
risk it. If both she and Regina had to stop their work, the
group would never survive.

Fiddlesticks, her conscience said. *You just want to see*
what Simon means by "intimate caresses" . . .

Like those he lavished on her now, his hand kneading
her breast as his mouth plundered hers with a hunger

that answered her own. Heavens, the strangest parts of her body were tightening, tensing, yearning for his mouth, his fingers . . .

Then he unfastened her pelisse robe and dragged it off.

"Simon!" she cried as her serviceable wool gown puddled at her feet.

"Naked flesh, remember?" He circled behind her to unlace her corset.

"But if anyone comes in—"

"Don't fret, sweetheart." With heated, open-mouthed kisses, he teased her sensitive ear, her flaming cheek, the pulse beating furiously in her neck. "The door's locked."

She swayed back against him, struggling to regain her sanity. "What about the servants? They have keys."

"Yes, but they wouldn't use them without permission. The footman is fetching my doctor. When he knocks to inform us of the man's arrival, I will go into the hall, and that is where your family will find me when they return."

"W-won't the doctor . . . say something to . . . someone?"

"I pay him well for his discretion." He peeled off her corset, then dropped it. "I will pay the servants to keep quiet, too, if I must."

It sounded eminently sensible . . . far too sensible for how he made her feel. His hand now cupped her breast to tease and fondle and drive her out of her mind. And his other hand . . . oh, sweet heaven . . . what was he doing?

He rubbed her between the legs as he had in the forest, but this time it was much more intimate, much more . . . erotic. Since she never wore drawers, only the thin linen of her chemise lay between his fingers and the most hidden part of her flesh.

"You're so wet and hot, sweetheart," he said in a guttural voice. "Do you know what that does to me?"

He knew about the dampness, the heat? Of course he did. No matter what he'd claimed about his celibacy, he'd probably had plenty of women in his life. Or he wouldn't know how to do *this* so . . . very . . . oh, heaven help her. What was he touching that made her feel—

A moan escaped her lips. Wildly she arched into his hands, craving more. He kissed a fiery path down her neck, and she turned her head to meet his lips.

When she spotted herself in the mirror, with his masterful hands all over her and his mouth ravishing her neck, the picture they made together excited her further . . . until she realized how anyone else would react to see it. "Simon, if the servants . . . do . . . unlock the door—"

"They'll find you lying in fashionable deshabille in your bed, awaiting the doctor." Taking her by surprise, he lifted her in his arms. "Because that is precisely where you will be."

With a gasp, she flung her arms about his neck. There was some flaw in his logic, but she couldn't puzzle it out when his gaze was raking her body with such exhilarating intent.

In her chemise, she could hardly be called naked, but it was less than she'd ever worn in a man's presence. And Simon seemed to see right through it as he stretched her out on her bed, for he hovered over her, his eyes darkening to that deep cerulean blue that always sent an errant thrill along her spine.

When he untied her chemise with a flick of one finger, then dragged the neck down to expose her breasts, her face flamed, but her shameless, flagrantly rebellious nipples tautened into points beneath his penetrating glance.

"Do you know how often I have imagined you like this?" he rasped as he slid onto the bed beside her. "How many stifling Calcutta nights I endured by conjuring up pictures of you naked beneath me? Wondering if your breasts were as full as they'd seemed?" He fondled them, teased them. "Wondering if your nipples would be pouty little cherries or rich dark damsons that puckered sweetly when I touched them?" He bent toward her breasts. "Or tasted them, like this . . ."

His tongue slicked over her nipple, and she choked back a groan. His words seduced her as thoroughly as his devilish caresses. Just the sight of his golden head at her breast shot a tremor through her.

This bargain had been a mistake. Much more of this, and she'd beg him to take her, if only to ease the yearnings in her breasts and belly. Not to mention the place between her legs that he was now unveiling, tugging her chemise up inch by inch. He even stroked her there, his finger tormenting the spot that ached for his—

Good heavens, she couldn't let him do this, or she would be lost. She wouldn't put it past Simon to ruin her if she were fool enough in the throes of her heedless desire to say she wanted him to.

But she'd already agreed to let him touch and taste her, and if she didn't hold to it, he would ruin everything she'd worked for.

Long as the woman lays there and lets the man do what he wants, he'll never know the difference.

Yes! That's what she must do—lie here and let him do as he pleased. Not allow her shameless feelings to tempt her into doing things back, like stroking his hair or thrusting her hips against him as she was doing this very moment—

She forced herself to ease back onto the bed. *Just let him 'do his business.' Then it will be over and your virtue will be intact.*

He shifted to suck her other breast, and she had to fight to keep from clutching his head to her chest. Instead she grabbed great handfuls of the bed covers and squeezed.

Think of something other than his curst mouth. Think of Newgate. She fixed her gaze on the bed canopy of white muslin above her. *White. Yes, think of the white-wood carver project. What you will do with the money.*

Had Simon and Mrs. Harris met again? She would have to ask him later. Perhaps—

"What are you doing?" Simon snapped.

She jerked her gaze from the canopy to where he hovered over her, scowling.

A guilty flush heated her cheeks. "I-I don't know what you mean."

"Yes, you do. Seconds ago you were aroused, and now . . ." His gaze shifted meaningfully to where she clutched the bed covers for dear life. "You're resisting me."

"Perhaps I'm not as passionate as you thought." She forced a cool smile to her lips. "Or perhaps I merely don't find this as engrossing as you do."

Anger blazed in his face. "And perhaps you're trying to put a swift end to our bargain the only way you know how."

A pox on the man and his uncanny ability to read her mind. "That's a rather arrogant way to look at it. You're assuming that I—"

"I am assuming nothing. I know you—you would

rather die than allow me to win. So you are circumventing our agreement."

With deliberate insolence, he bent to run his tongue in a circle around her nipple, and a delicious shiver coursed down her.

Desperately, she fought back. "You said you wanted to touch and taste me; you said nothing about my responding. Or doing the same things to you."

"Ah, but I am arrogant enough to want it all. So go ahead—resist me. Lie back and think of England and keep your hands to yourself." He seized her nipple in his teeth, arousing it with a sensual sweep of his tongue. Then he released it to flash her a darkly wicked smile. "But that will only make me more determined to have you writhing beneath me in the end, touching me and tasting me and begging me to give you pleasure."

Ooh, what conceit! How dared he? "Save your blustering speeches for Parliament, Your Grace. This is one fight you won't win with them."

The minute the taunt left her mouth, she regretted it. Now he wouldn't rest until he'd conquered her utterly.

"Then it's a good thing I don't intend to use speeches," he said in a harsh rasp.

And the battle was on.

She'd scarcely drawn another breath when he caught the hem of her chemise and jerked it up her body to bunch above her breasts. Now she lay fully exposed to him, from her chest to the garters tied just below her knees.

Simon scoured her naked body with a devouring glance. Then like Wellington at Waterloo, he swooped down upon her with merciless cunning, scorching her bared breasts and nipples with kisses, laving them with hot rasps of his tongue even as his hand delved fearlessly between her legs.

Only this time he didn't stop with rubbing her, oh no. He slid his devilish finger inside her slick passage in a motion as bold as it was shocking. She was still gasping at the audacity of that invasion when he began stroking her, in and out, up and down, first with one and then with two questing fingers.

Oh, heaven save her from his clever hand, which seemed to know just how to arouse her. She swallowed the cry that rose in her throat and squeezed the covers into knots in her effort not to squirm. She closed her eyes, but that only made her more aware of his mouth, now searing a path of open-mouthed kisses to her belly, his tongue darting into her navel for a fleeting caress before it trailed farther down to—

Her eyes shot open. "Simon, what are you—"

"I can taste you wherever I want, remember?" he lifted his head to growl.

His fingers withdrew from inside her, but only so he could part her tangled curls and bare her tender parts to his covetous gaze. As she held her breath, half in alarm, half in tantalized wonder, he covered her *down there* with his mouth.

Heavens! What on earth . . . what was he . . . ooh, that was not fair.

Now his tongue drove inside her, tempting her but not giving enough. If Simon had governed India anywhere as competently as he governed her body, no wonder everyone lauded his actions.

His tongue flicked her eager, throbbing petals and she heard herself moan as if in a dream, felt her hips arch up to meet his mouth. But she could no more stop it than she could stop the images flooding her brain . . . of Simon carrying her, worrying over her, conquering her as his tongue darted deeper and deeper.

She didn't even realize she'd grabbed his head, fisting her hands in his hair, until he demanded hoarsely, "Do you want me?"

The sound of his voice startled her into dropping her gaze to his face. Although she expected to see gloating there, instead his eyes glittered with a raw desire so electric, it sent a current through her. And so powerful that she could no longer deny it. She nodded.

"Say it, Louisa," he ordered. "Say 'I want you, Simon.'"

"I want you . . . Simon," she said even as she thrust her hips up, vainly trying to meet his mouth.

Eyes gleaming with a dark satisfaction, he returned to his sinful caresses. Soon he had her quivering and writhing, begging until her voice was hoarse from her cries, until she thought she would die if she didn't reach that summit his mouth seemed to offer . . .

When the lightning struck at last, pulsing energy through her from her curling toes to her tossing head and wringing a scream from her throat, she clutched him to her and held on without shame or sorrow, without even caring that she'd lost the battle. For it felt like she'd won.

Simon felt like she had won, too. He had tempted her into letting him pleasure her, but she still had not touched him, and he craved her hands on him.

With one last glance at the sweet delicacy he had just fed on, he slid up her body. "Touch me, sweetheart, please . . ." he growled, hardly conscious of the words, "Touch me, too . . . I beg you—"

"Where? How?" Unexpectedly eager to comply, she

started kissing his shoulders. The delicate kisses drove him mad.

He yanked his shirttails free, tore at the buttons of his trousers and drawers, then grabbed her hand and urged it inside. His heavy cock was so eager for her that it jerked at the first touch of her fingers. With a gasp, she let go, and he moaned.

"It's all right." He closed her hand around him. Thank God she let him, because he might die otherwise. "It's supposed to move." He showed her how to caress him. "Stroke it. Firmly." When she did, a heartfelt groan escaped his lips. "Yes, like that. My God, you have no idea . . . how good that feels."

"I have *some* idea," she teased with a sultry smile, then tugged hard, wresting a cry of pleasure from his throat.

"I knew that you are really . . . Cleopatra . . . not Joan of Arc." He thrust into her tight little fist. "Seducing men into surrender."

"Seducing?" She feathered a kiss along his throat. "You begged me, remember?"

He barely remembered his name just now, but he did remember begging. And her begging *him*. "Admit it, sweetheart, you surrendered first."

"You imagined that," she said with a silky smile, her strokes growing harder and faster. God, she was born for passion.

"The devil I did. I made you beg." He bent to brush her mouth with his. "And I'll do it again, too."

Then as he headed inexorably toward release, he kissed her mouth, fondled her satiny breasts, until she was once again wriggling and squirming beneath him.

Somewhere in the recesses of his brain he heard a

knock, but it had barely registered when another sound followed, of a key turning in a lock.

He didn't even have time to leave her before Draker's voice thundered through his fevered mind. "Damn you, Foxmoor, get the hell off my sister!"

Simon groaned. He had not wanted it to happen like this, for her to be seen like this. Fighting his burning urge for release, he rolled off her and onto his feet on the floor, dragging the cover over her.

With his back to Draker, he fastened his trousers. Staring down at her flushed, shocked face, he murmured, "I am sorry, sweetheart. Forgive me."

Before he turned, he heard other voices behind him, his sister's for one, saying, "Marcus, how is she?" Then a painful pause. "Oh, dear Lord."

That was all it took to fully banish his erection. Cursing, he faced them, taking in the horrified expressions of not only Regina, but at least three other members of the London Ladies Society, all of whom crowded around the entrance to the room. Then his gaze swept to Draker, and Simon sucked in a breath.

He had vastly misjudged what his brother-in-law's reaction would be. He would not suffer a beating at Draker's hands, after all.

Draker was simply going to kill him.

Chapter Fifteen

⤜⬥⬥⤛

Dear Cousin,
 Will you be surprised to learn that the duke and
my friend Louisa are shortly to be married? I was
present when they announced their betrothal. But do
not believe everything you hear about it—Foxmoor
was not found naked in her bedchamber. Though he
might as well have been, for she very nearly was.
                     Your shameless gossip of a friend,
                                              Charlotte

$\mathscr{C}$hoose your seconds, Foxmoor," Marcus said in a deadly voice that sent a chill through Louisa.

"No!" she cried at the same time as Regina. Dragging the cover around her, Louisa leapt from her bed. "No duels, Marcus. This is *my* fault, not his."

Marcus glowered at her. "He took advantage of you while you were wounded, for God's sake!"

She caught her breath. "How did you know about— And why aren't you at Tattersall's? You never return this early."

"A footman fetched me," Marcus retorted.

"At whose command? I did not send for—"

"*I* did," Simon said tersely. "While you were unconscious."

She was still trying to assimilate that when Marcus let out a roar.

"Unconscious!" Marcus stalked toward Simon. "Why, you wretched scoundrel, I'll tear you limb from limb!"

"Stop it!" Louisa put herself between her brother and Simon. "He didn't touch me then. And as soon as I awakened, he sent for a doctor."

After he'd already sent for Marcus. The full ramifications of that hit her. Heaven help her, he'd engineered this awful—

"You knew Marcus was coming." She could hardly breathe past the pain, and cast Simon a glance of pure betrayal. "When you agreed to my bargain, you knew he would find us together long before the doctor arrived."

"What bargain?" Marcus snapped.

"Be quiet, Marcus!" She fixed her gaze on Simon. "You knew, didn't you?"

He hesitated, then nodded.

"But why?" A shudder wracked her. "No, don't answer. I know why."

To accomplish what Sidmouth had wanted. She shifted her gaze to the women peeking into the room, then groaned. Oh, he'd done it so effectively, too. She could count on Regina and Mrs. Harris to keep quiet, but the other two . . .

Despair gripped her. One was a notorious gossip and the other a new member. It wouldn't be long before the tale swept through the group and women began to leave the London Ladies.

"I suppose you knew *they* were coming, as well," she choked out.

"Certainly not," he snapped. "Regina told me she was staying at the docks to pass out packets."

"We were going to, all of us," Regina put in quickly, "but Mrs. Fry said the Quaker ladies could take care of it and sent me home. Mrs. Harris and the others came along out of concern for your injury."

"Clearly that's not what they should have been concerned about," Marcus growled. "And I'll have his head on a platter—"

"Hush, Marcus!" Louisa and Regina said in unison. Louisa turned to Simon. "So it was just a happy coincidence for you that they came, too."

"If you want to look at it that way," he said warily.

And now she was ruined. If Simon didn't marry her, that is. And why should he? He'd achieved his goal—to discredit her before her fellow reformers. She'd let him do it, too, walked right into the trap like a rabbit hopping into the tiger's den.

Hurt exploded into anger. "You unconscionable devil!"

Remorse flashed over his face before it changed to sheer, unadulterated will. "I told you I meant to marry you. So I saw my chance and took it."

Louisa blinked, momentarily taken aback. "You . . . you didn't do this at Sidmouth's request?"

"No!" Shock suffused his face. "How could you even think it? I would never do that to you."

Simon *wasn't* working for Sidmouth. He *did* want to marry her—so badly that he'd purposely compromised her.

Torn between relief and anger, she didn't resist when he slid his arm about her waist and tugged her to stand beside him. "This is as good a time as any to announce that we are getting married, don't you think, sweetheart?" His gaze locked with hers, daring her to say otherwise.

Regina let out a breath, as did the other ladies, but Marcus only scowled and started toward Simon. "I would rather throttle you."

"You are not going to throttle him." Regina grabbed Marcus's arm. "It would ruin Louisa. She has to marry him now, and you know it."

Louisa glanced from Simon to Regina, her heart in her throat. Regina was right. But good heavens, what a choice. If she didn't marry Simon, she would lose everything she'd worked for. And if she did marry him . . .

"Louisa?" Simon prodded. When she continued to stand there woodenly, he shot the others a black look. "I would like a few moments alone with my fiancée, so if you could give us some privacy . . ."

"Privacy?" Marcus bit out. "You've already had far too much privacy."

"Marcus, for heaven's sake!" Regina said sharply.

His jaw tightening, Marcus glanced at Louisa. "What about you, angel? Do you want time alone with this scoundrel?

She forced a smile. "Yes, please." She needed privacy to wring his neck.

"Ten minutes," Marcus snapped. "In ten minutes, if you aren't both downstairs and dressed, I'll come up here and tear Foxmoor's heart out with my bare hands." His gaze shot to Simon. "Understood?"

"Understood," Simon murmured, though his fingers tightened on her waist.

The others were halfway out the door when Marcus paused. "Are you . . . able to go downstairs?" he asked

Louisa. "The footman didn't say how badly you were injured or even how it happened—"

"I tripped," she said before Simon could answer. "Getting out of the carriage at the docks. I tripped and hit my head. It temporarily knocked me out, but I feel fine now, truly."

She glanced to Regina, whom she implored with her eyes not to belie her. Regina gave a sketchy nod. Thankfully, the other ladies were already in the hall and hadn't heard. Louisa would have to trust Regina to make sure they kept silent, too.

Especially since Marcus looked skeptical. His gaze swung to Simon. "Is that what happened, Foxmoor? She tripped?"

Louisa held her breath. So help her, if he betrayed her now—

"Yes." Simon's fingers dug painfully into her waist.

Marcus hesitated. Then a faint, almost snide smile touched his lips. "I suppose it hardly matters. From now on, my sister and her activities will be *your* concern, not mine. And I shall vastly enjoy watching her give you hell."

As soon as her brother left, Louisa proceeded to do just that. She rounded on Simon, her voice trembling with rage. "How dare you? You schemed to get me alone, and then—"

"*You* were the one who suggested the bargain. I did not scheme to get you alone, for God's sake."

A pox on him for being right. Seething, she dropped the bedcovers and retied her chemise, then strode to her highboy for a dressing gown. She would never succeed in donning her corset and pelisse robe during the short time her curst brother had given her.

"Very well, but you schemed to have us found together." She jerked on her dressing gown. "You should have told me Marcus was on his way home. You shouldn't have *let* me make that bargain."

"I argued that it was unwise. You chose to ignore me."

It was true—she'd been reckless, and he'd counted on that. Because Simon, more than anyone, knew that her impulsive nature lay just beneath the surface, waiting for something like this to emerge.

"Come now, Louisa, would marriage to me be so awful?"

The hint of wounded pride in his voice further unsettled her. "I can't really tell, can I? I scarcely even know you."

That was the problem. Marrying the Simon who lifted sick children into his phaeton would be far from awful.

But the Simon who'd deliberately manipulated her into compromising herself . . . *that* Simon made her wary, even though he clearly felt remorse for his scheming afterward. *I am sorry, sweetheart. Forgive me.*

Approaching her from behind, the dratted devil slid his arm about her waist. "You knew me well enough to want to marry me before—what has changed?"

"Everything," she whispered. "You, me, my plans." She didn't want Simon's interference in her affairs. And if he'd been stubbornly overprotective before, only imagine how he'd be once they married.

"The only significant change is that we are even better suited now." He tugged her back against his lean frame. "We belong together. You know we do."

His achingly tender voice gave her pause. But did she dare believe it? "Do you love me, Simon?"

He stiffened, then countered with, "Do you love *me*?"

She winced. "Certainly not." It was true. It had to be true. Because if she ever dared to love him, he would use that ruthlessly against her.

"Then I don't see a problem," he said coldly.

"So this is to be a marriage of convenience, is it?" she choked out.

"Absolutely not." He dragged in a heavy breath. "I want a real marriage, Louisa. Surely there is enough affection between us for that. I like you. And if you could swallow your pride long enough, you would admit you like me, too."

"I desire you," she muttered. "That isn't the same."

"It's close enough for me." He nuzzled her cheek. "If you are not tempted by the prospect of an amiable marriage to a man who desires you and will treat you well, then consider this. Together we could do a great deal of good in the world."

"You mean, *you* could do a great deal of good." Wrenching free, she faced him. "And I could be the perfect political wife, never causing trouble, never engaging in controversial causes, so you can become prime minister."

A scowl darkened his brow. "I have never lied to you about my ambitions. But they need not keep you from participating in various charitable organizations. When you are not taking care of our children."

"Ch-children?" A pox on him, she'd forgotten about that. He would expect her to have children, *his* children. There would be blood and doctors—

"Yes, children." He eyed her closely. "I need an heir. Surely you know that."

Realizing how close she came to revealing her fears, she said quickly, "Of course." Then she frowned. "And you will expect me to put everything aside to raise them, I suppose."

"Not everything." He looked decidedly wary. "Regina has children and does charitable works. Indeed, a prime minister's wife is expected to do such things."

"As long as she chooses fashionable causes, correct? Would the London Ladies Society be one of those charitable organizations I'd be allowed to support, the way your sister does?" When he muttered a curse and glanced away, she nodded. "I thought not."

For a second, she considered that the marriage itself might have been part of her enemies' plan. That Simon had compromised her precisely so he could marry her and control her activities.

But that made no sense; surely Sidmouth wouldn't have asked Simon to do something so extreme. And even if he had, surely Simon wouldn't have agreed to it. Not when he could marry a less troublesome woman more useful to his career.

Unfortunately, that didn't make her feel any better. He still had her trapped.

Or did he? She set her hands on her hips. "Well then, here are my terms for our marriage. I must be allowed to continue with the London Ladies Society and all the charitable—and political activities—that such participation entails."

His gaze shot to her. "Damn it, you are in no position to bargain."

"And you like me in that position, don't you? Caught between a rock and a hard place. Only this time you have overshot the mark. For if I must give up the London Ladies either way, I'd rather take my chances with ruin than with marriage." When his scowl darkened to a glower, she hesitated, but she saw no other way to salvage the situation. "If you don't agree to let me continue with my group, then I thank you for your offer, but I can't marry you."

"The devil you can't." Fury carved deep lines in his brow. "If I tell Draker what happened today, he will forbid you to participate in your group anyway."

"And I will know that you're a liar and a cheat. Because you swore on your honor that if I let you make free with my body, you would hold your tongue."

With a curse, he raked his fingers through his hair, and a tiny part of her exulted. She had *him* trapped now. Simon might be a schemer, but when he gave his word, he didn't go back on it.

"Your brother will make you marry me. If he doesn't, my sister will."

"No one makes me do anything anymore. Not you nor your sister nor my brother. Surely you've already figured that out."

"So I am supposed to let you do as you please, gallivant about Newgate risking your life, risking the life of any child you bear—"

"I would never do that," she said. "We don't allow our other members to go to the prison if they're *enceinte,* and I'd certainly not ignore the rule for myself."

That seemed to give him pause. "You would refrain from your activities if you were with child?"

"Of course." Fortunately, she didn't intend to have children for a very long time. Now that she knew how to prevent them, she would make sure she bore his heir on *her* schedule and not his. Surely after a few years of marriage—after the London Ladies had succeeded in gaining their demands for prison reform—she would feel safe enough to have children. She had to give Simon his heir; it wouldn't be fair to him to do otherwise.

But only after she'd accomplished everything. And conquered her fear.

She glanced at the ormolu mantel clock. "Our time is almost up. What is it to be? Marriage to me on my terms? Or my ruin?"

"You know damned well I will not let you be ruined," he bit out.

She cast him a cool smile. "Then we are agreed."

He hesitated, but he knew when he'd been bested. Fixing her with a baleful glance, he snapped, "Yes, we are agreed."

Knotting the tie of her wrapper, she stepped toward the door, but he caught her arm and pulled her close enough to warn, "Don't think you will always get 'round me so easily, Joan of Arc." He lowered his voice to a seductive murmur. "I now know exactly how to tempt you, how to make you beg. And if the only way to master you in the marriage is to master you in the bedchamber, I will happily take on that task."

Though a thrill shot through her at the very thought of being mastered by him, she met his gaze steadily. "You forget, sir, that I know how to make you beg, too." She swept her hand down to his trousers, delighted when just the touch of her fingers made him harden. With a smile, she rubbed him through the rough fabric. "So we'll see who surrenders first. I wager it won't be me."

Leaving him cursing and trying to gain control of his errant arousal, she swept from the room. The battle lines were drawn. And despite her fears for the future and her uneasiness about how the marriage would play out, she looked forward to the fight.

Chapter Sixteen

Dear Charlotte,
   I did not credit the rumor about Foxmoor's naked-
ness, since he does not strike me as the reckless sort.
Miss North is another matter. After years of good
works, what woman could resist the promise of passion from a man as accomplished as the duke?

Your cousin,
Michael

Four days later, Simon watched as his new wife mingled
with the guests at their wedding supper. He could hardly
believe it—Louisa was his at last. He had traveled to hell
and back to get her, but he had done it, by God, and
surely everything would be easy sailing now.

As if she felt his gaze, she looked over and smiled, and
that smile thrummed through him like a sitar string
freshly plucked. She fairly sparkled today in her gown of
silver satin, with the Foxmoor diamonds about her throat
and orange blossoms speckling her dark hair. He couldn't
wait until she lay in his bedchamber wearing only those
diamonds and her Cleopatra smile.

What he felt must have shown in his glance, for her smile grew sultry and she raised an eyebrow. When he lifted his glass of champagne in a silent toast, she turned back to Mrs. Harris with a musical laugh. Every inch of him exulted.

It had all been worth it—Draker's draconian amendments to the marriage settlement and the rush to get the special license. Even the terms Louisa had demanded of him the day he'd compromised her.

He bit back a smile, remembering it. Any other woman would have leapt to marry a rich duke after he'd ruined her so publicly. But not Louisa, oh no. She had exacted her pound of flesh with all the righteous indignation of a wronged woman.

He had let her have her terms because she would have little chance to relish her triumph. By agreeing to quit her Ladies Society when she became *enceinte,* she had sealed her fate. He would put a babe in her belly in record time.

And he was bloody well going to enjoy doing it, too.

His sister strolled up beside him. "You look rather pleased with yourself."

"As do you." He drank deeply of his champagne. "God knows you have been angling for me to marry her for years."

"You will treat her well, won't you?"

"Your husband made sure of that—she now has enough pin money to start her own country. And her jointure—"

"I am not speaking of money, as you well know."

He stared off to where Louisa filled her plate with roast beef and pickles. "Do not fret, Regina. I would sooner cut off my arm than willingly hurt her."

He winced as he heard the words leave his mouth. It

was true, but the last thing he needed was for his sister—or his new wife—to know that. They had already taken enough advantage of his obsession.

He forced a smile. "I must congratulate you on your spectacular handiwork. My gardens have never looked so lovely."

His sister had planned and executed a simple church wedding and modest afternoon luncheon of astonishingly tasteful proportions. Their few guests were feasting on turtle soup and potted lobster beneath a hastily erected canopy of striped canvas. A violin player and a harpist played something appropriately matrimonial.

Only one oddity in the arrangements gave him pause. "I am curious about the Indian figures on the table," he said. "Your idea?"

"No, Louisa's, actually. She thought they might please you."

"I see." He wondered if his wife knew that the carved wood sculptures were of *devadasis,* Indian temple dancers of a decidedly sensual character. He would have to tell her later, if only to see her blush. He liked making her blush.

"Louisa went all the way to Petticoat Lane to find them," Regina added.

He frowned. "She didn't go alone, I hope." That part of town was dangerous.

"She had a footman with her." Regina shot him a glance. "But I do hope you realize that Louisa is used to moving about London as she pleases."

"I know that only too well," he said tersely.

"You have to understand—she's had a very difficult time these past seven years. Bad enough she had to endure the rumors about Marcus and her mother once she came into society, but then you and she . . . well, the gossip plagued her after you went off to India. I thought for a while that her friendship with Princess Charlotte might help, but then Charlotte died in childbirth and it devastated her."

"She was there?"

"Of course not. They did not allow the single ladies to attend the princess." She sighed. "But it still affected Louisa profoundly. I think that's why she throws herself into the London Ladies. It gives her life some purpose."

His fingers tightened on his glass. "Well, she need not do that anymore. She has me. Our life together. And soon, I hope, our children."

"Yes, but do not rush her. It is a huge change for her, so please try to understand. This has happened so fast."

"Of course." It was the least he owed her after how he had manipulated her into marrying him. Though he did not regret that in the least.

"I do wish you had chosen to wait a while longer to marry."

"You know we could not risk the gossip. And Louisa did not want to take time out of her activities to plan a more elaborate wedding." Nor had he wanted to chance her having second thoughts. The sooner he secured her as his wife, the better.

"But why not a wedding trip? It would be better for you both."

"We will, after Parliament is no longer in session." He smiled thinly. "If I can tear Louisa away from the London Ladies Society, that is. I should never have suggested that Christmas project. I will be lucky to get her alone for two days, much less two weeks."

"You should carry her to Brighton. She loves the sea, you know."

"Does she?" He had not known. Indeed, there was much he did not know about his wife.

"She always loved going there with the king and Princess Charlotte." Regina frowned. "And speaking of His Majesty, I am quite put out with him. I cannot believe he did not attend the wedding or the supper. Louisa is very hurt by his not coming, and I don't blame her."

Nor did Simon. But he did have a sneaking suspicion about why the king had not come. One that put a decided damper on his day.

She sighed. "I suppose it's because of your being at odds with him, but I honestly do not understand that. If Louisa and Draker and I are content with the marriage, I do not see how he could continue in his disapproval of you."

"His Majesty is fickle, as you well know," he hedged, reluctant to lie to his sister. Louisa had not been the only person he had wronged seven years ago. His sister had forgiven him, but that almost made it worse, for it emphasized what an ass he'd been to her back then.

"Nonetheless . . ." She slanted a glance at Simon. "You have nothing to do with his not being here, do you?"

"Of course not."

If he'd had his way, the king would be waiting in his study right now to hand him Liverpool's resignation. Simon had tried to see George ever since Louisa had agreed to the marriage, but His Majesty's lackeys had always made excuses for why the man was unavailable.

It was the only black spot in this affair. Simon scowled. He would not be surprised if the king was already trying to renege on their agreement.

And if he was?

Then Simon would work around it. Despite his threat

of going to the press, Simon could never shame Louisa like that. But surely there were other ways of making the king keep his promise, and Simon would use them if he must.

Later. "Tell me something, sister. How much longer must I endure this luncheon before I can forcibly evict our guests without appearing rude?"

She laughed. "Patience, brother. I still haven't even served the cake."

"Then serve it, for God's sake."

"After waiting all these years for your wedding night," she teased, "I should think another hour would not kill you."

"Another *hour?*" he growled, sending her hurrying off, laughing. She had no idea. After seven years, even another minute might kill him.

Unfortunately, it was more like two hours before they said good-bye to the last of the guests, and even longer before he could hustle Draker and Regina off. By the time they left, the setting sun already glistened on the verdant meadows of Green Park opposite Foxmoor House.

As the door closed behind them, Simon turned to Louisa with a frown. "I do believe your brother meant to spend the night here."

She laughed. "He was merely tormenting you, I expect."

"It's a good thing he relented," Simon said as he tugged her into his arms. "Because if I'd had to wait one more second to have you to myself, sweetheart, I might have tossed him bodily into the street."

He kissed her, a long, thorough kiss that only whetted his appetite. They'd had no chance to be alone in the last four days, and just the taste of her drove him insane. "It is long past time that we retire, wife," he murmured against her lips.

With a coy smile, she pushed away from him. "Not yet, Your Grace. You have to give me the chance to prepare."

"You look perfectly prepared to me—"

"I want to change into the special nightdress I bought." Her eyes twinkled as she backed toward the stairs. "You'll like it. It's of the sheerest fabric—"

"Unless it's transparent, I'm not interested." He stalked her ruthlessly.

"Ten minutes. That's all I need." Her teasing smile faltered. "Please?"

Do not rush her, Regina had said.

He sighed. "Fine. I'll go make sure no one let Raji out of my study."

"Thank you," she said, her smile ablaze once more.

His heart flipped over in his chest as she went up the stairs, hips swaying.

Besotted fool, his grandfather's voice intruded, the first time in days. The man was right. All she had to do was smile and swing her hips, and he leapt to give her whatever she wanted. Well, he could afford to be indulgent, couldn't he? He had convinced her to marry him. She was his duchess now, and nothing could change that.

His duchess. He liked the sound of that.

Smiling, he headed for his study and found the door ajar. He glanced inside, but his pet was gone, of course. Gritting his teeth, he hailed a footman. "Find Raji and shut him in my study, will you?"

As the footman scurried off to do his bidding, Simon put his pet from his mind and headed for the east wing. Seconds later, he was entering his wife's bedchamber after she answered his knock with a throaty, "Come in."

The sight that arrested him stole the breath from his lungs. With her velvety black hair rippling over her shoulders, Louisa stood beside the great state bed in a confection of sheerest linen. Like a fine glaze over her porcelain skin, it revealed as much as it concealed, highlighting the crimson buds of her nipples and glistening over the dark smudge of her pretty mons.

As his cock went on instant alert, he kicked the door shut behind him.

A smile trembled on her full lips. "Do you like it?"

"You could say that, sweetheart." Shrugging out of his coat, he strode toward her. "I mean to rip it off you with my teeth."

Her smile broadened. "I bought three just the same."

"Good." As he went, he unbuttoned his waistcoat and tore his cravat loose, then left them crumpled on the floor. "I will rip them off, too."

"They were very costly," she teased. "And I charged them to *your* account."

He caught her about the waist and dragged her flush against him. "All the more reason for me to do as I please with them."

When she chuckled, he grasped the ribbon ties in his teeth to tug them loose. But before he could proceed further, a shrieking mass of fur landed on his back.

He swore as Raji pulled at his hair like a demon possessed. "Bloody hell, not again!' he growled as he reached back to grab his pet, then wrench him off.

With Raji protesting, Simon held him at arm's length. "Sorry, scamp, but this is one battle you will lose. She married *me*, not you, and you simply have to accept it." Louisa's laughter spilled over them, and he scowled at her. "This is *not* funny."

"Of course it is," she sputtered between bursts of hilarity. "He's defending my virtue, poor thing."

As if in agreement, Raji chattered and struggled in Simon's grip.

"He can defend it all he wants—in another part of the house." He turned and strode for the door.

"Where are you going?" she called out behind him.

"To deposit him in my study," he shot back. "I'd throw him in the dressing room, but his caterwauling would drive us insane."

When he yanked open the door, she cried, "Wait!" Then she hurried over to kiss Raji on the forehead. The little devil stopped his complaining long enough to gaze up at her with worshipful eyes.

"It's all right, dear," she whispered.

Simon rolled his eyes. "Don't encourage him, for God's sake."

The sound of her laughter followed him out.

He strode down the stairs with his grumbling pet. He passed a footman, who cried, "Your Grace, I should tell you—"

"Later," he barked. "Tomorrow. Next week."

Hurrying into the study, he set Raji free, then froze. The king himself was bent over his desk, opening drawers and peering inside them. "What the devil—"

"Foxmoor!" The king had the good grace to look guilty. "I . . . was too late for the wedding, so I figured I'd duck in here and—"

"Search my desk?" Then he noticed the envelope lying there. "Is that Liverpool's resignation?"

George turned a sickly shade. "Er . . . not exactly."

Chapter Seventeen

❧

Dear Cousin,

Passion is all well and good, but better that a man give a woman love. I have had passion—it does not last. For Louisa's sake, I hope that the duke's passion comes from something deeper than the needs of his body.

Your cousin,
Charlotte

Louisa was still giggling in her new bedchamber when she spotted Raji's wooden canary beneath a writing table. Apparently that was where he had hidden to spy on them.

Poor Raji. She would have to find him a female monkey, because Simon's obvious affection for the scamp was clearly no longer enough to satisfy him.

With a sigh, she retrieved the toy, then wondered what she should do with it. She didn't want Raji to do without the one companion he *did* have. Bad enough he was banished to the study for the night.

After pulling on a dressing gown, she hurried out the

bedroom door. Simon must have taken the stairs at a run, for he was already nowhere to be seen. But she'd been to Foxmoor House many a time with Regina while Simon was away, so she knew exactly where the study was.

She hummed to herself as she strolled down the stairs. What a silly goose she was. Despite her initial misgivings about marrying Simon, she hadn't been able to stop smiling for the past four days.

His reaction to seeing her nightdress certainly helped. Perhaps this was *not* such a mistake. Simon had agreed to her terms, so she needn't fear for the London Ladies. And she had her sponges—one was lodged inside her at this very moment. The shopkeeper in Spitalfields had said that they didn't always work, but it was better than nothing, wasn't it?

And the truth was, she did want to share Simon's bed. How could she not, when he didn't even bother to disguise how fiercely he desired her? The way he'd looked at her a few minutes ago . . . good heavens, it was enough to turn even a Puritan into a wanton, and she was no Puritan. Not with him.

She quickened her steps, eager to have her husband back in her bedchamber. But as she approached Simon's study, she heard voices. Simon and a servant? Surely Simon could have no visitors on this, of all nights.

Then she recognized the other voice. The king. Her father.

"I swear, I will talk to him when the time is right," the king was saying. "I promise I will uphold my part of the bargain."

Bargain? What bargain?

"And that is why you are skulking about my study on my wedding night?" Simon snapped. "Of course not. You knew I would be occupied elsewhere, so you sneaked in here to steal our agreement. Then I could not use it against you when you trotted in tomorrow to announce that you had reneged."

The blood pounded in Louisa's ears. What bargain had he reneged on? And what agreement?

"I did not renege," the king protested. "It is just that the marriage happened so quickly I didn't have time to arrange—"

"You said that already," Simon remarked. "See here, I do not want to discuss this now. My wife awaits. But just so you will stop this foolishness, I should point out that I am not stupid enough to keep the damned papers here. They are locked up at my solicitor's. So your little search is all for naught."

"You won't use them, will you?" The king sounded panicked.

"I ought to."

"But you have to give me more time to gain Liverpool's resignation," the king said in alarm. "If you go to the press—"

"I am not going to the press," Simon said wearily. "I am not ready to commit political suicide just yet. And the last thing I want is for my wife to know that her father offered me certain inducements to marry her."

Just like that, the bottom dropped out of her world.

Certain inducements.

Oh, of course.

Clutching her stomach, Louisa prayed she could make it back to her bedchamber without retching. How could she have considered every possible scenario to explain Simon's interest in her, except the most obvious— her father and his machinations? She'd let the "falling out" between Simon and her father sway her, but it had so obviously been another of their schemes.

Bile rose in her throat, and she paused to steady herself with a hand on a console table. Oh no, what was she to do now? She was trapped in a marriage with him. Forever.

What an utter fool she'd been! How could she possibly have thought Simon had changed, that he would truly care for her? *This* was the real Simon. This was how he always worked.

She stumbled another few steps before Raji scampered out of the study and threw his arms about her leg. He must have smelled her.

She frantically tried to shake him off, not wanting Simon to know she was here, but he wouldn't let go. "Stop that," she whispered. "Go back!"

"Raji!" Simon came into the hall after his pet, then halted. "Oh God, no."

Slowly Louisa faced him, hardly even aware of the tears that stung her eyes. Feeling like an actress in some horrible farce, she held up Raji's toy canary. "I thought Raji might want . . ." She trailed off as the carving slipped from her fingers and rolled across the floor.

While Raji dashed after it, Simon stepped toward her. "This is not what you think." He looked stricken, even remorseful. But that only made it worse. "Your father and I—"

"Don't," she whispered. "Don't invent a lot of nonsense that we both know I'll never believe now."

"What is it, Foxmoor?" The king lumbered into the hall, then paled as he saw his daughter. "Er . . . good evening, my dear."

Her gaze still locked with Simon's, she choked out, "We missed you at the wedding, Your Majesty." Pain sharpened her tone. "Didn't you want to make sure you got what you paid for?" She waved her ring finger in the air, the heavy gold band feeling like a shackle. "Well, you did. I'm married to your friend and out of your hair at last. Happy now?"

The king's chubby cheeks flushed as he apparently realized what she'd heard. "Louisa, I only did what I thought was best for you—"

"Best for me!" Hot tears scalded her cheeks. "You bought me a husband whom you knew had always . . . despised . . . me . . ." The tears fell full force now, and she dashed them away, frantic to keep her dignity at least.

"I never despised you," Simon said in a ragged whisper.

"There now, poppet, you see? It's not like that." Her father came toward her. "I knew Foxmoor wanted to marry you. He just needed a little incentive—"

"Be quiet, will you?" Simon hissed at her father. "You have done more than enough damage for one night."

"But I want to explain, damn it," His Majesty shot back.

"Not tonight," Simon bit out.

"Oh no," Louisa said fiercely, the word "incentive" pounding into her brain. "I want to hear His Majesty's explanation. I want to hear what awful thing I did that would make him bargain to marry me off to the very man who once betrayed me."

Her father's eyes narrowed. "See here, you impudent chit, I warned you not to get involved with those Quakers. I begged you to consider what you were doing. But you were so blasted stubborn, worse than even your brother. And then the MPs started coming to me, complaining about your politics—"

"And you figured that Simon, of all people, would

know how to reel me in?" The pain of it threatened to destroy any remnants of remaining pride.

"Damn it, girl," the king bit out, "you were talking about putting up candidates for office. Radicals, even!"

She blinked, momentarily taken off guard. "You knew about Godwin?"

"Godwin!" Simon put in. "Charles Godwin? Owner of the *London Monitor? He's* your candidate?"

She leveled Simon with a cool glance. "And what if he is?"

"You see?" The king cast Simon a triumphant glance. "I told you she was a loose cannon. Reckless and thoughtless, that's what she is, letting herself be manipulated by radicals—"

"Enough!" Simon growled as Louisa stood in mute horror at her father's words. "Leave, damn you!"

The king drew himself up with royal indignation. "You cannot speak to me like that, Foxmoor, even if you did marry my daughter."

Simon took a step toward him. "If you do not leave this instant—"

"Fine, I shall go." The king sniffed. "But remember that you promised—"

"Get out!" Simon roared, his expression so enraged, it even frightened Louisa. "Before I throw you out!"

"All right, all right." Her father rushed past her. "I'll call on you in a day or so."

"Wonderful," Simon muttered as the king disappeared. "Now that you have ruined my wedding night, do come back and see if you can ruin my marriage."

"Don't blame *him,*" Louisa snapped. "You ruined your own marriage."

She headed for the stairs, needing to be alone to nurse

her hurt. But she should have known Simon would never allow it.

He raced up behind her. "So that's it?" he ground out as he kept step beside her. "You won't even let me explain? You're just going to march upstairs and closet yourself in your room to tally up my many offenses against you."

"Something like that."

Grabbing her by the arm, he swung her around. "The devil you are!"

"Was any of it true?" The seeming concern in his face wounded her even more. "The supposed interest in my group, your claims to feel affection for me, that . . . nonsense about how I've been a fever in your blood—"

"Every word was true," he said hoarsely. "I did my best not to lie to you."

"Except when you promised to let me continue my activities after we married."

"That, too. I swore on my honor, and I will hold to what I said."

"Until I am with child." A sickening realization hit her. "That's why you agreed to my terms, isn't it? Because you figured that you would have me *enceinte* within a short time, and then I'd have to stop anyway."

The flash of guilt across his face was her answer.

"Oh, I should have known . . ." she whispered.

"It was not as calculating as all that," he broke in. "Don't make it sound as if everything between us was just—"

"Part of your bargain with my father. Well, it was, wasn't it? You clearly promised him you would marry me and put an end to my work if he made you prime minister." Awareness dawned. "That's what you were fighting about—the letter of resignation that he didn't get for you from Lord Liverpool."

"All right, all right, yes. Your father did agree to make me prime minister if I married you, but—"

"So everything you said was a lie—every tender word and kiss."

"No, damn it!" He caught her by her arms and pulled her closer. "You can't believe that. You *know* I want you. From the moment I saw you again that first night at my sister's, I knew I had to have you. So when your father came to me, concerned about your activities, willing to offer me a few advantages to marry you, I admit it, I saw nothing wrong with—"

"Gaining everything you wanted—me in your bed *and* the position as prime minister."

"There was more to it than that, deuce take it," he said, eyes glittering. "Once your father told me what you were doing, I was as worried about you as he. And with good reason, considering what happened on the docks."

"Don't pretend you did this because you care about me," she whispered. "You used that incident at the dock to compromise me, to force me to marry you."

"That was *not* what I started out to do, and you know it. I called for a doctor, for God's sake!"

I will not risk seeing you end up dead.

She shook off the memory. Simon was very good at pretending to care. "You still turned it to your benefit, the way you do everything. You wanted to give my father what he asked for—getting me out of politics." Despair gripped her. "Was what I did really so very awful that you would go behind my back—"

"Men were talking about ruining your reputation to

stop your meddling, Louisa," Simon snapped, "so clearly *someone* thought you were reckless."

"And you?" She stared at him. "You saw the prison, the women, the children. Did *you* think my activities reckless?"

"When you're talking about putting up radical candidates, yes." As she opened her mouth to retort, he added quickly, "I am not going to discuss politics with you right now, when you are too angry to think rationally."

His condescension infuriated her. "I am perfectly rational, sir. Enough to know when I've been bested by a master." She drew herself up stiffly. "You set out to have your cake and eat it, too. And you would have succeeded if I hadn't—" A sob rose in her throat that she ruthlessly stifled. "Unfortunately, in this case the cake just happens to have an opinion about the matter."

Wrenching her arm free, she backed away. "There is nothing I can do to remove the cake from your grasp. Even if it were possible, a divorce is out of the question. A scandal would destroy my reform efforts as surely as marrying you probably will." She tugged her wrapper closer about her body. "But I'll be damned before I let you eat your cake, as well."

Whirling around, she headed for the stairs.

"What the devil does that mean?" he demanded as he raced to keep up with her.

"I will be your wife in public, because you leave me no choice. But you can forget about ever sharing my bed."

He swore a vile oath. "You are only saying that to strike back at me. When you calm down, you will realize—"

"I made one mistake. I shan't make another. You can't stop me from my activities if you don't get me with child, so I'll make sure you never do."

"What?" He stepped in front of her on the stairs to block her path. "You can't do that, damn you! I'm your husband!"

"Yes, because I was stupid enough to think you had changed. But you're the same Simon you always were, and I did *not* agree to marry *that* Simon."

Fury and candlelight lent his face an unholy glow. "Unfortunately, only one Simon signed the marriage certificate and made his vows, so you are married to *that* Simon whether you like it or not." He backed her down the stairs with implacable steps. "And if you refuse to honor the marriage in every way, then your association with the London Ladies will end right now."

A chill ran down her spine. "But you promised—"

"You swore in a church to be my wife, to honor, serve, and obey me. If you go back on your promise, I sure as the devil can go back on mine."

How dare he? She had a right to be angry after what he'd done. Yet he would punish *her* for what *he* had done?

She would *not* let him think he could get 'round her, the scheming scoundrel. "You can't stop me from doing as I please."

"You think not, do you?" He moved inexorably forward, forcing her down the stairs. "If not for my ambitions, you and I would already be on our honeymoon. Yet as much as I wish to stay in London right now, if I hear that you have even attempted to meet with the London Ladies, whether at the prisons or someone's home, I swear I will whisk you off to Italy or Spain or some other spot on the Continent. And we will stay there a *year,* if that is what it takes to bring you to your senses."

She thrust out her chin. "You wouldn't do that—leaving England would hurt your plans to become prime minister."

"No more than having a wife consorting with radicals would. So what is it to be, Louisa? A real marriage as we agreed? Or no cake for anyone?"

She stared at him, seething. "Go to hell."

He recoiled as if she'd slapped him. Then his eyes narrowed. "Not without you." And before she could do anything to prevent it, he dragged her up against him and kissed her hard.

Her temper white-hot, she'd already brought her hands up to shove him away when he drew back, his eyes boring into her like shards of ice. "I could *make* you share my bed if I choose. It is my right."

"Go ahead," she retorted. "But afterward you'd better sleep with a dagger at your side, because I swear I will kill you for it."

Twisting free of him, she dashed past him and up the steps. Thankfully, he didn't come after her, because she was half-afraid she would push him down the stairs if he did.

How dare he threaten her! *He* was the one in the wrong. *He* was the one who'd promised her father behind her back that he would curb her activities.

He also said he would uphold his promise to let you continue with the London Ladies, until you got his back up.

Oh, that was just his excuse. Eventually he would have trumped up some other reason for restricting her. It didn't serve his purposes to let her be part of the London Ladies, and Simon the Schemer always did what served his purposes.

As tears stung her eyes once again, she burst into her bedchamber and slammed the door. She was not going to waste tears on that wretch. She was *not*!

Dashing them away, she paced the floor. Nor would she let him get his way this time. Not for nothing had she spent the past few years teaching women how to get around their husbands.

Dictate her activities to her, would he? No cake for anyone, eh? Well, she'd just see about that. By the time she was done with the Duke of Foxmoor, he would rue the day he'd ever schemed to marry her.

Chapter Eighteen

Dear Charlotte,
Surely Foxmoor would not have married her with-
out feeling something deeper for her, not when there
are countless more eligible females to hand. Still, you
must admit passion has its place. It doesn't make up
for everything perhaps, but certainly a great deal.
Your cousin,
Michael

Two evenings after his thwarted wedding night, Simon strode into his dining room, then cursed as he saw the empty chair at the other end of the table. Still sulking, was she? "Where is my wife?" he asked the footman.

"She asked that a tray be brought up to her room. I took it up already."

So he couldn't even commandeer the tray in an attempt to see her.

Good God, he was thinking like a besotted idiot again. This was what his own wife had reduced him to, damn her.

And damn the king, too, and the whole bloody family. He must have been insane to get himself mixed up with them again. Louisa was volatile, her father a fool, and her brother a nuisance at best. He ought to wash his hands of the lot.

But he couldn't. He was married to her now, God help him.

With a groan, he took his usual seat at the table. His latest strategy wasn't working. After his temper had cooled, he had thought he would give her time for *hers* to cool, and then perhaps they could have a reasonable conversation.

Bloody stubborn female. "Reasonable" wasn't in her vocabulary.

Of course, his ultimatum had not helped. But he'd be damned if he would rescind his order. She was *not* going to twist him about her finger. He was the head of this house, by God, and she would learn to accept that if it took forever.

A sigh escaped his lips. Right. As if he could last forever in this limbo. He couldn't eat, couldn't sleep. During the day, he only half paid attention to what was said in the House, and at night, during his hunt through Grandfather's letters, he had to read most of them twice.

What the deuce did she do all day, anyway? She didn't go walking—he had charged a footman to accompany her if she did. Whenever he was home, he heard her moving around in the room adjoining his and saw the trays left outside her door. Apparently she ate in the dining room when he was in sessions.

The footman set a bowl of something white in front of him, and he tensed at this other, more tangible proof of her presence. "What is this?" he barked.

"Smoked fish soup, sir.' "

Made with milk, no doubt. Milk-based soups and sauces turned his stomach, always had. His cook did not know that because he had been hired after Simon's return, with the other servants. So all of them would accept whatever Louisa claimed about his likes and dislikes.

And where had she learned what those were anyway?

He had a fairly good idea. "My sister came to call today, did she?'

"Yes, Your Grace. How did you know?"

"Lucky guess."

He doubted Louisa had told his sister about their battle, or Draker would be beating down the door to throttle him for hurting her feelings. His minx of a wife had doubtless couched her requests for information about his preferences by claiming that she wanted to be a good wife.

He should have guessed what she was up to when his brandy began to taste noticeably less potent, and the fire in his room was allowed to go out frequently. But last night, when the servant told him it was his wife's idea to have his cigars tossed out so she could buy him better ones, Simon had finally realized what was going on.

She was using her "domestic warfare" tactics on him. And they were actually working. He had never been so uncomfortable in his own home in his whole life. Bloody conniving female.

Women are like horses, his grandfather's voice sounded in his head. *Give them their heads and they will trample you. They must be broken to the bridle if they're to give you a proper ride.*

"Yes, and you did such a good job of that, old man," Simon snapped. "That's why Grandmother cringed whenever you entered a room."

"Your Grace?" the footman said.

"Er . . . nothing. Just thinking through a speech." God, now he was talking to himself. That was what Louisa had done to him.

Simon pushed the soup aside. "Take this away, will you?"

The footman did it without comment, but when he brought the next course—a joint of beef ruined by a thick overlay of creamy sauce—Simon lost his temper.

Enough of this nonsense. He was not going to let her get away with this. She'd had plenty of time to get over her anger at his colluding with her father. It was going to end right now.

Shoving away from the table, he left the dining room and headed for the stairs. He was halfway up when he saw Louisa's maid slip out of her room with her discarded clothes. Good. Louisa had just dressed for bed, so he would catch her alone with her door unlocked. That was another thing that must stop, damn it—her locking her doors against him.

He jerked the door open, several husbandly admonitions leaping to his lips, but they died unsaid when he spotted her.

She sat by the hearth but she didn't see him, for her head was down and she was brushing her hair in long, slow strokes. He sucked in a breath at the picture she made, her inky tresses flowing to the floor and the firelight shining through her sheer nightdress to silhouette every soft, seductive curve. As if in a trance, he entered the room and headed for her, wanting nothing more than to haul her into his arms and kiss the stubbornness right out of her.

Then a sound arrested him. Weeping. She wept as she brushed, the sobs wracking her slender frame. Hearing them was like a knife blade to the gut.

He froze, half of him angry at himself for letting her tears affect him, and the other half wanting desperately to comfort her, to embrace her and assure her that everything would be all right.

That was exactly what she wanted, wasn't it? To bring him to his knees. To soften him until he allowed her to do as she pleased—consorting with radicals, ruining any hope of his being prime minister.

He would not let her do it, damn it!

He stood there another moment, uncertain. But in the end, his pride got the better of him and he left for his study, desperate to drive the sounds of her pitiful sobs from his head.

But being in his study only reminded him of her look of betrayal once she had realized that he had conspired with her father. He had hurt her badly. Not just once, but twice. Could he really blame her for wanting to strike back at him?

After an hour of such tormenting thoughts he went to bed, only to be plagued by them there, too. But sleeping was worse, for he saw her in his dreams, wearing her sheer nightdress on their wedding night, a hopeful smile trembling on her lips. Until her father walked in and the smile turned to shock.

When he awoke at dawn, hard as stone and restless, she was still asleep. And as on the past two mornings, though he dawdled, he ended up having to leave for Westminster Palace without ever hearing her stir in the adjoining room.

A few more days, he told himself. *Give her time.*

But how many more of these days could he stand, the hours bleeding into each other, one long monotonous torture?

Even being at Westminster did not help. With no important issues on the agenda just now, the lords had little interest in Parliamentary business and the speeches were dull as a rusty penknife. Halfway through the morning, he was contemplating going home when a voice hissed at him from close by, "What the devil are *you* doing here?"

He turned to see Lord Trusbut staring at him in alarm. "Why shouldn't I be here?"

"You said you would go with the ladies to Newgate. I counted on it when I sent my wife off with yours."

Simon stared at the man. Surely Trusbut was mistaken. Louisa would not have defied him so openly. Not after what he'd threatened. "They . . . er . . . went this morning?"

"Yes, just as they'd planned," Trusbut whispered. "Your wife told us the day before your wedding that today's trip to Newgate wouldn't be affected by your marrying, so I brought Lillian to your house just an hour ago."

Two men nearby frowned at them, so Simon motioned to Trusbut to go with him into the hall. Once there, he snapped, "Are you sure they went to the prison?" He'd given express orders to the coachman that she was not to take any coach anywhere without Simon's permission.

Trusbut eyed him as if he'd lost his mind. "Of course. Your wife asked if I meant to join them, and I told her I was going to my club. When I asked to see you, she explained that you were coming from here to join them at Newgate. That's why she requested that I carry her and Lillian to Lady Draker's house—so you wouldn't have to leave two equipages near the prison. I was happy to oblige—it was on my way to the club. But then I remembered I wanted to speak to Peel, so I came to find him. And found you here instead."

"Yes," Simon said grimly. Here in Parliament. While his wife trotted off to do exactly as she pleased. Domestic warfare was one thing, but out-and-out defiance was unacceptable.

He was not fool enough to admit to Trusbut that he couldn't even control his own wife. "Sorry, old man," he said tersely, "I forgot entirely about the trip to Newgate. And since I left before the duchess was awake, she had no chance to remind me." He headed for the door. "I am going there now." *And taking my wife in hand, damn it.*

"I'll go with you," Trusbut said. "I see that Peel isn't here anyway."

Moments later they were in Simon's carriage, silently trundling toward Newgate. Thank God Trusbut wasn't a chatty sort, because Simon doubted he could carry on a civil conversation just now.

When they reached the prison, a guard led them through several dank, gloomy halls. They moved at a snail's pace to allow for Lord Trusbut's game leg, so by the time they reached the women's ward, Simon's anger was at fever pitch.

But it faded at the sight that greeted them as the guard ushered them inside. Over two hundred women sat on the stone floor in small and orderly groups, diligently painting wooden carvings. Mrs. Fry, Mrs. Harris, and

Regina moved among them to help. Though the women wore meager clothing, it was clean and neat and, for the most part, proper.

A burst of laughter from the corner made the laboring women glance up, then smile indulgently toward where a group of children milled about, clapping at some entertainment that he and Trusbut were too far away to see. Which was, of course, being provided by Simon's wife, along with Lady Trusbut.

Simon motioned to Trusbut and they made their slow way around the crowd. As they approached their wives, Simon could hear a bird trilling over the buzz of female conversation. Then he spotted Lady Trusbut's canary perched on a chair, and beside it, Raji dancing with his usual glee.

Simon caught his breath. He ought to be angry that Louisa had brought his pet here without his knowing, but how could he when the children watched enraptured, their little faces animated with delight?

Lady Trusbut was the first to notice him. When she saw her husband, she broke into a smile so broad it wiped years from her aging face. Simon did not have to look at Trusbut to know that the smile was returned, the way a wife's smile *should* be. By a caring husband.

He winced.

Louisa had not spotted them yet, but she was smiling, too, as she watched the children enjoy the antics of Raji and Lady Trusbut's canary. Indeed, her face wore a look of such pure pleasure that a lump caught in his throat to see it.

And suddenly her defiance of him did not matter so much. The only thing that mattered was figuring out how to keep that look on her face.

So when she glanced over at them and her smile faltered, he cursed himself for ever conspiring with her father. If he had simply courted her like a proper gentleman before marrying her, would they now be estranged? Was it too late to make it right?

He hoped not. Because at this moment, he would crawl through broken glass if it would make her smile again.

Chapter Nineteen

Dear Cousin,

After seeing how Foxmoor looked at Louisa today at the prison, I have hope that their marriage may one day prove a love match, if they can refrain from discussing politics. Louisa tells me that her husband is not at all pleased by our choice of Charles Godwin as a candidate.

Your opinionated cousin,
Charlotte

Louisa jerked her gaze away in a panic. Good heavens, Simon was here. How had he found out?

Lord Trusbut, of course. She should have known she'd be caught. What had she been thinking? Her husband would never forgive her for this. He would whisk her off to Italy and that would be the end of her hopes for the London Ladies.

But what else could she do when Lady Trusbut showed up with her canary, eager to go off to Newgate? Tell her that Simon forbade it? She couldn't destroy the woman's budding interest in the London Ladies before it even had a chance to flower.

She sighed. What would he do now? Drag her out? Lecture her before her friends? Order Raji to dance on her head?

"Raji," Simon said, then added a command in Hindi.

The monkey made a pretty bow to the children, then began marching like a soldier, his hand in a salute.

As the children burst into laughter, her gaze shot to Simon. He was watching her, but he didn't look angry. He looked like an urchin gazing through a toy shop window at what he couldn't have.

It was a most unsettling glance, haunting her, chipping away at her anger. That had been crumbling for days, every time she heard him pace his bedchamber or saw him pore over papers in his study, with his cravat askew and his face weary.

Not that any of that compared to what he'd done to her, of course. And yet—

She had to admit that Simon's present betrayal differed vastly from seven years ago. For one thing, he'd actually married her. Considering that he'd already compromised her and destroyed her reputation, there'd been no need for him to carry it so far just to remove her from politics.

And he *had* said he'd married her because he wanted her. That must be true, or he wouldn't have lost his temper when she'd denied him her bed. He would have just trotted off to find a mistress.

She swallowed. How did she know he hadn't?

Oh, she should never have said what she did. Despite what he'd done, the thought of him sharing some other woman's bed tortured her.

And that was only the least of what he *could* have done if he'd wanted. Another husband might have locked her up or beaten her—such things did happen, even in the finest homes. He could even have demanded his marital rights by force. Her puny warning to kill him wouldn't have worried a real tyrant.

But Simon wasn't a real tyrant. Somewhere in that devious, scheming soul of his was a reasonable man—she just knew it. A man she could care for. The problem was, how was she to get to *that* man? Simply give in? Forgive him for his unforgivable behavior?

She had to do something. He was her husband whether she liked it or not. Did she really want the sort of distant marriage her own parents had endured?

She stole another glance at him, her heart thundering to see the yearning in his face as he stared at her.

When their gazes locked, Simon said hoarsely, "Raji, stop." After the monkey complied, he added something in Hindi and Raji scurried over to her. She glanced down to find the dear creature holding his tiny hand out. Not sure what to do, she took it, then caught her breath when he kissed it.

As the children squealed with delight, her gaze returned to Simon. His eyes held such brooding desire that her pulse began to thump madly.

"Your Grace!" called a voice from behind Simon and Lord Trusbut, and Simon turned toward it.

A guard with an eye patch approached them, and Simon broke into a smile. "Captain Quinn!"

When he offered his hand, Captain Quinn pumped it hard. "I heard you were here, sir. Thought I'd come and thank you. Mr. Brown told me you were the person who recommended me for this position, despite my bad eye."

Simon smiled. "Why shouldn't I? Your one good eye is probably twice as sharp as any other man's two."

"I gather it's sharper than those of the fellow I replaced," Captain Quinn said grimly. "Turns out the wretch made a practice of looking the other way while the prisoners regularly assaulted the women. Took money from the male convicts for it, of course. Must have been what got him sacked."

"That wasn't the only thing that got Mr. Treacle sacked, I assure you," Simon said tersely.

Louisa caught her breath. Brutus the Bully had been sacked? It must have been at Simon's instigation or how would he have known to suggest a replacement?

What's more, Captain Quinn clearly had a conscience. So while she'd been preparing for their wedding, Simon had been improving matters at the prison.

A slow warmth built in her belly. He must have done it for her. Heaven knew he'd have no other reason.

"How do you know the duke, Captain Quinn?" Lord Trusbut asked.

"His Grace and I were at the Battle of Kirkee together, sir. Never seen a man fight so hard or long without a lick of soldierly training. His Grace can wield a sword with deadly accuracy. But it wasn't his sword that won the day—it was his rousing speech. Turned that battle 'round, it did."

Simon looked more uncomfortable than she'd ever seen him. "Nonsense," he said tightly, "it was you lads who turned it 'round with your hard fighting."

"The sepoys would have fled if you hadn't bucked them up and then joined them in the fight. The only other Governor-General to fight beside them was Wellington, and he was a soldier by training." Captain Quinn broadened his gaze to include them all. "The duke was a hero, slashing and parrying like some mad—"

"Forgive me, you have not yet met my friends, have you, sir?" Simon interrupted, his voice decidedly strained.

As he introduced the Trusbuts, Louisa watched him speculatively. Why did talk of India always make him uncomfortable? The papers had lauded his performance at Kirkee. Was he simply too modest to acknowledge it?

Simon turned to Louisa. "And this, Captain Quinn, is my wife."

"Your Grace," Captain Quinn murmured as he bowed.

She had to resist the urge to laugh. She'd been Miss North for so long that being the Duchess of Foxmoor would take some getting used to. "I'm pleased to meet any friend of my husband's, sir," she said as she held out her hand.

Captain Quinn's face lit up at this show of congeniality. "The pleasure is all mine, madam." Seizing her hand, he pumped it as furiously as he'd done Simon's. "I always said His Grace must have some extraordinary female awaiting him in England, given the way he kept to himself in India."

As a blush stained her cheeks, Simon said in a husky voice, "Indeed, Captain, for what man could look at any other woman, with a lady like my wife filling his thoughts?"

Yesterday, the compliment would have grated. But today . . .

Today, she hoped desperately that he meant it.

When Captain Quinn returned to his duties, Louisa half expected her husband to give some excuse for whisking her off. Instead, he asked how he and Lord Trusbut could help.

With her heart in her throat, Louisa told him he could

entertain the younger children, since Lady Trusbut was eager to show her husband around the ward and explain what the ladies were trying to accomplish.

Louisa settled the older ones down for a lesson in reading, while Simon whittled the little ones simple monkeys and birds with Raji settled atop his shoulder. From time to time, she glanced over to see him earnestly listening to some three-year-old's chatter.

He made such a strange picture there in the prison, dressed in a fine bottle-green coat and buff trousers, with his immaculately tied cravat and his starched collar points wilting in the damp.

Her husband, the duke, helping in Newgate. It was hard to fathom.

They departed two hours later. Regina agreed to carry the Trusbuts back to Westminster to retrieve their equipage. That left Louisa and Simon to climb into his carriage alone, since Raji was ensconced on the perch with the coachman.

An awkward silence ensued once they pulled away. Now was his chance to lecture her, yet he sat across from her, staring out the window, deep in thought. Should she *ask* what he meant to do with her?

Not unless she wanted to remind him that she'd done what he'd forbidden. So she tried small talk instead. "Captain Quinn seems nice. A decided improvement over Mr. Treacle."

"Yes."

She twisted her hands together in her lap. "I suppose you were the one who had Brutus the Bully sacked."

"I did strongly encourage Mr. Brown in that direction."

"Thank you," she said softly.

His gaze swung to her, solemn, intense. "You're welcome."

"Captain Quinn will be a decided improvement."

A faint smile touched his lips. "You said that already."

She licked her own lips nervously. "He seems quite admiring of you. You'll have to tell me what happened at Kirkee—it sounds like an exciting tale."

His face grew shuttered and he shifted his gaze out the window once more, a frown creasing his brow.

That was the wrong thing to say. She didn't want him angry. She didn't want to be at odds with him anymore. The Simon who'd entertained the children at the prison was a man she could live with—as long as he stopped being a tyrant about her activities. "Simon, I know you're probably very angry at me for—"

"Defying me?" His gaze shot back to her. "Going off to the prison behind my back? Taking Raji to a place he's never been without me?"

Her heart sank at the edge in his voice. "Raji was fine, and you know it. Besides, you started this by conspiring with the king. Surely you see that was deplorable." When his jaw tightened, she groaned. "But that wasn't what I meant to say."

"No, I am sure it was not," he said bitterly. "You probably meant to point out yet again how horrible I have been to you by marrying you and sharing with you my name, my wealth, my connections—"

"I want cake," she blurted out. When he blinked, she added in a soft voice, "That's what I meant to say. I want cake. For both of us."

Chapter Twenty

❦

Dear Charlotte,
    A man may look affectionately upon his wife, but that does not mean that when faced with important decisions, he will allow her to influence him. I would not place too much hope in a tender glance, my dear.
                         Your forthright cousin,
                                  Michael

For a second, Louisa wasn't entirely certain Simon had taken her meaning. Then a look of such stark, wild hunger crossed his features that her breath caught in her throat. Before she could even think, he'd reached across the carriage and hauled her onto his lap.

"What are you doing?" she exclaimed, darting a glance at the window.

"Eating cake," he murmured. Then his mouth seized hers.

She forgot about the crowded streets outside the carriage windows. She forgot about her anger and his machinations and her father. There was only Simon, plundering her mouth like a marauding conqueror, his hands sweeping possessively over her body, his breath wafting hot and heavy over her face.

He paused to drag the curtains closed, but as he bent his mouth to hers again, she pressed a finger to his lips. When a scowl twisted his brow, she said hastily, "I want to make sure we're in agreement. We *both* get cake. Which means you'll let me participate in the London Ladies."

His eyes glittered a searing blue. "You will share my bed? And stop telling the servants to feed me things I detest? And give me back my cigars?"

She gave a shaky laugh. "I didn't think you'd noticed."

"Of course I noticed. The same way I noticed the trays outside your room and your absence at dinner and the cold, empty space in my bed . . ." His choked words seduced her as effectively as the kisses he now scattered over her cheeks, her nose, her brow.

"The London Ladies," she rasped while she still had the power to speak. "Will you let me—"

"Do you mean to defy me again?" he countered.

"I might." She scowled at him. "If you make unfair pronouncements."

"Wrong answer," he growled.

She'd already opened her mouth to retort when she felt his hands unbuttoning the back of her gown. "We can't do this here, for heaven's sake!"

"The devil we can't." He was disturbingly adept at undoing her clothing. "I'm not taking any chances with you this time, sweetheart. I mean to make you mine before you change your mind. I cannot go another night alone in my bed, thinking of you alone in yours."

Though his words thrilled her, they weren't the ones she wanted to hear. "But you haven't yet agreed—"

"If you want to negotiate terms, give me some incentive." After removing her gloves, he dragged her gown and chemise and stays down in one fell swoop to bare her breasts, then scoured her with his ravenous gaze, sending her blood into a frenzy.

As she warmed to his clear admiration, he bent his head to seize her breast in his mouth, sucking it so sensuously that she squirmed on his lap.

He devoured first one, then the other, while she buried her hands in his thick hair to hold him close. "Now this, sweetheart," he rasped, pausing briefly to tongue her nipple, "is what I call cake."

Cake, yes. The dratted seducer had made her forget about the cake. "The London Ladies, Simon," she whispered, though it got harder to speak when he was sliding his hands beneath her skirts. "Will you let me participate?"

"Do you promise never to defy me?" he shot back.

"It depends—"

"Wrong answer again." He found the aching spot between her thighs and thumbed it so that she gasped. "You are my wife. I will not have you going behind my back. Is that clear?"

"Yes, but—"

"Never again do I wish to have some lord accusing me of not holding to my word because my wife lied to him."

She winced. She probably *shouldn't* have told Lord Trusbut that her husband was meeting them at the prison. But how could she have known he would then run into Simon?

"Is that understood, Louisa?" He brushed his mouth against her ear as his forefinger delved suddenly, shockingly inside her.

She wriggled to get free, but that only made it worse when his finger swept along her cleft in a silky caress so erotic, she gasped. Then writhed against it in an attempt to feel more.

Simon's breath quickened as he laid her out across his lap to give him better access to her breasts.

"Understood, Louisa?" he repeated, tugging at her nipple with his teeth. "No going anywhere behind my back."

When he punctuated the demand with a maddening caress down below, she whispered, "Yes . . . oh, good heavens, yes . . ."

Then, realizing what he'd made her say, she stiffened. He was trying to seduce her into agreeing with him. And it was working.

Very well, seduction was a game for couples, wasn't it? As he teased her nipple with his devilish tongue, she untied his cravat and tossed it aside, then unbuttoned his waistcoat and shirt. He drew back only long enough to remove it all.

She blinked. Now *that* was a chest, very nicely swathed in muscle, the way a man's chest should be. She looked her fill, since it was her first look at her husband's naked body. Dark blond hair trickled from his throat to where it broadened to take in his whole chest, swirling about his male nipples, then narrowing to a thin line over a flat, taut stomach before disappearing beneath his trousers. Which were noticeably bulging.

And swelling even more beneath her gaze.

"Don't just look, sweetheart," he said hoarsely. "Touch me, too."

With a blush she dragged her gaze back to his face. "Wh-what?"

"Put your sweet hands on me." He practically ripped loose the buttons on his trousers and drawers. "Anywhere. Everywhere. Here."

He seized her hand and tried to force it inside his drawers, but remembering her purpose, she resisted. "And where's *my* incentive, husband? I get cake, too, remember?"

Eyes smoldering, he slid his hand beneath her skirts once more, but she stayed him with her other hand. "Not that sort of incentive, drat you. Since I agreed not to go anywhere without your knowing, you should agree not to restrict my activities with the London Ladies."

When a frown touched his brow, she slid her hand beneath his drawers to caress his thigh. His naked, brawny thigh. He sucked in a harsh breath.

Delighted to have such an effect on him, she slid her hand closer to his ballocks, skirting them, brushing them . . . teasing them. "You did promise me that when we agreed to marry, you know."

With a groan, he closed his eyes. "Yes, but . . . that was before I found out you were courting . . . radicals."

"According to my father," she said as she stroked everywhere but his rigid flesh, "you knew I was. You said that's why you married me. To stop me."

He squirmed beneath her hand. She slid one finger along his heavy arousal, but when he pushed against her palm, she withdrew.

His eyes shot open to blaze at her. "What do you want from me?"

"Our original agreement—that you won't restrict my activities with the London Ladies." She fondled his shaft, and he groaned.

"All right, damn you." Sliding her off him and onto the

seat, he knelt on the floor between her legs, then tugged her closer. "You can have your original agreement."

She beamed at him. "Thank you. That's all I wanted."

"I do have one condition." Eyes alight, he shoved her skirts back to bare her below the waist.

She grabbed his shoulders. "Oh?"

"Since allowing you to consort with radicals would damage my future in politics, you must let me advise your group on their choice of candidate. You owe me that, at least."

"Advise. Not browbeat."

"Advise," he repeated, then bent his head to suck her breast. "Come now, wife, I am being most accommodating, and you know it."

"Fine, though undoubtedly I'll regret it."

"I will make sure that you don't." Then a wicked smile crossed his face, and he shoved down his drawers and trousers.

"Oh Lord," she said as an instrument of rather sobering proportions sprang free. So that . . . beast was what she'd been fondling? It hadn't felt so large. How on earth did any sane woman "lay there and let the man do what he wants" when he was assaulting her with *that*? "Um, one more thing—"

"Negotiations over," he snapped as he aimed the thick rod of flesh between her legs. "The only words I want to hear out of your mouth for the next hour are 'Yes, Simon . . . more, Simon . . . please, Simon . . .'"

"Please, Simon," she whispered as the tip brushed her curls. "Try not to slay me with that beast of yours."

"Beast?" Simon halted to stare at her, then let out a choked laugh. "My God, you're a virgin."

"Of course!" She drew herself up. "You didn't actually

believe what I babbled in the woods about having been with other men."

"Certainly not," he hastened to say. "It is just that when I am with you I forget . . . I mean, you are so damned—"

"Wanton?"

"Wonderful." He nuzzled her cheek. "I get carried away, and I forget."

He angled his shaft up between her thighs, a hot, heavy reminder of what they were about to do. When he caressed her between the legs with it, rubbing it up and down against her damp curls, she caught her breath, torn between the pleasure it gave and the pain it promised.

"In the past seven years," he went on, "you and I have made love in my dreams so often . . . I have to remind myself that you have not actually done it."

"You really dreamt of me?" Now he was opening her with his warm fingers, smearing her with her own juices. "That wasn't just something you said so I would let down my guard?"

"God, you have no idea," he said hoarsely as he slid inside her.

To take her mind off the strange and rather uncomfortable intrusion, she asked, "What exactly did I . . . do in your dreams?"

"You tempted me with your hair and breasts and belly. You rubbed your nipples against my chest—"

"Like this?" she whispered as she did what he'd said.

He gave a harsh laugh. "Yes, Cleopatra, exactly like that." His eyes glimmered. "And you put your hands on my a— . . . my buttocks. Try that, too."

Although she blushed, she did as he ordered, but when she went a step further and squeezed the firm flesh, he surged inside her. Instinctively she tensed to feel him so thick there.

"It's all right, you're doing fine," he said huskily. He slid his hand between them to find that spot that always seemed to crave his touch. When he stroked it, she relaxed, allowing him to slip even deeper.

A groan escaped his lips. "That's it, sweetheart, let me in. That's even better than I dreamt."

"It's not at all what I dreamt," she said dryly.

"What did you dream?" He continued to stroke her where they were joined, which did make it easier to endure him inside her.

"I-I don't know." She remembered how Regina had once described it to her. "Angels . . . harps . . . like it was when you . . . did those things with your mouth to me in my bedchamber. Only better."

"Give me a chance, and you'll have that again. But first . . ." He drew back to stare at her ruefully. "I'm told that purgatory comes before heaven for virgins."

She eyed him skeptically. "Purgatory?" She'd heard varying accounts of a virgin's pain. The same varying accounts she'd heard about childbirth. And Lord knew how reliable some of *those* were. "Or hell?"

"You tell me." Giving her no time to tense up, he plunged deep inside her.

The pain was sudden, intense . . . and brief. It took a few moments for it to pass. Then she sagged against him, relieved that it hadn't been worse.

He brushed a kiss to her forehead. "Well?"

She wriggled experimentally, but there was only a lingering soreness. "Definitely purgatory," she pronounced.

"Thank God." He clutched her hard against him. "Because after seven years, stopping now would be hell for me."

He began to move, and she caught her breath. It was . . . intriguing, to say the least. Quite . . . invigorating.

Then he thrust particularly deep, and her pulse leapt. Good heavens. That wasn't like anything she'd ever felt, not even that night in the bedchamber. There was something so . . . amazing about being joined to him like this.

Now he was kissing her, his tongue hot and strong, surging inside her mouth the way he surged inside her body, and the multiple sensations began to swamp her. His thrusts beat in counterpoint to the swaying of the coach, the thundering hooves . . . the clamoring of her heart. Soon the wild rhythm quickened, building, growing, running away with her . . .

"Do you want me, Louisa?" he tore his lips free to growl, reminding her of that day in her bedchamber when he'd made her beg.

"Yes . . . I want you, Simon."

With a groan, he increased his pace. She grabbed at his buttocks to hold on, joining them even more intimately. He drove inside her over and over until her head spun and her body soared and she couldn't stay anchored to the earth . . .

"Yes, sweetheart, yes," he rasped as he plunged to the hilt. "Yes!"

And in that moment the heavens opened up, and angels and harps rained music down around her, blending with her cries.

With a guttural cry of his own, Simon flooded her with his essence, clasping her so tightly she didn't know where he began and she ended.

For a moment she felt suspended in the heavens, joined to Simon inextricably for eternity while his seed still poured inside her and her heart beat a madly exultant rhythm.

Then her heart began to slow and his breathing to settle. The creak of the carriage intruded in her thoughts, along with the realization that they were inches away from a city full of people who had no clue what they were doing.

A little embarrassed, she loosed her hold on him.

But he wasn't done. "You are my wife now," he whispered fiercely, still clasping her to him. "You are mine, Louisa. My wife. Say it."

"Your wife," she echoed, the words feeling more like a vow than anything she'd said at their wedding. "I'm yours."

Some of the fierceness left his face, and he buried his face in her neck, his arms so tight around her that she could hardly breathe. "Don't ever deny me your bed again. I don't think I could bear it twice."

She stroked his hair, the rough pain in his voice melting her heart. Their joining was clearly more than mere lovemaking to him, and that made her regret being so harsh before. "There's no need," she whispered.

Besides, today had made her realize the risk she'd taken. Denied an outlet for his urges, a man was liable to find it elsewhere. Especially a man like the Duke of Foxmoor, who could have any woman he wanted. The very thought of him doing something like this with another woman made her ill.

"You'll be a real wife to me from now on," he said.

"Yes." She hesitated, but she had to be sure. "As long as you're a real husband to me."

He pulled back to eye her warily. "What do you mean?"

"I won't tolerate a mistress, Simon. I'm not sure I could even tolerate your going to a bawdy house."

Relief, then amusement shone in his face. "Didn't you suggest only a few days ago that I do so?"

She glowered at him. "Now see here—"

"I am only teasing you," he said with a light kiss to her nose. "Trust me, the last place you will ever find me is a bawdy house."

He said it with such conviction that she believed him. "And a mistress? You won't take one?"

His amusement faded to solemnity. "Not even if you banished me from your bed forever."

She swallowed, not quite sure she believed him. "Why not?"

His eyes began to smolder as he lifted his hand to cup her breast. "Because I happen to like only one flavor of cake, sweetheart." He kissed her neck. "Yours."

As he thumbed her nipple, the heat rose in her again. Oh, she truly was her mother's daughter. And just now she was glad of it.

"You see how easy I am to please?" he said. "Give me cake, and you can do whatever you want. At least until you find yourself *enceinte.*"

She stiffened. Her sponges! Good heavens, she'd forgotten all about them. Too late to do anything about it now, but she must not forget again.

He nuzzled her cheek. "I suspect it won't be long until you are with child. Because when a man eats as much cake as I intend to, children inevitably follow."

The thrill coursing through her was tempered by the knowledge that she still intended to use her sponges. Just for a while. Surely she could be forgiven for that.

You should tell him about the sponges. Simon would understand.

Would he? No other man would. And Simon was more determined to have his way than most. No, she couldn't tell him yet. But it would be all right; they'd been married less than a week. What was a few more days alone together before she had to think about children? Surely she could get past her fear eventually.

And if she didn't?

She'd cross that bridge when she came to it. Which hopefully wouldn't be anytime soon.

Several hours later, Simon lay in his bedchamber beside his sleeping wife and wondered if he would ever be able to satisfy his sweet tooth. He'd had "cake" twice this afternoon, and already he craved it again.

He stared down at Louisa's tousled hair and the wedge of shoulder above the covers turned golden by the waning sun. Instantly his cock stirred. God, he was a randy devil.

But seven years of celibacy would turn any man into a randy devil. Even now, he wanted to lick every inch of her fine, porcelain skin, to dip his tongue in her navel, to drink his fill of the nectar between her legs before rising up to plunge his cock so deeply inside her that—

He swore under his breath. His cock was now painfully hard. And he truly *would* be a devil to take her again. Twice was more than any virgin should have to endure on her first night.

Throwing himself back against the pillow, he laid his arm over his eyes. He should sleep. He'd certainly had little enough of it in the past few days.

Yet how could he sleep with Louisa beside him after all these years? He groaned. This obsession with his wife must stop. Bad enough that he craved her every waking moment. But she had used her delectable body to wrest concessions from him that he should never have given. He could not let that happen again.

He was supposed to be getting her *out* of politics, not advising her on candidates. If he didn't watch it, she would be coaxing him to support some idiot radical who would ruin his future as prime minister. But what was a man to do when his luscious wife put her hands where he had wanted them for years? Especially when he wanted to *keep* her putting her hands on him?

That's what mistresses are for. His grandfather's voice grated. *To satisfy you in bed so that you can keep your wits about you with your wife. A mistress has no power. But a wife has the power to ruin you, if you let her.*

Grandfather might have been right, but he could never betray Louisa that way. He would take her in hand by standing firm on the things that mattered, and giving her freedom in the things that did not. Because living like his grandfather was not an option. The devastation the old bastard had caused to everyone surrounding him made that clear.

Which reminded him . . . He glanced over, but his wife slept soundly. He could either stay here aching for her, or get something done. Clearly he was not going to sleep himself.

He left the bed, dressed, and ambled downstairs to his study. The minute he entered, Raji hurried to his side.

"Hello there, scamp." Simon lowered his arm so Raji could climb up. "Sorry to abandon you, but you'll have to get used to it. No more sleeping in my bed, I'm afraid." He chuckled. "I don't relish fighting you to get to my wife every night."

Raji chattered happily as Simon lit candles in the dusk-dark study and dragged out the last box of letters. If he did not find anything here, he was not sure what else to do. He would help Colin to whatever extent he could, of course, but he might not be able to give him what he truly wanted and deserved.

Even if Simon did find the proof, he would still have to convince the king to support Colin's claim. So far, the man had not upheld any other part of his bargain. His Majesty had not gained Liverpool's resignation. He hemmed and hawed about its being better to wait until sessions were over.

Ignoring Raji, who was sniffing his hair, probably smelling Louisa's lilac scent on it, Simon took out the top batch of letters and began to read. He was well into his tenth when a sound from the doorway made him look up.

Louisa stood there wearing nothing but her wrapper and her smile.

His pulse quickened instantly. *Steady, man. She will not be ready for you again so soon.*

"I did not want to wake you," he explained when she continued to stand there, one eyebrow raised.

"I suppose I shall have to get used to a husband who rushes off to his study every chance he gets."

"It was either that or make love to you again, and I did not think a considerate husband should do that to his newly deflowered wife."

She strolled into the room, her smile turning coquettish. "Am I so hard for you to resist?"

He raked her with his gaze. *"Hard?* Definitely."

It took her a moment to grasp the double entendre. Then she closed the door behind her and reached for the tie of her gown. "Well, then, perhaps you need some relief for your condition, my darling."

Darling. His wife had called him "darling." She had never done so before, and just the sound of it on her lips delighted him. Especially when she came toward him with seduction in her eyes.

She did not get far, however, before Raji scampered across the desk to launch himself at her.

Simon gave a rueful laugh as the monkey settled eagerly into his wife's arms. "Raji obviously will not allow that." He sat back in his chair. "And in any case, you should give yourself time to recover. Or so I hear."

Conceding the point with a shrug, she rounded the desk to stand beside him and look down at the letters. "So what do you work on so diligently every night?"

He hesitated, but there was no reason not to tell her. If anything came of it, it would affect her, too. "I am reading through Grandfather Monteith's old correspondence to see if I can find any mention of Colin Hunt."

"Colin Hunt. Wasn't he your—"

"Aide-de-camp. Yes. And quite possibly also my cousin."

She stared at him. "Your cousin."

"By my Uncle Tobias. You know, the one who died in India."

"But I thought he died alone."

"Apparently not." Simon uttered a sigh. "There's little doubt that Colin is his son. Uncle Tobias signed his name to the birth certificate as Colin's father. I have already authenticated that signature from letters, so I know that much is true."

"And the mother? Who is she?"

"An Indian woman. She died when Colin was quite

young. He was raised by his mother's sister, who says his mother was my uncle's legitimate wife."

"Wife! But that would mean—"

"That Colin is heir to my maternal grandfather's title. Yes, if I can prove the claim."

She paused to take that in. "There's no record of the marriage?"

"Unfortunately, no. Though his mother supposedly married his father in a church, the place was destroyed by a flood shortly after Uncle Tobias died."

"Convenient," Louisa pointed out.

"Yes. But the church really was destroyed. That part is fact."

"And what of their marriage certificate?"

"That is where it becomes complicated. Colin's aunt claims that when Uncle Tobias realized he was dying, he wrote to my grandfather to tell him of the marriage. He enclosed the certificate as proof. That was the last anyone saw of it. Shortly after that, my uncle died, leaving his wife and son in dire financial straits."

He fingered the letter before him. "You may not know this, but around then, Indian widows of officers were cut off from being allowed the widow's portion. So according to Colin's aunt, when Grandfather Monteith offered a healthy sum to the widow if she never pursued the matter of her son's inheritance, she agreed."

It sickened Simon to think of his grandfather taking advantage of a poor woman that way, though it didn't surprise him. Grandfather Monteith would not have been pleased to have a half-Indian grandson. He had crafted his public persona too carefully to allow such a "stain" on the family line.

"At the time," Simon went on, "Colin was the son of a

second son, so his inheritance was not of any great import anyway."

She laid her hand on Simon's shoulder. "But once your other uncle died without issue—"

"Colin became the heir. Not only to the Monteith title, but to the Monteith estates. Which have increased substantially since I have taken them over."

Louisa's hand tensed. "That would certainly give someone great incentive to lie about their heritage."

He laughed. "Colin? Hardly. I had to twist his arm to get him to be my aide-de-camp after his aunt came to me with his story. He meant to continue serving in the *peshwa's* army, but I could tell he had inherited my grandfather's keen mind. His talents were wasted as a foot soldier. Nonetheless, he never had any interest in being the earl. When I tried to convince him to return with me, he refused, saying I should let the matter stand."

"Then why are you pursuing it?"

"Colin is a man without a country. Other Indians do not accept him, and the English do not, either. It isn't right. He and his mother deserved better treatment from my grandfather, so I owe it to him to set the matter straight. And not just to him, but—" He paused, wondering if he should reveal so much, but when she squeezed his shoulder encouragingly, he went on. "To his wife, too."

"Oh, I forgot he had a wife. She was Raji's previous owner, wasn't she?"

"Yes. She, too, was half Indian. When she lay dying, I swore that I would make sure Colin got what was rightfully his. Assuming I could prove his claim."

"But why would you make such a vow? Just because he was your aide-de-camp and possibly your cousin?"

"Is that not reason enough?" he hedged. How could he

tell her the truth? She already thought him devious and a liar, but at least she seemed to think him competent as a statesman. If she knew everything—

"I think there's something you're not saying." She pulled her hand back. "I know that those Indian women are very beautiful . . ."

Bloody hell, he had not realized how this must sound. "I told you, sweetheart, I was celibate in India. I never had an affair with Colin's wife, if that is what you think."

"Then why would you make her promises?" she whispered. "You can tell me, darling, really you can, even if you just secretly cared for her or—"

"It was nothing like that." Now he *had* to tell her, if only to keep her from getting the wrong idea. Besides, the secret had lain like a sore on his soul for too long. If anyone could help him lance it, it was his forthright, practical wife. Assuming that she did not regard him with loathing, instead.

"But you are right; it was not just because of Colin that I made that vow." A ragged sigh escaped him. "It was because of what I had done. You see, I am the one who caused her death."

Chapter Twenty-One

Dear Cousin,

    Surely you acknowledge that a tender glance is sometimes all a body needs or wants. Once in a while, a tender glance is even more important than having one's opinion solicited by one's spouse.

        Your romantic-minded cousin,
        Charlotte

*L*ouisa didn't know what to think or say to his astonishing confession. "Does this have to do with that battle you and Captain Quinn fought?"

Simon shot her a veiled glance. "How did you know?"

"Today you clearly didn't want to discuss it." Louisa perched on the edge of his desk, and Raji settled himself in her lap. "Colin's wife died in that battle, didn't she?"

"Actually, she died just before it, at the hands of the Marathas. They were warriors who served as soldiers-for-hire for the *peshwa.*"

"What's a *peshwa?*"

"A sort of prime minister of a region of India. Baji Rao

was the peshwa and ordered his Marathas to raid Poona. They burned the British Resident's home to the ground, then roamed the town, pillaging and slaughtering. Colin's wife was singled out because she was half-English and married to my aide-de-camp."

"Is that why you blame yourself for her death?" Louisa asked, laying her hand on his arm.

Shrugging it off, he rose abruptly to pace. "I wish that were so. But no, my part was more . . . shameful."

His refusal to accept her comfort stung, but she tried not to show it as she sat stroking Raji's silky fur and waited.

When he spoke again, his voice was cool, remote. "Weeks before the Marathas' raid, Colin told me his wife had gone to Poona to visit her mother and was hearing rumblings in the marketplace about a revolt. The *peshwa* was angry about the treaty the British had convinced him to sign."

He strode over to a pedestal table and poured himself some brandy from a carafe there. "So I questioned two native officers from the area. They assured me all was well in Poona. 'The *peshwa* would be a fool to revolt,' they said. 'He knows the great strength of the British army,' they said."

A harsh laugh escaped his lips. "I briefly considered that they might be part of a potential rebellion, but they were highly regarded officers. Whereas Colin had every reason to resent the British. I assumed he was exaggerating the situation.

He swallowed some brandy. "I had negotiated the treaty with the *peshwa* myself. The other two *peshwas* seemed perfectly content with their treaties. So why would Baji Rao dispute his?" His tone turned self-deprecating. "I was the mighty Governor-General, after all. I knew exactly what was happening in my fiefdom."

"Oh, Simon," she whispered, but he paid her no heed.

"Besides, Colin got his information from his wife, who had even more reason to distrust the British than he did. *Her* bastard of a British father hadn't married *her* mother. So she saw rebellions where there were none." He stared blankly into the brandy glass. "I assumed she wanted me to march down to Poona with an army and make a fool of myself."

As if sensing the tension in his master, Raji slipped from her lap to join Simon, but Simon paid him no heed, either. "I didn't know her very well, and what I knew I didn't like. She thought I was another posturing Englishman, and I thought she was a troublemaker."

Simon's hands shook, making the brandy glass tremble. With her heart in her throat, Louisa left the desk to take the glass from him and set it on the table.

"So I was not about to act on the strength of her word," Simon said hoarsely. "Colin and I argued about it after the officers left. I told him he should not listen to his wife, that women were fickle creatures swayed by every emotion and not to be trusted."

Louisa swallowed. "I suppose you were thinking of how I'd had you sent off to India."

Simon's gaze shot to her. "Certainly not. I deserved what you did—even then I realized that." He raked a hand through his hair. "When I cautioned Colin, I was not thinking of any specific woman. I was just spouting nonsense my grandfather poured into my ears when I was growing up."

His grandfather? No one ever spoke ill of the Earl of Monteith, whose tenure as prime minister had been regarded as brilliant by Whig and Tory alike. But that didn't mean he hadn't been a scoundrel in his private life.

Simon sank into a nearby chair. "In the end, Colin let me guide him. He didn't have a choice—he could hardly gather a force himself to march on the *peshwa*." He buried his face in his hands. "So when the Marathas set fire to the residence at Poona, we were thirty miles away, headed for Bombay. The news reached us quickly, and we raced there with the small force we had at hand, but we arrived to find Colin's wife dying."

"And that's when you made your promise to her," she whispered.

He lifted his face to her, his anguish carving lines in his handsome features. "She had always wanted to see him get what was rightfully his. It was the only thing I could offer to make up for . . . oh God, everything."

This time when she laid her hand on his arm, he didn't resist. "That's why you fought so hard at the Battle of Kirkee," Louisa said softly. "To avenge her."

"To avenge all of them," Simon choked out. "And to pay for my error. Do you know how many innocents were killed before the battle began? How much destruction was wrought on the town because I—"

"Made a decision based on limited knowledge," she told him. "You did what any leader does. You weighed the choices and chose what seemed best."

"You don't understand," he said with a shake of his head. "I should have gone myself to assess the situation. I should not have relied on the wrong officers. I should have listened—"

"To a woman you didn't trust?"

"She was right, damn it!"

"Yes. But if you'd acted on her information and she had proved to be wrong, would you blame yourself any less for whatever ensued?"

He stared bleakly at her, then dragged her onto his lap and clasped her so tightly to his chest that she could scarcely breathe. "You are too kind to me, sweetheart."

She stroked his hair. "And you are too hard on yourself."

"Not hard enough. You didn't see Colin's wife with her blood gushing from her wound, her eyes wide with terror as death took her. And Colin weeping over her body. The images . . . still haunt me at night."

"As well they should." When his anguished gaze swung to her, she caressed his cheek. "If they didn't, you would be a cold shell of a creature, incapable of feeling. Instead of a warm-blooded man dedicated to doing what's right."

"I am not sure I know what is right. If I could make such a monumental error once—"

"You could make one again, yes. That only proves you are fallible. As we all are." She nuzzled his cheek. "And surely you learned from your mistake."

"God, I hope so." The storm of his remorse seemed to have subsided some, for his hold on her loosened.

For a long moment, they just sat there clasping each other as the bracket clock ticked above them. After a while, she said, "I'm glad you told me."

"So am I," he said in a low rumble. "I have lived with it for so long alone, chafing every time people speak of my heroic actions at the battle—"

"They *were* heroic," she protested. "Don't think otherwise. You could have buried your head in the sand or denied your culpability. Instead you led the soldiers to victory. Don't let your guilt over how it began negate what you should be proud of." She gestured to the letters. "And you're still trying to make amends, after all."

"Trying, but not succeeding, I'm afraid," he said with a sigh.

"I can help, if you want. With two of us hunting through them, we might find what you're looking for."

"That possibility becomes more remote by the day. I've never been certain I could find anything, anyway. Grandfather was too crafty—and too conscious of his public image—to keep something that might cause a scandal."

She drew back to stare at him. "You don't seem to hold your grandfather in quite as high an esteem as the rest of the world does."

"The rest of the world didn't know him," he said tersely. "The rest of the world never had to endure his 'training.'"

Her eyes narrowed. "What exactly did your grandfather do to prepare you for replacing him as prime minister?"

Simon's expression grew shuttered. "He was a stern taskmaster."

"It had to be more—"

"I do not want to talk about that now." He slid his hand inside her wrapper to caress her bare belly. "Did you not mention something earlier about giving me relief from my condition?"

When she started to speak again he kissed her hard, with a fervency clearly born out of something more than desire. He really didn't want to discuss his grandfather.

She considered pressing the matter, but he'd revealed

more about himself in the past few moments than he had in the whole time she'd known him. She didn't want to discourage him from confiding in her in the future.

So she kissed him and let him think he was taking her mind off it.

She'd always thought of Simon as devious, but perhaps "secretive" was a better word. He kept secrets because he couldn't bear to face them in the light of day. And though she suspected that he still held his darkest secrets close, she could be patient until he revealed those, too.

After all, she understood what it was like to keep secrets. Except that her secret could affect her marriage enormously if she revealed it. And she wasn't quite ready to do that, not when they were only now coming to know each other.

That was why, when he led her up to their bedchamber, she was grateful she'd already put in a fresh sponge before coming in search of him.

Over the next few days, however, the sponges got harder to manage. At night it was no trouble, for she simply insisted that her maid undress her before Simon came to her bed. And though he hinted that they could both sleep in the master bed, she pretended that she slept better alone. How else could she hurry to her dressing room to remove the sponge and clean herself with warm water as the shopkeeper in Spitalfields had instructed?

Fortunately, Simon accepted her behavior. Both her parents and his had always slept apart; those who could afford separate bedchambers usually did. Still, it pained her to have to gently request that he retire to his own bedchamber after they'd made love.

It was the other times that were a real problem—the times when he kissed her in the drawing room or the dining room or the music room. Once her blood started to heat and his hands to roam, it took all her control to insist that they retire to her bedchamber instead of letting her overeager husband take her on some sofa. Which actually sounded intriguing.

So she'd begun spending her spare time in his study, where Raji held sway and wouldn't allow any seducing. But just this morning at breakfast Simon had joked about her hiding behind Raji. If she weren't more careful, jokes could soon turn to suspicion. Given their newly married status, Simon had every reason to expect them to enjoy each other often. She *wanted* them to enjoy each other often.

She also wanted not to be forced into having children just yet.

This evening, however, she needn't worry about being tempted. The London Ladies were meeting to discuss their candidate.

As part of their agreement, Simon planned to attend the meeting. She'd even held it at the end of the day so he wouldn't have to miss Parliamentary sessions.

He walked into the drawing room, where she was already seated with Mrs. Harris, Regina, and Mrs. Fry, right on time, and took a seat across from her at the card table.

The minute Mrs. Harris mentioned Charles Godwin, it was clear he meant to get his own way, as usual.

"You do know that Godwin is a radical," Simon said.

"And what's wrong with that?" Louisa asked. "Parliament could use a few radicals these days."

"Yes, it could," he surprised her by saying. "And with

the mood of the country the way it is right now, you might even succeed in getting him elected. His newspaper gives him an edge that other radical candidates might not have."

"That was my thought, too," Louisa said, a little mollified.

"But that doesn't mean he would help your cause." Simon sat back in his chair. "Did you ladies pay attention to what happened after the St. Peter's Field affair?"

Louisa scowled. "Of course. Parliament behaved abominably, demonstrating yet again that they are behind the times. When they won't even support reform of the election process—"

"They never will, if you keep throwing radicals at them," Simon put in.

"And I suppose *you* support parliamentary reform."

"Absolutely. If England is to continue to be powerful, it *must* give the vote to more than the same few landowners. The people must have a voice."

The fervency in his tone surprised her. Parliamentary reform was not supported by Sidmouth and his cohorts. And they, like the king, had wanted Simon to silence her by marrying her.

She must never forget that. It was why Simon was at this meeting, after all.

Yet he seemed sincere. "You begin to sound like a radical yourself, sir."

"Hardly. Unlike Godwin, I mean to work within the present system. He only wants to uproot it."

That sounded more like Sidmouth. "To supplant it with something better."

"Perhaps. Though I seriously doubt that having Godwin roam the country inciting insurgency will bring about real change. It will only spawn more Peterloo Massacres, and I know that you don't want that."

"He does have a point," Regina put in.

Yes, he did, and that annoyed Louisa. Simon wasn't supposed to be the voice of reason here. "But he is still one of Sidmouth's crowd, and striking fear of revolution into the hearts of voters is their favorite tactic."

Simon fixed her with a dark glance. "Surely you can trust me to give my own opinion in this, sweetheart."

"I trust you in everything else, but not when it comes to politics. You're still too much the statesman to be trusted in that arena."

Irritation sparked in his eyes. "Have you no other candidates to consider?"

"Two others," Regina said. "William Duncombe and Thomas Fielden."

Simon's face brightened. "Fielden is an excellent choice. Support him, and no one would quarrel."

"No one would listen to him, either," Louisa said. "It would be just like having Mrs. Fry's brother-in-law in the Commons." She shot Mrs. Fry an apologetic glance. "No offense."

"None taken, dear," Mrs. Fry said. "Still, Mr. Buxton *has* paved the way for us to present the situation to the Commons."

"But what good is that if they don't *do* something about it? How long can our group continue to afford matrons and teachers? And even if Newgate is markedly better, there are other prisons we don't have the resources to address."

"These things require patience," Mrs. Fry said.

"Which is not Louisa's strong suit," Regina said.

Louisa scowled at her. "We've bided our time for three

years. We need government assistance, and we need it *now,* not three years from now."

"Newgate has been a prison for hundreds of years, sweetheart," Simon said dryly. "I don't imagine it will worsen anytime soon."

The flippant comment raised her hackles, and she drew herself up with a haughty glare. "That's exactly the sort of thing Sidmouth says to justify ignoring the plight of those poor women."

His eyes narrowed. "No, Sidmouth says that they do not deserve help. I am not saying that. I am merely pointing out that everything moves slowly in politics."

Enough of this. "Tell me something, Simon. If you were given the choice between becoming prime minister or championing prison reform, which would you choose?"

The room fell silent and he glanced about to find the other women looking at him expectantly.

Shifting uncomfortably in his chair, he turned his gaze to Louisa. "Becoming prime minister, of course." When she bristled, he said firmly, "Because I can do more good as prime minister than as a duke on the fringes of politics, pushing for prison reform. And sometimes the greater good is more important."

"That's the excuse every tyrant in history has used to justify his actions. Liverpool used it when he suspended habeas corpus a few years ago."

"And there was such an outcry from the people that it didn't stay suspended long. That is how you hold tyranny in check in England. Not by electing radicals."

She glanced around at the other women. "I suppose you all agree with him."

"Not I," Mrs. Harris said stoutly. "I think Mr. Godwin

is perfectly capable of a campaign that doesn't degenerate into violence or anarchy."

"Ah, but Mr. Godwin is your friend," Mrs. Fry pointed out. "Of course you think that."

"You have your own bias, Mrs. Fry." Louisa shot Simon a cold glance. "Which my husband is taking advantage of. He knows that any possibility of violence, however remote, makes Quakers balk at supporting a candidate."

"I am merely pointing out," Simon said tersely, "that you should consider all three candidates thoroughly before putting your weight behind Godwin. Ask them what they would do in certain situations. Determine just how reckless Godwin is. I would be happy to help you interview them, if you'd like."

"I'm sure you would," Louisa muttered.

"Come now, Louisa, you would be there to hold me in check." A sudden gleam sparked in Simon's eye. "Bring Raji, too. Then you could have him bite me every time I said something you did not like. God knows the little rascal will do anything you command."

The gentle jest made the other ladies laugh, and even Louisa couldn't suppress a smile. "I seriously doubt Raji would bite you, no matter who commanded it. He's no fool. He knows who feeds him."

"Funny how he forgets that whenever I try to kiss you," Simon said in a husky voice. "Then he turns into the knight errant protecting his mistress from the evil seducer."

Louisa blushed and the other ladies exchanged knowing glances.

Regina glanced at the clock. "The hour grows late, does it not, ladies? Perhaps we should give our newly married friends their privacy."

"Oh, do not break up the meeting on *my* account," Simon said. "I have a whole night ahead of me in which to ... draw Raji's ire."

Torn between leaping into his arms and throttling him for dragging them off the topic, Louisa opened her mouth to speak, then froze when something touched her foot. Simon had slipped off his shoe and was caressing her slippered foot with his stockinged one beneath the table.

A delicious thrill coursed through her that she ruthlessly ignored. Casting him a warning glance, she pushed his foot away. "We're not ending this meeting until we decide what to do about our candidates."

"Of course." Simon's eyes locked with hers as he slid his foot under her skirts to fondle her calf. "I am willing to stay here as long as necessary."

"There's no need for that," Mrs. Harris said. "Much as I still think Mr. Godwin the best choice, it won't hurt to compare them thoroughly. His Grace is right—why not interview all three men? We can ..."

Louisa scarcely heard a word, for Simon's foot was sliding up past her knee, and she was terrified that one of the other women would notice.

At the same time, the wanton part of her wondered how far he would take it.

"Louisa?" Mrs. Harris said. "Do you agree?"

She jumped. "I ... er ... that is ..." Now Simon's toe was tracing lazy circles on the inside of her thigh. "What was the question again?"

When the ladies laughed, Simon flashed her one of his bedroom smiles. "Just say yes, sweetheart. So we can adjourn."

Mrs. Harris took pity on her and repeated the question

about whether she could hold the interviews in four days' time at Foxmoor House. Louisa nodded, cursing Simon and his distractions. Clearly the group was going to proceed with caution whether she liked it or not, thanks to him.

She seethed the entire time they were seeing the ladies out. As soon as they were gone, she scowled at Simon. "You did that on purpose, didn't you?"

He cast her a look of perfect innocence. "What?"

She headed for the stairs. "Drew them off the subject of politics by mentioning Raji. Then . . . tried to seduce me with your foot."

"I would have tried to seduce you with something else, but I think the ladies would have objected if I'd dragged you onto my lap."

"Drat it, Simon—"

He stopped her with a kiss, drawing her into his arms before she could even react. For a moment, she succumbed to the heady sweetness of his mouth.

Then she caught herself and pushed him away. "You're only kissing me to keep me from talking about politics." She hurried up the stairs. "Just as you brought up Raji to take my meeting off course."

He kept pace with her easily. "You credit me with more deviousness than even I am capable of. The truth is, I have spent the entire day thinking about the moment when I could return home to make love to my wife."

The husky comment melted her. A pox on her randy husband.

She reached the next floor and started for his study, but he stepped in front of her. "But I did participate in your meeting," he said. "I listened to your ladies' opinions and considered them carefully. Given the differences in our views—and the fact that my mind was on something else—I would say I was most accommodating."

She crossed her arms over her chest. "Until the discussion stopped going your way. Then you used one of your tricks to distract the ladies so you could influence them to your point of view."

He muttered an oath under his breath. "I hate to tell you, but you are alone in wanting to pursue radicalism. Even Mrs. Harris has an open mind. And the only reason you don't is because *I* disapprove, and it annoys you to agree with me."

"That's not true!" she protested, despite the kernel of truth in his words. "And furthermore—"

He kissed her again, this time holding her head still so he could really plunder her mouth. When he drew back, she stared up at him with dazed eyes. "You don't play fair," she grumbled. "You would never try this tactic on any of your political opponents."

He chuckled. "Can you imagine Sidmouth's reaction if I did?"

She caught her breath. "Sidmouth isn't your opponent."

Simon froze as he realized what he'd said. "I . . . did not mean that how it sounded."

The devil he didn't. "So you *do* agree with Sidmouth's policies? You want to see him continue in office?"

"Sidmouth is a necessary evil. I have to play his game—and the king's—if I want to become prime minister."

"And after that?" She remembered that he'd been on the wrong side in the issue of parliamentary reform. Perhaps that wasn't the only issue. "Would Sidmouth be part of your cabinet if you became prime minister?"

He hesitated a long moment. "No." When her face lit up, he added, "But that is *not* something I want generally known, even among your friends, Do you understand?"

"Perfectly," she exclaimed, too excited to contain her delight.

"I mean it, Louisa. Not a word."

"My lips are sealed," she said cheerily.

"I can't unseat Sidmouth right away. It will take time and maneuvering—"

"And patience and careful planning," she said, now able to tease him. "Yes, I know, my cautious husband. But how do you mean to do it? Who do you mean to put in his place? Are you seriously considering throwing him out?"

He kissed her hard, then drew back, his eyes smoldering. "Can we discuss this tomorrow?" Pulling her close, he ground his erection against her. "Right now, politics is the last thing on my mind."

And the dear man deserved a reward after his wonderful revelation. "Certainly, my husband." She flashed him a coy smile. "Just give me ten minutes to prepare myself before you come to my room." Turning, she darted up the stairs.

"I can undress you perfectly well, you know," he said as he stalked after her.

"You'll wreak havoc on my clothes," she said breathlessly. "And shock my maid besides." Thank heaven for her maid, whose presence always kept Simon at bay while she slipped in her sponge.

He grumbled something behind her, and she hastened her steps. This was clearly not the night to tax his patience. Besides, what he'd told her lent her feet wings. Simon meant to unseat Sidmouth!

After he'd admitted to supporting parliamentary reform earlier, she'd begun to think he was not quite the stodgy old Tory she'd assumed. Though he did share the Tory's belief about radicals, she felt certain she could change his mind about that once he listened to what Godwin had to say.

Tomorrow. Because tonight, she meant to enjoy lying in her husband's arms.

Chapter Twenty-Two

❦

Dear Charlotte,
  I hope you're right. If Foxmoor can't influence his wife with tender glances, he will no doubt turn to more restrictive measures, like packing her off to the country. It is what I would do if my wife caused me trouble.

Your cousin,
Michael

*E*ven without the help of his valet, whom Simon had dismissed the second he walked into his bedchamber, Simon undressed and donned his dressing gown in under two minutes. He had not lied to Louisa—rutting beast that he was, he'd been thinking of this all day. He only prayed that his craving for her lessened with time, because right now it was a damned nuisance.

Why else had he blurted out his plans for Sidmouth? God help her if she spread that among her radical friends. If it got to the press, that would be the end of his political aspirations. He did not have enough support in the Commons yet to unseat Sidmouth, and until he did he must appear not to oppose the man.

He could only hope that his wife would be discreet.

At least as discreet as she was in other areas. Like their marital relations, where she was almost *too* discreet. He paced beside the adjoining door to her bedchamber. She had made it abundantly clear that she preferred privacy when preparing to come to his bed. Until now, he had acquiesced, figuring that she had been a virgin and needed time to adjust to marital intimacies.

But damn it, he wanted to watch her undress. He wanted to undress her himself. He wanted to make love to her somewhere other than her bed. He wanted to sleep with her at night, wake up with her in his arms. And no matter how much he told himself to be patient, he craved those things to a maddening degree. How was he supposed to bring his obsession under control when she still denied him *those* intimacies?

He reached for the door handle. Surely he had given her enough time to grow used to being a wife. What mysterious preparations did she do anyway that he, her own husband, could not watch?

Opening the adjoining door, he stopped short when he saw her maid standing there alone, his wife nowhere to be seen. Beyond her the dressing room door was closed. It was as if the maid stood guard. That roused his curiosity even more.

The maid spotted him and started to speak, but he held a finger to his lips to silence her. Although alarm flickered in her face, he knew she dared not disobey. But the fact that she looked as if she wanted to gave him pause.

With grim purpose he strode to the outer door, opened it so as not to make a sound, and ushered her out. After closing it just as silently, he crossed the room to ease the dressing room door open and look in at his wife.

The candle upon her dressing table revealed Louisa standing in her unbuttoned nightdress with her back to him. But although she faced a mirror that showed him plainly watching her, she was too engrossed in what she did to notice.

At first he thought she was cleaning her privates, for she had her linen nightdress hitched up and one leg propped on the stool as she lifted a dripping sponge to her sweet little honeypot. His cock, already half-stiff, instantly thrust itself through the gap in his silk dressing gown.

Then he saw her insert the sponge far up inside herself. With his stomach sinking, he held his breath to see if it came back out, but her hand came out empty.

He had visited a brothel often enough to know what she was doing. And he could easily guess why. She had denied him greater intimacy because of *this,* damn her!

"How dare you!" he hissed.

She jumped, and the guilty flush that spread over her cheeks as she met his gaze in the mirror was enough to confirm his suspicions.

A sense of betrayal sliced into him.

"It's not what you think, Simon," she whispered.

"No?" Entering the dressing room, he slammed the door behind him. "So you are *not* trying to keep me from siring my heir?"

She jerked her leg down. "No . . . I-I mean . . . it has nothing to do with—"

"I spent half my youth in a brothel, Louisa. I recognize

a sponge meant to prevent children when I see one."
Stalking up beside her, he dipped his finger in the bowl of
liquid that sat on her dressing table, then lifted it to his
nose and sniffed. The pungent scent of vinegar assailed
his nostrils.

Angry beyond words, he thrust the finger at her. *"This*
is why you come to my bed with your privates so heavily
perfumed. This . . . this *travesty* is why you will not let me
undress you or make love to you anywhere but in your
bed—"

"You have to let me explain," she pleaded.

"What? That you still secretly hate me? That despite
every accommodation I make for you, you are determined to plot against me?" The pain boiling up in his
throat threatened to choke him. "No wonder you so readily agreed to quit your London Ladies when I got you
with child—you planned to make it so I never did."

"That's not true. It was just for a while, until—"

"You got your radical elected?" he spat, still hardly able
to believe she was so cruel as to deprive him of children
without his knowledge. "Thus destroying any hope I had
of becoming prime minister? Is that how you meant to
undermine my authority?" He emptied the vinegar into
the chamber pot, then dashed the bowl against the door.
"This will not be tolerated!"

While she still gaped at him, shocked by his sudden
burst of violence, he jerked up her nightdress, preparing
to remove the sponge himself.

Then she began to cry. "P-please, Simon," she blub-
bered. "I didn't . . . it wasn't . . ."

She could hardly speak for her pitiful sobs, and they
tore at him, making him curse himself for upsetting her.
Then curse himself for paying them any heed.

Good God, he was pathetically besotted with her. He dropped her nightdress. "I want it out," he said in a low voice. "Now!"

She nodded, then propped her foot back up on the stool. "You h-have to understand. I-I wasn't ready for children, that's all. I just n-needed some time . . . to prepare myself . . . for the blood . . . and the doctors . . ."

The way she said "doctors," in the same tone one might use in speaking of snakes, arrested him. She'd used that tone in her bedchamber at Draker's town house when saying how doctors bled and cupped women.

"I-I wasn't trying to u-undermine . . ." She continued sobbing as she removed the sponge. "It really had nothing . . ."

She couldn't finish a sentence for her weeping, and now other things came back to him. How even after his doctor had finally arrived that day, while he and Draker were negotiating the marriage settlement, she'd refused to let the man examine her, no matter how much they'd insisted.

Then there were the comments she had made at the school—about the prisoners giving birth . . . about the blood. But why was she so—

The conversation with his sister about Princess Charlotte leapt to his mind, and he groaned. Damn it all to hell.

He captured her trembling hand as she dropped the sponge on the table. "You were there, weren't you?" he said hoarsely. "You were present when the princess died in childbirth."

Unable to speak for her tears, she nodded.

This had all been about *fear*. Which he would have recognized if he had not been such an idiot.

Cursing himself for his quick temper, he swept her into his arms. "Shh, sweetheart," he said against her ear. "It's all right. Shh."

With a strangled cry she threw her arms around him, seeking comfort from her tormentor, and he gave it as best he could, murmuring soothing words, rubbing her back.

"I-I wasn't supposed to see the birth," she choked out, her tears soaking his dressing gown. "They banished nearly . . . e-everyone from her bedchamber."

He stroked her and gentled her, feeling like a tyrannical monster.

She struggled to gain control of her fierce sobs. "But she was m-my sister. I loved her. So I-I hid in her dr-dressing room."

"Oh, sweetheart," he said softly.

"The labor was bad enough," she whispered against his chest. "She screamed for hours . . ."

He could only imagine. He had heard that Princess Charlotte had spent a grueling two and a half days in labor.

"But then came the birth, with the baby stillborn. He was huge, too big for . . . and they wouldn't use the forceps and . . ." Her voice turned fierce. "There was too much blood, so much . . . not only then, but before, too."

She turned up to him a gaze tinged by outrage. "By the time she went into labor, they'd bled her and bled her, and practically starved her, too. What else did they expect once she came to her childbed? How could any woman bear a child after she'd endured such—"

She erupted into tears again, and the full extent of her fear clawed at him. He brushed kisses against her hair, her temple, her damp cheek. His throat was raw with the horror of imagining what it must have been like for her to witness such a thing. She had only been twenty-two, still young enough to let it eat at her. Almost the same age as the princess.

"You should have told me," he whispered. "I wish you had."

She went still in his arms. "And what would you have done? Told me that . . . my fear was nothing. That Regina had borne two children with . . . no trouble." She swallowed. "I know it's not always as bad as what I've built up in my mind. But every time I think about—"

When she broke off with a sob, he clutched her head to his chest. She was probably right. With everything that had gone on between them, if she had told him from the beginning, he would have assumed she was refusing to have children to strike back at him.

Now he understood why she had been so reluctant to marry. It had certainly not been a Joan of Arc determination to be a reforming spinster.

She lifted her face to his. "I-I do want to have your child. Our children. I want it more than anything. I shall r-resign myself to it. I can do that. I *can*."

Yet she was stiff in his arms, and tears still trembled in her eyes.

Bloody hell, what was he to do? If he indulged her fear, how long would it last? He had to have an heir. And she would make a wonderful mother.

But not if she died of fright going to her childbed first.

He groaned. How could he make love to her, knowing that she so violently dreaded the inevitable result of doing so?

"Simon, I'm all right now. You can throw the sponges away if you like. I'll—"

"Shh," he whispered. There was only one choice he could make. Cursing himself for being such a weak fool, he reached over and picked up the sponge. "Lift your leg," he said.

She stared at him uncomprehendingly. "What?"

"We will do it your way for a while. Until you . . . feel more comfortable with the idea of bearing my children."

"You don't have to do this—"

"Yes, I do," he said firmly. "I won't have my wife quaking in fear when she comes to my bed. Now lift your leg."

When she did so, he inserted the sponge partway before letting her push it the rest of the way.

She lifted her face to his, and her expression of relief tore at him. "Thank you," she whispered.

Then she kissed him, and he clung to her lips as he had never clung before, kissing her ardently, desperately. He wanted to blot out everything that had just transpired, to forget that his wife had just convinced him to allow what no other husband in his right mind would.

Never let a woman's tears plague you into doing what you shouldn't, his grandfather's voice sounded in his head.

He cursed Monteith, then cursed himself when his cock came to attention with the predictability of Raji spotting a bird. Christ, he was mad. Yet he could not seem to help himself when he was with her.

Louisa must have felt his arousal, for she broke the kiss, staring up at him with a heavy-lidded gaze. "Shall we go to bed now?" she asked in a throaty murmur.

He glanced away, only to see their image in the mirror, limbs entwined, him erect and her with her leg still lifted onto the stool. Her nightdress was hitched up to her waist, baring her silky-skinned privates to his gaze.

His cock swelled, and he was seized by an urgent need to take her here, like this. "Face the mirror," he commanded her.

When she started to take her foot off the stool to turn, he said, "No, leave it there. I want to see every part of you. I want to watch me touching you."

Though her face flushed, she did as he asked, shifting her body around until she faced the mirror, with one foot propped on the stool and the other on the floor, exposing her tender flesh in all its dewy glory.

His mouth went dry. He yanked her nightdress off over her head, then shrugged off his dressing gown. Moving behind her, he reached around to fondle her breast with one hand while he fingered the delicate flesh between her legs with the other. Her face turned pink as her privates, yet she let out a moan of pleasure that stiffened his cock to iron.

"Sometimes, Louisa," he ground out, "I desire you beyond all reason." He rubbed his erection up and down the cleft of her buttocks to let her know just how hard she made him.

Her gaze turning sultry, she reached back as if to fondle his cock.

"No." He brushed her hand aside. "Put your hands on the table. I want to take you like this, from behind, while you watch." With his mouth against her ear, he continued in a harsh whisper, "I want you to see what I see when I drive inside you." He nipped her earlobe. "I want you to see the intoxicating picture you make, the one that consumes me day and night."

Her eyes a smoky black, she did as he said, leaning forward to plant her hands in front of her. Her hair cascaded down before her, hiding her breasts, so he gathered it up and looped it over one shoulder to allow him to look his fill of her.

God, what it did to him to see her like this in the candle's dim glow. Her face alive with her blushes and her breasts dangling between her arms like ripe fruit, she looked vulnerable and sweet and so erotic, it nearly drove him mad.

Never let a woman lead you by the cock.

He shoved his grandfather's voice from his head, then roughly pushed her legs farther apart, exulting in her little gasp of surprise. Deliberately he turned that gasp into a groan by reaching around to rub her slick flesh. And when she pressed herself against his finger, craving more of his touch, he felt a swift surge of triumph. Perhaps she *did* affect him too much, but at least he did the same to her.

Then her eyes slid closed. "No!" he growled against her neck. "You have to watch me take your beautiful body."

Her eyes opened to fix him with a mutinous glance. "I want you inside me."

"Not until you cannot bear it anymore," he said, then tormented her tender little pearl, laving it, stroking it, just the way he knew she liked it. "I want you begging, Louisa."

She smiled at him in the mirror. "You will never last that long," she said, a minxish taunt.

And when she swiveled her hips back to angle her sweet little derriere against his rigid cock, he feared she might be right. His erection lay painfully heavy in the cradle of her delicious behind.

But he refused to let her win this round. After his time with the brothel whores paid by his grandfather, he knew how to regain control over his willful cock, and ruthlessly he did so. "I can last as long as it takes, my tempting little Cleopatra."

Let her have her sponges if she must, but he would have her begging for him, admitting that he was not the only one in this marriage who was besotted. He would master her—and himself—if it took him hours.

So he caressed her breasts, first one, then the other, thumbing the nipples to taut peaks, then delicately scraping the smooth pebbles with his thumbnail until she cried out and thrust her breasts against his hand.

"I am the head of this house, do you hear?" he choked out, the vision of her writhing beneath his hands almost more than he could bear. But the voice of his grandfather haunted him, making his own voice harsh as he added, "You have your sponges only at my indulgence, understood?"

She groaned, but nodded.

"No more of these covert rebellions," he bit out. "I will not have my wife make a fool of me."

"I never meant . . ." she whispered. "I would never—"

"Swear it," he demanded as he fondled her repeatedly between the legs. "Swear you will be honest with me from now on."

"Yes, Simon, I swear."

He dipped his finger inside her, just enough to tantalize, then jerked it out.

"You belong to me," he rasped as he pulled her hips farther back. Sliding his cock up between her legs, he caressed her velvety softness with it. "Say it. Your body, your mind, your will . . . they belong to me."

"And you?" Her eyes suddenly flashed. "Do you belong to *me*?"

"I have always belonged to you," he said, the admission ripped from him before he could stop it.

"Then take me *now*," she hissed. "I beg you, husband . . . show me that we belong to each other. . . ."

So he did. Shifting his angle, he thrust so deeply inside her that she jerked, then released a heartfelt sigh of pure, sweet pleasure.

That only enflamed him more. He drove into her again and again, stroking her dewy pearl in front as he slid in and out of her slick passage from behind. He sucked at the smooth slope of her shoulder, then nipped at the delicate nape of her neck, wishing he could devour her whole.

The harder he pounded into her and fondled her, the more her breath quickened and her gaze burned into his in the mirror, until they were both panting, struggling like two wild animals fighting for dominance, each determined to make the other lose control first.

In the end, they came at almost the same moment. Her body stiffened before she let out a piercing cry and collapsed in his arms. An instant later he reached his own rapture and poured his seed into her.

His seed that would never take root.

The errant thought dug into his consciousness even as he strained against her, filling her, his heart beating a frantic cacophony in his ears. He thrust the thought from his mind just as quickly.

Time. She needed time. He could give her time if he must.

It took several seconds for his breathing to slow, and several more for his sated cock to slip out of her. But as soon as she felt it, she turned so she could slide her arms about his waist and hold him close.

He kissed her, plundering first her mouth, then her ear and the hollow of her throat.

"That was very . . . interesting," she murmured as he ravaged her neck. "I never imagined . . . making love in quite that way."

"There are a hundred ways to make love, and I mean to have us try every one."

Even as excitement leapt in her face, she eyed him thoughtfully. "Where did you learn this assortment of lovemaking techniques? During the youth you spent in a brothel?"

He started, then remembered what he had revealed in anger. "I suppose," he said evasively, bending his mouth to kiss her.

She turned her head aside. "Why would you spend your youth in a brothel and then . . . be celibate in India?"

"I'd had my fill of them by then," he admitted.

If she ever learned the full truth about that time in his life, she would know the weakness that remained in him, despite his grandfather's cursed training. And then she would use it to control him. He had no doubt of that.

"Most men—" she began.

"—do not discuss their ill-spent youth with their wives," he finished. Lifting her in his arms, he headed out of the dressing room. "It was long ago, hardly worth discussing. I sowed my wild oats like every other young man. But now I am old enough to want to sow something more fruitful—"

He broke off with a groan. "Forgive me," he murmured as he carried her through her bedchamber and headed for his without pausing.

She buried her face against his chest. "It's not you who needs forgiveness. I'm the one who—"

"It's fine," he said tersely, not wanting to think about her sponges.

"I just want you to know how I regret being a coward and not telling you."

"It's *fine,*" he repeated. When she winced, he softened his tone. "We can wait a while to have children, sweetheart."

Reaching his bed with the turned-down covers, he laid her on it, then slid into it beside her. "But I do want one thing in exchange for my indulgence."

She turned toward him, her face instantly wary. "Oh?"

"No more separate beds, all right?"

Breaking into a smile, she cuddled up next to him. "If that's what you wish. I only did it so—"

"Yes, I figured that," he cut in, not wanting to hear one more word about how she had been sneaking out to deal with her sponges. "Do whatever you must in your dressing room. Just return to my bed when you are done."

A teasing light shone in her eyes. "What if *my* bed is more comfortable?"

"Then we will move into your room." He caressed her cheek. "As long as we sleep in the same bed, I do not care which one it is."

That brought a soft smile to her lips that sent his blood into a stampede. Tenderly, she brushed a lock of hair from his eyes. "You are not the sort of husband I expected you to be."

Catching her hand, he pressed a kiss into the palm. "Oh?"

"I never guessed you'd be so . . . possessive. Not after you had what you wanted from me, anyway."

What he wanted from her? He had nothing close to that. What Grandfather had never beaten out of him was his darkest weakness—his craving for the sweet affection and abiding love that he had seen the Trusbuts show each other.

But that would always elude him. Grandfather had made him incapable of giving love, incapable of feeling anything but lust and obsession. And what woman would show him the love he craved when all he could give *her* was passion?

"Does my possessiveness bother you?" He held his breath.

"Sometimes," she admitted. Then, with a sensuous smile, she ran her finger down his chest. "And sometimes it arouses me."

He hardened instantly. "Does it?" he choked out.

Her hand dipped down to his abdomen. "Oh yes. I may not have inherited Mother's need for variety in men, but I certainly inherited her . . . urges."

"Thank God," he rasped, as he covered her mouth with his.

Perhaps passion would be enough for them.

But later, as she lay sleeping beside him and the night stole into the room she had finally agreed to share with him, he stared up into the quiet and once again wished for something more, something deeper.

Something he knew he could never have.

Chapter Twenty-Three

Dear Cousin,
   I had no idea you were capable of being such a tyrant to your poor wife. Do you even have a wife, or is this the opinion of a bachelor who fancies that he can bully any woman into doing what he pleases?
                 Your surprised relation,
                     Charlotte

Two days later, the London Ladies finished interviewing their potential candidates. As Louisa sat with Simon, Mrs. Harris, and Regina in his study, she couldn't help feeling relieved to have it over with.

Raji swung about the room from shelf to shelf, but none of them paid him any mind. The same had not been true of their candidates. Simon had purposely kept Raji in the study for the interviews, one of his little tactics for throwing the men off guard so he could get some honesty out of them.

Unfortunately, the honesty he'd elicited from Mr. Duncombe was rather unexpected. Raji's antics had prompted the man to make disparaging remarks about the Indians Simon had governed. Obviously Mr. Duncombe had thought to ingratiate himself to Simon with such slurs. Little did he know.

"Well?" Simon asked her now. "What do you think of them?"

She sighed. "Obviously Mr. Duncombe is out of the question. I think we can all safely agree that he was . . . well . . ."

"As dumb as they come?" Simon suggested helpfully.

While the other ladies struggled to hide their smiles, Louisa shot her husband an arch look. "I would have said he showed himself to be—to use Miss Crenshawe's term—an 'ass,' but I suppose 'dumb' fits him well enough."

Chuckling, Simon turned to the others. "The rest of you agree?" When they nodded, he added, "So Duncombe's out." Simon sat back in his chair, but wouldn't look at her. "And . . . er . . . what did you ladies think of Godwin?"

She scowled. "You know perfectly well what we think, you smug devil. We're not fools. It was painfully evident that in person, Godwin is too fiery even for my tastes. Fielden was more level-headed and sound in his opinions, by far."

"Good of you to admit it," Simon said, a hint of relief in his voice.

"How could I not, when Godwin suggested such tactics as our forcibly taking over the prison to illustrate our determination to improve the conditions?"

"It was an interesting idea," Mrs. Harris said, gamely defending her friend.

"It would have got you all shot." Simon glanced at his

wife. "And much as I support your aims, I really don't want to become a widower just yet."

She shot him a look. "Go ahead. You may now officially gloat."

"I am not gloating," he said, though a smile hovered about the edges of his lips. "I am merely congratulating myself for my good sense in marrying such an astute and clever female. And one who is honorable enough to own up to being wrong, even when it pains her."

"If you think that flurry of compliments will turn me up sweet . . ." She gave him a small smile. "Then you are probably right, you cocky devil."

"So what happens now?" Mrs. Harris put in. "I've never been part of a political campaign."

Simon explained the process, then added, "We'll have to make sure that Fielden's speeches have the proper focus. And if we get him mentioned in the press—"

"You keep saying 'we,'" Louisa put in. "Does that mean you'll help us?"

Simon glanced around at their hopeful faces, then sighed. "Yes. I suppose it does."

"Good," she said. "Because he made it very clear that he would only run if you and I throw our support behind him." And it warmed her heart that her husband would do so. Indeed, his answer had quite astonished her.

As their political discussion turned to small talk, she admitted that Simon had been astonishing her often of late. First there'd been his shocking agreement to her sponges. Then his adept handling of the interviews and amazing willingness to help them with their campaign. What was she to make of it?

It contrasted sharply with the darker side of him she sometimes saw, like when he left their bed to spend hours hunting through letters. His obsession with finding out the truth about Mr. Hunt was disturbing. She began to think it was more than just his way of atoning for his perceived error. It had to do with thwarting his grandfather, as if doing so would purge some pain in his soul.

She'd asked Regina about the Earl of Monteith, but Regina could tell her little. The man had apparently only paid attention to Simon. Regina *had* said, however, that Grandfather Monteith had never spent one minute with Simon without instructing him—how to act, how to stand, how to speak.

Louisa glanced to where her husband talked with the ladies with his usual easy charm, and a chill struck her. As surely as Simon crafted his whittled creatures, the earl had crafted Simon's smooth statesman's manner.

What she wanted to know was how. By admonishing him? Or by using some other darker method? Simon clearly despised him, so the man must have done *something* to him. Why else did Simon sometimes turn into a ferocious creature she hardly recognized?

Like when he'd exploded in anger in her dressing room. Not that she blamed him for that; any other man would have done the same. But the way he'd taken her afterward, so fiercely, so urgently, had frightened her.

At the same time, she'd reveled in its wildness. Oh Lord, when he made love to her she became this incredibly wicked creature, wallowing in the secrets of the bedchamber that he taught her.

She tried not to think of where he had learnt them. Or why he seemed bent on tormenting her with her own desires, bringing her to the point where she craved him so badly, she would say or do anything to gain her release.

Her only consolation was that she could do the same

to him. And often did, even when he cursed her for it. It was as if a silent war of passions raged between them. Was that what marriage was, this stormy and constant conflagration? She hoped not. While it excited her now, she feared it could become wearying.

Especially once she had a child. She bit her lip. The idea of having a baby tempted her more lately. She still put her sponges in, but she'd begun to hesitate when she did. Only the lingering image of her half sister's torment kept her from giving them up altogether.

"Oh dear, look at the time!" Mrs. Harris exclaimed, drawing Louisa from her thoughts. "We have to go! You and I are to meet the toy shop owner at the prison today to show him the first batch of toys."

"Drat it, I forgot." Louisa shot to her feet, then glanced at the clock. "Can we make it there in half an hour?"

"You can if you take my barouche." Simon stood, too. "It is already waiting out front for me to go to sessions. I will go with you to the prison, Mrs. Harris's coachman can follow at his own pace, and once he arrives, I will go on alone."

"We don't want to inconvenience you—" Mrs. Harris began.

"It's no inconvenience. I can be late. Besides, I had a part in your project, too. I wouldn't mind meeting this toy person to see what came of it."

"That would certainly help us," Louisa said, flashing him a grateful smile.

Simon's excellent equipage enabled them to reach the prison in record time. Even better, the toy shop owner proved so delighted with the painted soldiers and fancy ladies they showed him—and so impressed by Simon's involvement—that he said he would carry as many as they could make. Louisa could hardly contain her elation.

As Mrs. Harris went off to show the owner where the women worked, Louisa walked with Simon toward the gates. She slipped her hand in the crook of his arm. "I can't begin to tell you how much the London Ladies appreciate your help."

"*Just* the London Ladies?" he said with a teasing smile.

"Of course not. And I know helping us has upset your plans somewhat, but—"

"Wait!" cried a voice behind them.

She turned to see a nurse from the infirmary running after them. "Thank heaven you're still here, Miss North . . . I mean, Your Grace."

"What's wrong?"

"Do you remember Mrs. Mickle?"

"Of course." Louisa had met Betsy Mickle when the woman and her husband had been imprisoned in the ward designated for debtors. Born into gentility and educated well, Betsy had fallen from grace during her youth and ended up in a bawdy house. She'd had a rocky life ever since, although Louisa had thought things were looking up when Mr. Mickle paid off his debts last year.

"Don't tell me she's back," Louisa said. "Can't her husband stay out of debt?"

"Afraid not. They came in this week, with her nigh on to bursting with a babe in her belly. This morning she went into labor, but now she's doing poorly."

"Oh no," Louisa said, her stomach sinking.

The nurse shook her head sadly. "The babe is turned the wrong way 'round. The doctor's with her and thinks he can set it right, but she's too agitated to stay still for it. We were hoping you might talk to her, settle her down—"

"*Me?* What about her husband?"

"He can't bear watching her suffer—they had to send the poor man out. But she was always partial to you. If you could come be with her in the infirmary, she might settle down enough for the doctor to do what he must."

"Of course," Louisa said, but the thought of it struck terror to her soul.

"My wife cannot do it," Simon said, laying a hand on Louisa's arm. "There must be someone else who can go. Mrs. Harris perhaps?"

"No, I'll go," Louisa said. "Really, Simon, I want to do it." She cast him a game smile. "I *need* to do it."

It was time she faced this fear of hers. For years she'd managed to be busy elsewhere whenever help was needed in the infirmary. For years she'd avoided doctors, even refusing to help Regina at Chelsea Hospital. But if she could put this behind her . . .

"Besides, this woman is a particular friend of mine. I can't stand the thought of her going through this without someone at her side who cares about her."

He searched her face, his eyes haunted. "Then I am going with you."

"Certainly not. The last thing she needs right now is some strange man looking up her skirts."

"Damn it, Louisa—"

"It'll be fine, I promise." She squeezed his arm. "Don't worry. Just go on to Westminster for your sessions."

"I'm not leaving," he said firmly. "I'll wait here for you."

Her heart gave a little leap. "It may be a while," she warned.

"I don't care."

His fierce protectiveness of her brought a smile to her

lips. "Thank you." She stretched up to kiss his cheek. "You're the best husband a woman could want."

She hurried off with the nurse. As they worked their way to the back of the prison, the nurse flashed her a concerned glance. "This is Mrs. Mickle's first child, you know."

"Had she no by-blows when she worked in the bawdy house?"

"I don't think she worked there long. She went right to a protector, and then when he proved to be a scoundrel, she was fortunate enough to find Mr. Mickle."

"She'd be more fortunate if he could stay solvent," Louisa said as they entered the infirmary, though Betsy's fellow really was a dear man. "And now they'll have a child to feed."

At least she hoped they would. As she and the nurse reached Betsy's bedside to see the woman's writhing form and sweat-beaded brow, Louisa wasn't so sure.

Her first instinct was to turn tail and run. That anyone should suffer this was horrible, but that Betsy, the most good-natured creature in the world, should endure it felt patently unfair. And how could Louisa bear to watch . . .

Then Betsy saw her, and any cowardly thoughts of fleeing vanished, for the woman's face lit up despite her pain. "Miss North," Betsy breathed, "I'm so glad you're here."

Miss North. This probably wasn't the best time to announce she was now the Duchess of Foxmoor. Taking the chair at Betsy's bedside, she seized the young woman's hand. "You didn't think I'd lose this chance to visit with my friend, did you?"

The woman managed a shaky laugh, then her face contorted as a birth pang hit her and she gripped Louisa's hand so hard she nearly broke it.

"I'm going to try turning the baby now, Betsy," the doctor put in. "You have to stay still a bit. Just keep holding onto your friend and talking to her."

Louisa didn't know the doctor, but she'd heard he was reputable. For Betsy's sake, she prayed that was true and tried not to think of how reputable her sister's doctors had supposedly been.

She focused on Betsy's face and not on the doctor pressing down on her abdomen. "What are you going to name the child?" she asked, doing her best not to show the panic tightening her throat.

"If it's a girl . . . Mary Grace," Betsy choked out, clutching Louisa's hand like a lifeline. "And if . . . a boy . . . James Andrew. After its father."

Despite her aching fear, Louisa smiled. "Those are lovely names."

Betsy let out a scream, and Louisa gripped her hand tightly to her breast, praying for all she was worth.

"Steady now," the doctor said to Betsy, "the babe is small. That's good. Makes it easier to turn."

"Isn't there something you can give her to dull the pain?" Louisa rasped as Betsy let out another, fainter scream. "Brandy? Laudanum?"

The doctor shook his head. "I need her alert so she can push once I've got the babe in place."

And if he *didn't* get that far? No, she wouldn't dwell on that. She had to be strong for her friend.

"Now, Betsy, hold still a bit longer," the doctor murmured, amazingly calm as he pushed and prodded her.

Louisa glanced over to see the doctor frowning in deep concentration. Betsy had returned to crushing Louisa's hand, but at least she wasn't screaming.

Suddenly, the doctor broke into a broad smile. "I think

the little bugger is moving! Hold it . . . hold it . . . That's it! He's turned!"

Tears sprang to Louisa's eyes as Betsy collapsed against the bed with a cry.

"We're not done yet, ladies," the doctor said. "We've still got to get him out. You've got to push now, Betsy. Push!"

The next part went so quickly that it left Louisa reeling. One moment, Betsy was bearing down, her face twisted with pain and concentration, and the next, the doctor was holding up a squirming, squalling infant.

Beaming from ear to ear, the nurse cut the cord and wiped the babe clean before coming 'round the bed to hand it to Betsy. "There you go. Turns out that the 'little bugger' is a girl. And pretty as a picture, too."

As Betsy took the infant, Louisa began to sob.

"Miss North!" Betsy exclaimed. "Are you all right?"

Struggling to gain control over her wild emotions, Louisa nodded through her tears. "She's . . . adorable." She bent over Betsy to look at the baby. "An angel."

And she was, too, despite her puckered-up red face and the damp wisps of black hair clinging to her scalp.

"Would you like to hold my Mary Grace?" Betsy whispered.

Louisa nodded, too overcome by emotion to speak. Betsy handed the infant over, and Louisa caught her breath. Mary Grace was as fragile as a white-wood doll, her mouth a tiny rosebud and her fists no bigger than parsnips as she waved them in the air.

"Came out fighting, didn't you?" Louisa cooed at the baby. "And aren't you just the strongest little thing?"

Louisa had held many a convict child, and she'd often dandled her niece and nephew on her knee, but this felt different. In a very small way, she felt she'd helped to bring this one into the world, and the idea filled her with exhilaration.

It was one thing to hear that women often gave birth without problems. It was quite another to see it happen.

She handed the child back to Betsy, then felt a pang of envy as the infant's little mouth started working, rooting toward Betsy's breast. A lump filled her throat. She wanted her own. She wanted Simon's child.

"Your husband will be delighted," Louisa murmured.

"Oh, James!" Betsy exclaimed. "I forgot about him!"

The nurse chuckled. "I won't tell him you said that when I fetch him." She hurried away to do just that.

Having already delivered the afterbirth, the doctor bustled off to tend another patient, leaving Louisa and Betsy alone with darling Mary.

Betsy cradled the child, brushing a kiss to its little brow. "It's my first."

"That's what the nurse said."

"I was afraid I was barren. Never had anything happen while I was working at that bawdy house in Drury Lane, so I was worried." Tears welled up in her eyes. "But here she is, sweet little thing."

Louisa squeezed Betsy's arm. "Yes, she's darling."

Betsy gazed at Louisa. "And I couldn't have done it without you, Miss North."

"Nonsense," Louisa said. She was just about to explain that she was no longer Miss North when Betsy glanced beyond her and gave a start.

"Will you look at that? I can't believe *he's* here, of all people. Haven't seen him in years."

Louisa turned to see Simon working his way up the crowded ward, sidestepping nurses and piles of soiled and blood-soaked linens. She shot Betsy a surprised glance. "Do you know him?"

Betsy nodded. "It's Lord Goring. Used to come to the bawdy house every Saturday night, regular as clockwork."

Louisa's heart began to pound and her mouth went dry. *I spent half my youth in a brothel.* And before his father's death, Simon had borne the lower title of Marquess of Goring. "Are you sure it's him?"

"He's well and truly grown now, but I'd know him anywhere. He's the only marquess I ever met. Poor boy, his grandfather behaved like an ass every time he brought the young fellow there. Bullied him unmercifully."

"Grandfather?" A sudden pain settled in Louisa's chest. "His *grandfather* brought him?"

"Started taking him there when the lad was fourteen. The grandfather was the man I told you about, remember? The earl who became my protector for a few months?"

Louisa could barely breathe, a thousand thoughts racing through her mind. "You never said his name."

Betsy frowned. "No, and I don't suppose I should have mentioned that I know Lord Goring, either. I was just so surprised to see him—" She broke off. "Shh, he's coming near."

Good heavens, and she still hadn't told Betsy that Simon was her husband. "Um, Betsy—"

"So how is everything with the young mother?" Simon's voice boomed behind her. When she turned, his gaze was fixed on her rather than Betsy.

"She's fine, and so is the baby," Louisa said, then added quickly, "Mrs. Mickle, this is my husband, the Duke of Foxmoor."

She heard Betsy gasp, but didn't look at her, for she wanted to see Simon's reaction.

"The nurse told me to let you know, Mrs. Mickle, that your husband is asleep." He shifted his gaze to Betsy's face. "And she didn't want to wake—Betsy?" He froze, his smile vanishing.

No doubt about it. They'd known each other. And probably in the biblical sense.

But though a pang of jealousy struck Louisa, it was nothing to the sadness she felt at the thought of Simon being bullied by his grandfather in a brothel at fourteen. Especially given how mortified he looked, as if a childhood friend had suddenly shown up to relate tales about his embarrassing boyish antics.

But he recovered quickly, giving Betsy a quick bow. "That *is* your name, right? Betsy? I'm sure my wife must have mentioned it earlier." He was babbling now, and Simon never babbled. "Forgive me for speaking so familiarly when we have just met, but after how she described you, I feel as if I know you already."

"Th-thank you, my lo— . . . Your Grace," Betsy stammered.

Feeling guilty for not having set Betsy straight sooner, Louisa seized her hand and gave it a warning squeeze. She didn't want Simon to know what Betsy had told her, at least not until Louisa could find out more. No point to embarrassing him and her friend, too.

"The birth went beautifully," Louisa said quickly to cover the awkward silence. "The doctor turned the baby with amazing speed, and here she is—a darling little girl."

"Good, good," Simon clipped out. He laid his hand on Louisa's shoulder. "So you're ready to go then?"

"Not yet," Louisa said. When his fingers dug into her shoulder convulsively, she pretended not to notice, plastering a smile firmly upon her lips. "I thought I'd stay a while longer with Betsy to help her with the baby. And don't you need to go on to sessions anyway?"

"But how will you get home?" he asked, a hint of panic in his eyes.

"Mrs. Harris is still here, isn't she? And I'm sure she's still expecting to take me back to Foxmoor House."

"Yes, but—"

"Go on, Simon. I'll be fine."

He glanced from Louisa to Betsy and back in clear agitation. It was strange—he'd already revealed that he'd gone to a brothel in his youth. So why should it worry him so much that she had met a woman from it?

Unless it had been more than just a coupling to him.

No, she couldn't bear to think that. But she would find out. Oh yes, she would find out for sure.

"Your wife is right, Your Grace." Betsy's voice was amazingly calm. She cradled her baby. "She'll be fine here with me. She's my friend. I would never, ever let anything harm her."

"Thank you," he said in a hollow voice. He met Louisa's gaze, anguish flickering in his eyes. "But don't be long, sweetheart. The session will probably not go very late."

She nodded before shooing him off. As soon as he'd left the infirmary, she turned back to Betsy, intent on answers.

Betsy held her sleeping baby close, her head bowed. "I made a mistake," she mumbled. "Got the wrong man. It wasn't him. Beg pardon, it wasn't him."

"Don't be absurd," she hissed. "I know it was him. And not just because of what you said, either."

Betsy started shaking her head. "I don't know what came over me to speak such a lie. Your husband is not the man—"

"Drat it, listen to me! It's all right—I already knew about the brothel!"

Betsy's head jerked up. "What?"

"I mean, I knew Simon had gone to one in his youth." Casting a furtive glance at the other patients, Louisa lowered her voice. "He told me himself."

The new mother's eyes were huge in her face.

"What's more, I know that it . . . did something to him. He hates his grandfather, but I don't know why, and now you tell me that the man took him to a brothel." She seized Betsy's arm. "You *have* to tell me what the earl did to him."

"Ask your husband," Betsy said.

"I already have. He won't tell me." She swallowed. "And if *you* won't tell me, I'll have to assume his grandfather did something horrible and perverse, like those awful men I hear about from the convicts, men who touch children—"

"No, no, nothing like that!" Betsy looked torn, then admitted, "Well, it seemed horrible to me, but it wasn't perverse."

"So he didn't lay a hand on him."

Her face clouded. "Well, he did thrash him from time to time something awful. But where he hurt him was more in here." She pointed to her chest. "Inside. Where nobody could see."

"Except you," Louisa whispered.

Betsy paled. "It wasn't like that between me and your husband, I swear."

"You mean," she said acidly, "you didn't share his bed?"

"I mean . . . he didn't care for me . . . that is, he cared, but . . ." She gave a long sigh. "For the lad, I was more like . . . someone to talk to. You know?" She swallowed hard, staring down at her babe. "Poor thing, his mother was a cold fish, and his father was always gambling, and his grandfather—"

"Enticed his grandson into wickedness."

"Enticed?" Betsy gave a harsh laugh. "Far from it." Leaning closer, Betsy whispered, "Lord Monteith called it 'training,' he did. Said that the lad had to learn that 'whores were for bedding and ladies for wedding.'"

"Surely that's a lesson most lords learn on their own," Louisa bit out. "I don't understand why he would feel the need—"

"I asked Lord Monteith about that after I became his mistress. He said one of his sons had married too far beneath him because he 'followed his cock,' and he meant to see that his grandson didn't do the same."

Louisa didn't know whether to be pleased by this evidence that Simon's uncle had indeed married his Indian wife, or dismayed that the marriage had brought so much pain down on Simon.

Betsy smoothed her baby's wisps of hair with a maternal touch. "So he set out to teach the lad that a man must keep his urges in their place. That he mustn't care for the women he beds. That women, no matter how pretty or talented or desirable, are interchangeable."

Louisa gaped at her. "How on earth did he teach such a thing?"

Staring down at Mary Grace, Betsy mumbled, "I'm not sure I should tell you. If your husband finds out that I did, what will happen to me? My poor Jim's life is hard enough without me having a duke for an enemy."

"Simon would never hurt you—"

"He might, after what I did to him. Especially if what I say hurts the woman he loves."

As a sudden pang struck her, Louisa dropped her gaze. "You needn't worry about that. Simon didn't marry me for love . . . he married me because—" No, she couldn't tell the woman why they'd married—it was too humiliating. "It was more for convenience than love."

"Perhaps so, but that doesn't change the fact that he loves you now. I could see it in his face when he looked at you."

Her heart skipped a beat. "I'll grant you, he feels affection, but—"

"It was love I saw, not mere affection. And I should know, because it's how my dear Jim looks at me." Betsy seized her hand. "You love him, too, don't you?"

Louisa caught her breath. Did she? Was that why her heart soared just thinking that he might love her? Or why she'd reacted so strongly to finding out that he'd conspired with her father?

Was that why she was suddenly willing to risk anything, even death, to bear his child?

A tear slipped down her cheek. Oh Lord, she'd gone and fallen in love with Simon. Again. After trying so hard not to.

Yet would loving Simon really be so bad? He'd proved a much more indulgent husband than she'd feared, and if not for his uncertain temper, she would think they had a very good marriage.

Especially now that she'd decided to bear him a child. But before she did that, she had to know what haunted him so, what kept him from admitting that he loved her. If indeed he did.

"I do love my husband," Louisa said. "And that's precisely why you must tell me everything. A terrible sadness eats at him, torturing him with black moods and sometimes goading him into anger. How can I help him if I don't know what it is?"

Betsy gave a weary sigh, then nodded. "You're right. If anyone can help him, you can. And after the cruelties the earl inflicted upon him, your husband deserves some happiness."

Chapter Twenty-Four

※

Dear Charlotte,
  *You know I cannot tell you about my circum-
stances or risk losing my anonymity. But rest assured
that I am familiar enough with the ways of women to
form opinions about how they should be governed.*

Your friend,
Michael

Simon could not concentrate at Parliament. He kept
seeing Betsy and his wife together, imagining what the
woman might say. And here he'd thought he only had to
worry about Louisa's reaction to the childbirth. Clearly, he
should not have worried about that—Louisa had seemed
very comfortable with the birth when he had seen her.

But who knew how comfortable she would be if Betsy
revealed the sordid details of Grandfather Monteith's
training? It curdled his stomach just to think of it. God, if
he had realized that it was Grandfather's Betsy in the infirmary, he would never have allowed Louisa to go in
there.

Still, Betsy had a husband now and a baby girl. Perhaps she would not be any more eager to discuss the past than he was. Even as a lightskirt, Betsy had been discreet. And she had nothing to gain by telling Louisa. She had to know that he would not tolerate her upsetting his wife.

Suddenly Lord Trusbut appeared and took a seat beside him, dragging him from his worrisome thoughts. "Did you hear that the MPs are considering creating a committee to write a Gaols Bill?" the baron murmured.

Simon straightened. "Really?"

"Your wife should be pleased," Trusbut went on. "And even if the Commons decides against it, with that by-election coming up, things could very well change. One new MP could tip the balance."

Which was precisely what Louisa had been hoping for.

Simon eyed Trusbut closely. "How do *you* feel about a Gaols Bill?"

"Probably the same as you—it's about time. You saw what our wives and those Quakers have accomplished at Newgate. It's astonishing." He sat back on the bench. "And if volunteers can do so much, think what a system instituted by the prison itself and funded by the government can do."

Simon eyed Trusbut speculatively. The man had always been an independent thinker—clever and competent, but unswayed by politics. He voted according to his principles. Simon admired him for that.

Perhaps it was time Simon started throwing in his lot with men like Trusbut and Fielden and even Draker, so that when he *was* able to separate himself from Sidmouth and his cronies, there would be allies waiting for him in the wings. Men of character. Men of resolve.

Sensible men, who did not see the horrors of the French Revolution around every corner. "Trusbut, would you join me for a drink at White's tomorrow night? You are a member, aren't you?"

"And at Brook's," Trusbut said, looking somewhat surprised by the offer. "We could make it tonight, if you like."

"Tonight I have an engagement." Simon was not going anywhere until he found out what Betsy had said to his wife. "But I should enjoy meeting with you tomorrow night after sessions are over."

"I would be honored," Trusbut answered with a courtly nod.

The interchange lifted Simon's spirits, enabling him to participate in that day's session and thrust from his mind, however temporarily, his worries about Louisa and Betsy.

It felt good to be moving forward. All this time he had felt suspended, waiting for the king to fulfill his part of their bargain. But as that became more uncertain with every day, Simon had grown restless. He wanted to *do* something, however small. This felt right, a step toward the future.

Unfortunately, he did not get to enjoy his good mood for long. As soon as the session was over, Sidmouth and Castlereagh cornered him in the halls of Westminster Palace.

Sidmouth wasted no time getting to the point. "There's talk that your wife's group plans to support Charles Godwin in his bid for election."

"That is patently untrue," Simon snapped.

"The information came from Godwin himself."

"Then he is a liar." It didn't surprise Simon to hear it;

Godwin probably thought to force the hand of the London Ladies by spreading such a rumor. He must have guessed that the interview went badly.

"So your wife did *not* interview him as a potential candidate?"

Simon gritted his teeth. Damn that ass Godwin. Simon would wring his bloody neck when next he saw him. "As a matter of fact, she did. And though the ladies have not informed him yet, they decided not to pursue him."

"But they have another candidate in mind."

Simon hesitated. He wasn't sure if he had the right to repeat that.

On the other hand, the London Ladies would soon endorse their candidate. They couldn't keep it secret for long. Besides, Sidmouth couldn't possibly disapprove of Fielden. "Yes, they do. The man they have chosen is sensible, sound—"

"And unacceptable."

Simon's eyes narrowed. "You don't know who he is."

"I don't have to." Sidmouth glanced at Castlereagh, then set his shoulders. "The London Ladies are determined to meddle in matters beyond their purview. Any candidate they choose is sure to damage the very fabric of English society."

"Oh, for God's sake—"

"You were supposed to steer the ladies away from involvement in politics. The king assured us that you would."

Simon bristled. "The king also made certain promises to me that he has not fulfilled. So perhaps you should take your complaints to *him*."

When he turned away, Sidmouth said, "If you mean to

replace Liverpool as prime minister, His Majesty isn't the person with whom you should negotiate."

Simon froze. "What makes you think I mean to replace Liverpool?"

"That was always your ambition, wasn't it? To be prime minister?"

Facing them, he forced himself to smile. *Careful, man. You don't know what the king told them.* "I have my ambitions. But I am young. I have plenty of time."

Sidmouth gave a mocking laugh. "Like most young men, you also have little patience. We understand that. We are prepared to give you what you want, as soon as you want it."

"Oh?" He did not want to deal with Sidmouth. But His Majesty had done nothing to further Simon's plans so far, and Simon began to fear he never would.

"Liverpool foolishly thinks he can brazen out this St. Peter's Field matter. But someone must be sacrificed to placate the mob, and he is the logical choice. We are willing to press for a change—as long as the Tories remain in power."

"Of course."

"And we retain our own positions."

Simon tensed. He had not meant to include Sidmouth in his cabinet, which Sidmouth probably realized. Simon's choice would have been Robert Peel. But with the king noticeably absent of late, he might not get *any* choice. Sidmouth and Castlereagh might be struggling politically, but they were by no means dead. "I see," he said noncommittally.

"We would also expect you and your wife to disassociate yourselves from the London Ladies."

Bloody hell. He took a steadying breath. "I cannot imagine why that would be necessary."

"We can't support a prime minister who allows his wife to dabble in politics. If you can't make her resign, we'll not only court a different man for prime minister, but we'll make sure you personally never have a chance at it again. Castlereagh and I have the power to ensure it, especially with the MPs so uneasy about the by-election and the possibility of Godwin winning it because of your endorsement."

"I told you that neither I nor my wife's group support Godw—"

"Ah, but most people don't know that. And by the time that information has been disseminated and confirmed, I could have your credit with the Commons so undermined that no one would ever dare offer you a position of power."

It was a clear and blatant threat. Continue to let Louisa support the London Ladies and his political career was over. Nor did he have the supporters to combat that yet.

"This is not just," he said in a low voice. "Those women have every right to press for reform, every right to put up a reasonable candidate—"

"And we have every right to choose who replaces Liverpool, don't we?"

"The king will never allow it," he hissed.

"The king knows we are having this conversation. He says that you have not done as he hoped with his daughter. So now it is our turn to persuade you."

Simon paled. He should never have trusted His Fickle Majesty. The man would sell his own mother to placate his ministers. Never mind that his people suffered at the hands of the bloody idiots; the king wanted only peace and quiet, however he could get it. And the leisure to enjoy his pleasures.

Yet was Simon any different? Because he did not want Louisa to hate him and deny him her bed, he was willing to capitulate to her group, even at the risk to his own career. Even knowing that his being prime minister would be better for the country—for her cause—in the long run.

Grandfather Monteith was right. Simon *was* a slave to his passions. But no more.

"Very well," he said, much as he loathed giving in to their blackmail. "I will make sure my wife resigns from the London Ladies Society. But understand that I cannot do anything about my sister or her friends—"

"We wouldn't expect that. Just sever *your* ties and we'll be content. That was, after all, what you promised to do from the beginning."

True. But that was before he knew how worthy Louisa's cause was. Before he saw that she and her ladies were intelligent women every bit as capable of reasonable involvement in politics as any man.

Don't think about that. The others will still have their chance. All you are doing is removing Louisa from the situation. Which she would have done herself once she conceived your child.

So why did capitulating to Sidmouth's demands feel like a betrayal of not only her ideals, but his own?

It didn't matter. Politics was a nasty business, and it was time his wife learned that. And as much as he didn't want to be the one to teach her the lesson, he had no choice.

* * *

Louisa awoke after 2 A.M. in the master bedchamber of Foxmoor House, with her book still propped on her chest and the candle merely a nub. And no Simon. He still hadn't returned from Parliament.

Sometimes sessions did go late, but *this* late? Even poor Raji, whom she'd brought up here to keep her company, was dozing on Simon's pillow.

Trying not to wake the monkey—or worry about where her husband might be—she drew on her wrapper and headed downstairs. There was no way she'd sleep now. So as long as she was up, she might as well look through more letters.

She and Simon were nearly finished going through his grandfather's correspondence. Simon's solicitor had sent a note saying that he'd unearthed a box of his grandmother's letters in the family vault, but Simon was skeptical about how useful those would be. He'd claimed that his grandfather would never have allowed his wife to keep anything so dangerous. According to Simon, Lord Monteith had kept his wife quite firmly under his thumb. Which didn't surprise Louisa, given what Betsy had said about the man and his tactics.

She felt that clutch in her belly again, the anger and horror that had hit her after Betsy had revealed the callous methods Simon's grandfather had used to teach him "that a man must keep his urges in their place." That women "are interchangeable."

What a horrible person. No wonder Simon hated him.

But should she tell Simon that she knew the truth about the earl? No. Simon was proud, and clearly mortified by his grandfather's cruel methods. Otherwise he would have told her already about what he'd endured.

She didn't want to shame him. She wanted to heal him, to show him that love wasn't a weakness to avoid. From what Betsy had said and the things he'd said himself, he seemed to believe that he couldn't feel love. But she didn't believe that. She'd seen Simon's kindness, his indulgence. He could feel a great many things, if only he would let himself.

But it would take patience and caring to undo the damage his heartless grandfather had done. One thing her work at Newgate had taught her was that wounded souls responded best to kindness and trust. The women at Newgate had flourished because she and Mrs. Fry had said, "We have faith that you can do it, that you can better yourselves. We want to see you do it."

She must show her faith in her husband, too. She'd already taken the first step by abandoning her sponges. Time to put her fear behind her, so he could put his past behind him.

She entered Simon's study, then stopped short. Her husband was slumped in the chair behind his desk, sound asleep. His coat was slung over a chair, his waistcoat neatly folded on his desk, and his cravat hung from the globe stand.

A smile touched her lips. Poor dear Simon. He must have come home late, found her asleep, and decided to work on the letters. Skirting the desk, she removed from his hand the one he was clutching.

That was enough to wake him, for he jerked up with a start. "Bloody hell, what—" He broke off as he saw her standing there in her nightdress and wrapper. A strange wariness passed over his features before he dropped his gaze to his desk and picked up another letter. "I . . . um . . . was doing some work before I came upstairs."

With a smile, she took that letter from him, too. "It's two in the morning, darling. I think you can rest now."

"Why are you still up?" he asked.

Her smile faltered. So he *hadn't* found her asleep. He'd come in and gone straight to his study. She swallowed. That probably wasn't unusual for a man like him, was it?

Yet he hadn't done it before. Even on nights when he'd decided to work late, he had come up to tell her first.

"Raji and I fell asleep waiting for you," she explained. "When I woke up and you still weren't home, I came downstairs."

"I did not mean to worry you," he said, then seemed to catch himself, for he added more coldly, "I went to my club. Men do that, you know. Stay out late at their clubs. Drink. Gamble."

Yet she didn't smell liquor on him.

No, he was pushing her away. And she suspected she knew why, too: because he was afraid of what she might have learned about his past this afternoon. Of how it might affect her feelings for him.

So she must show him that *nothing* could alter her feelings for him. "You've had quite the busy night then, haven't you?" she said cheerily and bent to take his hand. "All the more reason you need to come upstairs and get some sleep."

He inhaled sharply, then caught her hand in a firm grip, staying her. When she glanced at him, he met her gaze with a heavy-lidded one of his own, then flattened her hand against his groin.

Instantly, his flesh stirred beneath her fingers. "It's not sleep that I need," he growled.

He eyed her with an almost feverish intensity. She

knew that hungry look well. It came whenever he was tense or distraught, and it inevitably came before a swift, hard bout of fierce lovemaking that wrung them both out and enabled him to sleep.

She'd never questioned it before, but that was because she hadn't known about his grandfather's curst "training." Now that she did, she wondered if what he really wanted was something he dared not ask for. Closeness. Affection.

Which he probably thought he could only get from bedding her.

The earl had lots of rules for us to follow with him, Betsy had said. *No talking to the lad ever. And if he spoke to us, we were to report every word to his grandfather. Anything other than "do this, do that" earned him a thrashing later. He learned not to say anything foolish or sentimental. He learned not to request anything, only to demand his pleasure.*

Slowly, he stroked her hand up his burgeoning arousal. "What I need is satisfaction for *this.*" With his other hand, he tugged loose the tie of her wrapper, then pushed it off her shoulders to bare her sheer nightdress.

Her nipples tightened beneath the stark hunger of his gaze. He swept some letters aside, then ordered, "On the desk. Get up on the desk."

Though he often made such commands, a chill swept through her at this one. Because now she knew why. But this time she would also give him what he couldn't bring himself to ask for.

"Up on the desk, Louisa," Simon repeated.

"No."

He blinked. "What?"

Only certain positions were allowed.

Louisa had asked Betsy to explain that. That was when she'd realized that Simon only made love in positions where he was in control. And that there were other positions he could have used but didn't. Louisa had just been too inexperienced to know any better.

"I want to try something else," Louisa said, determined to erode his "training" however she could. Reaching down, she unbuttoned his trousers, then his drawers, so that his rampant erection sprang free. She lifted her nightdress and straddled his legs.

"How did you learn about *that*?" he rasped, even as his hands settled on her hips.

"From a book in that shop in Spitalfields where I got my sponges," she lied. "It looked interesting." Sliding up his legs until her privates cradled his rigid member, she held her breath, fearful of how he would react.

He just groaned. "You never cease to amaze me, sweetheart."

Relief coursed through her at his capitulation. "I do my best." She leaned forward to brush her lips over his tousled hair and his fine wide brow. "What else can you expect from Cleopatra?"

"Less talk, more seduction," he muttered, shoving his thick flesh against her. He reached for her breasts, but she pushed his hands aside.

"I'd rather play with you a while first." She unfastened his braces and tossed them aside, then unbuttoned his shirt and stripped it off.

"Playing" had been another of his grandfather's taboos at the bawdy house. The women were supposed to be mere vessels for Simon's urges. Anything that smacked of affection or kindness had been forbidden. Including flattery, since the women weren't allowed to speak to him.

"I love touching your body, Simon." Louisa ran her fingers down his lovely broad chest. "It's so finely made, like those exquisite carvings you whittle." With a coy smile, she tweaked his flat male nipple. "And it's fun to play with, too."

"Louisa . . ." he choked out, throwing his head back against the chair. "Oh God, don't tease me . . . I want you . . . too badly tonight."

"Just tonight?" she quipped.

He gazed at her with an oddly stricken expression. "Of course not."

Briefly unsettled by his reaction, she guided his hands beneath her nightdress to her breasts. "I love the way you touch me," she whispered. "The way you make me feel."

"Do you?" He fondled her, his eyes holding such yearning that it made her heart ache.

"I love how you look at me," she went on, determined to make this be about more than just swiving. "It makes me feel how much you care for me. It sends shivers down my spine."

"I can think of better ways to send shivers down your spine." He stroked her with his erection. "And haven't you played long enough, sweetheart?"

She choked down a protest. "Yes, I suppose I have," she said, reminding herself that changing his habits would take time. And quite likely Simon would never relinquish control entirely over their lovemaking. But this was at least a start.

Rising up on her knees, she impaled herself on him, delighting in the shudder that wracked him. But when he thrust up so hard he practically lifted her off his lap, she said, "Wait. I want to be in charge for once."

His eyes blazed at her. "You always want to be in charge, you with your London Ladies and your sponges—"

"No sponges." Casting him a loving smile, she squirmed on his lap. "I threw every one of them out after I got home this evening."

He blinked. "Really?"

"I want your child—*our* child." When his eyes lit up at that news, she rose, then came down on him with an aching slowness. "Today made me see that childbirth has rewards, as well as risks. And having your baby is a reward I can no longer resist."

She kissed him then, and the kiss instantly turned wild and raw, all tongues and teeth and uncontrollable passion.

So uncontrollable that it took her a few minutes to realize that he'd taken over the motion she'd wanted to claim for herself, and was pumping up and down inside her in short, quick bursts.

She tore her mouth from his. "Sit still, for heaven's sake! It's my turn to make love to *you.*" Her eyes gleamed at him as she rose up too high for him to fully thrust inside her. "You might like it, you know."

"You go too slow," he grumbled.

She came down on him hard, then repeated the motion swiftly. "Better?"

"Yes." Trembling with the effort not to thrust, he nuzzled her breasts through her nightdress. "But it would be better still if you . . . took off your gown."

Delighted that he hadn't commanded her to do it, she complied. But perhaps commands weren't such a bad idea, given what Betsy had told her. She pushed her breasts in his face. "Suck them, Simon," she demanded, then couldn't help adding, "Please."

Not only did his mouth seize her nipple with unprecedented fervor, but his flesh seemed to stiffen and grow even larger inside her. Her taking charge was arousing him. Perhaps there was hope for him yet.

"That's so good, yes," she whispered, wanting to reward him. "I love when you do that."

That sent him into a frenzy of caresses and kisses, each more delicious than the last. She increased her pace until he was moaning low in his throat, his fingers digging into her waist, his mouth frantic on her breasts.

"Touch me . . . down there . . ." she begged, "the way you do . . ."

"Like this?" He pressed his finger right where she wanted it.

She jumped. "Yes, yes . . . oh, heavens . . . just like that."

"That pleases you, doesn't it?" he demanded, his body moving in tandem with hers, forcing her up in violent jerks as she slammed back down against him over and over.

Pleasure was pounding in her now, like a team of horses thundering toward a precipice, closer, closer, as she rode him like a shameless wanton, grinding against him, exulting in her power over him, delighting in his power over her.

His hands gripped her arms like talons. "Do you want me?" he growled against her throat.

By now the litany was a familiar one, yet she couldn't resist giving him the words he seemed to need from her. "Yes," she whispered.

"Say it," he demanded. "'I want you, Simon. I belong to you, Simon.'"

"I want you, Simon . . . I belong to you . . . Simon." Then she added, deliberately. "I love you . . . Simon."

That wrung a cry from him, then sent him hurtling over the edge and taking her with him into her perfect bliss.

As he spilled himself inside her, clutching her to him with the fierceness of a conqueror, she kissed his hair and his forehead and any place she could reach, determined to let him know how deeply she felt.

Only after the tension drained from him and she was sure he could hear her and be conscious of the words did she whisper again, "I love you, Simon."

For a moment, he said nothing, just groaned and held her tighter, his lips ghosting kisses over her cheek and jaw and throat.

Then he drew back and cast her a look of such anguish that it made her stomach sink. And in that instant, she realized she'd somehow tipped her hand.

"You know now, don't you?" he said hoarsely. "She told you."

Chapter Twenty-Five

Dear Cousin,

Now you make me wonder, sir, about your real reason for anonymity. Is it genuinely because you wish not to harm my reputation, as you first claimed? Or does it come from your fear of engaging me in person? For I assure you, cousin, *that if you ever attempted to govern me, I would make you rue the day you met me.*

Your irate correspondent,
Charlotte

*S-*she?" Louisa stammered. "She who?"

"Betsy, damn it." He lifted Louisa off his lap and set her aside. Then with his back to her, he rose and began to button his drawers and his trousers. "She told you about . . . my grandfather and his 'training.'"

"I don't know what—"

"Don't lie to me!" He whirled around, his face suffused with anger until he saw her wary face. Then his expression softened. "Come now, sweetheart, I could tell from how you acted that she told you."

"Was I that obvious?" she asked, unable to keep the hurt from her tone as she drew on her nightdress.

"No," he said hastily. "Not until you said that you—"

He caught himself, but she knew what he'd been about to say. *That you loved me.*

Her heart twisted in her chest.

"It doesn't matter how I guessed it." He stabbed his fingers through his hair. "The point is I did. And now I want to know exactly what the lightskirt told you."

"Don't call her that!" Louisa protested. "She's not a lightskirt anymore. And she didn't want to tell me, I swear. I made her do it."

He laughed. *"Made* her. Right. What did you do—drag the woman from her childbed and beat her soundly?"

"Of course not, but you know how I am once I get hold of something." She crossed her arms over her chest as she fumbled to explain without making him more angry at Betsy. "I . . . um . . . saw that the two of you recognized each other, and I remembered that she'd worked in a bawdy house. So I demanded that she tell me how she knew you and . . . and it went from there."

"I see." Shoving his thumbs beneath the waistband of his trousers, he thrust out his chest belligerently. "I can just imagine how she put it, how pathetic she probably made me sound."

"Of course not," Louisa said evenly, determined to keep the pity from her voice. Simon would abhor being pitied.

"Trust me, my friends at Eton would have given their eyeteeth to be trotted up to London to a brothel once a week and offered their choice of whores." He began to pace. "What boy would *not* want a veritable feast of women who would do whatever he commanded?"

"Except speak to him," she murmured.

He spun around to fix her with a bleak glance. "I want to know every bloody word she told you, damn it."

Louisa met his gaze steadily. *Hide your pity,* she told herself. *Be matter-of-fact.* "She said that your grandfather had rules for you and the women to follow. And that if you broke them, you got a thrashing."

"Nothing worse than the ones boys routinely got at Eton," he bit out.

"She said that if the women broke his rules, they were sent away."

That shook him. "I don't suppose she told you where—that they were banished to the madam's other brothel, the one that wasn't so nice, where the patrons had a bent for . . . unsavory practices. Of course, I didn't learn that for some years."

"It wasn't your fault," she said softly.

"At first I didn't notice," he went on as if she hadn't spoken. "At first I thought it was just a coincidence that the women who were kindest to me, the ones I showed a preference for, who didn't lie there like mute statues while I did my business, weren't there the next time I visited."

He clenched his hands into fists. "But after a few trips, it was hard not to notice. He never let them say their names, but I knew them apart anyway. So when I asked for 'the pretty redhead' or 'the blonde with the long legs,' my grandfather thrashed me within an inch of my life. I stopped asking." He laughed bitterly. "The lesson was supposed to teach me not to care what happened to them, to realize that one woman was the same as the next. At least that's what he kept telling me."

"Instead it taught you to feel guilty."

"Yes, once I realized that my choices made them disappear. He didn't tell me where they went—just that it didn't matter. I imagined them cast into the street, starving and destitute because I expressed a preference." He shot her a self-deprecating glance. "Boys of fourteen tend to be overly dramatic."

"Boys of fourteen don't belong in brothels."

He strode over to the fireplace and leaned against the mantel to stare into the cold embers. "He didn't send many of them away. He didn't have to. Not after he established his rules so thoroughly that none of us dared break them."

A muscle worked in his jaw. "Of course, that meant the women were terrified of me, terrified I might like them too much and they would lose their nice berths. So they were careful not to do anything beyond following my orders in bed. They didn't look at me, they didn't speak to me, they didn't . . . respond when I spoke to them or . . . touched them. They lay there like . . . lumps of flesh."

Louisa's heart constricted in her chest. Even she knew that young men wanted to be petted and flattered a bit. Not treated like bulls sent out to stud.

A bitter laugh escaped his lips. "The irony is that if any of my friends had known, they would have begged to change places with me. Of course, I didn't dare tell them—my grandfather had made it very clear that it was not to be spread around, and I was so afraid what he might do to me that I never broke that rule."

He snorted. "Not that my blithe young classmates would have understood. Every randy young idiot thinks that having a pretty woman lie willing beneath him, demanding nothing while he takes his pleasure, would be ideal."

A shudder wracked him. "But none of them have ever seen terror pass over a woman's face because he said she had lovely breasts. Or had his every word reported to his grandfather by the madam who watched—"

"Watched? Someone watched you?"

"Of course. How else could my bloody grandfather make sure we did as he wanted?"

"But Betsy said that she and you managed to break the rules."

Pushing away from the fireplace, he strolled toward her. "Your friend Betsy wasn't the average lightskirt. She had been raised a gentlewoman." A cold smile touched his lips. "Betsy said she thought the rules were cruel. So the second time I bedded her, she passed me a note saying that if I was to give the madam a guinea, I could do as I pleased."

He shook his head. "I do not know why it never occurred to me to pay them off before. I knew even then that money could buy me anything. And my father certainly gave me a sufficient allowance to afford it. Instead I spent over a *year* like that, enduring his 'training.' "

"You were young. And terrified of your grandfather. You accepted it because that's how he told you it was. I'm actually surprised that the madam even agreed to go against him."

"She had grown impatient with him, I think. Anyone could see I was miserable—and she probably figured it would be better to cater to a duke's heir with plenty of years ahead of him for frequenting brothels than to an aging earl who paid well but made her girls unhappy."

"So you and Betsy started your . . . friendship."

He must have heard the tightness in her voice, for he

cast her a concerned glance. "It was not like that between us."

"That's what *she* said," Louisa choked out. It was hard not to resent the one woman who'd given her husband solace in the brothel.

"Oh, sweetheart." He came up to draw her into his arms. "You have no cause to be jealous of Betsy. It was nearly twenty years ago. And most of the time all we did was talk."

"I know. She told me." Louisa had even asked Betsy what they'd discussed.

School. His friends. How much he liked pudding. All sorts of silly things.

"You have to understand," Simon said, holding Louisa close. "Betsy was the only woman I could talk to. Literally. When Grandfather came to get me at Eton, he took me straight to the brothel. I never went home. I saw Regina only at holidays, and she was an indifferent letter writer."

Louisa knew why, but suspected that Simon did not. Regina was probably still too embarrassed to admit that she'd only learned to read and write after her marriage, when her husband had helped her past her strange problem with seeing the letters wrong.

Simon rubbed her back. "Grandfather paid my schoolmates to report on me if I dared speak to an 'unsuitable female' there, and if I did—"

"You got a thrashing."

He nodded against her head. "But Betsy would listen to me rattle on about nothing. She would tell me things. About women, what they liked. I thought she hated my grandfather as much as I did."

"Until she became his mistress."

Stiffening, he pulled away from her. "She told you about that, too, did she?"

"I already knew that she'd once had an earl for a protector. And that it didn't last long."

He looked surprised by that. "Didn't it?"

"No. She left him the first chance she got. She saved every penny he gave her, then fled to Bath and took a job as a milliner there. Until she met her husband and he moved them back to London."

That seemed to shake Simon. "I always assumed . . . he always said—"

"That she remained his mistress until he died? What else would he tell you? That a woman left *him?* Used *him?* He would never do that." Louisa laid her hand on his arm. "She feels bad about what she did to you, you know."

"Comes a little late, don't you think?" he said acidly, shrugging off her hand. "She certainly didn't feel bad back then. She put me behind her without blinking an eye. After he discovered us talking one night, he only needed a few moments of privacy with her to convince her to become his mistress."

Louisa's throat felt tight and raw just thinking of how that must have hurt Simon. "He gave her no choice. She could either become his mistress or be sent off to that other brothel. And she feared that if she didn't become his mistress, she'd never escape that life."

"That's what he threatened?" For a moment, Simon looked irate. Then he scowled. "No, I don't believe it. She would have told me. He left us alone to say our good-byes." The bleakness in his gaze struck her to the heart. "I begged her not to take up with him. I told her I would

make her *my* mistress, even though I knew I couldn't afford it on my allowance. But *she* said—"

"That she didn't care for you, was bored with coddling you." *That she wanted a real man in her bed.* Louisa couldn't torment him by reminding him of *that.* "Yes, I know what she said. Your grandfather gave her no choice there, either. She had to either crush your budding friendship or watch him thrash you for it. And she couldn't bear to see you thrashed."

He stared at her in stunned disbelief for a long moment. Then his expression crumbled. "Oh God. All this time I have thought that she—"

"Betrayed you. Pretended to like you when she really didn't. Of course you thought that." She put her arms around him, relieved when he didn't push her away. "It was better than recognizing the truth—that her defection was just another of your grandfather's awful 'lessons.'"

He buried his face in her neck. "But it should have occurred to me that he was capable of that."

"Such cruelty? How could you have imagined it? How could *anyone* imagine that someone who cared for them would treat them so horribly?"

He was trembling now, his arms tense with the effort not to let it show. "It wasn't all horrible, you know," he protested. "On the way to and from London, he taught me everything he knew about politics. He was an intelligent man and very knowledgeable."

"Very knowledgeable and very depraved." She stroked Simon's hair, wondering how Lord Monteith had ever been able to treat her dear husband so coldly. "He tried his best to make *you* depraved, too. You have no idea how much Betsy regrets her part in it."

His bitter laugh tore at her. "She should have called his bluff. I would have preferred a thrashing. Thrashings were nothing to me by then."

"I know that," she said, her throat raw with unshed tears. "But *she* didn't."

"Betsy always was tenderhearted," he choked out.

"If it's any consolation, she loathed being with your grandfather. Said he was a hateful man. And she's always wished she hadn't done what he asked."

He breathed hard and heavy for a moment, then with a quick squeeze left her arms. "Actually, she did me a favor," Simon said wearily. "After that, I balked at playing his games. I told him no matter how much he thrashed me, I would do as I pleased, would bed whichever women I pleased however I pleased. If they disappeared, so be it. Between my not caring what happened and the madam's irritation with him, he lost his hold over the situation. The brothel trips stopped."

"But the damage was done," she said.

"If you want to call it that." With unsteady motions, he picked up his shirt and pulled it on. "Infernal as his methods were, they did work. I did learn a valuable lesson."

"That women are interchangeable?" she said tartly.

"No. I never did learn that." Chucking her under the chin, he shot her a rueful smile. "If anything, going to the brothel taught me the reverse. One way I rebelled before Betsy came along was by trying to arouse my companions even when they were terrified of me. I tried everything, did everything. And that's how I discovered that each woman has different preferences." His smile faded. "And that paying for a woman muddies one's enjoyment of the experience."

"That's why you were celibate in India."

"Yes. That and the fact that I learned my grandfather's other lesson very well." He met her gaze steadily. "He did succeed in teaching me to put my ambition above all else. In teaching me not to let . . . passion cloud my judgment."

Passion. He used that word a great deal. She began to wonder if for him it meant something else. "What about love?" she whispered. "What is its place in your little hierarchy?"

He jerked away from her. "It has no place," he said in a hollow voice. "That's the one thing my 'depraved' grandfather managed to beat out of me—the ability to love. If you haven't realized it by now, you will. I am incapable of loving anyone."

"You don't believe that," she said, heartsick to hear him put it in such bald terms. "And neither do I."

"No?" Every muscle in his body went rigid. "Do you know who I was with at the club this evening, Louisa?"

A sudden premonition sent a chill down her spine. "Who?"

"Sidmouth and Castlereagh. We were discussing my future as prime minister."

"You did say you might need them to gain that position," she said warily.

"Unfortunately, I need them more than I anticipated," he said, his voice as distant as she'd ever heard it, "which is why I am . . . taking you to my estate in Shropshire in the morning."

He couldn't have astonished her more if he'd slapped her. "I don't understand."

His fingers curled into his palms, and he couldn't seem to look at her. "They made it quite clear that they would prevent my ever becoming prime minister if I did not immediately 'disassociate' myself—and my wife—from the London Ladies."

"What? How dare they!" She drew herself up, shaking from head to toe with anger. "They have no right to interfere if you choose to support my group!"

"I told them that. They did not agree. They left me no choice but to comply."

She stared at him, her stomach roiling. "So you're going to cut me off. Even though I upheld the terms of our bargain. Even though I changed my candidate—"

"They don't care about our bloody bargain, damn it!" He whirled on her, eyes blazing. "And they don't care who your candidate is, either. They simply want you and your ladies to stop interfering in politics."

Even knowing why he was doing this didn't assuage the hurt. "And since you told my father—and them—from the beginning that you would manage that, you immediately agreed to pack me off to Shropshire?"

"That was not their idea," he admitted. "They undoubtedly expect me to demand that you resign." A bitter edge tinged his voice. "Of course, they do not know how seldom my wife heeds my demands. So I am taking you away to make it easier for you."

She struggled to contain her anger. "For me? Or for you?"

"Both."

Panic seized her. "But you're going with me."

"Not to stay. Just to introduce you to the staff and—"

"Set up my prison." Her anguish threatened to choke her. "That's why you wanted to make love to me. Because you knew it would be our last time."

Guilt suffused his face. "Just for a while, until Parliament adjourns and I can join you." He dragged in a harsh breath. "You would have left the London Ladies soon anyway, once you conceived our child."

"What are you talking about?"

"That was our agreement."

"It was not! I agreed to stop going to the prison, that's all. I said nothing about ending my other activities, like pushing for reform and trying to promote our candidate. And anyway, when you said you would support Fielden, I thought you had come to accept my participation in the group. That you might even approve."

"I know what you thought. And it's true that I—" He broke off, then cleared his throat. When he spoke again, his eyes looked utterly implacable. "It does not matter what I intended. I did not realize how determined they were to scuttle your organization. Now that I do, I have to take different measures."

She couldn't believe this. Everything she'd worked for, everything she'd thought she knew about her husband was crumbling in front of her. "You're going to abandon Fielden."

"We both are," he said tightly.

A sharp pain lanced her chest. "But I already sent a letter by express to him to state that the London Ladies Society would be putting him up for office."

"Then I will inform him otherwise."

"He's a member of your own party, for heaven's sake," she cried. "There is no reason—other than their idiocy— that you should abandon him."

A shudder wracked him. "Things change."

"No, *you* have changed." Tears stinging her eyes, she hugged her arms about her waist. "You're willing to sell your soul to those devils to become prime minister."

Anger flared in his face. "When will you learn that politics requires compromise? I cannot do a bloody thing for reform if I do not have a position of power."

She shook her head. "Do you really think they're going to let you support reform once they put you in that position of power? You said you would unseat Sidmouth, but you won't dare to do that to the man who makes you prime minister. At least with my father as your champion, you had a chance of choosing your own cabinet. But if you throw in your lot with his ministers—"

"Damn it, this is the way it has to be for now."

"For now?" She strode up to seize his hands, desperate to reach him. "Sell your soul to them, and it's sold for good. They won't stop with this—Sidmouth isn't the 'compromising' sort. They'll drag you down into hell with them inch by inch until you forget every ideal you're fighting for."

He snatched his hands free. "I can build my own supporters. In time—"

"Sidmouth and Castlereagh aren't going to give you time, don't you see? They're not even giving you time to make this decision. It's either do as they demand now, or that's it."

His eyes blazed at her. "I have not been in England long enough to carry the Commons without them, damn it!"

"Perhaps not right now, but you still have your position in the Lords. Sidmouth can't do anything about that. As for the Commons, you have the husbands of some of my ladies, not to mention Mrs. Fry's brother-in-law. You'll have Fielden, if he wins. You can gather your supporters *without* Sidmouth—"

"In how many years?" he snapped. "By then, God only knows where the country will be."

She stared at his bleak face, forcing her anger back, swallowing the furious words that seared her throat. There was something more to this fierce ambition of Simon's. In the past few weeks, she'd come to know her husband well. He wasn't the sort of man to let men he despised force him into anything.

Yet in this one matter he seemed to lose all sense of character and integrity. If she was to change that, she had to know why. She had to restrain her temper, be reasonable. "What made you decide to become prime minister anyway, Simon?"

The question brought him up short. "What do you mean?"

"You can work in the House of Lords to bring about change, and perhaps do almost as much good. Why did you seize upon the ambition of being prime minister? It's a very unusual step for a man with your wealth and titles."

"Someone has to do it," he said flippantly.

She gritted her teeth against a hot retort. "That's not an answer. Why must it be you?"

He drew himself up. "So that it's done right. So that the country can move past its fear of the Reign of Terror and into a better place."

"And only *you* can accomplish that?"

"I was bred for it. Loathsome as my grandfather's tactics were, he taught me astounding things about politics. It would be foolish and irresponsible to waste that knowledge in a vain pursuit of my own pleasure—"

"Like your Uncle Tobias and your father, the duke, you mean."

He eyed her warily. "Yes."

"So you're doing it to prove you're a better man than

them?" she asked, confused. "Because you don't want to disappoint your grandfather, like his son and son-in-law did?"

"Certainly not!" He cast her a scornful glance. "Why should I care if I disappoint a dead man?" He snorted. "I disappointed *him* long ago. Grandfather never thought I could become prime minister. After my . . . error with you seven years ago, he said I was 'too much a slave' to my 'passions' to ever 'run a country successfully.'"

She began to understand better now. And what she understood broke her heart. "So you set out to prove him wrong. First, you ran India without ever giving in to your passions. But that was only preparation for the real test—running England." She caught her breath. "Except that I was still around when you returned, still inciting your 'passions.' And you can't prove him wrong as long as I keep doing so, influencing you, meddling—"

"No," he ground out. "This has nothing to do with him."

"It has *everything* to do with him," she said fiercely. "You need to prove to yourself that he was wrong about you, and to do that, you have to resist your passions. That's the real reason you're packing me off to Shropshire. Because you know you can't resist your 'passions' as long as I'm near."

He just stared at her with hollow eyes.

"But it's not just your passions you're trying to resist, is it?" she said, unshed tears clogging her throat. "You're fighting the impulse to care—not just about me, but about prison reform and all the issues Sidmouth and Castlereagh ignore. Because caring means feeling something, and nothing terrifies you more than that."

"That's enough," he choked out.

"If you feel something," she went on relentlessly, "you

risk being hurt, the way your grandfather's cruelty hurt you, the way your parents' neglect hurt you, the way Betsy's seeming betrayal hurt you—"

"Shut up, damn you!" he cried, seizing her by the shoulders. "You're wrong! It's not about that! It's only politics—"

"Nothing is ever only politics," she hissed. "Don't you see? You think you're proving him wrong, but all you're doing is *becoming* him! You're becoming the very man you detest. You're trying to turn your heart to stone so you'll have the strength to do what they ask." She lifted her hands to cup his cheeks. "And it's killing you, my love. Compromise by compromise by compromise."

For a moment, she thought she might have reached him. His eyes looked haunted, lost, and his fingers dug into her shoulders painfully.

Then with a heart-wrenching shudder, he thrust her away from him. "You do not understand how politics works, and you never will."

His voice had become so icily remote that it was no longer the voice of her beloved Simon. It was the voice of the great Prime Minister Monteith. And she had no doubt that somewhere in hell, that man was cackling in triumph.

"I am sorry it pains you, Louisa," he clipped out, "but this is the way it has to be. And we *will* be leaving for Shropshire in the morning."

She caught her breath, then steadied herself. She knew what she had to do now. Even if he hated it. "Go to Shropshire if you wish. But I will not."

Fury carved his features into coldest marble. "You are *not* going to destroy my chance at prime minister!"

"No, I wouldn't do that. For one thing, defying my

husband would harm my own reform efforts. For another, I love you, and that means I won't ruin your hopes for the future, even if I think you're wrong." When the mere word "love" made him flinch, her heart sank further. "So I'll stay here in London and be the dutiful wife, if that's what you require."

Some of the tension left him.

But she wasn't done. "That does not, however, mean that I'll abandon my organization without a word. It's only right that I prepare them for my resignation, that I meet with them and Mr. Fielden in person to explain, that I arrange for other members to take my place on the committees. Surely you won't deny me that chance."

"Louisa—" he began, his face clouding.

"I won't do it publicly, don't worry. And I won't do it here." She couldn't prevent the curtness that crept into her tone. "I wouldn't want it to get back to your 'friends' that you're allowing my ladies to come and go in your house." She glanced back to where dawn already lightened the window of his study. "So I'm going to Regina's."

That took him off guard. "For how long?"

"However long it takes." Until she could figure out how to live with *this* Simon. The one who couldn't seem to put his past behind him.

"There is no need for you to go to my sister's," he said hoarsely. "I am sure you will take care of your withdrawal from politics with discretion. As long as you are being reasonable, I would rather have you here."

"You planned to send me to Shropshire for several weeks anyway, so I don't see what difference it makes if I spend time at—" She broke off as the answer dawned on her. "Oh yes, I see. In Shropshire, you could have hidden from me the sort of man you've become. And if I stay here in our house, you think you can use our 'passions' to blind me to it."

When anger flared in his face, she added softly, "But I love you too much to hide from the truth. If I am to spend the rest of my life watching you relinquish your principles to prove something to your devil of a grandfather, I need time apart from you to prepare myself."

"To nurse your anger, you mean," he bit out.

"Tell yourself that if it makes you feel better," she whispered. "But the only person I am angry with right now is the Earl of Monteith. Because if not for him, I know without a doubt that my husband could become the greatest statesman England has ever known. Whether or not he ever became prime minister."

Swallowing her tears, she headed for the door.

"Louisa," he said behind her. "You said you love me."

"I do," she whispered.

"Then stay. Please."

Simon had never begged her for anything outside the bedchamber. He had demanded, commanded, coerced. And she was tempted, oh so tempted, to give in.

But though he might be able to accept compromise after compromise with comparative ease, she could not. "I can't right now. I'm sorry. I have matters to take care of that I just can't when I'm with you."

He snorted. "Who's hiding from the truth *now?* The only reason you're scurrying off to Regina's is because I admitted that I am incapable of loving you back. And that angers you."

"Angers me? No. Because you're not *incapable* of love, Simon. You're afraid of it. And that doesn't anger me—it just makes me sad."

He didn't leave his study while she packed a small bag

beneath Raji's watchful eye, then released the monkey from their bedchamber. He didn't step into the hall when she called for a carriage, and he didn't call out a good-bye when she walked out the door, with Raji fighting the footmen in a vain attempt to go with her.

But just as the carriage drove away in the early dawn light, she looked back to see him standing in the window of his study, watching her, stoic, distant. And that broke her heart most of all.

Chapter Twenty-Six

⟡

Dear Charlotte,
   Govern you? I would not attempt it. I happen to
like having my head attached to my body. But is it
true that your friend the Duchess of Foxmoor may be
resigning from the London Ladies Society?
                                                              Your curious cousin,
                                                                          Michael

*A*fter his wife's departure, Simon paced his study restlessly. Raji shadowed his every move with a sullen scowl,
behaving as if he'd lost his closest friend.

The way Simon felt.

Simon glowered at his pet. "Don't give me that look,
damn you. *She* abandoned *us,* old chap. It is not my fault
that she trotted off to Regina's. She's just sulking because
she's lost her cursed hold over me."

Exactly. *He* had won their ongoing battle. He had actually persuaded Louisa to resign from the London Ladies
Society.

So why didn't this feel like a victory? Why wasn't he

toasting his success? He had finally put his career in the proper perspective. Why wasn't he ecstatic to finally, *finally* have gained control over his passions? Because of some foolish nonsense his wife had said about passions and feelings?

He muttered a curse under his breath. She did not understand. She was a woman—they thought everything was about "caring" and "feelings." But some things transcended that. Politics, for one.

"'Nothing is ever only politics,' " he muttered. "What rot!"

What did *she* know about it? She had never been forced to compromise, never had a reason.

Except when he had given her one. Except when he had made demands.

He gritted his teeth. He doubted very seriously that any other statesman had to deal with such impudence from a wife. *He* was probably the only one who would even tolerate it. *He* was probably the only one who even bothered to listen to his wife's opinions.

She had forced him into this position. It was not his fault if she refused to recognize political necessities. That was why women were not statesmen—because they did not understand the nasty nature of politics. As Grandfather Monteith always said, *Women*—

Simon groaned. He was *not* becoming his grandfather. God forbid!

Yes, he had learned a great deal from the man and did occasionally recall his advice, but that did not mean Simon was turning into him. Absolutely not. He would never be his grandfather, never.

She was making him insane. He had to escape this place, and escape her ridiculous accusations.

But where was he to go? The session didn't begin until later, and he was not sure he could stand looking at Sidmouth and Castlereagh today anyway. What he needed was something physical to drive her voice from his brain. A good hard ride. Yes, to clear his head before the rest of London society awakened.

He hurried upstairs to change into riding breeches, but as soon as he entered his bedchamber, he cursed. The bed made him think instantly of her, and her lilac scent lingered in the room.

Raji jumped atop her dressing table, then chattered angrily at him.

"Get off there, you besotted fool!" Grabbing Raji, he tossed him onto the bed, where his pet promptly began to swing from the hangings and shriek.

"Do you think I like her being gone any more than you do?" Simon snarled.

His mind was flooded by images of her making love to him in his study, like some fearless Valkyrie determined to wipe out the past. He had never reached so fierce a climax. Or hated himself so much for it.

Because after foolishly thinking that one more time together would sate his need for her, he'd discovered that it merely increased his guilt.

Deuce take it, he had nothing to feel guilty about! He had done what he had to. It was better this way. She needed to see what was required of a statesman's wife, no matter how painful acknowledging the truth was for her.

No matter how much she loved him.

With a groan, he dropped into the chair beside her dressing table and buried his face in his hands. *I love you.* Those had been her cruelest words. He had never guessed how sweet they would sound on her lips until she spoke them. Until she dangled before him the one thing he craved, the one thing he had yearned all his life to have.

The one thing he had no right to, since he could never say the words back.

But romantic fool that she was, she didn't think him incapable. She thought him afraid. A coward. It made her "sad."

Sad, damn her! She pitied him! How dare she pity him?

His temper exploding, he swiped his hand across the dressing table, sending perfume bottles and rouge pots and brushes flying. Raji abruptly stopped swinging to hang whimpering from the bedstead.

Simon's head felt like it would explode, so of course his grandfather's voice came to torment him and egg him on. *That's it—show your wife who's in charge. Be a man. She's just a woman like any other.*

Except that she wasn't.

"I have to get out of here," Simon said as the stench of perfume threatened to choke him and the voice of his grandfather plagued him.

Jerking to his feet, he hastily changed his clothes, then plucked Raji from the bedstead. "Come, scamp. We're going for a ride." Someplace where nothing reminded him of Grandfather Monteith. Or her.

He spent the rest of the day trying to accomplish that. He rode in Brompton Vale, blessedly empty at that early hour. It should not have made him think of her, since he had never been near there with her.

Yet the sheltering oaks and yew hedges reminded him of the woods where he'd first kissed her after his return from India. And when Raji took a sudden leap into the boughs, he couldn't help remembering how he'd tricked her into kissing him the second time . . . and letting him caress and suck her sweet, scented flesh—

Brompton Vale was not a good choice for forgetting her.

Unfortunately, it took him a good two hours to coax Raji down so he could head for his second choice: his solicitor, who had found Grandmother Monteith's letters. Simon had intended to have them sent over, but he might as well fetch them himself. Nothing at the solicitor's office could possibly remind him of Louisa.

Unfortunately, seeing his grandmother's spidery script on the outside of the box stirred other painful memories. Of his grandfather bullying his wife, calling her a silly fool and ordering her about. The way Simon had tried to bully Louisa.

He gritted his teeth. That was not true; he had not bullied her. He had made perfectly reasonable demands. It was she who was unreasonable, she who could not see why he must act as he did.

The solicitor's office was clearly another bad choice for forgetting her.

His third choice proved better. After dropping Raji and the letters off at Foxmoor House, he headed for White's. Not only was it devoid of memories of Louisa, but it provided the perfect solution to his pain—he could drink himself into oblivion.

Simon wasn't much of a drinker. He didn't like losing control of his senses. But some occasions called for burying one's sorrows in a bottle, and this just happened to be one.

Unfortunately, he had barely embarked upon his quest for oblivion at White's when a familiar voice hailed him.

"Foxmoor?"

He glanced up. "Ah, Trusbut. Good evening." He lifted a bottle. "Port?"

With a nod, Trusbut lowered himself carefully into a chair across from Simon, settling his cane between his spindly legs. "I didn't see you in sessions, so I wasn't certain if you had remembered our engagement."

Their engagement? Christ, he had forgotten all about it. "Did I miss anything interesting at Westminster?" Simon asked as he filled a glass for Trusbut.

"Not in the session." Trusbut leaned forward to take it. "But I did hear some interesting gossip. A friend in the Commons told me that Thomas Fielden received a note from your wife yesterday, saying that you and the London Ladies Society mean to support him in the by-election."

Simon's fingers tightened on his glass. Damn, he had forgotten that Louisa had already informed Fielden of their choice. For the by-election she would now have to abandon.

But he could not tell Trusbut that. He owed it to Louisa not to reveal anything until she'd had her talk with Fielden and the London Ladies.

Trusbut sipped his port. "I must say I was pleased to hear it. There had been talk of the Society supporting Godwin, and that would have been very bad."

With a nod, Simon took a gulp of his port. He did not want to have this conversation. But he also did not want to alienate Trusbut by dismissing him.

"Fielden's a good man, very sensible," Trusbut went on. "And very interested in reform."

"So I gather," Simon said noncommittally.

They were silent a moment. Then Trusbut cleared his throat. "Actually, the news of Fielden has emboldened me to broach a matter of some delicacy."

The last thing Simon needed right now was to discuss matters of *delicacy.*

But before he could put the man off, Trusbut said, "It concerns Liverpool. And his cabinet."

Taken by surprise, Simon searched Trusbut's face, but could read nothing in the older man's rheumy eyes. "That is indeed a delicate subject."

"Some of us . . . that is . . . you probably are aware of the explosive situation that has arisen in England in the past few years."

"Yes." More aware than he'd like, given the havoc it wreaked in his marriage.

"A number of us think it's time for a change in government."

Simon blinked. Had Sidmouth and Castlereagh already started marshaling their forces? "I quite agree," he said evasively.

"Not the prime minister, you understand. Liverpool has his faults, but he is not a bad leader. The people would support him if not for Sidmouth and Castlereagh. *They're* who the masses blame for the recent troubles, and rightly so."

Gulping a generous measure of port, Simon sat back in his chair. *This* was not what he had expected. "So what exactly are you and your friends proposing?"

"We have spoken to Liverpool, discreetly, of course. And he seems to agree that those two ministers need to step down. He is even willing to let himself be guided by more moderate individuals in choosing new ones."

"Is he?" Simon said, his mind awhirl. How had he missed this particular bit of masterful machination going on around him?

That was easy to answer: he'd been distracted by his

wife *and* by the king and Sidmouth. They seemed to believe that Liverpool was entirely under siege by the Commons and the Lords, but the truth was apparently not so clear-cut. "What new ministers do you and your friends have in mind?"

"Robert Peel for Home Secretary, of course." Trusbut tilted his glass toward Simon. "You and your wife should approve, given his support of prison reform."

"Yes, Peel would be my own choice."

"George Canning for Foreign Secretary," Trusbut went on.

"Canning!" Simon exclaimed. "The king will not like that."

"No, but we don't mean to consult him. Liverpool intends to present this as a fait accompli. The king will have little choice but to accept it once he is shown the wisdom of it."

"I see." This new turn of events set Simon back on his heels.

"Canning is a brilliant statesman."

"Indeed he is," Simon admitted. Although Canning had once turned down the position as prime minister, he might accept a position as Foreign Secretary. The man was unfortunately against parliamentary reform, but perhaps he could be persuaded to change his stand. At least he supported other reforms.

Trusbut surprised him by taking a large gulp of port. "And . . . er . . . we've been thinking that you might consider a position, as well."

Simon's heart hammered in his chest. "Oh?"

"Secretary of War. Given your experience in India, we thought you would be an asset in that area." Trusbut held him with a piercing gaze. "Since your aspiration is to one day become prime minister, that position would provide you an excellent start. For the day when Liverpool *is* willing to step down. Which, given the current turmoil in the country, we hope won't be too soon."

Simon wondered if Trusbut knew that Sidmouth and Castlereagh wanted to unseat Liverpool. Surely not, or he would never be talking about this to the man they wanted to put in Liverpool's place.

But perhaps *they* had known that this was in the wind. That was why they'd made their offer, to trump the others by putting Simon in *their* court. In exchange for his selling his soul and grinding his wife under his thumb.

He swallowed some port, dizzy from having his world shifted on its axis. Because if Trusbut and his companions were successful . . . "Can you really bring this change to pass? Gain the resignations of both Castlereagh and Sidmouth?"

"We can. Especially if you join us. When you first returned, we weren't sure where your alliances lay, given your past friendship with the king. That day at my house you made it clear you opposed radical candidates, but couldn't tell if you supported the other extreme. Particularly in light of your connection to Monteith."

"My grandfather?"

"He always championed Sidmouth in the early days."

Simon had not known that. By the time he had been old enough to take his seat in Parliament, his grandfather had long retired as prime minister. A chill skittered down his spine as he remembered Louisa's words. That he was becoming his grandfather. God help him.

It suddenly occurred to him that Trusbut was nearly the age his grandfather would have been if he'd lived. "Did you know my grandfather?"

"Not personally, no." His clipped tone showed he was hiding something.

"But you knew enough not to approve of him," Simon guessed. When Trusbut looked wary, he added, "I understand, believe me. And I would very much like to hear your honest opinion of him."

"He was a solid statesman, a shrewd negotiator, and a brilliant orator, but—"

"But?"

Trusbut frowned. "I once overheard him speak privately to Lady Monteith at a party. His manner was most ungentlemanly. Indeed, I would be ashamed to say such . . . awful things to my Lillian."

"'Ungentlemanly.' A rather astute assessment of my grandfather's private character."

"But I can tell that you're not such a man, sir," Trusbut went on. "Indeed, I've been impressed by your treatment of your wife. One can tell a great deal about a man by how he treats the women in his care, don't you think?"

"I believe you are right," Simon said, his blood thundering in his ears.

Trusbut looked at his watch. "And speaking of wives, I promised mine that I would be home for dinner this evening." He shot Simon a questioning glance. "About the matter I mentioned—"

"Could I have a day to think about it, sir?"

"Certainly." He rose. "I trust you will be discreet."

Simon managed a smile. "Of course. No one will hear of this from me."

"Then I shall see you tomorrow afternoon at the meeting."

"Meeting?" Simon asked.

"I saw Lord Draker earlier today. He asked me to tell

Lillian that your wife has called a meeting of the London Ladies Society for tomorrow. Since Fielden is also supposed to be there, I assume the meeting is to announce your support."

No. The meeting was to announce Louisa's resignation. "Ah, the meeting," Simon managed to say. "Remind me again what time it is?"

Trusbut eyed him closely. "Draker said four P.M."

"Right." He forced a smile to his lips. "I am not sure if I will be attending. I may have another appointment. But I will try."

"Then I hope to see you there." Taking up his cane, Trusbut made his slow way from the room.

Long after the elderly gentleman left, Simon sat staring into his port. All this time, he had considered only one solution to the problems plaguing the present government—Liverpool stepping down. But that was because Simon had intended to take the man's place.

Trusbut's proposal opened up other possibilities. Peel was a Tory, but not quite the old guard. He was certainly more moderate than either Sidmouth or Castlereagh. And if men like Trusbut intended to back him, they were probably also eager to begin the process of reform, not only in the election process, but in other badly needed areas. Like the prisons.

That meant they might accomplish exactly what Simon had wanted to accomplish himself. And all he had to do to help was forget about becoming prime minister for now. Perhaps forever.

Why must it be you?

His wife's words rang in his ears as he set down his glass. Yes, why *must* the prime minister be him? He had said it was because only he could ensure that England was set on the right course. But was that truly his reason? Or had Louisa stumbled upon the truth—that he was really more concerned about proving himself to Grandfather Monteith than about doing what was best for his country?

A sobering thought, and quite possibly a just one. Even now, as Trusbut's proposal lay before him, his first instinct was to refuse. And why? Because he would have to temper his ambition.

Because he would not be able to prove his grandfather wrong.

He clenched his fingers on the glass. Louisa was right. He didn't give a damn about England—he was just trying to silence the curst voice of a dead man.

Suddenly no longer eager to drink himself into oblivion, he rose and set his glass aside, then left the club and headed home in a daze.

If he agreed to Trusbut's proposal, it would change everything. There'd be no reason for Louisa to resign from the London Ladies Society, no reason for his wife to look at him with such disappointment and pity that it chilled his blood.

There you go again, he could almost hear his grandfather sneering. *Letting your passions ruin your ambition.*

Ruin it? Or enrich it?

What if Louisa was right about that, too? What if it wasn't his passions he was trying to control, but his feelings? The part of him that cared about what happened to farmers wanting representation in government, and convict women who wanted only some kindness and a chance to start anew?

The part that yearned to have his wife regard him with pride and respect. And love. Definitely love.

Once home, he went right to his bedchamber, not wanting to make any major decisions when his body needed sleep so badly. But sleep eluded him in a bed whose sheets smelled of his wife.

So he left it to wander down to his study. If anything could help him sleep, it was those curst letters. He opened the box he'd brought back from his solicitor and skimmed the first few, sure that the exercise was pointless. Then he picked up a thick packet, and his heart began to pound. Not only were the edges charred, as if someone had rescued it from a fire, but it was postmarked India.

He couldn't prevent a little leap of excitement. Especially when he carefully separated the fragile parchment sheets to find an official document sandwiched in the middle.

Uncle Tobias's marriage certificate.

Swiftly, Simon separated out the pages of the letter that came with it and began to decipher his uncle's unfamiliar scrawl. When he finished, he sat back and stared blindly across the room.

Hard to believe that it had been in his grandmother's papers all this time. He remembered her as a mousy woman utterly cowed by his grandfather.

Saving this from the fire had been her tiny rebellion. She had probably realized that her husband would never expect her to defy him, would never look through her papers after she died. Since her oldest son was still alive when she died, she wouldn't have known if the paper might become necessary one day.

But she'd kept it just in case. As any caring mother would. And if *she,* his sad and pitiful grandmother, could ignore the demands of her bastard of a husband to thwart him beyond the grave, *Simon* damned well could.

Because the truth was, he did not want to listen to Monteith anymore. He wanted to listen to the demands of his heart.

Apparently he had one after all. Otherwise, why was his stomach in knots over the thought of losing his wife's respect? Why was there a persistent ache in his chest that worsened every time he considered a future in which they lived separate lives, like his parents?

He could not do it. Not now that he'd tasted love.

In that instant, he knew exactly what his path must be.

He waited for his grandfather's voice to plague him, to lash at him, to call him a fool—but nothing came. Just a blessed, blissful silence, a pure and holy peace. As if the ghosts of his uncle and grandmother had finally shamed Monteith into retreat.

All that was left was the sweet and lilting voice of his wife. *I know without a doubt that my husband could become the greatest statesman England has ever known. Whether or not he ever became prime minister.*

And with that hopeful, loving statement ringing in his ears, he was finally able to sleep.

Chapter Twenty-Seven

❧⟡❧

Dear Cousin,

I cannot imagine Louisa ever resigning her position unless some great reason required it. She might do it for love. I begin to think that she loves her husband dearly.

Your cousin,
Charlotte

At 3:55 P.M. the next day, Regina and Louisa stood at the front of the ballroom in Regina's town house, watching the members of the London Ladies Society mill about the rows of chairs with several of Mrs. Fry's Quakers. A few men who supported the Society's aims had come, too. Even Lord Trusbut was here with his wife, although he kept perusing his pocket watch with a frown.

"Simon has no right to demand this of you," Regina whispered as she scanned the room. "When next I see him, I shall tell him that."

"It will do no good." Louisa glanced over to where Marcus stood a few feet away, brooding. "You didn't tell my brother, did you? He thinks I really *want* to step down?"

"I didn't say a word, but he's not an idiot. He can tell from looking at you that something is wrong. But he's trying hard not to meddle. He does not believe in coming between a man and his wife." She drew herself up. "*I*, however, do not believe any such thing. If you would just let me, I would talk to Simon—"

"It won't change anything. Your brother is even more stubborn than mine. Once he sets a course, he doesn't waver, no matter how much anyone reasons with him."

Loving him didn't seem to work, either. Yet she couldn't stop. She'd spent last night churning her sheets, missing him, rethinking everything she'd said, wishing for what couldn't be.

Part of her had hoped he would show up this morning, begging her to return home. If he'd come here after her, it might have made her sacrifice easier.

Because the one thing she couldn't hope for was a reprieve. Simon's ambition had always usurped anything—and anyone—in his life. She'd be mad to think he would give it up just so she could continue leading her group.

Never mind that his cohorts were utterly unreasonable. Never mind that he didn't respect them or their aims, and that giving in meant the end of his own aims for reform. He was determined to prove himself to his dead idiot grandfather. And there wasn't anything she could do about it.

Tears sprang to her eyes that she desperately squelched. Surely she'd cried enough in the past day to fill a lake—must she fill an ocean, too? But how could she help it with the pitiful choices that the future offered her?

She couldn't leave Simon. Even if it could be managed

legally, she could never divorce him, for that would ruin his political aspirations. But they could live apart. She could busy herself at his estate while he spent his days in London. And when the season was over and he returned to the country, they could still live separate lives. It's not like they'd be stumbling over each other on his grand estate.

The trouble was, she didn't *want* to leave him or live apart from him. She wanted to be his wife, to bear his children, to live with him in harmony. But she couldn't when it meant letting him swallow her up, body and soul. How long before she became like his mother—brittle and distant, cold and uncaring? How long before she became just like *him*?

A footman pushed through the crowd to approach the dais they had set up. "Your Grace," he said as he reached her and Regina. "There is a man from the *Times* requesting entrance to your meeting."

Louisa sucked in a breath. "What? How did *they* find out about it?"

"Perhaps Mr. Fielden told them?" Regina whispered. "Before you had your meeting with him earlier?"

"Good heavens, I hope not."

Louisa glanced to where Mr. Fielden sat stalwart and grim. He'd agreed to stay until after the meeting, but his disappointment was unmistakable. "Mr. Fielden doesn't seem the type to court the press on his own." She turned to the footman. "Tell the gentleman from the *Times* to leave, if you please."

With a nod, the footman left, only to return moments later. "The gentleman refuses, Your Grace. He says he is waiting for the duke, your husband, to arrive."

She scowled. "The duke is not attending this meeting,

no matter what the press may assume. So tell him to be off, or I'll—"

"I'll take care of this," Marcus said, drawn over by the discussion.

After they left, she stood there, seething. "I wonder how the *Times* found out. If one of our ladies told them, I swear I'll get to the bottom of it."

"How?" Regina asked. "You won't be part of the London Ladies anymore."

Louisa's heart sank. "Drat it all." She stared out at the crowd, tears burning in her throat. Her members were settled in their seats, watching her expectantly. Best to get this done, before she fell apart. "Time to begin, I suppose."

Regina nodded and went to sit in the front row.

With a sinking in the pit of her stomach, Louisa took her place at the podium and waited until the crowd fell silent. "Good morning, ladies. I do appreciate your coming here today. It is with great sadness and regret that I announce—"

"—that her husband is deplorably late," finished a voice from the back of the room.

Her words caught in her throat and her gaze shot to where Simon was hurrying to the front, with several men at his heels. He looked harried as he gestured toward the chairs, and his companions slid into whatever empty seats they could find.

She tensed, not sure what to make of this. Was he actually daring to take over her meeting? After forcing her to have it in the first place?

As he reached the podium, she murmured, "Who are those men?"

"Members of the press," he said in a low voice. "I'm

sorry—I meant to be here an hour ago, but I had some trouble extricating myself from Sidmouth and Castlereagh."

"If you think I'll allow you to use *my* meeting for your political purpose—"

"Trust me." Seizing her hand, he squeezed it hard. "Let me have my say, all right? I promise you won't regret it, my love."

The words "my love" arrested her and she stared at him. He looked far different from when she'd left him yesterday in his study. The animation in his features lent a new brilliance to his beautiful blue eyes. And he was smiling so warmly that it couldn't help but light a spark in her, too.

With her heart clamoring in her chest, she nodded, then turned with him to face the murmuring crowd, her hand still caught in his. She spotted her brother standing in the back, an approving smile on his lips, which increased her hope.

Simon cleared his throat and the crowd fell silent. "As my wife said, we appreciate your coming here today. Because she and I are pleased to announce that we will be joining the London Ladies Society in endorsing Mr. Thomas Fielden for the upcoming by-election."

Louisa's breath hitched in her throat and she swung her gaze to Simon, hardly able to believe her ears. He was supporting Mr. Fielden after all?

To her shock, Simon winked at her—winked, of all things!

He squeezed her hand again and went on. "Would you come up to the podium, Mr. Fielden?"

Mr. Fielden rose, looking as flummoxed as she felt, and made his way to the front amid applause and ladylike murmurs of approval. Louisa stole a glance at the reporters, who were scribbling madly in their notebooks.

As the man reached the podium, Simon seized his hand and shook it vigorously, then turned back to the podium. "We are confident that Mr. Fielden will be a fine asset to the Commons, especially in light of his continued interest in prison reform." He stepped back. "Would you like to say a few words, sir?"

"Thank you, Your Grace." Mr. Fielden approached the podium. To his credit, he was able to think on his feet, for he gave a short and pithy speech that laid out his progressive aims well.

The whole time, Louisa stood there frozen, her hand crushing Simon's. Did this mean Simon had come to his senses?

Mr. Fielden finished his speech, then returned to his seat amid enthusiastic applause. Simon drew Louisa back to the podium. "In the past few weeks, I have had the great honor of watching my wife at the helm of this fine organization. In that time, her cause has become my own. That is why I am pleased to announce that, as of today, my good friend Robert Peel has agreed to head up a Parliamentary committee to draft a Gaols Bill."

A stunned silence fell upon the room. Then the ladies rose as one and burst into thunderous clapping. As Louisa's knees buckled under the weight of her rampaging emotions, Simon caught her about the waist to steady her.

"Sorry you had to hear it this way, my love," he murmured. "I meant to tell you before the meeting started, but it has been a day of meetings for me, and I only made it here because I drove the phaeton neck-or-nothing across Hyde Park."

"You have nothing to apologize for, nothing!" she said giddily. "A Gaols Bill! Do you know how long we've pressed for such a thing? I don't know what you did to accomplish it, but—"

"I will tell you later," he broke in. "But first we have to finish this."

He turned back to the podium as the applause began to die, and she stretched up on tiptoe to speak in his ear. "This *does* mean I don't have to resign from the London Ladies, doesn't it?"

He shot her a teasing smile, though his eyes were full of remorse. "And leave them in the lurch now that they are on the brink of achieving their highest goal? What are you thinking, woman?"

Her heart soared. *I'm thinking I love you.*

Simon faced the crowd. "And now I shall turn the podium back to my wife so she can continue the meeting, since I am not yet officially a member of the London Ladies Society."

That garnered him some laughs as Louisa stepped to the podium. "I fear that anything else I could say wouldn't compare to this wonderful news. But before we adjourn, I do want to thank the duke from the bottom of my heart." She cast him a smile full to the brimming with love. "Because today he has made me proud beyond words to be his wife." Amid another burst of applause, she adjourned the meeting.

It was nearly an hour before she could get her husband alone. Reporters besieged him with questions, which he answered with his usual aplomb. Meanwhile, she was swamped with Quakers and members of the Society offering her thanks that she felt almost guilty to accept. Simon had convinced Robert Peel to form the committee—she was sure of that.

Then Lady Trusbut pushed her way through to Louisa,

her husband following more slowly behind her. "What a victory, my dear, a complete victory!" she crowed. "I cannot wait to tell the girls. Opal will be positively giddy with joy." She leaned close. "She's the one who most encouraged my participation in your group, you know. On account of her aversion to cages."

Louisa laughed. "Then do thank Opal for me." She squeezed Lady Trusbut's hand. "Because we are delighted to have your support. You and your husband's."

Glancing around for Lord Trusbut, Louisa spotted him standing apart with Simon, engrossed in a secretive conversation. When the two men were done they headed back to their wives, Lord Trusbut smiling broadly enough to split his cheeks.

"Come, my dear," Lord Trusbut told his wife as they approached, "we must go. I promised Fielden that we'd stop by his house so he and I can discuss strategy." When Lady Trusbut looked as if she might protest leaving so soon, he added, eyes twinkling, "And Mrs. Fielden keeps parakeets. Three of them."

That was all it took to have Lady Trusbut chirping her good-byes and taking her husband's arm. Before Lord Trusbut left, he nodded to Simon. "I shall see *you* at Westminster Palace tomorrow, to meet with Liverpool, Peel, and Canning."

Liverpool, Peel, and Canning? Her gaze shot to Simon. That was an odd group, wasn't it?

Fortunately, Regina was already herding out the stragglers. She paused to blow a kiss at Louisa, then left the ballroom and shut the doors.

At last Louisa and Simon were alone. Her mind awhirl, she asked breathlessly, "What was Lord Trusbut talking about?"

"It is not completely settled yet, but a new government is being formed."

"Liverpool is resigning?"

"No. Sidmouth and Castlereagh are. Not yet, but soon. They were given no choice."

She gaped at him. "But that means—"

"I am not going to be prime minister." He cast her a faint smile. "Not for some time, anyway. I will be Secretary of War in Liverpool's cabinet. With Peel as Home Secretary and Canning as Foreign Secretary—once we convince the king."

"B-but how did this happen?"

He related a conversation he'd had with Trusbut and revealed how change had been in the works for some time.

Yet that didn't explain what she really wanted to know. "And you're happy about this? Not being prime minister, I mean?"

The smile he shot her looked genuine. "Fine, actually. You were right—I *was* only trying to prove myself to my grandfather. But if I had sold my soul to Sidmouth and Castlereagh, I would have regretted it all my life. Grandfather Monteith was from a different age, as are they. And I did not belong there." He took her hand in his. "I belong *here*. With you."

Hope swelled in her chest. "What changed your mind?"

"You have to ask?" he said hoarsely. "Yes, I suppose you do." He caressed her hand. "It was several things, actually. For one, I found Uncle Tobias's marriage certificate among Grandmother's papers. Along with this letter."

Stunned, she watched as he drew a sheet with charred

edges out of his coat pocket and handed it to her. She read it quickly. Addressed to Simon's grandmother, it began with his uncle's account of how he came to be dying.

But it was the last two paragraphs that made her heart catch in her throat:

> *I am sending this in hopes that you can prevail upon Father to do what is right by my dear wife and infant son. As my legitimate heirs, they should receive any inheritance due to them upon my death.*
>
> *I know Father does not understand my choice of wife, but that is because he fears love too much to embrace it himself. Instead he takes his cold comfort from his accomplishments. But tell him I die content, knowing that for however brief a period, I have had the best thing a man can ask for in this fickle world— someone to love.*
>
> > *Your faithful son,*
> > *Tobias Hunt*

Tears stung her eyes as she handed the letter back to Simon.

He took it and said in a choked voice, "It appears that Grandmother did try to prevail upon Grandfather, and he tossed the documents in the fire. She must have rescued them and kept them all these years.

"You can imagine what I felt when I read this. It hammered into my brain what you'd said. And I knew without a doubt that I would be well on my way to becoming my grandfather if not for you."

A tear trickled down her cheek. "I don't believe that. always had faith that you could be a better man if you chose."

"And your words have tormented my conscience eve since you spoke them." He lifted her hand to his lips, then kissed it. "That is what really changed my mind. That, and the fear of losing you."

"You wouldn't have lost me."

"No? You have too much integrity to live with a man who has none. And I could not have endured watching the woman I love lose her respect for me, 'compromise by compromise by compromise.'"

His echo of her words touched her heart. Then the rest of what he said registered. "The woman you love?" Tears of happiness clogged her throat.

He drew her into his arms, his eyes so tender it made her chest hurt. "I do love you. I think I've loved you for years. But I was terrified of it, as you said—terrified that loving you would mean Grandfather was right about my being a slave to my passions. He probably *was* right—and I don't care. Because *you* are 'the best thing a man can ask for.'"

He kissed her then, with the sort of soft, sweet affection that fed a woman's starving soul. When at last he drew back, she understood why poets spoke of hearts bursting for joy. Because surely hers would split its seams any minute.

"Come, sweetheart, let's go home," he said.

She couldn't resist teasing him. "Is that a request? Or command?"

His eyes gleamed at her as he led her to the door. "What do *you* think?"

"I think . . ." she said, giddy with happiness, "it's a good thing you didn't marry me seven years ago. I'm not sure I could have handled you then."

The tigerish glance he gave her set her blood to thrumming. "And you think you can handle me now?"

"No." When he laughed, she added, "But I shall certainly enjoy trying."

Epilogue

Dear Cousin,

My friend went into her confinement at Foxmoor House rather than her husband's estate. She did not want to be away while Parliament was in session, and I gather the duke did not want her away, either. Isn't that sweet? She says he is planning a christening party to rival the king's coronation celebration. I fear she is only half joking.

Your cousin,
Charlotte

Simon paced the hall outside his wife's bedchamber. Raji paced right beside him. Neither one was happy.

"The screaming has stopped, at least," Simon muttered to Raji. His wife's screaming *and* his pet's. He should have banished Raji to his study, the way Louisa had banished Simon to the hallway. But he needed the company.

"Damned doctors," Simon told Raji. "She just *had* to have the prison doctor to deliver our child. She couldn't let my own capable physician attend her. Oh no. Only the man who'd delivered Betsy's girl would do."

Raji chattered in answer, then seized Simon's leg.

"At least *my* doctor wouldn't have let her kick me out

of the room. All I was doing was begging the man to stop her pain. What's wrong with that?" Simon picked the rascal up, needing something to keep his hands busy so he didn't put a fist through a wall. "She said I made her anxious. *Her?* She's bloody well killing *me!* It's been fourteen damned hours. How long does it take to have a baby, anyway?"

The door opened and the doctor emerged, beaming from ear to ear. "You have a fine and healthy son, Your Grace."

Simon caught his breath, clutching Raji so tightly, the poor devil protested. "And Louisa? Is she . . . ?"

"She's doing well. Tired, but that's to be expected."

Tears sprang to Simon's eyes. "Thank God."

He headed for the door, then paused to thrust Raji into the doctor's hands.

"Wait!" the doctor cried. "What am I to do with him?"

"Just don't let him come in here, that's all," Simon said

As he entered the room and shut the door firmly behind him, he heard the doctor mutter, "I wasn't going to believe me."

Regina was helping the nurse clean off his son, but Simon had eyes only for his wife, who reclined against the headboard. He'd never seen her look so pale, so drained.

So damned beautiful.

Hurrying to her side, he seized her hand. "We'll never have another one, I swear. We'll use sponges and condoms and watch the phases of the moon—"

"Don't be ridiculous," she said with a weak laugh "We'll do no such thing." She cradled his hand against he heart. "It wasn't so bad, you know."

"You were screaming! Raji went almost out of hi mind to hear it."

"And you?" she teased.

"I was way beyond out of my mind." His voice grew hoarse. "I have never heard you scream like that."

"You'd scream, too, if someone were trying to shove their way out of *your* belly." Her eyes twinkled at him. "But given your bedside manner, I believe next time I'll banish you to a room farther away. In Shropshire, perhaps."

"That's not funny," he grumbled. "I was afraid I'd lose you."

She cupped his face with a tender smile. "I know. But I wasn't about to let something so silly as childbirth pangs keep me from spending my life with you." When Regina came over and laid the babe in Louisa's arms, Louisa added, "And our son."

A lump lodged in Simon's throat. *Their son.* It hit him at last. He had a son.

He leaned closer to look at the squirming bundle, at the closed eyes and the cherry of a mouth, then blinked back more tears. "He's absolute perfect."

"Of course he is. He's yours, isn't he?"

Simon gave a choked laugh, feeling light-headed. He touched the tiny fist, and the little fingers closed about his index finger, holding on with a surprisingly strong grip.

"Now tell me, what happened?" Louisa said eagerly.

"What happened where?" he asked, absorbed in marveling over his son.

"The Gaols Bill! Did it pass the Second Reading?"

Good God, he'd forgotten entirely where he'd been when she'd gone into labor. "Yes, Joan of Arc. It passed. They had just announced it when the servant summoned me home."

"That means it's sure to become an Act of Parliament." She gazed at him, her eyes alight. "Oh, did Mr. Fielden give his speech? The one I wrote for him?"

"Indeed he did, and it was every bit as stirring as the woman who wrote it." He chucked her under the chin. "You are quite a piece of work. You just bore your first child, and *that's* what you're thinking about?"

"Not only that." She grinned. "I also want to know the news about your cousin. Regina said the decision about his title was to be made today. I did not expect it so soon—what happened?"

"The king finally upheld one of his promises to me, believe it or not. He hemmed and hawed a bit, but after the way Trusbut and I forced him into changing his cabinet last year, he knew better than to cross me in the matter of Colin's title. I told him I wanted it done with all due speed and he made sure it was."

"So?"

"Colin is now officially the Earl of Monteith." He shot her a mischievous glance. "And my grandfather is now officially turning over in his grave."

"Good." She smiled down at their son. "I hope he turns a dozen more times once our boy grows up. Because little John David Henry Augustus is sure to be a far more progressive prime minister than your nasty grandfather ever was."

"No son of mine shall ever be prime minister," Simon said solemnly.

She cast him a bemused look. "Why not?"

"Because I want something better for him."

"Like what?"

His heart full, he brushed a kiss on her damp brow. "This, sweetheart. A deep and abiding love."

She gazed up at him with shining eyes. "Why can't he have both? You do."

"Ah, but I was lucky, and I doubt lightning will strike twice. Politics does not generally make for happy marriages. Look at my grandfather's."

"That only went badly because he was such a monster."

"Perhaps." He gazed at his son. "Or perhaps politics creates men like him—sad little Napoleons who can't bear not to be in control of everything, even their personal lives. Which means they have to beat down whomever they can't control."

Stroking his wife's hair, Simon marveled again at his good fortune. "Either way, if I have to choose between a happy marriage or a future in politics for my son, the happy marriage will win hands down."

Taking the baby from Louisa, he held him for the first time, tears stinging the back of his throat. Life was good. *This* was good. "Because as Uncle Tobias once said, the best thing a man can ask for in this fickle world is someone to love."

Author's Note

$\mathcal{I}$ admit it—I fudged with history a bit in this book, although not as much as you'd think. Of course there was no Simon as Secretary of War, and Lord Monteith was an invented prime minister (thank goodness). But many of the other political characters and events are real (although I admit to making the events more dramatic). Lord Sidmouth did resign as Home Secretary in 1822, having never recovered from the backlash after the Peterloo Massacre. And while Lord Castlereagh never resigned—he committed suicide in 1822—Liverpool replaced both him and Sidmouth with ministers who were more progressive than their predecessors.

Sir Robert Peel (during the era in which my book is set, he had not yet gained the title) did become Home Secretary, and he did push through the Gaols Act in 1823. George Canning did become Foreign Secretary.

And the new and improved cabinet was able, after Liverpool finally retired in 1827, to push through what Simon wants implemented in my book—parliamentary reform, which affected how people were elected to the House of Commons, and thus how much influence the aristocracy had on legislation.

The Reform Act of 1832 was considered groundbreaking in its time. It probably won't surprise you to learn that Lord Sidmouth, who was still knocking around in 1832, voted against it.

Other bits of real history in this book include the material about Newgate and prison reform. Mrs. Fry's Association genuinely changed how prisons were governed, and her brother-in-law did serve in the Commons. And Louisa wouldn't have been the first duchess to dabble in politics. Long before the time of my book, Georgiana, the Duchess of Devonshire, stumped for her husband's political party, along with all her friends.

Sadly enough, the material about Princess Charlotte is also true—she did die horribly in childbirth after two days of labor, although history is still not sure whom to blame.

And there really was a razing of Poona and a Battle of Kirkee. The British did win against overwhelming odds, but the Governor-General had no part in it. The real man who inspired everyone to fight was Mountstuart Elphinstone, the British Resident at Poona. He'd never fought in any army, but still managed to lead them to victory after assuming command. With such an impressive man for a model, how could I resist giving his role to my hero?

Pocket Star
proudly presents

The School for Heiresses

A collection by Sabrina Jeffries, Liz Carlyle,
Julia London, and Renee Bernard

Available in January from Pocket Star

Turn the page for a preview of
The School for Heiresses . . .

*W*hy are you running away from home?" Collin asked his captive.

Her head swung around, her eyes full of panic. "How did you know I was run—" She broke off with a groan, realizing she'd confirmed his guess.

"You might as well tell me everything. I'll get it out of you eventually."

"It has nothing to do with you!"

"Once you decided to 'borrow' one of my horses, you involved me."

"You're the one insisting on an entanglement. Just let me leave and I'll *walk* to Honiton."

"The hell you will. I'm not letting some fool of a young woman out on the road alone to be raped or killed."

The harsh words made her tense. "Fine. Then be a gentleman and drive me there."

"Not a chance. Not until I know what you're up to." He led her into the house, releasing a grateful breath to be out of the infernal cold. "Hand me your cloak and gloves," he ordered as he shut the door.

She blinked at him. "Why?"

"You'd be an idiot to run off without them in this weather, and I'm not taking the chance that you'll knock me over the head while my back is turned."

With a roll of her eyes, she peeled off her gloves, then untied her cloak. When she drew it off, the sight of what lay beneath struck the breath from him.

He'd guessed her to be a girl of about sixteen. He'd guessed wrong. God help him, that was a woman's body half-bursting out of the ridiculously tight male apparel she'd apparently "borrowed" from a man much thinner than she.

It was impossible not to stare at the fetching picture she made in a waistcoat half-unbuttoned to make room for her plump breasts, and breeches too snug for her hips. Her unfortunate choice of a tail coat made matters worse, since the nipped-in waist only accentuated her curves.

So did the shimmering cascade of copper-gold hair that fell to her waist unfettered, although a few lingering hair pins twinkled in the candlelight.

This time it wasn't just his blood that stirred.

And the last thing he needed was a reckless runaway firing his blood. When he married again, it would be to a steady, quiet female who wanted peace as much as he. Maybe some settled widow who wouldn't be bothered by his mixed blood. Certainly not an impudent wench with more curves than sense.

"What's wrong?" she asked, coloring beneath his intense gaze.

"You thought you could pass for a man in that costume?"

"Well . . . no. I'm too plump in . . . er . . . certain places for that."

Luscious, more like.

"But that's what the cloak's for. And even without it, from a distance—"

"You'd look like a cherry ripe for the picking," he snapped. "Just how old are you, anyway?"

"Nineteen." She cast him a mutinous glance. "Old enough to go where I want and do as I please."

She had a point. In India, she would already be married. And her lucky husband would already be happily initiating his blushing bride to the pleasures of the bed, unveiling those creamy breasts and dimpled belly, winding himself in the luscious silk of her copper-gold hair as he buried his—

Colin swore under his breath. What was he thinking? She was trouble. The chit was probably running off to elope with some equally clod-pated idiot. Although if that were so, why hadn't the idiot come to fetch her?

Whatever her reasons, no young female with her attractions and rash tendency to land in trouble should be roaming the English countryside at midnight.

"Old enough or not, you shouldn't be on the road alone." He held up his free hand. "So give me the cloak and the gloves."

Rebellion flared in her face and she flung the gloves at him. As he lunged to catch them, she deftly swung her cloak over his head, then took off.

He swore, momentarily blinded, and fought free of her cloak just as she sped past him toward the door. "Oh no, you don't," he growled as he snagged her around the waist, then jerked her up against him. "Nice try, my dear. But it would take a better 'man' than you to best me."

"Very . . . funny," she gasped as she struggled against him. "Let me . . . go!"

"You're plucky—I'll give you that." Also incredibly foolish. And it was time he made her aware just *how* foolish.

"My patience is at an end." He stuffed his pistol inside his waistband, then caught her by the throat. "You have one minute to tell me your name, where you live, and why you're running away."

Although she stopped struggling, her hazel eyes narrowed to slits. "Or what? You'll throttle me?"

"As tempting as that sounds, no." He slid his thumb down to brush her top shirt button. "I'll simply remove the rest of your clothes piece by piece until you do."